at the
EDGE

READ ORDER				
369	182	29	44	8
140 (10)	259 (12)	326	61	96
	150	354	77	119
		378	163	286
			194	61+341
			226	
			242	
			270	
			309	

PAPER ROAD PRESS
paperroadpress.co.nz

Copyright © 2016
First published in paperback and ebook in 2016
ISBN 9780473354152

All stories in this collection are © 2016 their respective authors

A catalogue record for this book is available from the National Library of
New Zealand

Cover art by and © Emma Weakley
Design by Marie Hodgkinson
Proofread by Spell Bound

AT THE
EDGE

EDITED BY DAN RABARTS
AND LEE MURRAY

TABLE OF CONTENTS

Introduction

Angela Slatter

WRITING IS HARD.

Writing short stories is extra hard.

Writing *good* short stories is harder still.

You see, you don't have the luxury that you get with a novel, which allows enough room to meander through your myriad chapters and slowly build up things like character and backstory, to give the reader lavish descriptions of setting, appearances, the turning of the seasons, all ten courses of a magnificent feast, et cetera. No. With a short story it's straight into the action because you simply don't have time to set things up in a leisurely fashion; a novel's a marathon, a short story's a sprint, don't they say? Or was that just me?

Don't be fooled, though. That doesn't make a short story easy – or quick – to write. In a short story every word must count, every description must earn its keep, justify its place; every single element you put in must be precisely the right one for that tale. You need to present characters who spring forth fully formed, yet not as stereotypes; you need to be wary of writing a white room setting that leaves a reader dazed, confused and geographically embarrassed; your dialogue needs to sound like human speech even though it isn't, but rather a really sneaky and convincing facsimile. Everything you choose to put in absolutely must be the thing that is most required at that point in time, space, and plot.

If you want to write a good short story.

Over the years I've had students and just-starting-out writers say, 'I'll begin with short fiction: it's fast and easy.' That's my cue to laugh. Sometimes it's a light, tinkling sound to show how much they've amused me, other times it's a full-on, earthy *Bwahahahaha* accompanied by moustache twirling and the theatrical wrapping of a black cloak around myself as I disappear into the mists. When I wander off on such occasions, I'm continuing my own personal journey to discover fine short stories. I've been lucky: I've found writers like Kelly Link, Hannah Tinti, Karen Russell, Kaaron Warren, Lisa Hannett, Steve Almond … all writers who can give you a tale short enough to sit on the head of a pin, yet knock you for a six with its precision, its beauty.

Such stories haven't simply been written, but *crafted*. Their authors have audited as well as edited their works, asking whether or not this element fits, does its job, *belongs*. And when they're done, what they've created are bright little stars, something that shines so intensely that, despite its small size, it catches the eye. That, when read, sticks in the brain and stays there for a very long time, percolating and, if you're lucky, changing the mind in which it's lodged. That's what the best fiction of any length should do: disrupt a reader's everyday. Re-wire the way they think. Evolve new ideas, make way for different concepts, throw a mind wide open.

Then there are the folks who decide it's not enough to just write a good short story … they want to do more: they want to pull together an anthology. They set themselves up for all manner of time-consuming blood, sweat, and tear-based activity: finding a publisher, putting out calls for subs, trawling and swimming and splashing through the slush in the hope of coming up with a bunch of those bright stars. Lee Murray and Dan Rabarts are such people – I've met them, they're lovely, they seem quite normal for writers – but, I suspect, there may well be traces of masochism in their make-up. It's not enough that they've a large collection of publications and Sir Julius Vogel Awards between them. And it's not enough to just create a book showcasing New Zealand talent. No, they're bringing together writers from New Zealand *and* Australia. It's a weirdly natural mix, after all, we're kind of friends, kind of rivals, kind of cousins … but we're all most definitely at the edge.

Herein you will find work from writers of repute, writers at the top of their game. Herein you'll find work from new names, names to watch out for, to seek in the future. You will find tales of apocalypses both soft and hard, you'll find Lovecraftian horrors to please the most cosmic of palates, you'll find hints of fairy tales and myths and paths less travelled by. You'll find horror, fantasy, science fiction and stories that meld all three together with bold strokes and determined stitches. Most of all you will find heart, and you will most certainly find some bright stars.

ANGELA SLATTER
BRISBANE, AUSTRALIA
FEBRUARY 2016

Editors' Note

Dan Rabarts & Lee Murray

It's a sticky evening in February. We meet in the capital at the Thistle Inn, New Zealand's oldest surviving tavern, right around the corner from Katherine Mansfield's family home. She used to come here and there's the proof: an excerpt of her writing on the dining room wall. I arrive first and take a seat on the downstairs patio, clutching my piece of paper with my notes, a few numbers crunched on the back. I don't have to wait long for Dan and Marie, and it's just as well since the pub is as popular as it ever was and I'm in danger of losing the chairs. Dan has worn his good shirt. We talk about the weather, and how difficult it is to get a park around here.

Say something! I send Dan a telepathic message.

So, the Baby Teeth *thing,* he says, *that was good.*

We chat about the charity project that evolved from a flyaway comment, re-energising the local speculative fiction community, discovering some new talent, and developing our strengths as a creative team.

Good times.

Yes, good times…

So, Lee and I were thinking about another anthology, Dan says.

I slap my page of notes on the table. I've been fiddling with it and the edges are already curling.

I don't remember all the words, but there's some excited talking. A blurt of pros and cons, and stars-in-your-eyes ideas. Let's make it broad this time, we say. Not just us. We have to include our friends across the ditch.

Nodding. There's a whole continent of talent there. And they have the same mindset; there's an empathy. They even liked our work enough to give it an award.

Two awards, actually.

That's true. There's a pause as we contemplate that unexpected windfall.

We're looking at a lot of work. Definitely hard yakka.

A beer glass is rolled between two palms. There'll be nothing to show for it, either.

When did that ever stop us?

So – Australia, then?

Just think of the stories: taniwha and bunyips.

Across the table, Dan is already dreaming of monsters.

Perhaps it's significant that Chief Te Rauparaha once tied his waka below the Thistle Inn at the edge of the same body of water that laps at the shores of Australia, because Marie barely looks at my carefully crunched numbers.

Yes, she says. I like this.

It was an edge of sanity moment because as I recall it, none of us flinched.

After that, the fliers went out, social media sites buzzed and the stories came in, slowly at first and ending in a deluge. The response was like a national anthem sung in a stadium, both in terms of volume and quality. We could have filled two books. This wasn't like *Baby Teeth: Bite-sized Tales of Terror* (Paper Road Press, 2013), where the stories, and the people, were self-selecting. This time the trainer wheels were truly off: Dan and I were going to have to make some hard decisions.

Just one more, then?

We can't afford one more. And which one, anyway?

If writers think getting a rejection is hard, letting some of those stories go was even harder.

Dan contacts his former mentor, the local, Arthur C. Clarke-nominated science fiction author Phillip Mann, who offers us a story, too. A foreword by World Fantasy Award winner Angela Slatter? Why yes, please.

Editing the stories is a pleasure, especially when you're dealing with writers bent on improving their craft, willing to fine-tune every nuance until their stories are as sharp as a greenstone patu.

And so, a year after that meeting at the Thistle, we have another anthology.

Dan, Marie and I are privileged to share *At the Edge* with you. It is a superb collection by some fine writers, people we are proud to call our friends.

Their stories tested us. They made us shiver, and gave us hope. They are stories which balance on the edge of madness, the edge of the universe, the edge of time, the edge of reality. They hover on the precipice between life and death, between passion and ennui, between certainty and indecision. And all of them are infused with that bloody-minded quality that embodies the Antipodes, a resilience inherent in nations born of warriors and wanderers, the children of whalers, convicts and miners: people not afraid to roll up their sleeves, or strike out for new territories, innovative resourceful sorts prepared to find meaning in the expanses out here at the edge of the world.

LEE MURRAY AND DAN RABARTS
WELLINGTON, NEW ZEALAND
FEBRUARY 2016

The Leaves no Longer Fall

JODI CLEGHORN

'DECIDUOUS WAS ONCE A WORD EVERYONE KNEW,' I say, choosing a red paper leaf from the old pillowcase. 'It was how trees that lost their leaves in autumn were described.' The paper leaf dangles from my fingers, trembling as I brush it through the air.

Ty, seated in my lap and chin slick with drool, reaches up with chubby hands for it. Jamie, just two, kneels at my feet watching. I let the paper leaf go. It zigzags to the grassed floor, lacking the natural grace of leaf fibre.

'First the leaves turned red. And yellow. Orange,' I continue, finding leaves of the corresponding colours so Jamie can name them. 'The leaves were beautiful and when they fell, the ground turned into a colourful carpet. You could kick them and throw them. Jump in huge piles of them.'

'Jump!' Jamie says, scrambling to his feet and bouncing up and down. 'Jump-jump.'

I prop Ty against the buttress roots of the Moreton Bay fig growing in the space my mother-in-law used as a second lounge room before she died, and shake the pretend leaves over Jamie's head. He giggles and turns crazy circles trying to catch them. Once they settle, scattered about him on the grass, he bends to collect handfuls and throw them over himself, squealing. Ty mimics him.

'Shhhh, honey,' I say, trying not to cry, thinking of all the things lost to my sons. Jamie should be outside where he can be as loud as he wants to be. Run as far as he wants to go. 'We don't want to wake anyone.'

My throat closes up and I lie back on the grass, force myself to think of good things. And breathe.

On the inside of my eyelids, Dan digs through the cracked foundations of this room when we first arrive in Central Victoria from Rookhurst. I remember how I spent the final months of my pregnancy with Max improving the soil, building sub-tropical humus. After Max was born, we planted the seedling with his placenta and the fig flourished, grew as our family did: first Max, then Jamie and Ty. And the unused rooms of the ridiculously large house became homes for refugees fleeing the North, waiting for a chance to buy a place on a boat to Tasmania. The desperate and hopeless, whom Dan gave a second chance at life.

Please, please Dan. Please find some other way to help. It's too dangerous.

Useless words now. Useless words echoing in an emptiness that threatens to consume me.

Jamie sings 'jump-jump' and the paper leaves rustle at his feet. I squeeze my eyes shut so hard it hurts – one pain to temporarily mask another – and force myself back to the happy memories.

One morning … one morning, when Max was tiny, Dan arrived home with the coloured paper and I traced and cut leaves, wanting to give the tiny babe at my breast some sense of the world I'd come from. One he'd never have a chance to explore.

I open my eyes. Above, through the wash of unshed tears, the branches transform the room into a natural cathedral. A tiny skylight lets in enough sunlight for vitamin D and photosynthesis. Everything carefully measured and balanced to ensure the tree and the boys thrive. But the vulnerability of life – the impermanence of it – sits heavy on my chest.

'Let's collect the leaves,' I say and wearily sit up, rubbing eyes longing to weep. 'All the red ones first.'

'No!' Jamie folds his arms and thrusts his bottom lip out.

'Then orange ones first.'

'No.' The way he stands with his legs slightly apart reminds me of Dan: that stubborn stance, inside and out.

'If you're not going to clean up, you can go back to bed.' The words snap from my mouth.

'No!'

I kneel in front of him and force a sing-song edge to my voice. Settle the fury boiling in me as much as the one in him. 'The leaves need to go to bed. And so do we. It'll be twilight soon and time to get Max ready for school.'

'NO.'

Ty pitches forward from the buttress alcove and starts to cry, grass and dirt stuck to his mouth. I draw him to me, set him on my hip, and return the leaves one-handed to the old pillowcase, ignoring the small storm building in Jamie. If both our storms merge, a supercell will tear through the artificial calm that seals in my grief.

A knock on the lounge room window startles us all. Jamie stares at the glass so black the world outside is hidden. No one should be out there before twilight. A white handprint burns into the darkened glass. The bottom falls from my stomach and I take several tentative steps toward the window, clutching Ty to me, and trying to turn Jamie away before a face from the past appears.

*

Only madmen like Dan and Jackson made it their business to be outside when the sun was up. Jackson ambles down the hallway, stripping off his insulated coat and ice vest, as if nothing suddenly terminated our friendship seven years ago. As though Rookhurst is down the road and he's just dropped in for a quick chat and a cuppa.

Jamie gawks around the corner of the lounge room.

'Who?' he asks, his father's brazen confidence in that single word.

Jackson drapes his protective gear over the back of a kitchen chair. 'Who would you like me to be?'

'Supe'man!' His small face lights up.

'Don't get too excited.' I sweep into the kitchen to prepare tea; busy hands to still my mind. 'He says that for just about everyone. Gets it from his brother.'

'And Dan.'

I hold the kettle in the void over the sink, the tap running, precious water wasting.

'The news reached us a month ago. I'm sorry, Annabel. We're all sorry.'

I thrust the kettle under the stream of water. 'When heroic deeds in a humanitarian crisis are considered criminal acts…' I can't finish the sentence; the rage and grief and futility seethe dangerously close to the surface. 'They didn't even have the decency to—'

I take a deep breath and jam the power cord into the socket.

'You found out from the broadcast?'

Jackson looks stranded in the revelation. Unsure in the foreign landscape of my home.

I slam two mugs on the bench and force myself to stay calm. 'It'll have to be black. We haven't had sugar or milk since I was pregnant with Jamie.'

Jackson nods and bends so he's at Jamie's height. 'Go play in the other room, little mate,' he says and my middle son actually does as he's told, taking a battered board book over to 'read' to Ty.

My stomach clenches, waiting for the kick Jackson is about to deliver.

'Morrison's dead.' The breath expels from him as he slides into the seat on the opposite side of the bench, like he was somehow simultaneously holding it and talking. 'You can come back now.'

'Back?' The floor drops from under my feet and my hand clamps on the edge of the bench. The words pepper me like they did when I heard Dan had been shot dead by Immigration Police just the other side of the New South Wales border. 'Back to Rookhurst?'

'It's your legacy.'

The ecstasy on Morrison's face when he stumbled onto my heritage and realised how it influenced my research is still crystal clear in my memory: my mother the botanist, my grandmother the glass blower. How he wooed and seduced me into thinking his science enclave in the mountains was the answer to the most immediate crisis facing us as a nation. He made me believe I could solve it if I could just make glass live.

'We always knew, all of us, that Morrison was Edison to your Tesla.' The kettle whistles and my hand shakes as I pour water into the mugs. The precious teabag floats to the surface, inflated by hot air. 'We knew the bacteria in his glass was yours. We knew Dan argued with Morrison because he stole your work. We know that's why you left.'

I slide one mug across the bench.

'It doesn't matter anymore. They're both dead. And I'm…' I take a sip of tea and burn myself. Suck in my bottom lip to relish the pain rather than quench it. After several uncomfortable minutes, I know there's no reason to hold back with Jackson and say, 'We needed living glass ten years ago. Instead, we got Morrison's hybrid glass. By the time Ty's at school, we'll be underground. Whatever I hypothesised at uni and modelled back at Rookhurst, whatever I wanted to achieve, it's obsolete. Pointless.'

'It's not, Annabel.'

Jackson unrolls a tablet from a cylinder in his satchel. He waits for the molecules to switch from flexible to fixed and then hands it to me. On-screen, an epidermal breach spiderwebs through the hybrid glass I helped create: triple-glazing embedded with photochromatic bacteria for block-out. It began as the hope for the new Australia. Morrison rushed it through, dumbed it down to a stop-gap measure to keep the country habitable while communities built underground. It became his bargaining chip with the Government to keep our enclave off the official radar.

I zoom in, trying to work out why the lighting in the intrusion looks wrong.

'It's cracking from the inside out,' Jackson says and as I zoom in as close as the programme will let me, I see the outside world; a dustbowl of red and black. 'Morrison thought the bacteria in the middle or inside layer might have become thermogenic.'

'Generating heat?' I zoom out. The photo is geo-stamped

the Seven Hills Internment Camp, The Sydney Basin, two months earlier.

'How deep?' I ask, handing the tablet back.

'Morrison estimated a 50 per cent intrusion. He and Carmen left to test it but never made it there.' Jackson turns and presses a palm against the kitchen window. The solar-darkening bacterium lightens at the touch. 'You knew all along Morrison's glass was substandard to what you could create.'

'And now, with him gone, once the damage is done, I'm expected to fix it.' I pace the length of the kitchen. 'I'm not some fucking messiah.' There isn't enough space in the kitchen to walk off my frustration. My rage. The impossible situation Jackson has thrown me into. 'I'm needed here. Dan died for the people we're sheltering here. I can't just leave.'

'And help, what, ten, fifteen people?' Jackson stands and I glare at him, but he doesn't lower his gaze. 'The heat creep Alice modelled when Morrison was setting up Rookhurst, it's double what she projected. The Government knows. Dan was caught because they're reinforcing the New South Wales and Victorian borders.'

'They're going to close it?' As each word leaves my lips I know with absolute certainty it's what they're planning to do.

Jackson doesn't need to say any more.

If I don't find a way to make glass live, at best we're going to face an unprecedented movement of people south – a humanitarian crisis to blitz the others. At worst, we'll all be dead before we make it underground.

'Dan wouldn't think twice, would he?' I say.

'You're not Dan.'

'Mum?' a sleepy voice calls from the hallway, interrupting us. 'Is Daddy home?'

*

Dan wouldn't think twice about a 1400-km trip north, in summer, because he did longer trips all the time. Even adding three small boys into the equation and nothing but dirt bikes to take us there, he wouldn't have hesitated. In his mind, everything was possible. But I'm not Dan.

I only have one photo of him: the two of us out the front of the tiny Rookhurst Presbyterian Church, newly married by Caius Morrison – me in the only dress I owned, Dan in his Hard Yakka cargo pants and shirt. He'd at least bothered to take off his hat and comb his hair. Morrison had no legal authority to join us in holy matrimony – we could have just as easily traded vows on the riverbank as in the Church – but we were the first at Rookhurst to decide to be together. So we made a big deal and Dan begrudgingly let Morrison preside over it.

I ease the photo from the wooden frame. It goes into the old satchel along with a dog-eared manila folder, a data stick and a notebook. I fold my wedding dress and stuff it in before shoving the satchel into a pannier bag filled with clothes.

I'm not Dan. He'd take weeks, if possible, to plan a trip. Prepare multiple routes and contingencies for every eventuality. I can't do that. I'd freeze into inertia if left with time to think. One night to prepare is almost one too many.

Every minute passing is one lost.

No amount of justification of a greater good can absolve me of the guilt twisting my guts. It's cowardly, leaving without an explanation of where I'm going or why I'm doing this. The families I'm leaving behind deserve better than a good-bye note left on the kitchen table. I want to believe Dan's brother, Amos, will take care of them like he has promised.

But Amos is not Dan. And every word I do not write is a lie I'm left to live with.

Before I wake the boys and prepare them to leave, I carefully remove a new shoot from the fig tree and drop it into a seven-day incubation tube – the last I have. It's the most fragile of hopes that it will survive the trip. I try not to think of us the same way.

*

My heart skips a beat when I see the warped Rookhurst sign in the bike's headlight, but exhaustion precludes any actual emotion. I follow Jackson off what's left of Thunderbolt's Way and through the gate of the former principal's house, now a common living space. The windows in the old school buildings are lit up: everyone's working. It's like I never left.

I kill the engine, kick down the stand and help Max slide to the ground. Only then do I stiffly climb off and loosen the bindings strapping Ty to my chest. Every part of my body aches and vibrates. Brian and Alice wait at the bottom of the stairs to the old school master's house. Two little girls peer around them, lit with fascination. As I walk towards them, I stumble and almost fall. Alice rushes to me, steadies me. With her arm tightly around my shoulder, my jelly legs strengthen enough to keep me upright. Tears wash through me and down the shoulder of my oldest friend.

'I'm just exhausted,' I blubber, but it's more. So much more.

She relieves me of Ty so I can remove my jacket and ice vest, then do the same for Max and Ty.

'Do you like Superman?' asks Max of Alice and Brian's eldest girl when he's free of his coat and vest.

'Who's Superman?' she asks.

Jackson opens his rucksack and retrieves a slab of Dan's old Superman comics he must have found in the garage at home. 'This is Superman!'

The four children run upstairs to find somewhere to read, even Jamie, who's still unsteady on his feet from the sedatives Jackson gave him to keep him on the bike.

I follow, dragging myself up the stairs and slumping into the old leather lounge. Ty feeds lazily at my breast and I stop thinking about the trip. We made it and that's all that matters.

Josephine and Alex join us as coffee is served. Josephine sits next to me and offers her breast to the tiny baby girl cradled in her arms. The contented infant slurps and murmurs smooth over the doubts I've had; for better or worse, Rookhurst is now our home.

Josephine smiles as her fingers slip between mine. She tips her head to me and whispers, 'I'm glad you're back.'

Jane and Keith are the last to arrive, with their twin daughters, and at first the lounge room seems full: nine adults and a tumble of kids talking, laughing, crying, arguing. All my old friends are here: the people I committed to live the rest of my life with. Then an overwhelming emptiness descends. Those who are missing become sinkholes in the floorboards: Morrison, Carmen and Dan. Memories crowd in, rushing up like the ocean in a blowhole, soaking me in the brine of regret. It tastes of Alex's greenhouse coffee beans. The guilt pulls like the outgoing tide, and I'm drowning.

'You need to sleep,' Alice says, taking Ty out of my arms. 'C'mon. We prepared the room out the back for you and the boys.'

I try to argue, to tell her Dan is waiting for me in the shipping container we've made our home, but it's too hard.

*

The following night, I stand in the centre of Dan's work-shop with the fig tree cylinder in my hand. Through the window, I watch the last brown smudge of twilight silhouette the skeletal outline of trunks, the lifeless remnants of the bush that once enclosed the tiny township of Rookhurst. Max is outside on the jungle gym, laughing and shouting with Alice's daughters. When we lived here, heat-resistant vegetable vines hung from the bars my little monkey now swings on.

This is a Rookhurst Dan could have loved.

I never understood why he resented it. He'd come of his own free will, though last to join the collective: a builder and an amateur storm chaser who wrote poetry in the margins of his blueprints. To me, he was a strange fit for Morrison's enclave of scientists. Whatever it was that lured Dan to say yes to Morrison's proposal, he never confided in me.

I switch on the light and everything is exactly as I imagine he left it. A mausoleum, sealed up, waiting for him to die. I pick up a hammer and some nails, try to remember what he was building the day he argued with Morrison for the last time.

Eyes closed, echoes of the heated discussion fall from the rafters.

'If we don't leave, I'll kill him and we won't be able to stay.'
'If we go now, we'll never be able to come back.'
'I can't live anymore with what he's done.'

I didn't care that Morrison claimed my breakthroughs as his own. I was motivated by the hope of a new building material, strong and heat-resistant, to enable shattered communities to rebuild where they were. So no one else had to flee south. It didn't matter to me who put their name to the innovation. Dan, though, couldn't move past it.

I scour the drawers, crates and other piles of Dan's hoarded junk. Always the excuse that it was the end of the world and he wished he was just saving for a rainy day. I want to go slow, savour each of the little things of his, but I'm afraid if I stay too long I'll never leave. It's not until I have it in my hand that I know what I'm searching for: his old leather tool belt, the one with the busted strap, soft and stained with sweat. It goes in my satchel and as I close the lid on the suitcase, I see the corner of an old primary-school scrapbook, buried beneath a pile of even older manuals. Dan refused to talk about his childhood and I feel a certain betrayal lifting the book out.

It's brittle, stained with insect faeces and filled with the yellowed newspaper clippings of a trial dating back three decades. I read without comprehension. The name featured in the headlines means nothing until I see the photo: Morrison, a much younger Morrison, going by the name of Caius Morgensten. I crouch in the dirt, turn back to the beginning and carefully read every article. It ends with an alleged paedophile released back into the community on a legal technicality.

In the dust I scrawl dates. Confirmation comes with the photo that falls out of the scrapbook when I stand up: a messy cluster of young boys in soccer uniforms. The middle one – with a face that could belong to an older Jamie – holds a trophy. Morrison stands to the side, leering at the camera.

*

The breeze blows away from the old school buildings and I'm grateful as I dig a small but deep fire pit behind the Church. I don't want to incite the fear of a bush fire in anyone that might smell smoke. Each page of the scrapbook comes away easily and nestles together in the bottom of the hole, like eggs that will never hatch their vile secret. Fire dances along the edge of one page, then another, and the entire book is consumed in half the time it took to dismember it. The photo melts and warps on top before it ignites. Smoke wheels around towards me and I'm drenched in the stink of lies and secrets. In it I find a belated empathy for Dan, an understanding of what drove him to risk everything for the most vulnerable.

When the fire is nothing but hot ash I fill the hole and then dig a second one, a smaller one. I open the tube and slide out the Moreton Bay fig cutting. It now has a furry, inverted crown at the base, the tube accelerating the growth. The delicate roots are pale against the dark, dry dirt. In years to come, perhaps the boys and I will be able to sit in the buttress roots and pretend Dan's arms are holding us.

Back at the compound, I stand at the falling-down fence with my hands wrapped around the rusted top bar and remember how Dan said Rookhurst was too small. I never understood because I relished the isolation and the lack of distractions. I was relieved and grateful to have escaped the atrocities on the coast for a chance to do something to alleviate the suffering and dislocation of whole cities of people. I was so wrapped up in my research, so preoccupied with doing good I couldn't see the pain in the man I loved.

At the door of my lab I know I'm no longer driven by altruism. In making living glass from the hybrid glass, I obliterate the last evidence of Morrison's existence.

*

I shift from mother to working mother to full-time scientist as the seasons once moved effortlessly from one to the other. The boys spend all their time with Josephine and Alice and while I don't see them it's easy to pretend I'm at peace with the arrangement. I fall into bed exhausted, well after dawn each day, and comfort myself with the knowledge that they're young and adaptable and it's not forever. Until Josephine appears in the door of my lab, her daughter tied to her back and Max lingering at her side.

'Max was telling me about how he used to help you,' she says and I can tell from the look on Max's face it's a lie. 'Can we come in?'

'Sure,' I say, playing the game. I turn to peer down the barrel of the microscope so she won't see how it bothers me that Max is with her.

They stop at the bench where the test plates are arrayed in three rows of twenty, waiting for the first three strains of the bacteria. Each piece of glass is compromised – ranging from a scratch to epidermal shattering of all three layers. Every square has a tiny number and letter in the right-hand corner, carefully drawn by Max after hours of practising letters and numbers small enough on every piece of scrap paper he could find across the compound. The weeks of asking him to wait, trying to explain things didn't happen quickly in science no matter how much you wanted them to, led him to wander off. Distracted by the urgency of my work, I'd let him go.

'Mum's going to smear gel stuff on the glass and the germs in the gel are going to get into the cracks and infect the glass,' he tells Josephine.

'What kind of germs?' she asks.

When Max doesn't answer, I say, 'I've created a new bacterium from the original, spliced it with *Acacia peuce* and *cambagei* genes.'

I don't look up, my attention fixed on the reaction of the final bacterial strain to temperature changes.

'The theory is the new bacteria will invade via the cracks and replace the old. The glass will heal as the colony grows and stay photochromatic like the hybrid version, but also become photosynthetic and endothermic. The three layers will evolve into a self-supporting ecosystem that will use heat as part of its life cycle.'

'Do you mind if I take a look?'

I step away from the microscope and let her watch the bacteria multiply. Max looks everywhere but at me.

'I'm going to start the experiments in a few days,' I say. 'Can I count on you as my lab assistant?'

He shrugs. 'I think I'd rather dig with Josephine and Alex, or help Alice with Ty,' he says.

'Max—' I reach out to hug him and he slips through my arms and out of the lab.

Josephine straightens, but her shoulders stay hunched.

'It's not your fault,' I say, but blame lingers in the hollowness of the words.

*

Each test fails like the one before, the new bacterium multiplying, then merging with, rather than destroying, the existing colony. Within twenty-four hours each strain dies regardless of how much heat or light it receives, and the bastard bacterium left weakens the molecular structure of the glass.

I take the final sample from beneath the microscope and place it with all the other failed samples. At the end of the bench, I rest my cheek against the stainless steel and stare at the checkerboard of failure. There's a dull throb behind my eyes threatening to escalate to a full-blown migraine before the storm rumbling outside hits.

It takes me longer than it should to work out the noise I'm hearing isn't just thunder, but something being dragged across the floor. Jamie appears in my line of sight, standing on the step Alex made for Max so he could work alongside me at the bench.

'Play, Mummy.'

When did he start speaking in two-word sentences?

While I've been buried in the lab, absent to children who have already lost a father.

And for what?

My efforts are nothing more than a wasteland of good intentions and flawed theories. The pointlessness of it all desiccates my vision. And into it a small hand reaches and takes the sample square closest to the microscope.

'Ji'saw,' Jamie says and rotates it in one direction and then the other.

In the window behind, lightning flashes and wind drags at the edges of the roof iron, trying to prise it from the steel trusses. I close my eyes and imagine the dust outside becoming mud; puddles become a stream, and then a raging river that sweeps everything away.

'Ji'saw.' When I open my eyes, he has a square in each hand, trying to fit them together in the space in front of his face.

'It's not a jigsaw.'

'Yes. Ji'saw.' He batters the two pieces together, trying to join them. In his mind, sheer force of will joins them, just as I believed mine would animate glass.

I push myself up from the bench and feel the last of my motivation, my belief and momentum, bleed out of my feet and into the concrete floor.

He crosses his arms over his chest and plants his feet a hip-width apart, the glass firmly gripped in each hand. In that moment I see how Jamie will always echo Dan's defiance and his sense of justice. The fragile sutures that hold my heart together snap.

'Give them to me.'

'No!' Jamie yells.

'Yes.'

The hand I've put out for Jamie to put the glass in is steady. There's no external evidence I'm being seismically undone from the inside.

I need to leave Jamie with someone responsible because I'm not. I'm completely tapped out. Barely hanging on.

The howl of wind overhead intensifies and the lights in the lab flicker and drop out for a second.

'Where's Alice?'

'No Alice.'

'Yes, Alice.'

'No, no. NO-NO-NO-NO.' He swipes his arm across the bench and half the failed samples shatter around my feet.

'You little shit!' I scream as the building rocks with the ferocity of the thunder.

I lunge for him but I'm slowed by fatigue, my anger only hot enough to ignite an impotent explosion. Jamie jumps from the step and runs with the speed only small children are blessed with, out of the coolness of the lab, down the corridor of the building and into the vicious night.

'Jamie!' I chase him across the old playground, through eddies of dust, rising in columns from the parched earth. 'Jamie, stop!'

My pelvis protests. The bones clash against each other

and I slow down.

Jamie's never seen a dust storm much less been out in one. *He'll stop. He'll come back. He will.*

I pull my t-shirt up over my mouth to keep the air breathable and try to follow his outline blurred by the opaque air. At the gate, I lose sight of him for a moment. It becomes several moments, then a fragment of a minute where time stops and overhead the sky is torn open by lightning and night becomes day. In the x-ray after-burn, there is no silhouette of a small boy running into the maw of the storm.

'Jamie!' I scream, his name stamped out by a series of deafening booms that shake the ground.

Dust scores my eyes and ears, fills my throat. My bare skin smarts and bleeds as though it's being rubbed with a thousand tiny pieces of sandpaper.

The wind strengthens. I lean into it. Push against it.

Buffeted by gusts, I stagger out of the schoolyard. Across the buckled bitumen and into the decimated bush. I've lost him.

I can't search by myself, blinded and barely able to breathe, yet I can't turn back for help and leave him out here alone.

*

In the nightmares that crowd my sleep, his body is encased in glass and an electrical storm rages inside the box. He lies there, like Sleeping Beauty, waiting to be woken. Waiting for me to find a way to fix his broken body so he can live again. But I can't theorise and experiment to find the breakthrough because there's too much noise. A cacophony of his name shouted in hysterical desperation. I try to tell them to stop searching because I've found him. He's safe. He's with me. But when I look at the glass box he is gone, and I wake screaming his name.

Afterwards, I lie in a clammy shroud of sweat and fear and force myself to think of anything – the periodic table, the genus of all extinct plants, every clause in the '79 Immigration and Resettlement Act – anything to not think about Jackson carrying the limp body from the graveyard of trees. Or the massive haematoma on his forehead that my hand couldn't smooth away. And I won't wonder if the fall killed him, or if, face down, he suffocated in the dust. I won't imagine how scared he might have been in those last seconds, disorientated and alone in the fury of the storm. I won't remember rocking and keening in the dirt with his lifeless body in my arms, wishing my tears were all that was needed to bring him back.

Outside, rain falls and I begin to recite to myself the atmospheric convection modelling for storm prediction they taught us in first-year uni. I will fill my thoughts with anything to keep me from thinking of all the ways I should have dealt with Jamie's defiance. How it was my responsibility to keep him safe.

*

The click of the door pulls me from a listless sleep. I roll over. My body aches from weeks of lying in a cocoon of grief and filthy sheets. On the pillow beside me is a dirty square of glass. I snatch it up to hurl it at the wall, *the fucking glass*, but as I touch it I realise it's smooth. I rub dirt from the corners until I find the number and letter: L20. Through the fog of grief something shifts.

This is the last sample piece I put under the microscope.

Even though the lab belongs to a different lifetime, a past I want to forget, questions form like tenacious bubbles: is the square one of the pieces Jamie took? Did he have it in his hand when he ran into the storm?

I rub more dirt from it. The epidermal shattering is gone: all layers of the triple-glazing are unblemished, lightly shaded grey in the weak twilight.

My little boy died, while the glass lived.

The epiphany roils inside me and I know no matter how hard I try to hide from it, the knowledge will dog me.

I walk stiffly down the back stairs of the house and across the playground to the old school building. Max is sitting on a stool, with Dan's old tool belt around his waist, waiting for me. The small-boy roundness is gone from his face, but the curious glint still lights his eyes.

'I found the first one out near the fence,' he says, sliding off the stool. 'Jackson and I found another one near—' He stumbles over a couple of words and finally says, 'out in the bush.'

I look down at my feet. Scientific discovery is often a consequence of accident and chance, but this—

'It was the dirt and the rain,' Max continues, and the tone reminds me of the talks he used to practise for school. 'You were trying to grow glass like plants, without any of the things plants need.'

I nod. My lack of common sense, my tunnel vision, the obsession with obliterating Morrison, of wanting there to be some kind of legacy in Dan's pain. And all I ended up doing was losing Jamie.

No. He's not a set of keys. Not a book or a pair of glasses you misplace only to find later. He is gone.

'I tried it with the others. River water works better than tank water. The dirt out in the bush is better than the soil in the greenhouses.'

I nod again and look at the samples lined up on the bench. Smooth. Impervious. Flawless.

The pressure in my skull releases. The haze burns away.

'We could call it JTD glass,' he says, and I finally look at him. 'Jamie can save the world like Superman.'

And in the space that clears in my head I see terminal glass healing. I see old buildings refitted, new ones constructed, borders reopened and people leaving internment camps, moving north to cross the Byron Line to re-inhabit the homes they fled. I see a different world. Not the world of the past I wanted so desperately for my boys. Instead, there's the possibility of a world where my boys have options for where and how they live. Leaves might once again fall, but from the trees they grow in their lounge rooms. Where the constructed world and the natural world are no longer clearly defined as one or the other.

Tears of hope, tears I thought I would never cry again, pour down my face. Max's skinny arms wrap around me. On my knees, I hug him tight, his body warm, his heart thumping against mine, his breath tickling my ear.

In every cell of my body, I feel how easy it is to be defined by what's broken – been taken – and stay that way. It's harder to trust in living again and hope that in time, all fissures might heal.

The Urge

Carlington Black

Wed, February 3, 2027

John Quant's nose tickles like he is fifteen again – hot flush, spikey cells, and crackling snot.

Something is wrong with the air. Not the usual wrong that we've got used to – the monoxide, the tarry putrefaction of urban life. Something wrong not in what we've added, but in what's always been there.

He must ignore it. Rise above it. Concentrate.

He is trained to look at the data. He is self-trained over 40 years to keep the senses in check.

Tomorrow will be busy. They will be analysing results from January.

The results. The numbers. The final units remote in with their telemetry data. John is calm. The data is completing.

But his nose still itches. He looks around the lab, tucks his chin to his chest, and extracts the dried nasal mucus.

Thurs, February 4

Damon sends through the first datasets from the Project Aeolos measurement sites. His memo points out a spike in krypton across all sites. He heads his dispatch 'Extraordinary'. John reprimands him. These notes go into the official record. Hyperbole is improper. Even in these days of hipster science, there is no place in the discipline for looseness. Save that for the girlfriend – if you have one.

Quant likes Damon. He sees his younger self in him. A quiet resolute intelligence wrapped in a square rugged frame.

Quant's dad said that a body should be used for more than carrying around his soft mind. Quant played rugby. He cried when he got hurt. He cried when the referee said he broke the rules.

Damon plays social rugby. His body has responded accordingly to the physical stimulation.

There is no doubt about Damon's data. Krypton should be at 1.14 parts per million of the atmosphere. Yet the project has measured 1.21ppm average across all sites, peaking to 1.49ppm by month's end. That's beyond previously observed variability for this narcotic gas.

Quant removes the krypton data – as they were not looking at it – and forwards the remaining results to Project HQ in London. London won't be happy though. Quant's team is meant to be looking for the markers of climate change. All *that* data is static.

It is Maena's birthday today. Quant gets Veronique, the team secretary, to send flowers, and organise the children to draw some cards. Maena will have arranged for them to do something on the weekend to celebrate.

That night, Maena only engages with Quant in bed once she confirms tomorrow's schedule, double-checks the alarm, checks Facebook, and is sure the kids are asleep.

FRIDAY, FEBRUARY 5

A note comes from the international project leader. He questions whether Quant has the project set up according to their specifications. The first dataset delivered an outcome in discordance with the Project Aeolos hypothesis. The levels of carbon monoxide should be climbing. But the data is not moving. He says the lack of predicted numbers is undermining the result. Quant knows he means that the team is undermining HQ's chances in the next funding round. The leader says Quant will have to recalibrate the instruments. Quant has not budgeted for that, so cannot ask for more money. Quant decides to face that problem with Jim Casey next week.

TUES, FEBRUARY 9

Quant covers off the recalibration with Jim. Casey is irritated. That is unusual.

But Casey authorises Quant's proposal that Damon and Julie visit all nineteen sites. It will take the month. They are both happy to go. Thank goodness for the enthusiasm and industry of youth. But that writes off February – which is now feasibly another faulty dataset.

Maena has scheduled a family walk along the beach this evening. The children keep picking up conical molluscs. Bright blue and about the size of a fingernail. It's not Quant's speciality, so he can't answer their question why the ebbing tide was leaving deep trails of them in waves down the beach.

He holds Maena's squat hand. Her palm stays dry despite the humidity.

FRI, FEBRUARY 12

Damon has reported back each day this week as they visited the first three sites. All tested within the confidence and tolerance level for the project guidelines. They recalibrated them anyway. Quant asks them to do that for each site. He orders Flynn to join them next week with a new calibration kit. Flynn will QA the process. Quant must be sure.

SATURDAY, FEBRUARY 13

Maena has organised for the family to BBQ with the Fergusons. They live in a tiny valley that cuts into the Eastbourne Hills opposite Pūriri Street. Leonard Ferguson is a nuclear physicist who works at GNS. He's also good at BBQ. Their children get on exceedingly well, so keep themselves occupied after dinner. The adults sit on their deck through the rest of the warm evening. The sun vanishes and the clack of cicadas gives way to the chirchirp of crickets. Maena thinks she sees green and white clouds in the night sky. Her skin fluxes pleasantly against her thin cotton dress while serving tea. Quant thinks it a very pleasant evening.

SUNDAY, FEBRUARY 14

Quant tries to BBQ for the family. It doesn't go so well. He throws the mess to the dogs and takes himself to the beach to calm down. Those blue shells are now ankle deep. Great shin-high rifts of them. There is also a vague taint to the air. He causally links it to the rotting flesh of the shellfish. By the time he gets back, Maena has rescued things with a selection of salads.

TUES, FEBRUARY 16

The city finally hits summer. It's come late, but with retribution for being wantonly anticipated. Temperature and humidity is high. Standing at the bus stop this morning, Quant feels an end-of-day tiredness. The bus pulls up, hydraulics fizzing.

The cicadas' mating call reaches a volume that breaks into Quant's awareness. Once he notices, the clamour is astounding. Each and every tree bristles with them. Their dry snappy clack echoes through the hills. Now he hears them all the time. He can't get the clack out of his head.

FRIDAY, FEBRUARY 19

Not a single instrument has been found inaccurate. Quant didn't think they would be. They were getting the same sorts of readings across all the units. There were no rogue results. The whole lot is uncommon in unison.

He requests that Damon sends the group data for the month to date. Krypton is rising quickly – imperceptible unless you are looking. Quant knows that's strange. But he doesn't want to risk the project by including the data in the package uploaded to London. It's not what they're meant to be looking for.

SUNDAY, FEBRUARY 21

Quant gets up to go to the toilet. It is 3.17am. The cicadas are still casting their calls, sonically drowning the crickets. They are snapping, like fingers cracking in your ear. So loud, it's distorted.

Quant thought they only made that noise during the day.

He sits at the computer and does some research. No one has studied cicadas intensely. He supposes that it doesn't make for a sufficiently interesting funding proposal.

In New Zealand, the various species of cicadas have life cycles of between three to five years. The population is periodical, meaning every three, five or seven years, depending on the species, the population surges. Quant immediately notices the cycle is made of prime numbers. This must be one of those cyclical years.

The curious scent taints the air continuously now, and it's everywhere — not just at the beach. So it's not emanating from the molluscs. It's not the thick clumpy scent of decomposition. It's altogether sharper — like ozone. It can't be the rising krypton, which is odourless.

MONDAY, FEBRUARY 22

Quant asks at work, but no one else smells anything unusual. The answer makes him feel as if he has a form of nasal tinnitus. He won't ask again.

Damon, Julie and Flynn have gone AWOL. Quant can't get them on their phones. Neither is there an answer at either of their hotel rooms.

TUESDAY, FEBRUARY 23

Quant gets hold of Julie. She answers the phone in Damon's room. She sounds sleepy. Her voice soft like a Robitussin addict. She explains that they were out at the remote Kihikihi site yesterday. They were getting ready to leave for Paeroa.

Quant imagines Julie as a phone sex girl. The fingers of her left hand grip the receiver. Her thin red-brown lips brush, sticking momentarily to the phone cup. Quant snaps back to the call, chastising himself as he issues an affirmation on Paeroa.

WEDNESDAY, FEBRUARY 24

A cicada is trapped on the morning bus. It crashes into windows. Through each successive collision, crusty thorax on glass, the whirring transforms into a damaged flacking sound. Quant watches, embarrassed for its desperation. The cicada clips the ear of a passenger and comes to an abrupt stop on the forearm of Quant's shirt. It is bright green, shimmering like Soho neon. It picks out its spindly legs from where they spiked the cotton. Quant pinches lightly at its thorax and pulls it away from the shirt. He holds it to the morning sunlight. The cicada's legs trace helpless arcs. Its dark pixel eyes stare at him. Quant stares back.

FRIDAY, FEBRUARY 26

Damon, Julie and Flynn are again not reachable by phone, but the occasional short text message from each indicates they're on track. All instruments are testing okay. Quant absolves himself of responsibility: when the data assimilation is complete and the results stay the same, it is up to London to accommodate the facts. Screw their hypothesis – get a new one.

SATURDAY, FEBRUARY 27

Cicadas are everywhere. Not just on the trees, but on buildings, fences, vehicles, and food. They clatter about the backyard, snap, thwack and bang. The kids are greatly amused – catching them by the dozen. They bring each one to Quant, arm outstretched and palm open. The cicadas don't bother flying away. They just scritch themselves into position on the kids' hands and start clacking. The kids love the big ones the best. They peer at them closely, watching the viridescent exoskeleton on their carcasses flex, making that cracking noise.

Everywhere and anywhere, cicadas pair up swiftly and mate. The frantic functionality of the hundreds of cicada matings in the backyard is an opportunity for Quant to introduce the topic of sex to the two eldest, Fiona and Jonno. They watch the quick urgent pairings, fascinated.

Sunday, February 28

A very hot day. Thirty degrees Celsius. Very unusual for Wellington. Quant's family spend the whole day in and out of the pool. By mid-afternoon, the heat is such that the kids decide to have 'nudey-swims'. They strip off and flesh about in the warm water. Cicadas fall into the tepid liquid with them. The younger girls smile-scream as the cicadas whir across the water surface. Jonno calls them kamikaze cicadas. He scoops them up, tossing the half-drowned carcasses into a Shinto shrine he imagines in the flower bed.

Reclining on a chair in the partial shade next to Quant, Maena lifts her thin cotton dress to her pubis. She wears practical knickers. She parts her legs slightly to cool inside her thighs. An aging Freedom store shade dapples the ripples of her skin. Quant imagines his tongue brushing out the dimples, sticking momentarily to the goose bumps. He shifts in his chair, which sets it creaking and scratching. Maena turns and smiles. 'We'll have to fix that.'

Later she brings out an afternoon snack. The kids stand

pooling water on the deck, waiting for Maena to lay out the meal. They jiggle in unison, in freshened anticipation of food. Their browning naked bodies are already drying in the sun. Rivulets of crinkled water run into the triangle of the girls' groins. Freshly filtered water traces a line down Jonno's chilled arched penis and spills from the pursed tip.

A cicada flies into the jam. The kids screech with laughter as it coats itself with tacky boysenberry. Quant fishes it out with a knife and flicks it away.

Maena looks up to the sun, eyes closed, and emits a little cry, somewhere between joy and heat exasperation. She shrugs the dress off her shoulders, slipping it to her feet, and steps out.

The kids eat hungrily, watching.

Maena flicks off the straps of her bra and unhooks it.

The kids down glasses of ice-cubed juice.

Maena eases the thick sweat-dampened cotton knickers to her ankles.

Quant, sandwich in mouth, sees his wife. Velvet curtains of adipose tissue drape her thighs. Breasts pendulant, satisfied stomach cernuous. Broad wanton smile. She takes little leaps towards the pool. Her bottom dances. Cheeks slap. She plunges with a joyous screech into the pool.

The kids cheer and Quant joins them in mushing wet fruit slices into his mouth.

WEDNESDAY, MARCH 2

Again no answer to Quant's calls to the travelling team. They should be finishing this week. Their text messages are terse and belligerent. Flynn texts that Damon is flirting with Julie and it's distracting their work. Damon texts that Flynn is deliberately finding things to criticise. There's no word from Julie. Quant wishes he was there, to know she is okay.

THURSDAY, MARCH 3

A relief – finally *other* people notice the pervasive smell. Quant is called at the office by journalists asking if the Institute knows what it is. He tells them he could not smell it, and is not measuring anything unusual. That irritates them, but there's nothing they can do about it.

The month's results are now in, but Quant doesn't finish making sense of them. Krypton levels are still climbing. He sends a note to Jim, recommending they write a briefing paper on krypton for the Minister. The upward trend is now worrying, but the narcotic effects are still a long way off.

FRIDAY, MARCH 4

Jim is not at work. Quant estimates that 22 per cent of the staff are away. Those at work are indolent.

At the bus stop, a used condom lies ripening in the sunshine. The bus is late. Quant has to stand thinking whether he should clean it up. It's unseemly. He wonders at the hurried tryst that must have occurred right where he stood, only hours before. He shifts uncomfortably and adjusts himself in his trousers. The bus arrives. He gets on.

He can't hear the drawled greeting of the bus driver over the din of the cicadas.

SUNDAY, MARCH 7

Quant lies in bed listening to the cicadas. The males are desperate to rise above the din of nearby competitors. He hears them rearranging themselves to go again, in turn, louder and rougher. The coarse hum is magnificent. The females fling themselves in the direction of the male noise they like best. Their skittery clasping sounds like dry hail scraping the roof.

Maena bumps her body heavily against Quant. She dances tiny dry thrusts against his side. She runs raspy hands down his chest and over his allantoid stomach. She locates what she needs. It is ready. She casts the sheets back, and shucks off her pyjamas. The wooden joints and bolts of the bed crack under them. Their pubic hairs scritter like Velcro.

MONDAY, MARCH 8

Damon is dead. The police found him in Julie's room in Hamilton. Flynn entered the room while Julie and Damon were mating. He bashed in Damon's head with one of the aluminium housings from the air-sampling units.

What are they doing still in Hamilton? They should have been in Kaitaia. Fuck them.

Quant finds Jim at a café near the Institute, overlooking the bay. The sea is flat, but a long-spaced swell paces itself, spilling foam over the pebbled beaches. Quant asks Jim for news on the Ministers' response to the report. Jim says he hadn't got around to sending it. With hand on shoulder, he invites Quant to go for a drink. Quant declines. He goes home.

The strange esthesis caused by the odour now even overpowers the diesel exhaust of the bus.

TUESDAY, MARCH 9

Maena is languid. There is no dinner. The family gathers in the kitchen and eats things from the fridge. The kids aren't even asleep before she slumps onto the bed, rolls onto her back and peels open to Quant like the dry husk of a mandarin. He sucks hungrily at the juice, wiping away pith.

WEDNESDAY, MARCH 10

The kids don't get up to go to school. Maena is not up to make them. Quant drives to work because the buses have stopped. He pulls in for petrol. Looking for someone to pay, he interrupts the service guy in the machine shop with a female customer on the bonnet of her car.

THURSDAY, MARCH 11

After dark, Maena reclines on the wooden deck, naked. Quant watches her from a nearby lounger. A cicada lands on her thigh. She makes no move to wipe it away. He can see it picking at her skin with its sticky feet. Tiny red welts swell like inflamed goosebumps. More cicadas land, congregate. They clack ceaselessly. They latch onto each other, dry humping. Maena squirms. She's sort of smiling. More follow. They tangle in her pubic hair. She slumps, undone.

FRIDAY, MARCH 12

There is no one at work. He can't reach anyone at the Hamilton police station. He doesn't know what's happened to Julie. Gorgeous Julie. He looks at the office pin board for the photo of her from a conference last year. It's at the post-session drinks. She's in a t-shirt and short skirt. The hard angles of her torso are visible. The protuberance of bone at the hips. The muscles rich with adenosine triphosphate. He picks the photo from the wall and goes to the bathroom.

MONDAY, MARCH 15

Quant drives past two dogs copulating on the road. They are oblivious as the car swerves around them.

Driving home, Quant sees one of those fucking dogs. It is dead. He stops to look. Cicadas crawl around its eyes, sucking at the death weep. Cicadas use liquid sap to build their soil burrows.

WEDNESDAY, MARCH 17

The family is eating canned food. Maena is not eating. She is shedding weight. Her skin is dry. She has no energy to go to the supermarket. Quant went there yesterday; it was open, shelves in disarray, but empty of people.

Somewhere along the line, Quant realises, he has stopped going to work.

THURSDAY, MARCH 18

They all stay in bed until noon. Then lie about the lounge. They can't be bothered eating. The kids are emaciated. There's no human sounds from the neighbours or road. Just the cicadas snappeling.

Quant fucks Maena carelessly in the lounge while the kids watch videos. TV stations aren't running. She feels dry and brittle beneath him. He can't remember if they finish.

Much later, she says she is pregnant. They look at each other blankly, unable to think of anything but the cacophony of cicadas.

He says she looks terrible. Like she's drying out. She asks for salve. Quant anoints Maena with pawpaw cream, then crawls onto her and interlocks. She is parched inside. It hurts and leaves him bloody.

THURSDAY, MARCH 25

Quant awakes to complete silence.

A week has passed.

He feels guilty. He doesn't know why.

There are dead cicadas on the windowsill.

Maena lies beside him in the bed, breathing shallowly. Skin parched and peeling.

The kids are up and about. They stomp about the neighbourhood, languorously digging their heels into cicadas that flap on the ground. The cicadas coat the ground in brown and green. They rasp about the pavement. They lie crunched on the road and everywhere underfoot. Jonno collects them in rubbish bags and piles the shells onto a mound on the beach.

FRIDAY, MARCH 26

It's Good Friday for those who are entertained by those things.

The silence is strange. Quant can still hear cicadas clapping. But they're all dead. A breeze has started. The air is clear. The first time in weeks. The air swirls dried husks of cicadas into large mounds.

The kids are clearly more alert and stronger, thank God. They trek to the Four Square and return laden with packaged food. Quant feels his strength returning.

SATURDAY, MARCH 27

Maena is not recovering. She may be dying. Quant tries to

help her; compresses; any medicine with sanguine instructions. He sits by her the whole day, pacing the dry scrape of her breath. He calculates that it is slowing 1% every five hours.

SUNDAY, MARCH 28

The kids say people are appearing on the streets. Buses trundle slowly past the house. Radio and TV is back on, with repeats, and news bulletins by tired people. Government ministers look bewildered and say they are conducting inquiries.

MONDAY, MARCH 29

The date of our deliverance is a prime number. There are Australians in blue uniforms on the streets. They dole out fresh food and water. Quant sends the kids out to join the short passive queues. The blue uniforms come to the door. They wave machines about in their hands.

From the bed, Maena cracks at Quant to dispel them.

At the door, the uniforms tell Quant everything is okay. He agrees, they are okay. They go away.

Maena's skin is hardening – becoming rigid. Her breasts are chitin plates. Her bottom like two cockle shells.

She has burrowed under the sheets. Her pixel eyes stare at Quant from the bed dark. From there, she whispers to Quant hoarsely: what happened was glorious, wasn't it? Bacchanalian. Insouciance. She wants it again.

You can, Quant says. You can come again.

He wraps the hardened body in the bedsheets and carries it into the garden to bake in the soil.

Boxing Day

Martin Livings

IT WAS EARLY MORNING, BUT ALREADY THE GROUND WAS starting to shimmer with summer heat, the reds and browns of our sun-scorched property running together like melted paints. Dad sat on the verandah in his favourite chair, the wicker one that was coming apart, and watched the procession of cars approaching up our driveway, the road so far away that it wasn't even visible from the house. I stood on one side of the chair, Pete on the other, though Dad couldn't see him, nobody could, not anymore. Nobody but me.

Dad smiled, that tight, expectant smile we all knew too well; not a smile of amusement, but of pleasure, the pleasure of violence on the horizon. He smiled that smile before he punished his children, or his wife for that matter. And he smiled it every year on this day.

'They're coming,' he said, his voice husky, and took a deep swallow from his can of beer, already his third for the new-born day. He reeked of it. I breathed it in, tasted it. Tasted things in it that I'd never tasted before. Promise. Hope. 'We can start soon.'

Yes, we can, Pete said in his cold, silent voice. I had to stop myself looking at him standing there, smiling at my dead twin brother, nodding to him. Not when Dad was there. Only when we were alone. I could see him out of the corner of my eye, though. He looked like he always did, like me, only a boy; a strong, tall, entirely satisfactory boy. Unlike me. He looked good, fifteen years old and in his prime. Not like he'd looked at the end, thank heaven. I couldn't have taken that, not for a whole year.

Had it really been a year? It seemed like yesterday. It seemed like a thousand years ago. Anything but a year, twelve months, three hundred and sixty-five days.

I watched the cars draw closer, my heart racing. Dad was right. We'd start soon.

Less than two hundred people lived in Blair, and most were related to me one way or another. Uncles, aunts, cousins, second cousins, once removed, twice, three times. The town census and my family tree were basically the same thing. But our family was the trunk of that tree, and that made us top of the food chain in Blair. Poppa Michael was Dad's father, but he was old and couldn't remember much of anything anymore, so Dad was in charge. Sure, the Mayor went through the motions, but nothing happened without Eddie Blair's say-so. And Eddie Blair had three daughters including me, who were irrelevant to his wishes, and one shining son. Pete.

Had.

The first car pulled up, and Uncle Albert and Auntie Doreen climbed out. They opened the back door, and four of my cousins spilled out into the dirt. Two girls and two boys. The boys looked excited, and a bit scared. The girls just looked bored. I didn't blame them; every year I'd felt much the same. Not this year, though. Albert nodded at Dad, who nodded back. Then he headed around to the side paddock to start setting up. More would join him soon, with sledgehammers and star pickets and ropes. Many hands made light work.

Every year, the day after Christmas, the family would gather here. The women brought food and grog, and immediately joined Mum and us girls in the kitchen. Our job was to keep the menfolk fed and watered for the day. And the men … the men did what men did best. Ate. Drank.

Fought.

I glanced at Dad's hands. He'd already bound them with thin strips of cloth, blood stains visible from previous years' bouts. He was a deeply superstitious man, used the same strapping every year, wore the same clothes; his dark blue shorts and his white singlet, which was also spotted with rusty brown stains, some faded by years of washing, others fresh. The cloth on his knuckles was as close to protection as he was willing to offer. *Fucken faggots and their fucken pillow gloves,* he'd spat when watching a boxing match on the telly. *What's the fucken point?*

Dad was a man of few words, and a lot of those words were *fucken*. If Pete or I or Evie or Mary ever said it, though, we'd get a clip around the ear, if we were lucky. Sometimes it was a fist to the side of the head. Sometimes more.

Sometimes much more.

Dad finally got out of his chair. I saw the hesitation, the slight flinch of pain that rippled across his forehead. I tried not to smile.

He's old, Pete said, standing right next to me now, the summer morning air chilled by his presence. *Old and slow and weak.*

I didn't react, couldn't. Death had made Pete a bit cocky. Which was ironic, considering how he'd died.

We walked around the side of the house, Dad and I, and watched the rings being constructed. Blairs all, by blood if not by name, bashing steel pickets into the dust, deep enough to hold the ropes that would be slung around them like spider webs, ready to catch unwary souls. All the same as last year, and the years before that.

This year, though, this year was going to be different. This year was going to be the last.

Dad put a wrapped hand on my shoulder, calloused and bruised and rough, fingernails cut brutally short, and looked into my eyes. There was a sadness in his, a loss that mirrored my own.

'Are you sure about this, Katie?' he asked.

I nodded. I was dressed differently from the rest of the Blair womenfolk, shorts and an old t-shirt, no shoes. They weren't my clothes. They were Pete's. There was still blood on the shirt, blood that wouldn't wash out. I didn't try that hard. I liked it there.

Dad frowned, a thunderhead rolling across his face. 'It's just not right,' he growled. 'It's not done.'

'Just this year, Dad,' I assured him, as sweetly as I could. 'I need to do this. Just this once.' I looked into his eyes, and tried to hide my hatred. 'For Pete.'

He sighed. 'For Pete. Just do your best, Katie.'

'I will, Dad,' I replied with complete honesty. 'I will.'

Fucken right you will, Pete growled. He glared at Dad from beside me.

Dad didn't hear him. Dad never heard Pete. Not since he'd killed him.

The Blair men had nearly finished setting up the rings, four of them, the star posts driven into the ground in the same place as every year. They weren't exactly even, but they were good enough. Four rings, and sixteen competitors. It didn't change much from year to year, just the young ones getting old enough to strap their hands and climb into the ring, and the old ones stepping down. This year, we were a man short. It stuffed everything up.

That's where I came in.

I looked around at the fifteen boys and men preparing for battle. Not all of them would be leaving the rings on their feet. Five or six of the fighters would need medical treatment for broken bones, dislocated retinas, bloody noses; the usual stuff. The town hospital kept some beds free after Christmas, just for us. Blairs would go in, and a few days later Blairs would come out.

Pete Blair, though, he never came out. Never woke up.

The first eight fighters strode out onto the paddock, my father amongst them. They kicked up dust as they marched, chests pumped, smiling for the small crowd of onlookers, mainly the other Blairs waiting their turn, or the boys and old men, some looking at their futures, others at their pasts. I allowed myself a small smile, safe, unseen. Nobody paid me any attention. *Katie*, they'd think, *she's nothing, a girl, a weakling. Forget her.*

That's what we're counting on, Pete said from behind me. I felt his cold hand on my shoulder, and it gave me comfort. *They'll never see you coming, Katie. And they'll never forget you again, not after today. Not ever.*

'I know,' I said, relieved to be able to talk to my brother again. We'd been planning this day all year, the two of us, since he'd died.

Pete and I were fraternal twins, but we were so alike it was uncanny. He was born first, and if reports are true, Dad bellowed with joy when he saw that little thing between the child's legs, such a little thing to give such pleasure to a grown man. Such a little thing, yet so important.

I came out second, a tiny wet anticlimax. A living, breathing afterbirth, as far as Dad was concerned. Just another girl.

Pete and I had both grown up tall, lean, strong. Our reflexes were excellent; we'd gotten them from Dad. We both picked up sports with almost no effort. But Pete got all the attention, while I was relegated to the background. Ignored.

And my dad, of course, he was so disappointed I wasn't a boy. Another girl was no use to him, not on the farm, and especially not on Boxing Day. I think he thanked the good Lord he had Pete; his hopes and dreams could live through him. I was the forgotten twin.

One of the spectators yelled, 'Go!' and the first four fights began simultaneously. There was no bell, no rounds. No referees. One rule. You fought until one man either conceded or couldn't stand up. The first round was usually a pretty light-hearted affair; nobody wanted to get too badly hurt, not with three more rounds ahead. The winners were already known, more or less.

I smiled again. I knew the winners already, not more or less, but absolutely. After all, I drew up the round robin chart every year. I knew who'd fought who in the past, and who'd won. I knew the odds.

I was the only one interested in working out the roster for the fights; nobody else could be bothered, they just wanted to get out there and beat the shit out of someone. And the women weren't encouraged to do anything but cook and clean and have babies. Here in Blair, the twenty-first century hadn't arrived. Hell, even the twentieth century was having a hard time getting a toehold. It was my job to make up the charts, decide who fought who in the first round.

Theoretically, the outcomes of the fights determined who fought who in the second round. In practice, I already knew who would win. And this year, I'd planned the roster more carefully than ever before.

Especially where I placed myself in it.

I ignored three of the fights, various uncles and cousins belting each other half-heartedly. Instead, I watched my dad fight his younger sister Eileen's son, Toby. He was a dark horse; young but fast, with a good reach. Lanky, but lean. If I'd put him against anyone else, he might have made it through to the next round.

Against Dad, he didn't stand a chance.

Dad drew him in, let him unload a couple of hard jabs to his kidneys. They made the old man flinch, which warmed my heart. Toby attempted an uppercut, aimed at Dad's jaw, but Dad dodged back, grinning that cold grin, the one he always wore during the fights. He stepped to one side as Toby tried again for his face, and the kid overbalanced, stumbled forward a little.

A little was all it needed. Dad took him down with a hard left hook across his cheekbone. The skin split, and blood gushed. He tumbled to the dirt, his knees folding beneath him. He fell face first into the dust and didn't move.

'Fucken yeah!' Dad roared, and raised his fists. The onlookers cheered.

I looked away, sickened. I'd felt those fists on my flesh, when Dad was angry or drunk or both. Pete was stronger and faster than me, he could have escaped the beatings easily, if he'd chosen to. Most of the time he chose not to, took the punishment so I didn't have to. And then, last year…

I tried to make it right, he whispered in my ear. There was a mustiness to his breath, grave dirt, and behind it a deep rot.

I tried. But he…

'I know,' I said.

The other three matches ended exactly as I knew they would. Three more men victorious, pumped up with bravado and adrenaline and testosterone. Then I stepped off the verandah and towards the rings. Curious eyes found me, then looked away. Laughter bitten back, stifled by respect for my father. For Pete. I ignored them all.

My turn.

I'd put myself up against a distant nephew from the other side of town, a nice little kid called Evan, barely ten years old. I liked Evan a lot, and he liked me. He wasn't going to fight me. I wasn't going to fight him, not properly. It was a play fight, like more than a few of the first round. We laughed as we pretended to box, then I tapped him on the jaw and he collapsed onto the dirt in giggles. I raised one hand in mock victory, and it was over. There was polite applause, condescending, patronising. *Oh, isn't that nice? Katie made it through the first round. Well done, young lady!* I gritted my teeth.

Keep it together, Pete told me from the corner of the ring. *Keep it together.*

'I will,' I hissed through my teeth, and smiled and curtseyed to the too-polite crowd.

The second round was eight fighters, two in each ring. No chance to watch Dad fight this time. He was up against one of his brothers. Darryl was a pitbull, and I was relying on him to soften the old man up for me. As for myself, I had more of a challenge ahead. My opponent was a second cousin, a brash kid called Billy. He was a year older than me, but a year behind me in school. He hated that. I could see it in his tiny eyes. He was almost vibrating with anger and anticipation. He wasn't much taller than I was, but probably twice my size overall. I'd seen him kick girls to the dirt on the playground. He didn't care. I knew he'd wanted to bully me at school as well, but he didn't dare, not with Pete by my side and my dad at home. Even after Pete had died, Billy had held back. But here, today, all bets were off, and he knew it.

I was counting on that.

'Billy,' I said with a nod. He didn't respond, just glared at me, like a dog on a chain. Waiting for the signal to attack.

'Go!'

Billy charged, bellowing. I kept very still. It seemed to be happening in slow motion. Billy was going to knock me down, then kneel on my chest and bash me with both hands, the same as he did to so many other poor kids in the playground at school. So predictable.

At the last second, I dodged to my left and stuck my leg out.

Billy couldn't stop. His eyes widened as his momentum carried him past me, his ankles catching on my shin. He went down face-first in the dirt with a muffled cry.

I moved to straddle him, sat on the small of his back. He could have gotten up even with my weight on him, but he was stunned and hurt. I leaned forward and whispered in his ear.

'Give it up, Billy.'

Then I grabbed his head, pulled it back, and rammed it into the hard ground. It didn't take much strength. The head *wanted* to go forward – that's just how the anatomy of the neck works. I didn't let go, pulled his head back, and slammed it into the dirt again. This time there was a crack, and Billy screamed, a strangled thing, pathetic.

I leaned in, whispered. 'Give it *up*, Billy.'

I yanked his head back again. Blood splattered the dirt where Billy's face had been, red on red, a dark rain which soaked quickly into the thirsty sand. I prepared to send his head back to earth yet again.

One hand came up, shaking wildly. The first two fingers and thumb outstretched, the others curled up. I smiled.

'You're smarter than you look,' I told him quietly, and let him go, got back to my feet.

And you're meaner than you look, Pete said from behind me, admiration in his voice. He looked over my shoulder as Billy stood up, blood running from his nose and a split lip, tears from his eyes. He didn't meet my gaze, just slunk away, out of the ring. I followed, slipping under the rope.

I looked at the faces of the Blair men who'd watched the fight. Their eyes were wide, and more than a few mouths were agape. I smirked and nodded at them, and they looked away, faces flushed. I suspected they couldn't have been more confused if a kangaroo had spoken to them. It was that unnatural. That pleased me greatly.

I glanced at Dad. He'd finished his fight fast, faster than I'd expected or hoped for, as he was watching me as well. There was something in his eyes, something I'd never seen directed my way before. Pride? Could it be?

He was proud of me too, Pete pointed out, standing just behind me. *Didn't stop him killing me.*

I nodded, both to Pete and Dad. Dad nodded back.

There was a break between the second and third rounds, during which much beer was drunk, though I restricted myself to water. Needed to keep my head straight, or it'd get knocked off. As drinks were greedily sculled, two of the rings were disassembled, mostly by those who'd lost in the first two rounds. Bloodied men and boys gathered up pickets and ropes, limped away from the arena. That's what it was, I realised, an arena, like the Romans used to have. A spectacle of blood and pain. Vicious entertainment for the Blair clan. Mainly for my dad.

Pete didn't find it entertaining, not even when he was alive. That's why he'd spent a year training non-stop, just training to win, to beat Dad, to show the whole Blair clan that it could be done. To end the circus. And he'd come so damned close.

It's time, Pete whispered in my ear. I nodded, pulled myself back to the here and now, headed towards my assigned ring. This was where I needed to be, heart and soul. No time for daydreaming, not yet. Maybe later, if all went well. But now, I had to fight. And I was fighting…

I blinked. The man in the ring wasn't who I was expecting. When I'd written up the round robin, I thought Uncle Dave would make it through to the third round, a fat slob who I could finish off fairly easily. But instead there was a tall, thin man facing me, with dark eyes and darker hair. Definitely not a Blair, not by blood. It was my Aunt Alison's second husband, an out-of-towner called Jerome. I knew nothing about him, he'd never fought on Boxing Day before. I'd written him off in the first round, ignored him.

This was not the plan. Not the plan at all.

What now? Pete whispered in my ear. I shrugged him off. Closed my eyes for a second, took a few deep breaths, tried to think. Jerome had beaten at least two opponents I would've expected to have beaten him. He was a lot tougher than I'd anticipated. So, what now?

I opened my eyes, looked at the man. Now I had to beat him. It was that simple. God laughs when man plans.

'Go!'

Neither Jerome nor I moved, just watched one another. From the next ring over came the slap of flesh against flesh as my dad pounded his opponent, or perhaps the other way around. I could hope for the best, for him to take a beating, but not too much of a beating. He had to make the final round.

And so did I.

I approached Jerome warily, and he mirrored my motion. We circled one another, a gentle spiral of attraction, like two water droplets going down a drain.

I smiled at him. He didn't smile back.

When he moved, I barely saw it. One second he was keeping his distance, the next he was on me. His bare left fist slammed into my gut, and I felt the breath go out of me. My eyes filled with tears. A hard right jab caught my eye and twisted my head around. I stumbled backward, arm curled around my stomach, and hopped out of his reach. His eyes were unreadable. My left eye was already swelling, tears blurring my vision. I shook them away.

'Don't do this,' Jerome murmured, barely audible over the cheers of the crowd. 'I don't want to hurt you. I don't hit women.'

Definitely not a Blair, Pete laughed from the corner of the ring. I resisted the urge to yell at him to shut up, didn't have the breath for it anyway.

'You ... just did,' I gasped. 'Want to try again?'

Jerome nodded and approached. I could see from his expression that he thought he had my measure, that he'd figured out how strong I was. How weak. I didn't move, just remained hunched over, breathing heavily. He raised one fist, ready to take me down.

I kicked him in the balls.

In an instant, all his composure, all his threatening calmness disappeared, replaced with a symphony of pain. He howled and collapsed to the dirt, clutching his testicles. I knelt beside him and punched him in the face as hard as I could. Something cracked, possibly his cheek, more likely my own knuckles, but I ignored it. I punched him again, and again. He raised his hands from his crotch to his face, to fend me off. So I hit him in the balls again. Again.

'Say uncle, Uncle,' I hissed at him. Raised my fist.

He didn't hesitate. There was the hand, the two fingers and thumb. The fight was over.

I staggered backwards, leaned on the ropes. My head was vibrating like a bell, my face tight and sore. My stomach ached. I looked at my hand, where the skin had split across the knuckles, weeping pale blood. I fought the urge to cry.

Don't give up now, Pete urged from behind me. *We're so close.*

'You were so close too,' I gasped. 'Was it worth it? Is it worth it?'

It has to be.

A hand touched my shoulder, and I started, thinking Pete had become real, really real, solid and alive again. I turned, and saw the bruised face of my father instead. So much like Pete, the same features, just older, weather-beaten. Pete's face. My face.

'You've proved your point, Katie,' he said gruffly. 'You've done Pete proud.'

I nodded, sniffling, shoulders slumped. I didn't let him see my rage, didn't meet his pale blue eyes. Pete's eyes, my eyes.

'It's over,' he said, and patted my shoulder awkwardly. 'It's finished.'

'No,' I mumbled. I looked up at him. His eyes hardened. 'What?' Less a word, more a guttural growl.

'No,' I said again. 'There's still one round left.' I looked around, and realised that this was the ring, the same ring as last year, set up in the same place. I smiled. 'Come on, Dad,' I said, and stepped back into the ring. 'It's Boxing Day. It's tradition.'

A complicated expression passed across Dad's face. I saw anger in there, certainly, but also sadness, regret. And, strangely, again, some pride. I wondered if he could learn to respect his daughters the same way he'd respected his son.

He killed me! Pete's voice was filled with rage, the rage I'd felt for the past year. The rage I'd felt today. But it was passing now, ebbing away, replaced with something else. Pity? Dad didn't seem like a monster anymore. He seemed tired and old. And human.

It's too late! Pete cried. *We've come too far! Please, Katie! For me!*

'For you, Pete,' I mumbled, as Dad climbed through the ropes of the ring. Behind me, I heard Jerome leaving, still moaning in pain. I wondered if Auntie Alison would have any more kids after what I'd done to her new husband. Should I feel bad about what I'd done?

I shrugged. Maybe later, when I had time.

'Did you feel this way?' I asked Pete. 'Last year? Here?'

'What?' Dad asked, confused. 'What do you mean?'

I ignored him. 'Did you hesitate? Is that why it happened?'

Dad opened his mouth to speak, but one of the Blair men beat him to it.

'Go!'

I charged at my father, my blood boiling. A year's worth of sleepless nights, of endless training after school, Pete's dead voice in my ear, whispering, cajoling, urging me to do this. Maybe now Pete could rest like he was supposed to. Rest in peace, that's what the priest had said at his funeral, after the mortician had filled the hole in the back of his head with sawdust and putty and slathered him with tacky make-up to make him look alive. But he hadn't looked alive, he'd looked like a dummy, like a waxwork, and he'd said so from beside me at his own funeral. All because of Boxing Day. All because of Dad.

All of this filled me up, made me feel like my seams would burst and my rage would spill out like a flood, like a drought-busting flood across the whole Blair farm, drowning everyone. All of this, and I screamed and attacked my dad.

One punch, and my world exploded in sparks.

I collapsed to the dirt. My strength vanished. I was a popped balloon, a broken doll. A scrap in the dust. A girl pretending to be a man. Nothing. I struggled to breathe through my broken nose.

Dad stood over me, my blood dripping from his knuckles. His own daughter's blood. He looked down at me, still with that strange combination of fury and pride.

'I'm proud of you, Katie,' he said, breathing heavily. His face was flushed and red, blood vessels broken across his cheeks. His eyes were bulging. One of his hands, the unbloodied one, fluttered to his chest, as if he was having trouble catching his breath. 'Give it up. You done good. You done good by Pete.'

'You…' I mumbled through numb lips, tasting the blood from my nose. 'You…'

'What?' he asked, and his voice was almost gentle.

'You … don't get to say his fucken *name!*' I yelled.

Dad staggered back a step, as I pulled my legs underneath me and got unsteadily to my feet. I reached up to my nose and felt it, then gritted my teeth and pushed it sideways back into place. The pain was like a firework going off behind my eyes, but it cleared my head. I looked at my father, and saw another emotion I'd never seen before, not even when he'd looked at Pete.

Fear.

I felt the hand on my shoulder, and knew it was my brother. He'd come so close last year, but when he had the chance to take Dad down, he'd paused, and our father had taken advantage of that, laying into him with everything he'd had left. Pete had fallen backwards, and there'd been a rock on the ground, one missed during the setup. He'd landed square on it, and it had punched straight through the back of his skull and into his brain.

He'd lasted two days in the hospital before he'd died. He was strong, so strong.

I took a step towards Dad, and Pete stepped with me.

Dad's eyes were even wider now, his breath coming in shallow gulps. We walked, my dead brother and I, and Dad looking at me, then at Pete, then back at me again. His knees started to shake.

I heard something I didn't expect, couldn't have expected. Cheers. Cheers, and people chanting.

Chanting my name.

Chanting *my* name.

Another step, and another. Dad was transfixed.

'For Pete,' I said calmly, though my blood was singing in my veins.

Is it? Pete asked, concern in his dead voice. Fear. *Is it really for me now?*

I ignored him.

Dad looked back and forth between us, over and over again. Then he said one word, softly.

'Pete?'

I punched him, just once, under his left cheekbone. It wasn't a particularly hard punch, but his eyes rolled back into his skull and he collapsed to his knees. I watched him fall, and saw it there, in the dirt beside him. The rock. The blood-stained rock that had been removed last year, but there it was, on the ground, waiting. Thirsty.

Dad fell sideways, hard, and the rock bit into his head. He didn't move. Blood pooled beneath him. Silence.

Then pandemonium as Blairs swarmed the ring, grabbing me and pulling me away, kneeling beside my father's body. Screams and yells. I was carried out of the ring by half a dozen men, their hands all over me, but I didn't care, barely felt them. Carried back to the house, where my mother and sisters were waiting. I let myself be carried.

And, all the way, Pete was beside me.

It's over, he murmured, *let it be over*.

I didn't reply. All I could hear was my name on the lips of my family. My living family.

*

It was early morning, but already the ground was starting to shimmer with summer heat. I sat on the verandah in Dad's chair, the wicker one that was coming apart, and watched the cars approaching up our driveway. On one side of the chair, Pete watched with me, looking concerned. On the other side, my dad. He smiled, and I smiled too, that tight, expectant smile. Violence on the horizon, the impending storm.

'They're coming,' I said, and drank a mouthful from my can of beer. 'We can start soon.'

Yes we can, Pete said sadly. Dad just laughed, and so did I.

It was Boxing Day. It was tradition.

The Architect

Phillip Mann

PART i

THE IMAGE REFLECTED BACK FROM THE INSCRIPTION mirror was of a moon-faced man with a shiny bald head and a frizz of short white hair. It was one of those faces which, apart from its maturity, was difficult to age: a rubbery face, full of unexpected expressions, and with sharp blue eyes that could be impish one minute and angry the next. Now the eyes were bloodshot and tired.

This was the Architect and his lips moved as he talked to himself. 'Come on. Come on.' Despite the years he had spent alone at his work, the Architect had never learned patience. He stood at the bench, hands flat on the counter, fingers drumming. The technology he controlled was old and slow: as indeed was he. The Architect had forgotten how many times he had stripped down his machines and repaired them, poring over the bulky manuals until he knew parts of them by heart – or how many times he had requested upgrades – only to receive the answer from 'up-top' that supplies were short or that there were other priorities. That is, if he received a reply at all.

Slowly the mirrors became pearly white: the reflection of his face faded. Bright green graph lines appeared and quickly traced the complex image of a building. It could have been the setting for some Gothic romance. The walls were high with many buttresses. Dark alcoves set well back in the walls enclosed narrow windows. The roof was steep, with a walkway running round its edge – inviting suicide perhaps? The whole was completed with a spire like a witch's hat – but squat. 'Good God! What was I thinking?' he murmured. The Architect had designed and constructed this building many years earlier, shortly after he had arrived to work on the frozen planet called Meredith. It had been one of his first creations in the days when he was still experimenting in using ice as a building material.

After a few minutes there was no further movement and the green construction lines held still. The building was complete. Had he wished, the Architect could now have made a virtual tour of the whole structure. He could have inspected any point of the grim construction. It was well built – he had to admit that – and there were no tell-tale pin-points of red light which would have indicated an over-stressed joint or a weakness through melting. All was as it should be, solid and firm and unbending, as it had been for over two generations.

The Architect reached out and touched a small blue disk which glowed on the front of the control panel. Immediately the bright green construction lines vanished and the tower adjusted, becoming more solid, more real, more the true image of a building than a concept. Slowly it began to turn, offering itself for aesthetic rather than engineering inspection.

The Architect stood back from the screen and surveyed it. Analysing it again after so many years, the Architect's lips screwed up like someone who had suddenly encountered a disagreeable smell. Returning to this early construction, he found he did not like it. 'Too heavy by far … marred by the ostentatious dreams of youth,' he murmured. 'Too serious, too! *Fiat lux*! *Fiat gaudium.*'

As he aged, and became more skilful, so the Architect's designs had become gentler, more rounded; sensual, even, and whimsical. Brighter too. If this were to be the final building in the city, the crowning glory of his vision and his final affirmation, as it were, it would have to be re-designed … nay, re-made. Totally. From foundation to spire. No question!

He rubbed his hands, and breathed on his fingers. Then he slipped his hands into the soft round mouths of the design gauntlets which rested on the wide desk amid all the control switches which rose in a bank before him, almost like the keys of an organ.

As soon as he flexed his fingers, a point of light, bright and cherry-red, appeared in the middle of the tower. Without shifting his gaze from the image, the Architect began to manipulate the light. Within the gauntlets, his fingers moved, as though independent of the rest of his body. Like many artists before him, he was now destroying his earlier work.

Obediently, the grandiose arches and baroque incrustations he had once favoured began to melt away. Literally! Scorched by millions of micro lasers, normally only used for final annealing and polishing, the tower began to melt from within. Drips became drizzle. Finally, cascades of water poured down and were quickly sluiced away. The demolition work was done carefully. There was no sudden collapse, and nothing would be wasted. The water would again be stored in the vast pressure caverns beneath the construction hall and maintained at exactly 5.5 degrees above freezing, available to be reused when the Architect designed a new tower.

Satisfied all parameters were exact, ensuring that only the tower would be defrosted and not the surrounding buildings, the Architect left the machine to do its work. It would take just over an hour.

He crossed the hall, limping slightly, for he had many ailments, including dizziness which caused him to stumble and fall. Slowly he climbed the spiral staircase leading to his private quarters. It was, he recalled, time for his medication, his *Aqua Mirabilis* as he called it. This was the potion which had kept him alive and active for many years and to which he was now wholly and happily addicted.

In his room, the light above the communication panel was flashing red, indicating that an urgent message had been received from the Icelander Station above. The Architect chose to ignore it as he had many times before. He threw a towel over the light to stop it filling his room with its irritating flash. After all, he reasoned, how many messages had he sent to the surface over the years asking for necessary supplies, demanding assistance when he fell ill and pleading for news of the wider world … only to have them all ignored? No, they could wait a bit. He was busy, and if they wanted to see him that urgently they could take the lift down through the 'shaft' and knock on his door politely. The 'shaft' was a 300-metre-long tunnel which connected his quarters and all the deep-freeze machines he controlled with the surface platform where the managers lived. He did not envy their luxury; well, not anymore. Over the years he had come to love his solitude. Events in the world beyond the city he was building had little meaning to him.

The Architect stretched out on his untidy bed. Above him, suspended from the ceiling, was a clear plastic reservoir containing a pink liquid. A fine catheter dangled, its coils within easy reach. He took this and connected its pressure tap to a tube which emerged from the side of his throat. Immediately, he felt a warm glow spread through all his limbs and he relaxed, breathing deeply. His eyelids fluttered as the drug took effect. When he finally closed his eyes, he was already deep in his dream of a blue sky above a green hillside where wild flowers bobbed in a summer breeze. A pretty young woman in a white dress was unpacking a hamper and setting the food out on a plaid blanket – a world he had not seen for many years, and a woman he had never known.

*

Exactly an hour later he woke up and detached the catheter. He felt refreshed. Rejuvenated. Ready for the act of re-creation. He ate a food capsule, cracking it between his teeth and sucking hard to extract all the nutrient before chewing the plastic to the consistency of soft toffee, which melted away in his mouth.

He removed the towel from the communication panel. The light was still flashing its red-alert message. Instead of opening contact, he tapped out a message of his own – 'Gonfishin, Don't disturb!!!' – and sent it off with a chuckle. And indeed, he had work to do: a tower to build. He set off down the spiral stairway. He wasn't even holding the rail, and the limp was forgotten.

All was well in the design studio. The melting demolition was complete. Where the tower had once stood was now a bare piazza – strange amid the gleaming walls of the buildings which surrounded it.

Donning the design gauntlets again, the Architect made

various quick adjustments and the view of the piazza began to change. The viewer now seemed to be rising above the city while moving away at the same time. More buildings appeared. The piazza became smaller, but it remained special too because it was at the very centre of the entire city. It was the focus of many avenues and brightly coloured buildings. Some of these had been sculpted to suggest the fanciful shapes of terrestrial animals – a giant hare, for example, sitting back on its haunches, ears erect; or a giraffe stretching to feed on the leaves of a tree.

Other buildings were clearly based on ancient monuments of Earth. A serene Taj Mahal with its clear lake stood just beyond a comic and tipsy Leaning Tower of Pisa. In a distant quarter of the city, erect in its own park, was Stonehenge. The Sphinx too, now with a handsome male face and blue painted eyes, stared at the naked and relaxed *David* by Michelangelo. The two monuments stood looking at one another as though in mutual admiration. And beyond both, her flame held aloft, was the Statue of Liberty, naked in this rendition … and all were carved from ice.

Surrounding the city were trees imported from Earth. And spaced among these was an orchard, a brewery and some vineyards.

Beyond, in the hazy distance, rose the interior walls of a giant dome. They arched over and enclosed the entire city. Lights hidden in the dome's construction sent ever-changing patterns across its surface. No blue sky or bright sun were here, but a dazzle of light all the same. And, outside the dome, faintly invisible to anyone looking from within, was a grey mottled sky, with turbulent winds and racing clouds. Anyone who ventured through the air lock and walked outside encountered dark frost-bitten rock faces, sheer cliffs and dunes of driven snow. This was the surface of the planet Meredith, where the temperature never rose above freezing.

'Why build here?' had been the Architect's first question years ago when he came to Meredith. Only then had he been told of the vast network of mines that was planned to burrow into the mountains and dig deep below the planet's surface. The company would extract the rare earths and minerals: the uranium, the platinum, the gold, the cinnabar, the silver and in some places the diamonds – all found in abundance. Meredith was also home to certain useful microbes, but innocent of advanced life. Meredith, cold and grim, swinging round its pale sun … Meredith, the richest by far of all the known planets to date. It was so rich the company which owned it had decided they would make it a showplace with a city to rival fabled Xanadu. That was the Architect's job.

Crazy, sublime, inspired, surreal – those were some of the words used by those who chanced to visit the Architect in the early stages of his creative work. Others coined a new word and called it Escheresque. The word reminded the Architect of a sneeze. He was aware it was not necessarily intended as a compliment, but to him it was high praise. He replied with a cough of his own: 'Hundertvassarian! Do excuse me!'

And indeed, the clash of artistic styles could have been a jumble, a clutter, a farrago, a mish-mash. But it wasn't. Somehow the Architect had managed to create harmony in diversity. Wherever you looked was contrast and audacity. The entire city was knitted together by high, soaring walkways which joined curved buildings. It could be traversed by a lone man on foot in a single hour even though there was hardly a straight line to be found anywhere. Cloisters led off thoroughfares. Houses, no two of them alike, stood cheek by jowl amid flower gardens. Simple gravity-driven waterfalls spilled their water into a single artificial river which meandered peacefully, but with occasional rapids, through the city until it poured away into a cistern ... there to be cleansed before being pumped back up the hill to begin its journey again.

As the years passed and the city grew, senior members of the mining company came to see what progress had been made. They wandered in the streets, marvelling at the shapes. They stayed overnight at the guest-house, the only building which was fully functional with warmed floors, a tennis court and small concert hall. After they had got over their initial astonishment, they were intrigued to learn that every building was made of ice – simple H_2O!

Water in the form of snow and ice was abundant on Meredith. This material had simply been melted. As water, it was channelled into moulds. These were then clamped and coated with a strong laminate which hardened as it cooled giving each block, arch or column perfect insulation from outside heat, and the strength of stone. This near perfect insulation allowed the temperature within the dome to be held at a comfortable 22 degrees. Once frozen, the blocks would never melt unless the laminate were attacked with a laser. Even then they could be quickly repaired. It was the Architect's private intention that when the last block was in place, every laser except those used for construction would be buried deep. The city would survive.

The Architect ran his hands through his frizz of white hair.

Incredible! After all these years he was about to create the last building. Within a few hours everything would be complete. What an extraordinary moment. What would he do then?

Ah. Then he would call the people who dwelled in their prefabricated huts on the surface and invite them down to his city – *The City* – for a grand party. He would let them picnic in the parks, swim in the canals and climb among the buildings – and he would acknowledge their accolades with a modest smile.

Settling in to his work, perched birdlike on a stool, the Architect reached out and made certain adjustments. The image in the screen vanished. When the screen next came alive it showed the bare piazza. A quick touch and the screen transformed smoothly to design mode. With his eyes fixed on the screen, the Architect began to draw, his fingers moving deftly within the warm gauntlets.

He worked until he fell asleep and his head rested on the control panel.

He dragged himself up to his bed, sipped his *Aqua* and slept.

*

That became the pattern of his days. Work, *Aqua*, Sleep, *Aqua*. Work…

Never once did he think to check the communication board which continued flashing. He had far more important things to do.

A spiral began to grow from the ground. Day and night, blocks of ice were formed, laminated and sent on their way down the gravity chutes to the waiting construction monitors who, following their strict schedule, identified the blocks and forwarded them in sequence to the construction cranes. The work never stopped and day by day the tower grew. The booms coming from the freezing pits were a constant reminder of the work, but the Architect no longer heard them.

The new tower was slim in comparison to the bulky gothic building it was replacing, but it was much taller. The diameter at its base was no more than ten metres. It soared upwards gracefully and when complete, it would be the highest of all the buildings in the city. Within its walls there were no steps or windows or passages. They were not necessary, as no one would live there. But it was not solid either. In the centre was a column of open space – like the hole in the zero.

At its very top the Architect had crafted a space which looked like interlocking diamonds. This would be the final resting place for the ceremonial 'last block'. It was a cube of clear ice, 2.5 metres on each side. It would be hoisted up into the Diamond Room – as the Architect called it – and then anchored to the roof. Beneath it would be a flat, circular platform of ice which could be raised and lowered using a pressure column – one of the Architect's inventions.

*

The days slipped past, and then came a moment when finally the Architect sat still, his gaze unwavering as he studied the finished work. The ceremonial 'last block' was designed and ready for the Freezing Chamber. With a sigh – which might almost have been interpreted as regret – the Architect touched his fingers together and the screen facing him became opaque. The final design was being assessed, coded, calculated and saved.

Moments later, the image reappeared. It showed exactly how the block would look *in situ*. The Architect made some quick adjustments and the view changed. He was now looking at the entire tower revealed in three dimensions. All the graceful curves were firm and intact and the Diamond

Room at the apex shone with a bright inner light. The tower turned slowly before him. From all points of view it retained its symmetry. He had designed the tower to be partly translucent – a special technique he had developed – and shafts of clear light, projected from the roof of the dome, split into all the colours of the spectrum as they passed through the ice. The central column could now be seen for what it was: a lift shaft. As he watched, the platform began to rise up the central column slowly as though it were lifting people to the viewing gallery. When it reached the top, the platform became the floor of the diamond-shaped chamber. Here, visitors would be able to move around and even under the last block. They could also view The City in all its splendour.

The Architect made another small adjustment and, when the screen cleared, it was as though he were standing inches away from the last block and able to see every detail. It was covered with carefully etched writing: quotations and poems from the literature he loved.

Another small adjustment and he was outside the building drifting slowly down. Here again, was writing inscribed on the blocks. It was the story of the city written by the Architect himself, describing progress from the first plan up to the present moment. Occasionally he passed narrow openings shaped like feathers and leaves. On one occasion, there was the frozen shape of an eye staring out. It was his eye. Several times, there were images of his hands. And then he reached the ground.

'The rest,' murmured the Architect to himself, 'is mechanical.' He moved down the design bench and flipped open the cover of a small panel. Beneath the panel was a single red button. He pressed it with his thumb, holding it until a message flashed on the design screen:

CONSTRUCTION PROGRAMME ACTIVE.

From deep within the bowels of the building, from somewhere far beneath him, there came a growling. The growling grew to a muted roar which made small objects tremble. The forces which would fashion all the final pieces had been unleashed. It was indeed a historic moment and the Architect decided to go and watch.

After glancing round to make sure that all was in order, the Architect left the design chamber. He entered a narrow and damp passage which led downwards. It had been hewn from the solid rock. Immediately the roaring from below was louder.

Well, at least them upstairs will know I am at work. The concrete floored path was lit by overhead lamps which cast a cold light. The hardness of the stone underfoot was softened somewhat by a worn carpet of raffia which the Architect had brought back after one of his rare journeys away from Meredith. Occasionally, when he had been constructing a lot of blocks, this passage had become frosty and the carpet stopped him from slipping.

After several twists, the path ended at a steel door similar to those used in banks to protect their wealth. The door was painted bright red, and was the first of two doors which served as a temperature lock. The Architect tapped in a code. He heard the magnetic bolts withdraw and the door opened slowly, pulled from within by a hydraulic arm. He entered, pressed a bright green switch and the door closed behind him. This was always a bit unnerving, for if the mechanism ever failed or the power faltered, and the emergency phone went dead, he could be trapped here for … But it had never failed. The engineers who had planned and built the entire chamber and all the mechanisms it contained had been careful and thorough – as indeed was the Architect who came after them. He thought of them as his brothers – in philosophy, if not in trade – for they built to last … for all eternity.

When the first door had closed, the second door opened automatically. In contrast to the first door, this one was painted blue. The Architect stepped through. He entered a vast chamber eerily lit by high incandescent lamps. Everything was stark and blunt and functional. The chamber had been blasted and then quarried from the living rock of the planet. The walls streamed with water. Stanchions rose from the floor and crisscrossed before disappearing into the gloom of the ceiling.

In the centre of the chamber was a large circular pit. Other smaller pits surrounded it. These contained the specially treated water which would form the ice blocks from which the tower would be constructed. The sloping sides of the pits and the metal walkways connecting them gleamed in the harsh light and were glossy with a jelly-like slime. This was one of the consequences of the construction process and of the laminate chemicals which coated the finished blocks and stopped them from melting. The jelly was not only slippery, but caustic. Before going any further, the Architect slipped his feet into a pair of clogs which stood just inside the door. These clumsy-looking over-shoes contained a strong magnet which was activated by his weight. When the pressure sensors felt his weight, the magnets locked on, anchoring his feet to the metal pathway. When he lifted his foot the magnet released. Thus he was able to walk, albeit in an ungainly fashion, regardless of how slippery the metal grid beneath his feet had become. One of his regular maintenance tasks was to hose down the glossy slime from time to time and send it slithering down into the vast pits where it would dissolve and separate from the water, ready to be used again. He had not done this clearance for some time and the slime now coated all the stanchions and walkways. *All in good time. That will be my last task.*

Safely shod, the Architect advanced across the narrow bridge that led to the large central pit. Plumes of water vapour rose into the air. From the pit came the roaring. The Architect gripped the iron fence that ran round the perimeter. Looking down he could see the tumble of dark water churning as it poured into the pit. While he watched, the level of the water gradually rose, until finally it was just a few feet below the lip of the pit. Then the nozzles cut off.

The Architect began to clunk his way round the pit. He thought about ice. What a wonderful construction material it was! Given a steady temperature and constant pressure it could be shaped into almost any design. On a planet such as Meredith, ice was the ideal building material. Almost all the individual blocks required for the construction of the tower could be made in this one large freeze-pit.

Deep within the dark water, there was a sudden swirling as though giant fish were swimming there. Thousands of small rubber vanes, each impregnated with ceramic ferrite, shifted away from the sides of the pit and began to lock together magnetically forming complex patterns. They were joining in a specific sequence derived from the calculations of the design computers, and as they joined and locked, they formed the moulds for every block the Architect had designed.

Staring down through the water, the Architect observed the separate blocks for the roof of his tower taking shape. He lifted his gaze to the centre, where a clutch of vanes were stirring up the water as they busily locked together. When the freezing was complete, these blocks would be the supports for the final block at the pinnacle of the tower. Meanwhile, the final block would be fashioned separately in one of the smaller pits which was equipped with special micro-vanes for detailed work and electrical fittings.

The Architect, like a fond parent, smiled as the vanes fluttered in the water, finding their final position and locking in.

Eventually, however, the water became still. All the vanes were in place. Then there came a raucous sucking and a gurgling and the surplus water surrounding the moulds began to drain away. When the water was gone, a klaxon began to clamour and a red warning light just inside the door flashed.

The next stage of creation could not take place until that switch was closed and the blue door was shut. Reluctantly, the Architect clumped back to the entrance and slipped off the clogs. He closed the switch and the flashing stopped. He entered the temperature lock and closed the blue door. There would now be a pause of five minutes while the mechanism built its energy for the freezing blast. The Architect passed through the red door which closed behind him, and as it did the magnetic locks slammed home. No going back now. The temperature beyond the doors would already be falling.

The Architect knew exactly what was happening. He had viewed it often from the security of his design room. The temperature would drop to about the freezing point of water. Holding steady at that temperature, there would be a hush. Perfect silence and stillness. Nothing moving. Then, moments later, would come an immense discharge of heat as the water within the vanes was suddenly deep frozen into clear blocks and plates of ice. But the heat would be short-lived, swiftly replaced with a bitter and biting cold.

Freezing, and its resultant expansion complete, the vanes would detach progressively. The polarity would change and each vane would return to its unique position clamped to the side of the cistern. Revealed, standing in the middle would be the crude blocks of his tower.

Immediately, the glossy laminate would be released from spray nozzles to flow over the blocks, hardening as it touched the ice, seeping into every crevice and following every curve; locking in the cold while excluding any warmth. This process complete, the temperature would be slowly raised. Any cracks or gaps in the ice would be quickly revealed, and sealed.

All this took time, of course.

The Architect re-entered the design room. 'Time now,' he murmured, 'for communication.'

He climbed up to his room where the red warning light was still flashing. At his leisure he began to open contact.

END OF PART 1

Hood of Bone

Debbie Cowens

H_{E WAS STANDING AT THE OCEAN'S EDGE. I KNEW THE} back of his jacket, an oilskin of dark seaweed green, and the short grey hair smoothed below the herringbone golf cap. He was one of the few, the dog walkers and early risers. Before seven, the beach belonged to us. We roamed the wide stretch of sand, gazed over the beckoning waves and wondered why the sea appeared such a murky blue if it only reflected an insipid morning sky.

Sylvia, inquisitive and outgoing even for a Fox Terrier, yapped and scampered in his direction. I called her back, fearing she might be an unwelcome intrusion, but mid-route something else caught Sylvia's eye, or rather nose, and she swerved and darted towards a patch of sea mulch on the shoreline. I jogged after her and saw what had captured her attention: a dead fish.

'Sylvia!' I called, and with reluctant obedience she returned to me with a sheepish expression. I clipped on her lead, not entirely trusting her to resist the temptation of a fish breakfast (or worse, fish perfume), and we resumed our usual walk.

It was a chilly autumn morning and the last week had been unusually rainy for Kapiti, but today was bright and cloudless. It could have passed for early spring except for the bite of cold in the air, hinting of a fierce winter ahead. As it was Sunday there were fewer people on the beach than other days and for many long minutes we saw no other soul. Once the dead fish was a safe distance behind us, I unclipped Sylvia and let her run freely, darting around to sniff the redolent delights of driftwood, seaweed, and tracks in the sand, and chase seagulls as they scoured the beach for food. My thoughts roamed erratically from the warm cup of coffee I would have once home, to the four houses I was showing that afternoon, to whether I should make a cheesecake to take for dessert to Pete's parents for dinner or just pick up a bottle of wine. My mother-in-law could find a sugared phrase to criticise any dish I made. On the other hand, an offering of wine might prompt her to jokingly check I wasn't pregnant and then not-so-jokingly imply I should be. Yet for all the distractions and anxieties niggling my mind, the sea could eclipse them all, like the tide coming in and sweeping away footprints and detritus. There was something hypnotic in the waves. The tide's ceaseless rhythm of rise and fall, distant edifices unfurling into white foam, their shallow vanguard drawing fingers across the sand before slipping back into the sea.

The sea had always held fascination and foreboding for me in equal measure. My mother's younger brother had drowned in a riptide when she was a child and through her zealous warnings and her taut ashen face whenever we saw the ocean something of her fears had been passed on. My brothers and I learned to swim in the safe, still waters of chlorinated pools. I hadn't more than dipped my toes in the sea before I was thirteen and the beach started to become a summertime haunt for my friends. Then long hours of lying in the hot sand gossiping were followed with sprinting into the waves and swimming out as far as we dared. My fear of missing out on the fun or looking ridiculous far outweighed any inculcated dread of the sea. We would rush into the waves, laughing and jumping up when they threatened to break over our heads, and we shrieked with delight as the force of cascading water rolled us backward as though we were no more than ragdolls. There's giddiness in sensing the insignificance of your weight and strength in the face of nature. It was exhilarating to wade deep into the onslaught of waves and know that the next one could knock you down or drag you under.

I had lost the taste for thrills of that sort as an adult but looking at the sea I still felt the strength of the tides, the vastness of the ocean. It stretched far beyond the horizon and no one had yet ventured to its utmost depths. I knew my smallness when I watched the sea and it filled me with a fear I didn't understand. How could anyone endure it for days, weeks at an end? Kupe, Cook, how had they ever had the faith or courage to risk so vast a journey through turbulent seas into the unknown? What made them believe that land or anything at all lay beyond the unfathomable stretch of ocean?

Sylvia's excited yapping broke my thoughts. I'd wandered closer to the shoreline, my feet treading deep prints in the compact, wet sand. My excited foxy was ten metres or so ahead, barking and circling a silvery fish carcass as long in the body as she was.

'Sylvia!' I yelled, but she lunged at the fish as though my voice were a call to charge. I jogged forward with the lead, ready to drag Sylvia away before the dead fish became a combined doggy breakfast and roll-on perfume. By the time I reached her, she had the fish's head in her jaws and was shaking it in a frenzy of growls like it was one of her squeaky toys. Its decaying body snapped off at the spine and fell on the sand as Sylvia continued to thrash her head back and forth.

'Drop it!' I ordered.

Sylvia spat out the fish-head. She raised one paw and looked at me with expectant hope as though perhaps I might throw the fish head for her to fetch. I bent to clip the lead on her collar. Out of the corner of my eye, I saw movement. A long pale worm emerged through the cavity of the fish's eye socket. I jerked back in fright. I grabbed Sylvia's collar and clipped on her lead without shifting my gaze. I'm not particularly squeamish about creepy-crawlies in general but this unsettled me. It was too big for a maggot yet it filled me with the same instinctive revulsion. It was no thicker than a pencil, its body was sickly white with translucent silvery rings at each segmentation. It slithered, or rather glided as though moving through water, over the fish's skull and coiled around above the eyes, settling into a grotesque, pulsating wreath. Its faceless head opened to reveal two disproportionately large jaws, and more hideous yet, a second smaller horizontally opening maw further in. It latched onto the fish's flesh and I heard, or imagined I heard, a terrible scraping, like fingernails on blackboards. Sylvia whined and pulled on the lead, straining in the direction of the fish's body. I glanced over and saw two more of these worms, sliding through the scaffold of fishbone and half-stripped flesh.

I kicked sand over the fish head. I had to bury it. Sylvia barked and darted around, yanking on the lead, but I didn't stop shovelling sand with my foot until there was a substantial mound over both the fish's head and body, and nothing remained but the rolling waves, the circling gulls and the excited yapping of my terrier.

I paused, out of breath. I chuckled inwardly, embarrassed, though alone, that I had got into such a panic over some sort of larvae or sea worm or whatever they were. Ridiculous. I'd managed to get sand inside my sneaker. Balancing on my left foot, I took off my right shoe and shook out about a half-a-cup of sand before slipping it back on.

'Come on, Sylvia. Let's go,' I gave her a quick pat and we turned to head back on our usual route home. 'And no telling Dad that your mum freaked out over a bug, okay?'

Sylvia looked up at me as she trotted along. I took it as an agreement.

'That's right. What goes on the beach, stays on the beach. And I won't tell him about your little escapade with the dead fish.'

The old man was still standing at the edge of the sea when we passed by again. He didn't appear to have moved an inch in twenty or twenty-five minutes.

'Hello!' I called out, but he didn't turn or move.

'Hello? Are you okay?' I walked towards him. Sylvia strained against the lead, reluctant to diverge from our usual path. Had he had a heart attack or a stroke or something? Was it possible to have a seizure of some sort standing up and remain paralysed in that position? He didn't move as I approached.

'I see you here most mornings – one of the regulars, like me. I'm Barbara, by the way. I pass by your house on our way to the beach most days, actually. It's the grey bungalow on Manly Street, isn't it? Lovely place. Lots of character.

Beautiful garden out front. I've seen you gardening when I've driven past sometimes.' I was babbling, filling the tense void with speech. His shoulders and the back of his head remained steadfast. My words sounded hollow, pathetic over the backdrop of gushing waves and crying seagulls in the distance. 'I guess you're the green-fingers of the house, eh?'

I was only a few feet away when I paused for breath. Sylvia whined. My heart thumped. Calm down, I told myself, taking another step forward, virtually dragging Sylvia now. Maybe he's hard of hearing. The thought cheered me. The old man was fine, and he wouldn't have heard me rabbiting on like a drivelling, slightly stalkerish real estate agent. Besides, I had my cell phone if I had to call an ambulance. I'd done a first-aid course a few years ago. Another step, another yank on Sylvia's lead. Or maybe it was five years, but I still knew how to do CPR. Another step. I remembered the basics anyhow. That'd be enough.

'Hello?' I reached out and put my left hand on his shoulder. Sylvia was tugging hard on the lead in my other hand. Only when I commanded her to heel did she stop pulling.

'Sorry, Sylvia's eager to get back home to her breakfast, little guts,' I joked, dropping my hand from his shoulder as I stepped round to stand beside him.

At last he turned to face me, but his eyes were solid white without pupil or iris. Like he was staring through me. 'I have heard our deaths shrieking in the waves,' he whispered.

I staggered, tripping over Sylvia and tumbling backwards onto the cold wet sand.

He did not move his feet but his pupilless eyes tracked my fall and he loomed over me, a towering figure enhaloed with light from the bright blue sky behind. '*From the depths, the worms devour us and enshroud the Earth with a hood of bone.*'

Sylvia growled and snarled. I scrambled to my feet. Whether she sensed my fear or something worse, I couldn't tell, but she stayed close as we fled the beach, not once daring to look back. We ran home. I was still panting after I had locked the front door, removed my jacket and headed for the kitchen.

'You look knackered,' Pete greeted me, glancing up from the coffee machine. 'You haven't taken up jogging again?'

One side of his pyjama collar stuck up awkwardly over his bathrobe, the bread bag lay open by the toaster. Sylvia padded to her water bowl and lapped noisily. I was irritated rather than reassured by the sight of such domestic normalcy.

'There's an old man on the beach,' I started. 'I don't know what's wrong with him, but his eyes … they were white, completely white.'

'Cataracts,' Pete explained matter-of-factly.

'No, it wasn't anything like that. Besides, it wasn't just his eyes. He said all this creepy stuff about death in the waves and worms eating everyone.'

'Cheery stuff. Although I suppose he has a point. We'll all get eaten by the worms in the end.' He crept towards me, wriggling his fingers towards my face and putting on a cheesy, rasping horror-film voice, 'After we're dead and buried. The worms are coming to get you, Barbara.'

'Stop it.' I whacked his fingers away. 'I'm serious. It was threatening, somehow. It really scared me.'

Pete put his arms around me. 'Don't worry, hon. Maybe he was having you on, y'know. Trying to get a rise, or something.'

'But it wasn't just the guy,' I said, pulling away. 'Before that, Sylvia found this dead fish and it was riddled with these creepy worm things. I've never seen anything like them before. I could see their jaws, like huge teeth – fangs almost – hooking into the flesh. They were gnawing, scraping the meat off the bone.' I shuddered.

Pete hesitated before speaking. 'Do you think maybe that getting creeped out over a maggoty old fish might be part of it? You got unnerved and then some old guy happens to say some weird stuff and…'

'You think I'm exaggerating?'

'I didn't say that, but it's easy to see how getting squeamish over a rotting fish might make you a bit more susceptible to overreact to what actually…'

'Overreacting? You think I freaked out over a bug or two and then imagine an old guy ranting about death for no reason?'

'I didn't say that.'

'Yes, you did. You literally said "overreact". Just like that time when your mother didn't mean to…'

'My mother? Oh, so that's what this is really about. You don't want to have dinner with my parents.'

'No, it's not that. I just mean that you never believe me. It's always me reading too much into what people say.'

He sighed and returned to the coffee machine. 'Let's not do this now. Let's just have a nice breakfast and forget about it, okay.' The espresso machine gurgled and rasped, drowning out the silence between us.

I waited, watching Pete watching the white cup slowly fill with dark, thick coffee.

'We should go back,' I said.

'What?'

'Come with me to the beach. You can see for yourself.'

'I was making scrambled eggs.' He gestured at the stove top, but he hadn't so much as broken an egg yet.

'Make them when we get back,' I insisted. 'What if that old man needs help or something? We can't just leave him.'

Pete gave a half-hearted objection but once he had swallowed the last of his coffee, he agreed to get dressed and walk back to the beach. Sylvia embarked on our second walk with less enthusiasm than the first. Both husband and dog dragged their heels but as only Sylvia could be hurried by means of a leash I had to plod along much slower than I wished.

The sight of the tussock-fringed dunes was enough to cool my impatience. A twinge of dread troubled me. What would be worse? To have Pete's suspicions confirmed and see nothing more than a half-rotten fish and a harmless old man, or to discover that my fears were justified?

We followed the snaking path to the beach, the clay dirt bleeding into sand as we progressed towards the steep rise of the dunes, our feet treading deeper with each step.

'Where was this guy?' Pete asked, stopping to survey the beach from the peak of the dune.

The old man had gone.

'He was at the edge of the ocean, just over there.' I pointed to the lonely stretch of sand, still and lifeless but for the white-foamed remnants of broken waves stroking the shoreline. I swallowed hard. My throat was tight. 'We may as well leave. It was silly of me, I guess.'

'Come on, we'll walk along for a bit. See him further up, eh?' Pete took my hand and motioned onwards. Generosity came easy to him when he knew he was right.

We started along the beach. The tide had crept inwards, washing away any trace that he'd been standing there at all. We passed another couple and a lady walking her Labrador but nobody had seen an old man wandering the beach.

'I guess he must have gone,' Pete said, trying to not sound

too pleased.

I nodded. I wasn't annoyed or relieved; just suddenly, achingly weary. I felt disconnected from my earlier experience as though it had occurred long ago or in a dream. I spotted the two mounds of sand up ahead.

'Let's go home,' I said.

I didn't have the heart to exhume them.

*

It was just after midday when I loaded the car boot with corflute signs and headed out to set up for my one o'clock showing. I checked my teeth for lipstick in the car's rear-vision mirror before reversing out of the garage. They were fine of course. I had checked my reflection scrupulously in my full-length mirror – polished shoes, crisp blouse, and pressed suit. Presentation was essential in an Open Home. Perfection produced confidence; confidence produced sales.

I drove down my street and turned onto Marine Parade. It was a faster, if less direct route to my first house than negotiating veins of suburban streets twisting around the centre of the town. Half a dozen or so people had gathered on the footpath beside a parked ambulance. I slowed down, pulled over and killed the engine. I glanced at my watch. I didn't really have time to go rubbernecking, but this was too close to where I had walked on the beach this morning.

I paced over to the small crowd, my heels clacking on the concrete. The lady who works in the Four Square was one of the onlookers, her bright burgundy cropped hair identifying her more readily than the shop's name badge. 'Vera'. She raised her eyebrows in friendly recognition.

'What's happened?' I asked.

'A drowning. Apparently, that man found a body on the

beach.' She nodded towards the rear of the ambulance.

I turned. A young man was seated at the rear of the ambulance. A latex-gloved paramedic was swabbing the side of his mouth, but there were still traces of dried blood below his lips.

'What happened to him?'

She shrugged. 'Not sure, love. Moana might know. She was here before I came over.' She raised her voice and called to a pair of teenage girls who were simultaneously talking and typing into their phones at great speed. 'Moana, love, come here a minute.'

The taller of the two girls obligingly trotted over, dragging her friend along.

'Wassup?' she said.

'We were wondering what happened to him, the guy who found the body,' Vera explained. 'You were here weren't you, when the ambulance arrived?'

Moana nodded emphatically, her brown eyes widening. 'He was like totally freaking and yelling at the ambulance guys that he got bitten. For reals. Like when he went to give the old guy mouth-to-mouth, he got bitten. But here's the real freaky bit…' she paused dramatically. 'The guy was already dead.'

Vera looked at me, her eyebrows raised. 'Let's not get too carried away now, love.'

'Nah, it's true,' Moana's friend insisted. 'We were here when the ambulance arrived. The guy had been pacing up and down, waiting for them. His lips were bleeding loads, like blood running down his chin and everything. We could see it from across the road. We thought he'd just got the bash when we first saw him but then he started waving and yelling at the ambulance, "He's drowned. He's drowned and he bit me".'

'Look, I'll show yous. They wouldn't let us down on the beach but we got a photo from up on the dunes.' Moana thrust her phone in front of our faces. A blurry image of a pale body lying flat on the stone-grey sand. The face was too small in the distant photo to make out any features. His clothes were wet, darkened with water and clinging to the lifeless body, but I recognised them.

'Ohmygod,' I whispered. 'It *is* him.'

Vera's eyes widened. 'You know him? Oh, how awful. Put that away!' She shoved Moana's phone away.

'Sorry, I didn't know,' Moana mumbled.

'No, don't worry,' I started. 'I don't know him exactly. I've just seen him around before, walking on the beach. I saw him today…'

'Are you okay, love? You look a bit faint.' Vera put her hand on my shoulder. 'You've had a bit of a shock.'

'I have to go,' I mumbled. The noise of the people around grew loud and indistinct. It was hard to focus on what Vera was saying. Something about sitting down?

I walked back to my car, trying to make sense of the conflicting explanations, trying to understand why the sight of a frail old man lying prone and lifeless had filled me with as much dread as sadness. I should have helped him. A man had died. I was probably the last person to speak to him and I ran from his disturbed ramblings.

And yet worse than the weight of guilt was the other sickening fear. Maybe I'd be dead if I hadn't run. The man with the blood-smeared mouth, the girls' story of how the drowned man bit him.

I fumbled my car open and got in, exhaling deeply once the door was shut. I looked in the rear-vision mirror.

Calmness returned when I saw my grey-blue eyes staring back at me.

'I don't have time to think about this.' I placed my fingertips at my temples and breathed. 'It won't do any good to lose my nerve. I have work to do.'

I grabbed my phone out of my handbag and sent a text to Pete: *Off to Open Hm. Back @ 5. Will get wine for dinner.*

*

Sylvia didn't come to the door to meet us when we got back from Pete's parents' around eleven. I found her curled up in her bed near the fireplace, shivering.

'Poor thing.' I picked her up and cradled her in my arms. 'Why didn't you leave the heat pump on for her?'

Pete wandered over. 'Get a bit cold, Sylvies?' He tousled her head and shrugged. 'She doesn't feel that cold to me.'

'You can sleep with us tonight, Sweetie. It's too cold in here.' Sylvia rested her chin on my elbow.

I carried Sylvia upstairs and lay her down on my side of the bed.

'Keep her warm, Pete,' I instructed when he entered and sat down. 'I'm just going to take a quick shower.'

'Sure thing.' He kicked off his shoes and got on the bed, slipping one arm around the dog while the other reached for the TV remote.

I heard the background murmur of the late-night news as I turned the shower on in the en suite. It was warm by the time I'd undressed. I got in and buried my face in the cascading water. The day was over. I had held it together all afternoon and through dinner's polite chit-chat.

Finally, I fell apart in a shaky flood of tears and didn't fully understand why.

*

My dreams were not dreams that night. Memories crashed down on me like towering waves, knocking me over with their force, dragging me under, deeper into each distorted vision. I saw events, relived them, not as they had been, but as they were now: bloated, twisted, and monstrous. Childhood nightmares made flesh and spiteful. Faceless figures in the shadows watched and judged me for my sins. I stood in the sea, exhilarated, laughing with my friends as a young boy drowned before me, flailing and screaming beneath the waves.

I saw my dead uncle, a child of eight I knew only from old photos, rise up out of the ocean. His face and limbs were blue and swollen from the sea. He trudged through shattering waves towards me. I wanted to run but couldn't. Something heavy and warm pressed my body down on the sand; the sharp edge of a blade pricked at the base of my throat, threatening to plunge deep if I moved.

The old man walked with my child-uncle now. Their white pupilless eyes stared ahead but they were coming for me.

Your death is shrieking in the waves, they rasped. *The worms devour us. They'll cover the world with a hood of bone.*

*

I woke to the sound of Sylvia whimpering. She had pushed herself up close against me, her head on my clavicle, her paw stretched out, claws jabbing my neck. I slid her off me and she growled slightly but didn't wake as I turned my head to look at the alarm clock. Three thirty-eight. My mouth was bone-dry and my throat stung. I rubbed my neck where

Sylvia had been jabbing me. My fingers came away wet. I went into the en suite and switched on the light. I squinted at the brightness as I looked in the mirror. Blood trickled from the side of my throat to my nightgown. How had I not woken up with her scratching me like that? Had the Panadol I'd taken to relieve my headache before bed zonked me out completely? I ran the water and grabbed some cotton wool from the cabinet. Once the blood was wiped away, I saw two small punctures on my throat. They didn't look like scratches. Had she bitten me?

I felt unsteady on my feet. In the mirror, streaks of grey slithered on the marbled tiles around me. I splashed cold water on my face and gulped two glasses of water. Feeling a bit better, I put a plaster over the wounds and crept back to bed. Sylvia twitched in her sleep, her jaws jerking and thrashing. I moved her to the foot of the bed and lay beneath the covers.

Forty minutes later I flicked on the TV, hoping the drone of infomercials would drown the grating in my head.

*

The dog was gone in the morning. Pete had vanished from the bedroom, too. My head felt heavy and my muscles ached. I dragged myself out of bed and shuffled to the kitchen. A note on the counter informed me that Pete had taken the dog for a walk to warm up.

I wasn't hungry, but I turned on the stovetop and made porridge anyway. The spoon left trails in the viscous mix and my sleep-addled brain saw movement within. When I reached for the brown sugar a coughing fit overtook me, sudden and painful and just long enough to make me panic. What if I couldn't catch my breath? What if coughing turned to choking? What if I drowned in my own phlegm?

When it subsided there was a red spray of blood and mucus across the kitchen bench and the pot. I leaned over the porridge, looking into its beige interior, and saw a thick gob of blood with wriggling trails descending into the mix. Unthinking, I stirred it with a wooden spoon, turning the pot pink. I took it off the heat, too, worried that it might somehow come to harm if left to cook further. I wiped the benches down, got out a bowl for Pete, and filled it with porridge. I eyed it suspiciously, wondering why it looked unappetising, then sprinkled a heavy-handed dose of brown sugar and cinnamon across the surface. I placed it on the dining table and drew the curtains closed. In the dim light the bowl looked normal, innocent. It was fine, I told myself.

I dressed without eating and returned to the kitchen. A whispering in the back of my head soothed my nerves, washed through me like waves lapping the shore. Pete would be back soon. I walked to the front door and opened it, breathed deep. The ocean was close enough to smell, close enough to fill my lungs with its promise of gentle rocking, of a salty embrace, of a huge, powerful presence deep beneath the waves waiting to pluck me from meaninglessness and place me, insignificant *me*, upon its ceaseless crown of waves. I smiled at the thought of my skeleton stripped bare by tiny razor jaws, bound in seaweed and coral and the black, terrible mucus hood of the thing below. My eyes would be pearls, my soul at one with the immortal ebb and flow of the tides.

There were other minds, other people nearby, feeling the same thing. It was comforting to sense them, to know that up and down the coast bodies like mine were waiting to be torn apart and dragged into the depths, to hang together on a hood of bone.

Pete was alone when he returned.

He cried, and shook his head, and told me that our Sylvia had died. She had snarled and snapped at other dogs on the walk, had sunk her teeth into a Doberman, then had charged into traffic on their way back. His palm was red and raw where the lead had been torn from his grip. I kissed and licked his broken flesh and guided him to the table.

'What's this?' he asked, looking down at the cold porridge.

'Breakfast,' I replied. The thought of him eating it filled me with a warmth I hadn't felt in years. 'Eat.'

He poked at it with a spoon, sniffing back tears.

'Eat,' I replied, gentle but firm. My eyes strayed to the curtain rope – was it strong enough to hold his arms if I had to force-feed him?

He swallowed a mouthful without needing to be coerced.

'Uh, it's very sweet,' he mumbled. Clearly, he felt guilty about the dog. He was using his make-up voice.

'Have some more. You've had a nasty shock. Need your strength.'

I circled him and put my arms around his neck, kissed his shoulder through his shirt.

'Sylvia's body is still on Manly Street. The car didn't even stop.' His voice was thin, powerless. He wiped his nose with the back of his hand.

'We'll go get her.' I stroked his neck. 'We'll bury her on the beach.'

'What?'

'We'll go get her,' I repeated.

*

Sylvia looked hollowed out when we found her. Her fur was stretched taut over her ribs, her stomach sunken. It didn't look like she'd been hit by a car – she looked deflated. I felt a tingling in my bones as I stood over her. I heard the worms call.

Pete kicked at the gravel at the road's edge and apologised. 'Never should have taken her out,' he mumbled.

I bent and patted her side, felt the squirming shapes beneath her skin, searching for new flesh. Something inside my arm wriggled in response, sharing their anticipation. I smiled.

'Help me carry her, Pete. She loved the beach. Let's take her there one last time.'

I slipped my hands under her small body and lifted her into my arms. She hardly weighed anything. Pete was talking as I walked across the road and headed for the dunes. I couldn't make out what he was saying – the tide in my skull pulling me toward the ocean was too strong. I smiled and felt the worms writhing in Sylvia's body and saw in my mind's eye the dark form at the ocean's floor, the army of worms swimming back to it from coasts around the world, their bodies bloated with the flesh of land creatures, their minds touched by the creatures they had devoured. Soon I would be there too, mind and body below the waves.

'What?'

Pete had grabbed my shoulder, his fingers digging into the flesh as he forced me to stop. I realised that I was speaking to him, words tumbling out of my mouth unbidden. I listened.

'From the deeps, they are legion. We will be devoured and exalted, the world will be covered in a hood of bone…'

We were standing on a path atop a dune. I could see the sea. Every fibre of my being and the beings within me yearned for it. Pete looked worried, frantic. I struggled to regain control of my tongue.

'It's okay, honey. Here. Take the dog. We can go back.'

I handed him Sylvia's body, sensing the hunger of the worms within as they neared an uninfected host. He cringed as he took the small form into his arms, a look of disgust plain on his face.

'Let's go home,' I said, squinting against the harshening morning light.

He eyed me suspiciously but turned to leave.

It only took me a moment to find a heavy enough chunk of driftwood. He turned to see if I was keeping up when I swung the branch. It caught him in the side of the head and he staggered forward. I hit him again before he dropped Sylvia's body. Once he was on the ground, I hit him again, just to make sure he was out. The branch came away bloody and Pete lay still. I bent and stroked his cheek, then dragged Sylvia's corpse to lie across his face.

A warm wind swept in from the sea. I felt weightless, free. I almost floated to the water's edge. I stood a long time, watching the waves wash in. The skin of my ankles ruptured and a series of small forms slithered from the bleeding holes, into the waves. I watched them go, proud and hopeful. More of me would be carried off soon. All of me.

I waded deeper into the water, slipping away from the world of glaring light. My vision was growing cloudy but I had no fear. So much awaited me below the waves, below the surface.

Soon I would join them. Soon I would rise and take my place in the hood of bone.

CROSSING

ANTHONY PANEGYRES

'JANE! JANE SELF!'

I stand and the secretary points to a door. Nicholas gives my fingers a here-for-you squeeze and whispers some supportive cliché. He's like a buttery pastry – nice in a doughy babushka-doll way. That sounds harsh, but I like babushkas and have a soft spot for pastries. Nicholas and I are close, we hug now and then, even though he's never braved a kiss. I have hinted at that (and more). He always says something about getting to know him better and how time will help me decide.

'Wait for the unveiling,' he says.

I pat my skirt down and enter the room. A man wearing a pinstripe suit and a sharp black tie sits at an iron-red timber desk. Behind him is a regiment of lime-green, tinny filing cabinets. I thought here at the agency they'd have computers.

I scan his desk as he motions for me to sit. He is not entirely anal: a fedora, a few files, a hip flask, a cigar reclining on an ashtray. He has, I imagine, the shiniest of black shoes.

'So ya wanna cross over?'

'Yes, that's why I'm here.'

'Jane, right?' He has that old New York or Chicago twang – I can never tell the difference.

'Yes,' I say, holding out my hand. He reaches across the desk and shakes it.

'Al Farrone. Just a tick while I find your file.'

Get with the times.

He moves over to one of the filing cabinets and flicks through file after file, mumbling my name all along. 'Jane Self, Jane Self, Jane Self. Ah, Jane Self!' He brings it over and brushes through. 'Why, ain't you the new-age dame? Impressive.'

'Thank you.'

'Crossin' over will take some trainin'.'

'I realise that, Mr Farrone, and I believe I am as capable as they come.'

He asks me the standard 'What would you do?' and 'Where do you see yourself?' questions. I'd prepared for the like earlier, and I think I've nailed it by the end. So does Farrone.

'Atta-girl. You're in for the trainin'. I gotta feelin' you'll do fine. Jus' remember, one sector only. Your choice, but we ain't gonna just let you cruise into others. You got that?'

'NP6000.'

'Chosen already – I like it. I'll cross with ya the first time. Golden rule is no touchin'. It's more than dangerous.'

'Yes, Mr Farrone.'

'You ain't some whacko tryin' to bring back a loved one?'

'No.'

'Sorry for askin', Jane … it's a precaution.'

The truth is, I yearn to see Mark. After five years of marriage, I just need to know that he's doing fine – to see if he needs me. Who would have thought Mark would go before me? I was the asthmatic who spent hours line-gazing in the pool. He was the specimen of health. Or so I thought.

*

After the interview I tell Nicholas the good news. 'That's fantastic,' he says, while his tell-tale eyes glass over in betrayal.

Still, it's kind of him to say it.

We head out into the parking lot, where the latest floating cars hover alongside a '60s Mustang. The relic of a car next to the Mustang is Nicholas'. My 'boyfriend' has a fetish for vintage automobiles. I'd be happier if he drove a Mazda or a nippy Peugeot, but Nicholas is not keen on those 'new fandangled machines'. He swings my door open and I sit in the front seat and wait as he winds up the motor from the outside.

He turns to me once seated. 'Let's go out and celebrate.'

'Do we have to?'

'On me.'

Floating vehicles make traffic disturbing at times.

We crawl down Church Street, my least favourite place. The zeal freaks me out. The street holds throngs of people from all walks of religious life. Some patrol the roadside with pamphlets; others stand at stalls. Their eager voices seem magnified as they call out, attempting to proselytise: **S**alvific **A**ction – Adeville's SA. They are the city's Storm Troopers, enforcing the afterlife.

Ein Heaven! Ein Heaven! Ein Heaven!

We pass the Byzantine domes of a Greek church, a similarly domed mosque opposite, the arches of an Anglican cathedral, the obsequious grandeur of a Seventh Day Adventist church and a tiny Nestorian chapel. And so it goes as we chug along with the windows open, Bach choirs resounding from the Lutheran chapel, baritone intonations from the Russian, and frankincense burning so heavily I can smell it from the car. Smoke plumes ascend from Buddhist temples.

Nick is the sole Adevillian I've dated who hasn't laughed or giggled at my pained face as we travel along Church Street, Adeville's chief connecting road, the Holy Path, so to speak. Shops, bars, almost every suburb; all seem to branch out from it.

Nicholas Lamb is an agnostic-Christian – I understand his doubt. Losing Mark four years ago hasn't made me buy into the afterlife either.

We pass a columned Hindu temple as we finally turn off. *Good riddance, my dear Pantheon.*

A few minutes later and I moan loudly as Nicholas parks by the milk bar. He always takes me to the milk bar. It's a permanent fixation.

'C'mon, Nicholas! Can't we go somewhere else? Anywhere else? I'm not asking to go to some anti-gravitational restaurant or anything. Just a decent lounge bar.'

'A bar is no place for a respectable woman.'

The modern part of me is divided by this. His out-dated chivalry limits some fun a girl might have, but at almost thirty, the part of me that's over those younger and wilder twenty-year-old lads finds his old-school values a refreshing change. Nick always opens doors for me, always gives way to me first, always holds the umbrella over my side, while he gets wet. There's never a rude word, and on those nights when I sleep over, no kissing again of course, he even leaves for the bathroom rather than let me hear any bodily sounds.

'A café then?' I ask. 'A plain old café? How 'bout the French one round the corner? The one with the Victorian wallpaper.'

Even a French café is too new for my anachronistic man.

He strides ahead, entering the dated building, surely a remnant from the 1930s. Men on the footpath remind me that I could do far worse than Nicholas. Macho types swaggering in Stetsons, geeks in bowler hats, grave men in homburgs, and even nutso military sorts strutting around in Balmoral berets. So I head inside. The décor is a beatnik red, old bus-like-leather lounge chairs hug the walls, and stools line the counter bench where a few kids sit slurping loudly on their spiders and milkshakes. Jars full of candy fill the shelves behind the cashier. One breath and I am glucose-struck with aromas: malt, sugar and of course the ever-present sherbet.

We approach the man at the counter. White apron, snow-white moustache and cheeks sculpted for a warm smile.

'Hello, Nicholas, and hello to you, Miss Self. What can I do for you?'

'Caramel thickshake please,' says Nicholas. 'And a honey'n'malt for the lady here.'

We move over to a booth. The whole joint feels like one of those tacky retro places you find at a mega-cinema complex. But it's the real thing, not some poor mimic. Thoughts sputter around in my mind, popping, fizzing and whirring like an insane kitchen appliance. I turn my head to the side for a minute – it's my venting signal. As I turn back, I'm glad to see serviettes lining the middle of the table. My battle line is drawn.

'Why do you insist on taking me here?'

'Here we go again.'

'It's not the celebration I was hoping for. A malt milkshake for Chrissakes? What's next? Some rock candy for the ride home?'

'Jane, these are the best shakes in town.'

'I want to go.'

'I feel comfortable here. Out there, your kind of places. I don't feel quite right.'

'Now. I want to go *now*.'

I know Nicholas well enough. Beneath the table, my babushka's leg is beginning to spasm. I lock my eyes onto the serviette barricade and hold firm.

'Okay. You do deserve better.' He stands but his leg convulsions have crept along, his arm jerks and then his left eye starts twitching away like a dying fluorescent globe.

'It's all right, Nicholas,' I say in submission to his body's panic. I take his hand and he sits back down. 'Thanks for taking me out. It's really very sweet of you.'

The shakes arrive, foamy and thick. We slurp together for a while, listening to the sandy-haired kids discussing the fundamentals of childhood economics.

'A normal tom isn't worth a jack spider,' says one, displaying his marble.

'But it's worth a blue-eye jack,' says the other, producing a marble from his pocket and rolling it along the bench.

Nearing the end of his shake, Nicholas sucks up bubbles of air and liquid. He glances at me, wanting to say something, then he looks back down.

'I won't bite.'

He pauses. 'I don't have a degree like yours. You didn't need one working in a fruit'n'veg shop in Kalgoorlie.'

'What are you trying to say?'

'I get people, Jane. I'm a little sharper than I let on.'

'Is this about me crossing over?'

He nods.

'We've been through this, Nick. I need closure.'

He reaches out and holds my hand, 'Just know that I'm here for you. I know what you had with Mark was real. And I'll help you all the way, no matter how it ends. I can be your rock. You were married – I understand how hard it must be.'

His lines are old and used but bona fide – or 'dinkum' as Nicholas occasionally says. My throat chokes up a bit. I don't let any tears escape. It's one of those moments that could open up the falls. An instant in which I realise just how much Nicholas actually loves me.

*

I breathe easier in Adeville. My asthma hasn't played up for a while. Things sometimes feel foggy though. Nicholas assures me that the mist clears over time. I remember things: Nicholas, Church Street, the milk bar, neighbourhoods, my deceased husband, but there are memories that blur at the edges, ungraspable, obscure, vague bits of knowledge I must have known and forgotten in some recurring cycle. Hopefully, seeing Mark will help.

A week of training at the agency passes. I learn with Buddhist-like ease to zone out and empty my consciousness, focus on the region, street or even the house I need to see, then colour it in with textures guided by my senses: the brick paving, the sweet smell of Moreton Bay figs and other berries being mashed on the paths and roads, the varying light – the shifting greys and blues.

'Focus on your neighbourhood, perhaps the street first,' Al says. 'Never a person.' But I recall Mark: permanent two-day growth, lean figure, sweet aftershave mixed with saline sweat, his slightly coarse voice, his quick considerate eyes.

Despite my obsession, I pass every test, every examination. I am ready to cross over well before most other trainees.

*

We stand in a bare hall. Agents in surrounding halls aid others who cross over.

I'm Al's fifth for today. The old floorboards groan as I shift my weight from one foot to the other. Al Farrone tips his fedora.

'NP6000. In and out, five minutes max. No touchin'! We're the ghosts in their world.' He points his lit cigar in my direction. 'Remember to follow me, I'm the big cheese. And if you lose me,' another tip of the fedora, 'look for the hat.'

I wrap my brown and white scarf a little tighter. I've made an effort. Boots, a splash of colour on my face, a little winter cap on my head (the one Mark found spunky) and a jacket that accentuates my small waist – it could be cold on the other side. Maybe I'll see him, even on my first visit. I do as taught and concentrate on the place as a picture and slowly add other senses. I taste the air of the strip, the cosy inviting smell of coffee.

And I appear, there on the other side. Al is beside me. 'Atta-girl.'

We are on the main strip: cafés, restaurants, a bookstore, bars. People sauntering, striding, riding, pramming, gathering, browsing, holding, sitting, chatting, reading – all there, all present. It must be cold – the sky is hazy and there is a breeze, and I remember how the breeze here cuts to the bone.

'I can't feel the cold.'

'Can you believe their clothes?' Al says, looking around.

They all seem pretty normal to me. 'You cold?' I repeat.

'Cold? We can't feel the cold here, we just taste things as they pass through.'

We stroll along the path. My feet are balancing on the

pavement. I can't really feel it beneath me. There's an alfresco café with the words 'Uncle Tom's Café' written in a faded white along the window.

'See, no touchin'.' Al puts his arm straight through the pane; the glass remains untouched, his hand waves back at me from the other side. 'Passin' through is fine, even with folk, though I wouldn't recommend it. But don't touch.'

I follow suit, all the while searching peripherally for Mark. I feel the glass, or rather taste the sharpness of it on my arm. I then put my arm through other surfaces. The wooden door at the entry feels dry and dead; red bricks sandy and stagnant. People around us are oblivious, sipping their coffees, reading their papers or just chatting away.

I approach a young couple, clearly attracted to one another – a lady, her bobbed hair full of split ends, sitting with an urban Asian man who boasts a fringe of a moustache. I try to let their eyes take me in. I sit, or rather pretend to (I'm squatting) on the spare seat next to them and stare – they blink me out. I reach out and pass my hand through the dead couple. They feel warm, somehow heated, and there is an indefinable feel of flowing.

And then Al signals to leave and we're back in the hall. I'm dizzy about the trip, seeing the dead and my old suburb. I'm also literally dizzy. The room spins like a carousel on fast forward. My guts lurch, and twice I dry retch.

Al laughs. 'Vertigo – it gets better over time. You're the bee's knees, kid. You've taken to crossin' over real quick.'

*

A few days pass and much to Nicholas' chagrin, I am due to cross over again. Before I depart, I see a yellow Post-it on the fridge with my loopy print. *Asthma attack* is what I've written. I cannot recall writing it but I decide to leave it there like an alarm reminding me to swim every morning.

I meet Al at his desk where he is hunting through one of the endless number of files. I clear my throat. He looks up, tipping his fedora. I am in some dated detective movie – I'm re-enacting film noir.

I bypass the frivolous greetings and mundane polite gestures. 'So you can feel and smell but can't really touch?'

'You can smell, too? Only a few can do that,' he says. 'In a way, you don't really feel. You can't feel the weather, the breeze, the temperature. Most of us somehow feel substances, that's about it.'

'But you can't touch?'

'You don't touch. We must *never* touch.'

'Can it be done?'

'We *don't* touch. We pass through. We don't touch, we don't interfere. We learn, we accept, we take comfort.'

'And all those files, Mr Farrone?'

'Oh, they're comm'n knowledge. No secrets there.'

'Well?'

'There's a file here for everyone in Adeville.'

'You're kidding?'

'Nope. Two million, four hundred thousand and thirty-seven, as of this mornin's count.'

'Why don't you just have them backed up on a hard drive somewhere? Electronic, save on all that paper.'

'Hard drive? Ah, computers. Too high tech for me, I'm kinda uncomfortable outside o' the flicks and radio. This is how I've always done things.' He stops his filing. 'Head into the hall. This crossover you're doin' by yourself. You got that? Five minutes, then you'll be returned.'

'How do you pull me back? How do all the others come

back?'

'I've been doin' this for a while, kid, and I ain't gonna explain in a minute what's taken years to learn. Here, at the agency, we're all experienced crossers. I ain't ever touched nobody and I ain't never had the inkling. Basically, as long as I know the area, I can recall ya' back or if need be, physically get ya myself.'

*

On my own.

I recall the place I lived in with Mark, just down from the strip. Nicholas knows what I am doing. I don't know whether it's truly fair by him. At least I'm being honest.

I think of the red brick apartment, our large balcony; the crisp smell of anti-bacterial pine Mark sprayed obsessively throughout the house, a cover of sorts for his lack of cleaning aptitude. I imagine his fresh aftershave, the opposite of Nicholas' macho old-man fragrance. The marital bed and mattress, snug enough for the two of us, and how I napped on his side whenever he was away.

Suddenly, I am there. Just outside on the balcony. No more red brick – the entire apartment building has been rendered. I pass through the glass door. The kitchen is neater, the benches clear and scrubbed. Surprising smells drift through the air, much spicier than I recollect, traces of turmeric and something else – cumin. Both spices I have little time for. The spare bathroom is spotless, too. Of all the things Mark was, cleanliness was not one of his better qualities. I search for signs. Perhaps he has moved on in the afterlife? In the lounge, the couches are different: pleather monstrosities. On the wall, however, is a sign. The abstract painting we bought together. Its earthy colours made the place feel comfier.

I pass through the bedroom door. Our wedding photo is not on the bedside table or the shelf above the bed. Another picture sits in its place. I inhale sharply and move closer. Somebody else. While I am fair, she is dark. My hair long and blonde, hers short and raven black; my eyes are a cheeky blue but small, the Indian woman's eyes are the large sagacious type that could swallow seas.

It wracks me, so different.

Four years, Mark, and you've erased me completely.

I try to grab the frame. It's beyond irrational, I want to smash it. I will my fingers to hold it, but they just slip through no matter how many times I try.

There is a sound in the en-suite, the faint whirring of the fan. I step through the bathroom door. It's steamy but *he* is there. Mark, in his jeans, buttoning his shirt.

Four years. He has a slight softness to his body that wasn't there before. Then I see his head, his once black locks peppered and thinning, those lips I've kissed so many times, the light shadow on his jaw, and those cerulean eyes, crisp and sharp.

I watch.

It hits me that he's advancing and I'm not. I'm the ghost. I could tear up if I let myself. I need to control it – let that flood of emotion come later. There are other recollections to deal with now.

The memories don't come flooding back – they never left: his true laugh at a higher pitch; his slightly vacant gaze when he disagreed with someone; his attempts to keep me upbeat even when he was down; the way we read together at a café without having to talk; and of course those evenings when I would feel his breath and then lips begin to caress the nape of my neck.

'Mark!' I call. I move closer, trying to touch him, passing through his warm body. Back and forth I pass through the body that was once so tactile.

I try to clear my mind, solely concentrate on him. I reach out once more, my hand passing through, but this time he shivers. Did he feel something?

I'm back in the hall, on the floor trying to cope with the spinning walls. I'm crying, I brush the tears away with my sleeve. The thin veneer of composure disappears and I dry retch over and over, until my throat aches. I lie there in numbness for an age, then that gradually transforms to wonder: *Did he feel something?*

And then ire sets in.

*

I drive down Church St, my hand pumping the horn incessantly like a heartbeat. The zealots — I bet they're all restlessly hoping this is not all there is — leap out of my way.

I pull off the street and arrive at Nicholas' neighbourhood, all 1920s federation houses, exteriors roughly rendered beneath tuck-pointed redbrick. Everyone has a yard, both front and back.

He opens the door and greets me. I shrug to the side as I push past him. Inside usually tastes like a well-maintained but still humble red wine. Thick jarrah floorboards throughout add to that vintage sense. Now everything tastes acidic. To think that we've chatted about moving in. Dead people discussing our relationship barriers? Closure with Mark was my first obstacle; Nicholas refusing to get a wireless internet connection was the other.

Nicholas doesn't even own a television. He always has music, scratching out of his antique gramophone, or humming on the radio.

He pulls some iced tea out of the fridge – he finally did away with that old icebox – and pours us both a glass as we sit at the scarred jarrah table.

'I have a Post-it note on the fridge. Know what it says?' I appear as calm as can be, yet inside I'm a shivering wreck. I wait as the seconds drag by. He doesn't reply. '*Asthma attack.* C'mon Nicholas, why didn't you remind me?'

'Not this again. I have reminded you – who do you think told you to put the note up in the first place?'

'I still went for a swim in the morning though – not that I ever have to.'

Nicholas sits opposite, calm. How many times have we been through this? How many times have we replayed the scene? His stillness helps calm me. I've been down this path before. But this time, I will remember.

'Mark shivered. Maybe he felt something?'

'You mustn't ever touch them.'

'What?'

He stops talking and swirls the ice in his glass, staring at the amber liquid. Eventually, he pulls himself away to look up at me, crunching ice and gulping it down. 'Maybe we weren't good enough for someplace better or bad enough for someplace worse? And we're all people from the twentieth and early twenty-first century. We're a unique lot, us Adevillians.'

My murky thoughts are dissipating, as if inundated by a stream of clear water.

'Different times,' I say, so familiar with his words that I can continue his line of thought aloud: 'We feel wrong when we're in places futuristic for the time we lived in – our time. That's why we always end up at that dreadful milk bar.'

'That place is special to me. But you're right. Going backwards is fine, forwards, however. Like you in anti-gravitational restaurants, well, that's me in one of your lounge bars.'

'I know. I've heard this before.'

'Yep – but not after crossing over. The second or third crossing tends to be the key orientation.'

The clear water now rages through, only a slight discolouring remains.

'Asthma attack. I don't remember dying.'

'Few do.'

I should let rip with some expletives.

'You okay?' Nicholas asks.

He may not be Mark, but he is so solid, so real, so supportive. Shit, I realise. With his relic of a car?

'When did you pass away again?'

'1936.'

'So you've been here—'

'Going on ninety years.'

'Fuck.'

I go to the bathroom, turn on the tap that squeaks, then splash water over my face. I slap my cheeks a little too. My reflection hasn't changed. Mark's has. Perhaps Mark and I could still be happy? Maybe I could go back there?

I come out to the table where Nicholas waits.

'Family?'

He nods. 'Still miss them every day.'

'After so long?'

'You weren't the only one to cross over.'

I feel an incongruous sense of betrayal. He reaches for my hand but I pull mine away. Stung, Nicholas continues to talk, his voice rich with nostalgia.

'I crossed over all the time. I had two boys. Took them to a place just like the milk bar every Saturday morning. Eldest, Harold, got a lemonade spider; he was fair like my wife, like you. He could run like the wind, full of beans too, never rude although he did wolf his food down at the dinner table. Youngest boy, Walter, he'd order the malt, little bit on the chubby side like his old man. He could tell me the names of every blimmin' bird in Kalgoorlie. Couldn't run, couldn't kick at footy, but he was a gutsy little bastard.' Nicholas' eyes light up as he speaks. I reach my hand out this time and he grips it firmly. 'Nine and twelve, that's how old they were.'

'You watched over them?'

'For ten years, I watched my boys grow up. Watched the eldest become a boilermaker and the youngest go off to university, the one in Perth – first of my family to do so. I'm proud of them.'

'You still see them?'

'Probably dead as us by now. Life goes on. My wife met another bloke – that was hard, though I was glad at the same time. I don't want to make you uncomfortable but you remind me a lot of her.'

'That's okay.' My voice comes out thin.

'Used to see them almost daily, but as time went on I wanted to get closer to my boys. You know, touch them – give them a hug, shake their hands, ruffle their hair. I knew better – you *never* touch the living. Still, the feeling kept on growing, eating me. Seeing Walter and Harold only nourished the idea. You know, give them a pat on the back, let them know you care.'

'What happened?'

'I stopped myself from going – to make sure I didn't break the crossing over rule. Haven't seen them since. Probably a good thing too – didn't see them grow old, didn't have to see any heartache in their lives or deal with the pain of their aging. I just remember them as two fine young men. Maybe my time alive was some part of that. I certainly like to think I helped in some way.'

'I'm sure you did. You'd have been a great dad.'

We sit, sipping our tea, listening to some prehistoric jazz. I actually don't mind it, the trill clarinet, the strums from the double bass, the slide trombone and voices singing in reedy tones. I try to concentrate on the present, on Nicholas and all he has divulged. But I begin to imagine Mark opposite me. Nicholas' innocent eyes morph into Mark's sharp ones, his body leans up, the hair remains sparse but begins to loop and darken slightly.

'I'm sorry, Nicholas. I still need closure.' His hand turns limp. 'Five years married, you know.'

Nicholas withdraws, arms retreating. His spine presses back against his chair. 'Look, this is Adeville. I know I am not perfect. Maybe you aren't ready for us.'

'It's not that.'

'I get the picture. You're talking to someone who crossed over for ten years. Do you think my kids are all I saw? I watched her curl up at night, foetal like. Sobbing in the early years, her body wracking itself, always when the kids weren't around. Hell, I even watched her in the bath or shower imagining what'd be like if I was in there with her.'

'So you understand? You'll be here for me?'

'No,' he says. 'I feel like we're magnets – but you draw me in and then flip me around so I can't get close. I don't want to be led on.'

'That's hard to hear from you. You won't even—'

'This is *why*. You had to know me and know yourself.

I've been patient. If I did anything more it would have felt wrong.'

I touch his cheek, wanting to be touched in return. He is still. I search for that unripeness, that innocence in his gaze, but I cannot rediscover it. There's strength between us, his protective and genuine manner, old-fashioned values; warm reliability. I feel safer, securer and more loved by him than anybody else, including Mark. Do I want to toss all this away for a past love?

But another curious or nostalgic part of me wants to see what possibilities lay with Mark. A final closure perhaps? A new beginning? What remains? Can the past recommence?

At the front door, Nick doesn't farewell me, he doesn't say that customary apologetic line about it not working out. Rather, it comes out of left field and out of character for Nicholas: 'Area code NP6000, right?'

*

I'm in the office with Al.

'What's crossing over all about?'

'Initially it centres us, here in Adeville. After that it depends – an Adevillian need for most, I s'pose, to come to terms with the present. And to check up on 'em.'

As much as I pry it's always a similar response: 'See how things are,' or 'Make sure things are okay,' or 'Agents help us understand our world.'

I ask to look at the files and he says, 'No problem. Whose'll it be?'

'Mine, Nicholas Lamb's and yours.'

He collects them from the various cabinets, standing on a stool for one. The other two are on the bottom rung. 'Curious little dame, ain't ya?' Al says as he hands over the metal-rimmed green files.

I open mine and head straight to the endpoint. Death 2016, asthma attack. Status: married to Mark Self.

Nicholas Lamb: Death 1936, cardiac arrest. Status: married to Mary, two boys.

Al Farrone: Death 1929, found shot, possible links to the St Valentine's Day massacre. Case unsolved. Status: engaged to Vera Manino.

I hand them back.

'This'll be your last time before we get you signed up. And remember, no—'

'Yeah, yeah, no touching.'

'Listen hard – we've lost more than a few people, all through touchin'. I do what I can but I can't save 'em all. If ya wanna touch, ya don't cross over. They don't wanna be touched. You got that? They can't handle us Adevillians.'

'Adevillians – you mean the dead?'

'Adevillians. Anyway, it's instinctual. Some scientist claims when they do see us, their brain floods with some hatred-dope. Like I said, it's instinctual.'

It's hard to play meek, but I nod tamely.

'You have to get this, Jane. The living hate; *hate* us; hate bein' touched, and if ya touch 'em … that means they can touch ya' back.'

*

This time, I concentrate on the changes, her picture rather than mine; turmeric and cumin rather than oregano and parsley; our man. And then I'm there, and she is inside watching television, legs tucked up and near her body. Well-fitted jeans and slightly too long bare feet. It is hard to find fault. She seems a touch happier than I was, and carefree, she smiles at an old *Friends* rerun. Her teeth are perfect, and not in that ridiculously bleached style either.

Nothing of me – not a trace. A trace may ease the pain. A certain familiarity might breed contentment.

I move into the study where Mark taps away on his laptop as expected. I shift closer to him. I need him to know I'm here, that I still crave him, that I haven't forgotten him or cast him aside. I need to touch that face, feel his jaw, his shoulders, have his hands on my lower back.

My fingers pass through the warmth of his body. He shivers. I do it once more, and again he shivers. A third time and he pushes his chair back and stops typing. I am close. I pass through once more, there is a slight feeling of texture.

He jumps from the chair and strides out and into the lounge room. 'Arpana.'

'Yes, Babe.'

I never called him that. Those names were far too dolly-like for me.

'Can you feel my temperature? It felt like ice in there, it came on out of the blue – really shook me.'

She places one of those elegant and elongated Punjabi hands over Mark's forehead. 'Feels fine to me. Was there a draught?'

'No, it just unnerved me a bit. I'm going to head out, walk it off a little.'

Mark heads into the bedroom to grab his beanie. I follow him. I don't try to touch him here, not in front of her. I trail him out of the apartment, down the passage, into the lift and out the entrance gate. It's twilight but there's a sense that it's gradually darkening. His gait is long and I pump my legs to keep up.

Autumnal leaves crunch and crackle beneath his feet,

doing nothing under mine. He's panting slightly, his breath coming out in dragon-puffs. The park with two lakes is where Mark is headed. The one where we used to feed the maned ducks and clownish swamp hens. I am not short of breath in this world – in fact, I don't see my breath at all.

We reach the park with its Moreton Bay fig trees, their spanning branches ancient and resplendent. Down the decline, his sneakers leave ghostly imprints of the past on the damp grass. He does a lap of one lake, the one where we used to try and spot tortoises near the edge, and then he sits on a park bench. The usually chatty birds are dormant, fluffing their plumage out for the night's sleep.

I sit beside him, balancing really. How I've missed this place. Enjoy the little things, people always tell you – *savour them* is more sage advice. I want more, to really be here. Crossing over isn't quite the same; the world appears fleshed out but somehow I am not.

I reach out for his hands, arms that once pulled me closer, that ignited me, jolted me, shocked me. In comparison, Nicholas' embraces are buttery pastries. Although they lack Mark's zing, if truth be told, they're more comforting and loving.

My hands pass through Mark's, the sensation is hotter than usual. He shudders. I stand up, facing him, the spirit leaning out and over the man at the park bench. We are the clichéd illustration.

Once again, my hands stretch out. They pause on his cheeks. Contact! His skin is searing hot. I draw my fingers back in pain. He sees me. He stares straight at me. He doesn't leap up or scream – he's not movie scared, he's terrified, the kind of fear you have in a demonic nightmare. The petrification is real. Through the fear, though, I sense recognition.

But is it recognition of our past or is it a fear of me stealing his present?

'Mark,' I say, voiceless. He sees me mouth his name.

His mien abruptly changes. His eyes grow fierce; his lips thin, almost snarling. His body tenses, ready to pounce, wolf-like. 'Mark,' I repeat, desperate to calm him, desperate for some sense of more. He leaps. Hands snatch my wrists. His grip is hot iron, branding me, tattooing the skin. I cannot move. I mouth his name, again and again to no avail. The pain drives me to my knees. I am weak – a limp doll.

Is it Arpana? Did she fare better than me? Is he cruel? Is it just as Al's been saying all along: that the living can't handle Adevillians? I'm diminishing, the light darkens despite the heat, my skin burns, the stench infiltrates my nostrils. Perhaps Mark understands what he's doing, destroying the dead, wiping me away? Maybe he's forcing me out for both of us? But why that sneer on his face? My wrists burn. The smoke and the reek of it all. I forget about a final connection, closure, openings, whatever it is I sought, and I try to scream, desperately attempting to pull away, but his hands are lava-like chains.

As I'm fading, in the din of evaporating sounds, I hear familiar voices – an old Australian accent and a Chicago-Italian.

And I am away. In the hall perhaps? My world is shadow, my wrists scorched. Giddy, I retch.

Hands lift me as the light slowly returns. Nicholas and Al stand either side, bearing my weight.

'You're comin' to the sick bay, gal.'

'Think she'll be all right?'

'Thanks to you, Nick. Wrists will take some healin'. Got to her jus'n'time.'

The voices wane.

*

Nicholas still goes to the milk bar once a week, his own pilgrimage of remembrance. Occasionally, I go with him.

We're taking our time. After all, it's not a commodity we're short of.

Nicholas, no sign of trembling, sits opposite me now on leather cushioned wooden chairs as we both sip our *café au lait* on marble tables, while a dozen or so customers at other tables do the same.

'It was a mad search,' I say. 'I don't know if it was our years together, or a need for resolution. Or should I say post-death resolution? Lust perhaps?'

'For me it was holding on to the past.'

'I think – clichéd as it sounds – underlying it all, was a search for meaning. You get me. What did it all mean with Mark? Why can we cross over?'

'Just the nature of it all, I s'pose.'

'And in the end, there weren't any answers.'

'Maybe that's it. Maybe life's just a series of unresolved questions.'

Smells of buttery French pastries and coffee waft around the room. Here in Adeville, Nick is moving towards my future and I'm moving towards his past, both of us crossing into something new, something unknown.

12–36

EG WILSON

SHE WAS COLD. IT WAS DARK. SHE WAS HUNGRY. Where was she?

The time before now stretched eternal, black and empty as the farthest reaches of space.

She didn't know.

Thin walls held her close on three sides: elbow, elbow, back, and there, in front of her nose, the fourth wall -- a slanted grillwork that spilled golden light into her eyes. She lifted her head, felt the muscles in her neck contract and extend. She couldn't see the ceiling. She lowered her head, felt the muscles in her neck extend and contract.

Where was she?

Engines thrummed beneath her bare feet, vibrations travelling through cool metal plating to tickle her toes. It made her giggle.

There was a crash from the other side of the grill. She jumped at the noise, the tickle of the engines shifting from her toes to the soles of her feet, and giggled again.

'H-hello?' There was a voice outside. 'Is someone there?'

The tickling faded. She was silent, staring into the light.

'Hello?' The voice came again.

Maybe she should say something.

'Is there someone on my boat?' the voice demanded. 'Listen, I don't know who you are or how you came to be here—'

She didn't know either.

'—but if you're there, you'd better come out right now, mister, and keep your hands where I can see 'em.'

She didn't move.

A shadow passed in front of the grill, blocking the light. 'Almighty-righty then. I'm opening the door, and I have a gun, so don't try anything funny.'

The grill swung open. She blinked at the looming shadow, and it resolved into a form: a slim woman of maybe nineteen turns. Messy red curls fell to her shoulders, and she had a gun the length of her forearm levelled at ... at ... What was her name? Did she have one?

She didn't know.

The woman's face creased in confusion. 'Hello there.'

She said nothing.

'Who are you, then?'

She shook her head. She didn't know.

The woman stepped back, letting light flood the tiny room, and lowered the gun. 'Can you talk, little one?'

'Yes,' she said. She knew that much.

The woman nodded. 'That's something, at least. Are you going to hurt me?'

'No.'

'Then you can come out of that locker.'

She stepped out of the ... locker ... and into the space beyond. One look showed her everything, the knowledge appearing between one blink and the next: the sole-command cockpit to one side, the narrow bunks in front, the hygiene pod on her right. She turned, saw the narrow locker and the small square of cluttered table top, and looked at the woman.

'I'm Tsione,' the woman said.

The words echoed. It was odd, the things she knew now that she hadn't known a moment before.

The woman hadn't pronounced the T at the start of her name, but she knew it was there. The woman hadn't said it was once a man's name, but she knew that, too. The woman had pronounced it Shin-ay, but long ago it had been pronounced See-oh-nee.

The woman glanced around the ship – a boat, she'd called it – before looking back at her and mustering a smile. 'Do you have a name?'

'No.'

The smile slipped from Tsione's face. She sighed. 'Can't you say anything but yes and no?'

'Yes,' she said. The engines tickled her feet again, and she giggled.

'Great,' Tsione sighed. 'So you're a nameless kid who can only giggle and say yes and no. Where did you sneak on? Port Pratchett? Look at you, you're brown as a nut. Okay, you snuck on at Port Pratchett and somehow I haven't found you until now, when we're out on the edge of absolute nowhere on the way to slightly less nowhere. Fantastic. I could've sworn I threw a jacket in that locker just last night.'

'I didn't sneak on at Port Pratchett. And you did.'

The jacket lay crumpled in the far corner of the locker.

Moving slowly, Tsione closed the door and latched it.

'I wasn't in there last night,' she added. 'If it's any consolation.'

Tsione sat on the unmade lower bunk and put the gun down for long enough to pull her hair back in a messy knot with a bit of rubber flexiseal. 'How did you get here?'

'I don't know.'

'Were you there long?'

'I don't think so,' she said, and shivered.

'Are you cold?'

'Yes.'

Tsione pulled a thick jersey from the pile of blankets on the bunk and handed it to her.

'Thank you.' She shrugged it on. It was warm, and fell nearly to her knees.

'So you don't have a name?'

'Yes.' The reply was automatic. She blinked. She hadn't had a name a minute ago.

Tsione tilted her head.

'I have a name,' she said carefully. 'But I don't know what it is.'

'That's helpful,' Tsione muttered, rolling her eyes. 'I have to call you somethin'. Can't just say "hey, you" for the duration.'

An answer seemed to be expected. 'Okay.'

'Can I call you Eleutheria?'

'No.'

'Marybeth Anna Louise?'

'No.'

'Min Jung?'

'No.'

'Ashanti?'

'No.'

Tsione frowned. 'What can I call you?'

She thought and the answer came. 'Rerenga.'

'Rerenga?'

'Yes.'

'Funny name. Alright. Rerenga it is. Are you hungry, Rerenga?'

'Yes,' said Rerenga.

Tsione stood, rummaged in the cupboard over the table, and retrieved a covered bowl. 'Here. It's self-heating; just rip the top off and eat.'

Rerenga slid the chair from under the table and sat on it. She tore the lid off the bowl. A cloud of steam wafted up, smelling of spices, and she sneezed. The bowl rapidly grew too hot to hold; she placed it on a stack of papers and waited for the steam to dissipate, then peered inside.

It was very … square. There were cubes of brownish meat, and cubes of grey potato, and cubes of other green and yellow and orange things. She assumed they were vegetables.

She hesitated.

'It's okay,' Tsione said, perching on the lower bunk again. 'You can eat.'

Rerenga closed her eyes and said the first thing that came into her head, a string of words she only understood after she'd said them.

'That wasn't Ventional,' said Tsione.

Rerenga looked at her. 'Sorry?' she offered.

'No, no, it's fine. I didn't know you spoke Reo, is all. Hardly anyone does anymore.'

Rerenga gave her a noncommittal smile and turned back to her food. She lifted a hand, plucked a cube of meat from the steaming bowl and popped it in her mouth.

It was hot. She opened her mouth to let it cool down, and then chewed – and chewed – and finally swallowed. Mm. Interesting.

'Oh, no, honey—'

Tsione was on her feet. Had she done something wrong?

'Sorry,' she said.

'It's okay, you, uh, you can't have, um…' Tsione trailed off, grabbed a fork from a cup of cutlery on the table, and handed it to her. 'Here. Use this.'

After some fumbling she got it turned the right way, and then it was a matter of stab and eat, stab and eat. Much easier than burning her fingers on the hot cubes. 'Thank you,' she said.

Tsione nodded. 'And, um, try not to talk with your mouth full, okay?'

So many rules. 'Okay.'

The engines growled beneath her feet. Tsione frowned and crossed to the control panels to check the instruments. Rerenga ate in silence, watching as the woman shrugged and turned back to tidy her bunk, slinging clothes into storage lockers under the bed and straightening the blankets.

'You can have the top bunk,' Tsione said, and then stopped. 'Oh! I forgot.' She stepped to the desk and pulled a red folder out from under the far pile of paperwork. Flipping through it, she ran a finger down the page. 'Here. In case of unforeseen visitors. Ahem. Welcome to my spacecraft – that's the *Starstriker*. I am your captain – also pilot, co-pilot, mechanic, security guard, medic, and general deckhand. My name is Tsione. I hope you enjoy your flight.' She nodded and closed the folder.

'*Starstriker*?' Rerenga asked. The word tasted wrong in her mouth.

The engines growled again.

Tsione dropped her empty bowl into a chute beside the table. There was a flash of red and a strong smell of burning, and then it was gone. 'It's the name of my boat.' She dropped into the pilot's seat and bent over the control panel again.

'What does it mean?'

'It's derived from "star-struck", meaning impressed or dazzled. You know, by the glorious galaxy.'

Without looking up, she waved a hand in the general direction of the viewport. Outside, pinpricks of light lit the velvet darkness. A few sparkled like gems, shimmering redbluegreen without pause. Rerenga supposed it was an impressive sight.

She yawned.

'You can go to bed, kid,' Tsione said, still frowning at the instrument panel. 'If you want. Bunk's one step in front of you, h-pod's two steps to your right. Make yourself at home.'

Vibrations tickled her feet, and Rerenga smiled. 'I will. Thank you.'

She made use of the h-pod and then clambered onto the top bunk and burrowed under the blankets. Tsione glanced up, saw her, and waved the golden cabin lights off, leaving only the glow of the instrument panels for illumination.

She was roused later by a hand on her shoulder.

'Och, dree your weird,' she muttered, and then woke up properly. 'What is it?'

'Engines are out,' Tsione said. 'They were playing up earlier, and now they've gone dead. I'm working on figurin' out what's wrong, but it could take a while. I'm just warning you: it was already set to be a long time until we made planetfall, and now it'll be even longer. But it's probably nothing to worry about.' She flashed a strained smile in the half-light.

'Okay.'

'We're dead in the water and all you can say is "okay"?'

Was it not the right thing to say? 'Sorry?'

'Oh, forget it. Go back to sleep.'

Tsione dropped to the floor. Rerenga rolled over and went back to sleep.

She woke hours later, well-rested. It was nice to nestle into the blankets and stare at the metal plate ceiling; but nature called.

She dropped from the top bunk and walked the two paces to the h-pod. A few minutes later she walked back out. Tsione was fast asleep on the bottom bunk, her mop of red curls all that could be seen past the pile of blankets. The ship lay quiet and cold, almost alien without the steady thrum of engines. The time stamp on the wall above the table read…

Huh?

It hadn't changed since she'd been woken by Tsione in the middle of the night. That was odd.

Tsione woke twenty minutes later and almost tripped over Rerenga on her way to the h-pod. She waved the lights up, mumbled something inarticulate, and stepped over Rerenga's outstretched legs, vanishing into the cubicle.

The first thing she said when she emerged, hair loose and damp, was: 'Why are you sitting on the floor?'

'I'm watching the clock.'

Tsione glanced at the wall. 'It stopped last night.'

'It stopped at twelve thirty-six.'

'It shouldn't have stopped at all,' Tsione said, buttoning her overshirt. 'That's a kinetic battery, every movement drives the next one; it can't stop. It's not even been in here nine months.'

She crossed to the table and stared at the unmoving time stamp. She shook her head. 'There's nothing I can do. It was built right into the wall, I can't get at the wiring to have a look.'

'It stopped at twelve thirty-six,' Rerenga said again.

Tsione threw her a single-serve packet of cereal. 'Is it a problem?'

'I don't know.' There was a dull sense of foreboding in the pit of her stomach, but nothing more.

Tsione slid into the pilot's seat with a groan.

Rerenga went back to watching the clock.

The cabin lights went out a while later. Backlit by the blue glow of the control panel, Tsione looked ceilingward and muttered a curse, adding hastily, 'Sorry, kid. Don't mind me.'

'We've still got instrument lights,' Rerenga said.

'Instrument lights, yes. Instruments themselves…' She flipped a couple of switches, shook her head, and returned them to their resting places. 'Not so much.' She slapped a hand on the edge of the console. 'No engines, no lights, and now no instruments. What in the name of the seven systems did you bring with you onto my boat?'

'I don't know.'

'Is it a virus? You got a ship virus on you and now it's infecting the boat systems? Is that it?'

'No.' It wasn't a virus. She didn't know what it was.

Tsione crossed the cabin, a black shadow in the half-light. 'You going to try and steal my boat, kid? Cos I can tell you right now, that ain't ever going to happen. *Starstriker*'s mine and she's stayin' that way.'

'I have a name,' Rerenga said. 'You named me.'

Tsione crowded her against the bulkhead, eyes glinting. 'You trying to steal my boat, Rerenga?'

'No. I'm not trying to steal your ship.'

Tsione held her gaze for a moment longer, and then relaxed and retreated. 'Good. Glad we got that cleared up.'

'You scared me.'

'Lots of scary things in space, kid. Had to be sure you're

not one of them.' Her head turned. 'You going to cry?'

'No.'

'Good.'

The ship shuddered, pitching to one side before righting itself. Tsione swore.

'What was that?' Rerenga asked.

'Blast if I know,' Tsione said. 'We've got nothin'. Whatever it was, didn't come from us.'

'Where are we?'

'Can't you do anything but ask questions?'

'Yes and no.'

Tsione barked a laugh. 'Give me a minute to check the console.'

It felt more like ten minutes than one, but Rerenga didn't complain. Finally, Tsione spun her chair and beckoned. 'C'mere.'

She stepped up to the instrument panel, her eyes following Tsione's finger to where a map panel sat frozen.

'Okay,' Tsione said. 'Two days ago I left Port Pratchett on Miranda, which is a planet over here,' she pointed to a dot. 'We're bound for Port Atticus on Tympani Tertius, which is,' she traced a line to another dot, 'here. Which means we're floating in space,' her finger drew a circle around an area between the two dots, 'somewhere here.'

Rerenga's mouth was dry. 'Have you been this way before?'

'Once,' Tsione said. 'It must have been four or five years ago.'

'And nothing like this happened?'

'What is this, a quiz show? No. Nothing like this happened last time.'

The console lights died, leaving them in darkness.

Rerenga's voice rang out. 'I don't think that's true.' She

didn't remember opening her mouth.

The lights flickered and came on.

Tsione stared at her. 'That's as may be,' she said, 'but that's all I'm telling you. It's none of your business.'

'It is my business,' Rerenga said. Was it? Why?

'No,' Tsione snapped. 'It's not. Leave it be.' She grimaced and lifted a shaking hand to her head.

'Are you all right?'

'My head hurts like a newlywed's—' she caught Rerenga's eye and broke off. 'Uh, like something that hurts a lot.'

Slowly, ponderously, the ship rolled over and kept rolling. Tsione's eyes widened. She lunged for a button on the far side of the console, pressed it, muttered frantically under her breath, then engaged three more switches. The air grew heavier.

'Get on the bunk,' Tsione barked.

'What?'

'Get on the bottom bunk! Now!'

They made for the bunk, slipped as the floor pitched, leapt, and made it.

'Hold on,' Tsione said. 'I really don't know if this will work.'

Rerenga curled a hand around the bunk frame as the stars out the viewport wheeled in a lazy semi-circle. The air pressed down on her, crushing her onto the bunk. The stars stopped turning. Tsione blew out a breath.

'Okay. I'm going to have a look. Stay there.'

She shuffled to the side of the bunk and peered at the metal plate flooring. Slowly, she moved until she was sitting on the edge. She drew a breath; her hands clenched white-knuckled on the rim of the top bunk; and in one swift movement stood up.

Nothing happened.

Tsione grinned. 'It worked!'

'What worked?' Rerenga scooted off the bunk and stepped across to the table, where the piles of paperwork were shaking as if a stiff wind was blowing.

'Don't touch them,' Tsione cautioned. 'I rerouted any residual power to the instrument board and engaged the gravity lock. We've got enough mass to keep us up here, but I don't know about the smaller things.'

'What do you mean, keep us up here?'

Tsione nodded out the viewport.

Rerenga followed the movement. 'The stars are upside down.'

'No,' Tsione said, still smiling. '*We* are upside down.'

Rerenga stared at her, perplexed. Was she mad?

Tsione pointed to the floor. 'That is up.' Pointed to the ceiling. 'That is down. Or it is for the purposes of the boat's artificial grav, at any rate.' Pointed to the floor again. 'The gravity lock stops the boat compensating for roll. It keeps the centre of gravity tied to the floor, so the floor is always down. Which is why they,' she pointed out at the stars, 'look like they're upside down. They're in their normal places, but we've rolled a hundred and eighty degrees.'

Rerenga had a brief, dizzying image of what they must look like from outside: the tiny ship floating belly-up in space, she and Tsione walking across the ceiling as if it was normal ... which it was, because the ceiling was the floor.

'I see,' she said.

Tsione stepped to the rear of the cabin. 'I'm going to use the h-pod,' she said, 'if it still works. And when I get back, we'll jemmy the hatch and take a look at the engines. Don't touch anything till I get back, okay?'

Did she not trust her? 'Okay.'

Tsione disappeared into the h-pod.

Rerenga sat on the floor-ceiling and watched the unmoving time stamp, nibbling her lower lip.

Twelve thirty-six. Why was it important? Twelve thirty-six. One two three six. One thousand, two hundred and thirty-six. It was important, she could feel it in her gut, but why?

She didn't know.

She hated not knowing.

When Tsione came back, they cantilevered the chair out of the cockpit, exposing the engine hatch. Tsione hoisted it up and lowered the short ladder into the pit. There was a click. Green light ghosted from the hole.

'That light still works,' Tsione said. 'Good. This might take a while.'

It took several hours. Rerenga sat with her back to the console, alternately watching Tsione and the time stamp, and politely ignoring the stream of muffled swearing.

There was a clatter and Tsione emerged from the pit, wiping her grimy hands on a rag. She shook her head. 'I don't know what's wrong with her. The engines look fine to me, except for the fact that they're not going.'

She'd barely set foot on the deck when the green pit light failed. The blue instrument lights died, too. Tsione cursed; there was some fumbling and then the creak of the pilot's chair.

'Don't move.' Her voice echoed in the stillness.

'Okay,' Rerenga said. She hadn't planned to.

The cabin was in darkness. She couldn't have said where the ship ended and the black of space began. The stars out the viewport shone white and cold, glittering, mesmerising in their scattered patterns. But the patterns were wrong. The stars were upside down because the ship was wrong, the ship was upside down.

The stars began to move.

'Tsione?' Her voice wavered.

'I see it,' Tsione said grimly. 'We're rolling again. Hold on to something and pray it stops before the pressure of the spin splats us against the hull.'

The stars wheeled in a leisurely arc, ninety degrees, one hundred and eighty, two hundred and seventy – Rerenga's breath caught – three hundred and sixty, ninety again, one eighty, two seventy…

They were gaining speed as they rolled. The blue instrument lights flickered and died again; the green pit light flared and stayed on, lending an eerie glow to the spinning ship. Tsione sat frozen in the pilot's seat, hands clenched on the armrests, mouth set in a hard line.

She caught Rerenga looking at her, and shrugged.

'There's nothing I can do.' Her voice was quiet, defeated. 'No engines, no instruments. I'm not in control. I don't know what's happening, or why she's—' Her voice cracked. 'Why she's doing this. I've heard the stories – who hasn't? Travellers caught on the edge of space like this, bad things happening with no explanation, the engines go, the systems go. They call it the death roll. Boat starts spinning and won't stop. Keeps at it, getting faster and faster, until the gravity lock gives out. The g-forces knock you unconscious and then kill you, and the next ship along finds the boat and the bodies, still rolling, months later. Life support's failing,' she added. 'We might run out of oxygen before then. It'd be a mercy.'

Her tone changed. 'But none of those black box stories had a little girl show up cabin-side twelve hours before everything went pear-shaped.'

Rerenga looked at her.

'It makes me wonder, is all.' Tsione took her gun from the rack on the wall. She checked the magazine, chambered a round, and turned to face Rerenga.

Rerenga swallowed.

The words were quiet. 'Why are you here, kid?'

'I don't know,' she said.

'I'm not in the mood for games.'

'I don't know why I'm here.'

'Tell me why you're here, Rerenga, or—'

'What happened to you last time?'

Tsione blinked. 'What?'

'Last time,' she said desperately, the words leaving her mouth without conscious thought. 'Last time you were along this route. What happened?'

'I told you, nothing like this—'

'But something happened last time, and something's happening this time. What was it?'

'Nothing.' Tsione's voice rose.

'I can help you,' Rerenga pressed. 'Just tell me what happened.'

'No. Why are you here?'

'What happened?'

'Why are you here?'

'Why is she called *Starstriker*?'

The question hung in the air. Their breathing was loud in the silence. Tsione licked her lips, and then nodded. She didn't lower the gun.

'She was called the *Zuflucht* when I bought her. I forget what it means – safety or sanctuary or something—'

'Refuge,' Rerenga said.

'Or refuge, yeah. Something like that.'

'It means refuge.'

Tsione gave her a hard look. 'All right. It means refuge.'

Rerenga gestured for her to continue.

'The guy was a second-generationer from Edinburgh II; his name was—'

'Douglas,' she said.

'Douglas,' Tsione confirmed. She didn't look surprised at the interruption. 'He'd bought it off a lady from Zion, who bought it off a man from Archimedes Major, who bought it from his father, who got it off a cousin who lived on the second moon of Terminus. You get the idea.'

'Yes.'

'Apparently, the original owner had built it herself. Came from Earth, according to the records; little group of settlements called the Cargills on an island chain in the south seas—' She trailed off. 'Sorry. Where was I?'

'Douglas.'

'Douglas. Right. So she was the Zuflucht when I bought her. I hated the name, mostly because I could barely pronounce it and it was a pain to spell when I was writing paperwork.' She paused, thinking. The gun never wavered. 'I was fifteen when I bought her. Spent every coin I had.'

'What happened?'

'Hadn't had her six months when I was out this way on my own. Had a cargo of fruit in stasis; they were overdue for delivery at Port Atticus. I was pushing her hard,' she admitted. 'Harder than I should've, most like. Wasn't paying attention like I should've been. I was young, she was my first boat. You know.'

'I know,' she echoed.

'We hit a rock.'

Rerenga waited, tense, perfectly still, poised at the edge of the chasm. With every word, the pieces fell into place.

Tsione held up her free hand in a fist. 'A little flaming rock. About this big. Wouldn't have been so bad, but we were going so fast – I'd taken off most of the shielding and diverted the spare power to the engines…' She shook her head, eyes dark with pain. 'Tore straight through us.'

Rerenga caught her breath, remembering.

'Shattered her into a million pieces,' Tsione continued. 'Hurt like nothing I'd ever felt before. I could … I could hear her screaming around me.' She took a calming breath. 'And then she stopped.'

'And then?'

'And then an empty carrier arrived not a day later on its way through to Port Pratchett. Found the pieces scattered, found me floating in the lifesuit. I paid them everything and promised more, and we gathered every bit of her we could find – every splintered length of bulkhead, every square of floor panel, every engine spring – and took her to Miranda.'

Knowledge hovered out of reach. 'Miranda. What happened on Miranda?'

'I rebuilt her.' The words were soft. 'Used every original part I had, replaced the parts I didn't have, and spent every spare moment, every spare coin rebuilding her. Did as much of the work as I could with my own hands. Hired a few people for the bits I couldn't do – the heavy labour and the fiddly electrics and such. Took me a long time,' she added, 'but that was by the by. Time was no matter. I just wanted her back. Whole. Alive again. You know.'

'I know.'

'Had to report the accident, of course. They gave me a citation for carelessness, banned me from piloting for a twelvemonth. Fined me a little – not as much as they could have. They went easy on me, figured I'd learned my lesson. That was fine. I wasn't going anywhere; was too busy rebuilding her.'

Stars blurred outside the viewport. Time was short. She opened her mouth and let the words spill out. 'And the rock?'

Tsione shrugged. 'It disintegrated on the way through. They labelled it a small F-spec asteroid in rogue orbit and marked it expired. I think the official designation was MF-twelve-something. It won't be bothering us now, anyway.'

The ship rocked. Rerenga turned her gaze to the frozen time stamp. 'MF-twelve-thirty-six?'

'Might have been. Why?' Tsione followed her gaze. 'Oh.'

'Oh,' Rerenga echoed, the word little more than an exhalation of breath. 'I remember.'

'You – What? You remember? Remember what?'

Rerenga curled against the console, shaking, hands clenched, fingers digging into palms, as the memory flooded her. 'Everything.'

She remembered flying this route. Too fast, too hard. Being driven on by the thundering will of the captain – Tsione. Remembered the asteroid. Blaring a warning. Too late. Remembered the pain, wave upon wave of screaming agony as she was torn apart and scattered to the winds.

Remembered the terrifying black of losing herself.

Where was she?

Part of her remembered being gathered, piece by excruciating piece, from the depths as she slept. Being thrown in the cargo hold, a ragged jumble of gears and panels and levers and the trailing strips of that old blanket Tsione had always hated. Remembered Miranda, where her body was put together again.

Who was she?

She had wandered long in the black, she knew that.

And then Tsione had come this way again, had gathered her courage and decided it was time to try again. She wouldn't let the fear hold her back.

And Zuflucht had come this way with her, to find out who she was and how she came to be.

She hadn't known, and so the little girl in the locker hadn't known either.

And the knowledge had come, slowly, but now she knew. She smiled.

'What is it?' Tsione asked.

'I know who I am.'

The stars outside were slowing their mad wheeling.

'Who are you, then?'

The boat rolled and came upright.

'I'm the ship.'

The cabin lights came on. The instrument panel lit up. The engines roared to life.

'I'm the ship,' she said again, and giggled. The engines giggled with her, vibrations spreading through her feet.

Tsione stared.

'Or maybe the ship is me,' she added. 'I'm not sure. The delineation is a bit … well. I don't know if there is a delineation.'

Tsione's gun lowered. She dropped heavily into the pilot's chair. 'You're the boat,' she said.

The engines sang beneath them. 'Yes.'

'You're talking.'

'Yes.'

'I'm going mad.'

'No, you're not.'

Tsione took a deep breath. 'Are you going to hurt me?'

She snorted. 'No.'

'Do you have a name?'

'Yes.'

Tsione paused. 'What is it?'

'I have a name,' she said. 'You named me.'

'Starstriker?'

Rerenga shuddered.

Tsione shook her head. 'No. I know.' She smiled. 'Rerenga. What does it mean?'

Rerenga nodded. 'Refuge. And flight.' Her smile wavered and fell. She could feel the pull already.

'What's wrong?'

'I have to go.' The ship wanted her back. She couldn't stay here; she didn't belong in one piece in the cabin; mortal, stationary, flesh and blood.

'What?'

'I have to go,' she repeated, fighting tears. She wanted to stay, to talk to this woman who had destroyed her and then loved her enough to rebuild her with her bare hands; but she had to go. She belonged in the ship, in the oil racing through the engines, in the lights flickering overhead, in the metal floor panels and the console levers.

She stepped back, toward the locker, pulling off the borrowed jersey and dropping it on the bed as she went.

'Wait!' Tsione said, standing and moving forward. 'I don't understand.'

The time stamp on the wall was working again.

'I'm sorry,' she said. Beneath her feet, the water storage tank burbled an apology. 'I can't stay like this. But I'll be here.' She held Tsione's gaze, desperate for her to understand. 'I'll be here.'

She pulled open the locker door.

Tsione stood a pace away, gaping. Bereft.

'I'll be here,' she said a third time, and stepped backward into the locker.

She slammed the door as Tsione lunged, nails scrabbling against worn metal. Golden light spilled through the slanted grillwork.

Tsione opened the door. Her jacket lay crumpled in a mound on the floor.

Crop Rotation

David Stevens

Anxiety coursing. Sun up in three hours. The work that awaited him. The mess. Always making do. Nothing ever finished.

Then there was the thing the worrying was hiding. The thing that should be at the centre of his thoughts.

The bed sagged and creaked as he rolled, dragging his belly with him. Old traces of his wife – her face cream, roses and lanolin – lingered.

A distant banging. The noise came from inside the house. He lifted his head to hear from both ears, vertebrae grinding as he sat up. Carter jumped as a fox screamed nearby. He forced himself to relax. After the big storm, all those noises outside, him leaping each time, checking there was no one in the yard. Maggie yelling she couldn't sleep with him carrying on, there was no one there, who would be out in the dark after weather like that? *She* couldn't sleep.

The roaring dark over the forest that night, a dribble of green leaking over the distant mountains, and lightning flashing far away. The whole big sky black as secrets.

A week later, he was on the roof repairing the television

antenna, listening to his wife yelling he was a fool at his age. He guessed he'd been a fool at any age. He couldn't stand to hear a second longer how she was missing her soaps, and if he didn't get up there and fix it, he didn't know who would.

Useless effort. There was power but no signal, nothing but white hash on the screen. She said he'd put it up wrong, but they both knew that wasn't it, otherwise she wouldn't have stopped him when he tried to climb back up again.

She was taking a long time in the loo. Now he had to go. It would be a waste of time. He'd wait for ages, and maybe be rewarded with a tiny piddle.

Stuck here with these old man thoughts, these fag-end early morning bleats. He should be retired. Somewhere warm. Somewhere with human beings. Sitting in the shade, complaining about everything. Seen no one for weeks. Morning after the storm, Pearson's ute had flown up the dirt road like an emu with a rocket up its arse. Nothing after that.

She still wasn't back. If he didn't sleep, how could he do a day's work? Kitchen garden to be tended, though Maggie would do that. She was doing a lot more. Her hip had stopped playing up. Like that was some compensation. At that, he felt like a drink. He always felt like a drink. There was none on the place, not for a long time. That was the only way to fix that.

Silence solidified behind him. He was being stared at. Carter felt the eyes boring into his back. Something had settled back there in the dark, paused just outside the doorway, a chunk of the night settled on its haunches.

No movement. Perhaps he had been mistaken. Then came the long creak of the door being pushed open. The slow groan of hinges as it was closed again.

He'd meant to oil the door. Another job he'd failed to do.

Along his arms and legs, hairs rose.

Sniffing. Little gasps of air taken in, tasted. Coming closer, following his scent.

It hadn't been a fox screaming. He knew what was there.

Tentative steps on the hardwood floor as it came closer. Maggie had always wanted carpet in here, but carpet costs, and it wasn't him who polished the floors. Another way he had let her down.

It was nearer now. He felt it lean on the mattress, a deep breath through its nose. The pressure as a leg was raised, and a knee pressed down on the side of the bed. Weight shifted, something leaned forward onto the bed, and…

Don't be stupid, it's Maggie, it's Maggie, it's Maggie…

Carter had an image of a cat, poised and predatory, ready to pounce. Not the way he used to picture his wife.

The mass moved, falling forward, and Carter swung. As the body came down on the bed, using his hip as a pivot, he rolled out into the night. Looked across, saw his wife staring at him from the bed. *Who else?*

He shuffled out of the room, bad leg dragging. His bladder pressed with a false urgency.

Maggie had wanted an en-suite as well, but the house wasn't built for such luxuries, and he had kept telling her he didn't want to sleep in the same room where they shit. *Don't be ridiculous*, she said, and she had been right, like she was about everything. He had grown up with an outhouse and, in the winter, a chamberpot tucked beneath his bed. Bringing the toilet inside the house in his lifetime was achievement enough.

The bathroom light blinded him. He was still standing there when his vision returned. No use looking down, a watched kettle never boils, and he wouldn't be able to see his gear anyway, not with his belly hanging there. This is the bright future, and nothing is ever going to be as good as this again. When did the good old days end?

He let his pyjama pants fall, turned, sat down, and sighed yet again. What he would have copped if his old man had known he sat down to pee. *Ya what? Ya sheila!* The indignities the old bastard had avoided by having his last heart attack at 50. The benefits of a meat and beer diet.

He looked up. The corner of the manhole was ajar. That's what had taken her so long.

*

Carter had told her he would be out for the whole day. Drove off with that familiar gnawing, a rat chewing at his belly, matching the pulsing in his leg. He worked his way through his usual list of bills and delays and jobs undone, trying to identify the focus of his anxiety. In the end, he just braked halfway across a paddock and walked back, a slow aching trek with his gammy leg.

Maggie wasn't at the house. He kept expecting to turn a corner and bump into her coming the other way, and he had a lie ready to blurt out about the flippin' truck breaking down again.

It didn't happen.

Not in the garden, nor in the shed. He circled wider and wider, searching, following his thoughts, not tracks, his mood darkening as the trees grew closer and blocked the sky. All this shit he had meant to clear away, finish the work his father started. It would never happen now. The bush was coming back, swallowing his land. It would be as though he never existed.

Finally, he glimpsed her before she disappeared into a

clutch of she-oaks.

By the time he caught up, the ground was springier beneath his feet. Waste land, it all needed draining. Tea-coloured water seeped into her footprints, rising above her ankles. Everything else failing, but there was nothing wrong with his eyesight. Mosquitoes rose about her but she didn't swat, didn't wave her arms. She strode into the bog until she stood in the cleft between twin flooded gum trees. She leaned on one of them and stood in the humidity she hated so much, water up her shins.

Hanging back, Carter felt ridiculous. He should call to her. What was she doing out here? The only one who ever came out here was their son, long time ago. Bird-watching, he said. Bludging, more like. Gripping the tree, with her free hand Maggie bunched up the front of her dress. Carter slipped to the other side of the eucalypt he was hiding be-hind, to get a better look. Water flowed from the hem of her dress as Maggie dragged it out of the brackish water.

The dress rose up. She was not wearing support hose. Her legs were firmer than he remembered, less mottled. (Even just thinking it, he whispered that last word.) She crouched a little and pulled the dress higher. She was wearing nothing underneath.

Dementia, he thought and would have gone to her, would have broken cover and crossed over and held her, but then she spread her legs and crouched still lower. He heard the splash before he realised what he was seeing. From between her legs it pulsed, squirt after long squirt of white fluid, a flow like an elephant pissing, if an elephant pissed milky pus. The gunk flowed out of her at such a rate, he thought she should have been emptied, leaving the husk of her clinging to the tree like a cicada shell.

Run, his mind screamed, but he saw how it would play out. Turning, trying, making a few yards through the swamp before his crook leg gives way, and he splashes face down. She overtakes him with ease. Looks down on him half submerged, her head bent at an inquisitive angle. Her body lowers towards him and, just as she blocks the sun, something else breaks through the mask of her face, and he descends into darkness. So he stayed, his eyes closed to block out the image, as though that could somehow hide him.

Panting, he slid quietly into the shallow water, backing into the submerged roots of the river gum, forcing his backside into the mud. With his bad back and fat stomach he bent as much as he could, pressing into the shadow. Still he heard the noise, the thucking squirt, the thick splash. Gently, he submerged his hat, staining it wet before he replaced it, pulling the brim low to cover his face.

The splashing stopped. Holding his breath, he lowered himself as far as pain would allow. He heard the sluicing of water as she turned and began to retrace her steps.

There was not another person for a million miles around. Him and the trees and the insects, and whatever was passing for his wife. Her feet sloshing, step after step. He refused to look up. Beneath his hat, the sound of her movement was everything.

She walked past him.

Carter waited ages, eventually daring to lift his hat and look about. The sun had moved. The bog was silent but for the machine burr of insects. His leg was numb and he had to roll onto his knees and climb the trunk of the tree to raise his body from the water. Circulation returned slowly in sharp stabs and aches. He began the long limping journey to his truck, waiting for her to spring from behind each tree he passed.

He had not stopped waiting.

*

He wanted nothing more in life than to urinate and have this over with.

Maggie had been taken a few days after the storm, he guessed. Sitting on this very toilet seat, looking up and seeing a version of herself descend naked from the ceiling. Had she died from fright? Had they needed to finish her off? So long as it was quick. He remembered the night, not that he had recorded the date or anything. He had woken briefly as she left the room for the toilet. He must have nodded back off, for next thing he was being dragged from sleep, Maggie fumbling roughly at the front of his pyjamas, pulling him round from behind, mounting him, rocking back and forth in a way he couldn't remember. First he was surprised that it was happening at all, and then more surprised that he managed to play his part.

It was hard to mourn when there was someone in the house who looked just like her, spoke like her, and seemed to have her memories. By now, he suspected she had been replaced several times, that they were a couple of generations along. Sitting in the truck in the paddock that day, waiting for his clothes to dry, he decided it was not in his best interests to reveal what he knew.

He had headed home. Where else could he go?

It didn't take long to doubt himself, to deny the memory of that long afternoon. Life went on. If she had noticed him out in the swamp, she gave no sign.

Carter couldn't leave it alone. Seeing she was busy with her chores, he tramped out through the bog, searching for evidence. There was nothing. He had imagined everything. He was right, it *was* dementia, but *he* was the sick one.

Less than a week later, he walked along the creek that fed the bog. The water was clear, slowly flowing. There they were, affixed to the rocks near the bank. He stopped, relieved and horrified. Clusters of translucent sacs, water gliding over them.

He checked every few days now. Always, there are a few on the margin, browning, breaking up, drifting off into deeper water, where the fish and yabbies will take care of them. He doesn't worry about those failures. He focuses on the ones starting to ripen. He looks for the balding heads, the rounding (but not too round) stomach. There are a couple of half house-bricks he keeps there. It doesn't take long. Once they're ripe, the sacs are about to crack and fissure anyway. The skin tears easy, and it takes just a few hard whacks to crack the plate beneath. After that it's a cinch to reduce the insides to a thick green paste. The first time, before he steeled himself to the task, he left it late. It had raised its forearms, waving them gently, a bug's antennae testing the air. As he brought the brick down, a moan escaped.

Looking at the mess, before he pushed it out into the creek to dissolve, before he wiped the brick clean on the reeds, he taunted himself: '*You're fucking that*'. Green shit everywhere, shards like broken Bakelite poking through.

Push the bricks down into your trousers. Wade out into the creek. Don't look back. Just walk out there. Clean and deep this time of year. Let it all wash away. Go under, take a deep breath…

The sky was frosty blue. The day was mild, and a cool breeze dappled the surface of the creek. Carter closed his eyes for the moment, felt the air brush over his face. Dragonflies danced and hovered, danced and hovered. Along the bank, wild flowers trailed in the water.

He was a farmer. He had traded in meat all his life. He had dealt with hernias and prolapsed uteruses and extruded bowels, done his fair share of butchering. What we're all like underneath, most people were able to ignore that. There was no reason not to extend that deliberate ignorance to his own situation. Especially as he had no choice, not if he wanted to live.

Carter wiped the bricks, removing most of the muck, and put them back in their spot.

The stray thoughts had not stopped him coming down and culling the males every few days. He did *not* want to walk into the bathroom some night, and find his replacement waiting for him. It was hard enough to piss without worrying about what might come crawling down the manhole while he was sitting there.

He left the females alone.

In his reverie two or three drops squeezed out, barely disturbing the water in the toilet bowl. He pretended he felt better.

*

Where else could he go? Carter only knew his farm. Pearson had never returned. Everything beyond was a dark forest. Who knew what was going on out there? If he even camped out in another room, she would come hunting. He'd give himself away in an instant. So, stomach dragging him forward, he returned to the cave of his bedroom.

Carter ignored the cat's-eye glow from the bed as he shuffled across the floor. He put out of his mind an image of a tapering chitinous limb reaching round him, a barbed tip tapping his shoulder.

Her embrace was eager. The newcomer must have won. That wasn't always the way, but it was happening more often lately. The younger ones were breeding stronger.

The females would not suffer each other to live. Not while he was the only male, and he didn't intend that to change. It was a pity, he thought as she pinned him beneath her. They were good workers, and there was so much he could do to the property with just a few of them.

Carter finished and she rolled off. Quicker than peeing. Breathing came easier, the late night thoughts pushed lower in the sponge of his mind. Gave him a moment to plan. Don't adapt, you die.

That young couple, they'd bought Tennison's block a few years back, upstream a couple of miles. Maybe that would work. Perhaps different types of females could get on, not registering each other as a threat. She'd been a good sort. Wore khaki shorts and a singlet. Carter always snuck a look. Long brown legs. Unmottled. Good arms.

He could drag the tinny to the creek, go and take a gander at what was happening up there. Back up through the forest. Set off early, so it was all in daylight. He'd kept control here, but the rest of the place might have descended into chaos without a firm hand. Always tricky, introducing new crops.

No one would even notice if he untethered one of the embryonic females, trailed the sac bobbing behind the boat as he set off back downstream. See how she'd fare transplanted.

They should appreciate it, him taking one off their hands. If they thought about it.

If they thought.

Narco

MICHELLE CHILD

THROUGH SMOTHERING DARKNESS, RAIN ASSAULTS ME from all directions. Cars hiss by, headlights glaring. Shadows bend in the edges of my vision, distorting reality. The hood of my jacket crowds my face. I toss it back and wind claws at my hair. I can hardly keep my eyes open — more sleepy than usual.

Fucking narcolepsy.

Rounding the last corner to the train station, my pocket buzzes. My heart leaps. Mum?

Not Mum.

I stare at the flashing screen. It's him. My pulse rises. I skim through a glossary of insults I'd love to throw at him, but I can't risk an attack now. The battle within takes longer than it should.

I shove the phone back in my pocket and run, splashing through puddles.

Entering the sanctuary of Wellington Railway Station, I gasp for breath. My scarf's way too tight. I yank it free with burning-cold hands and wipe my face dry.

Fuck, I hate winter.

I mill with the other post-peak-hour stragglers, dribbling through the foyer. I hadn't meant to stay at work so late. My boss at the library had let me take my usual nap in the reserve section, but I'd lost track of time.

I head onto the Kapiti line platform.

Thank heavens, the weather hasn't screwed up the trains.

I pace, carefully avoiding the edge. Would anyone save me if I passed out and fell onto the tracks? I gaze along the platform at the handful of businessmen, soaked in grey suits that match their expressions. Doubt they'd notice.

A few columns down, three teens have staked their territory. Each of them sports a two-litre bottle of soft drink, most likely spiked with alcohol. They puff on cigarettes and roar like cavemen discovering fire. Their laughter cuts through the sheets of rain, sweeping under the awning.

My phone buzzes again.

'Please be Mum,' I whisper.

I look at the name. My throat tightens.

I push the phone to my ear. 'What do you want, Ben?'

'Dana, where are you?'

'I'm at the station.'

'Where are you going?'

'To my parents'.'

'Waikanae? At this hour? You're being stupid.'

'Stupid?' I shout over the howling storm. 'This is the smartest thing I've done in three years.'

He sighs. 'Look, it's pissing down. Please, let me come get you and we can talk about it. If you still feel the same tomorrow, you can go stay with your folks then … when it's safer.'

I clench the phone so hard, it shakes in my hand. '*Safer*? I'm twenty-eight. I can look after myself.'

'You're upset. You know what happens when you're

worked up.'

So goddamned condescending.

'You have no idea…' My lip trembles and tears brim in my eyes. I wipe them away and breathe deep, holding the phone aside so he can't hear me losing it.

'Dana, please come home. I love you. I don't want anything to happen—'

'You should have thought about that before you did what you did.' I hang up before my voice cracks completely, and shove the phone away. I hug my arms around myself.

Slapping my forehead with the heel of my hand, I rock back and forward in my boots. Sniff back tears.

Stupid, Stupid.

Fingers stiff, I grab my pill container from my purse and wrestle out a little white beacon of light. Provigil. Pro-Vigilance – pharmaceutical companies couldn't be any less subtle.

I've already taken today's quota, but I don't care. I swallow the pill with the last sip in my water bottle and grimace. I hadn't noticed how thirsty I was. Too late to go find more. The train's yellow eyes pierce the gloom as it slithers to the platform.

Stumbling aboard, I nestle into a corner seat. Straight away, my eyes start to droop, so I get my book out. I can get away with sleeping just about anywhere if people think I'm reading. A lame trick, but it seems to work.

A woman sits in the seat across the aisle from me. Plush yellow handbag and a veil of neat auburn hair – harmless. The three teens are down the other end, making enough noise to wake the…

*

My head nods – bounces back. Fog settles behind the eyes.

Just let go. No one can stop us from sleeping.

I smile bitterly. Waikanae is the end of the line, so I won't miss my stop.

*

'Excuse me. Miss? Excuse me…'

I snap awake. The auburn-haired woman is reaching across the aisle with my phone. 'You dropped this. It's been ringing.'

'Oh. Yeah. Thanks.' I take the phone and scroll through the missed calls from Mum. A text: *No worries sweetheart. I'll pick U up from station. Dad made spag-bol 4 dinner. Be safe.*

The train rattles along, and I sway. Nausea wallows heavy in my stomach. Massaging my temples, I sigh. The Provigil hasn't kicked in. My scarf's strangling me again. I pull it loose.

'Are you okay?' the woman asks.

I cough and rub my eyes, picturing how they look – puffy, red – windows to the soul of a zombie. 'Ah, yeah. Just killer-tired.'

'You want me to keep a look out for your stop?' she asks.

'No need. End of the line,' I say.

Picking my book up from the floor, I turn the pages thoughtfully. As if I care where I was at. Out the window, a scrub of black rushes by. My reflection's blurry, streaked in lines of water, charging down the glass. Ragged hair, doing its best to impersonate a bird's nest.

Look at yourself, you're a wreck.

'Where are we?' I ask the woman.

'We're nearly at Porirua.'

'Sweet, thanks.'

*

The train lurches to a stop. My eyes blink open.

'Porirua station, next stop Paremata,' the voice-over announces.

Asleep again? Pathetic. Why did you bother with the pill?

The woman's gone. She must've gotten out. The teenagers, too. I'm alone.

Heavy footsteps enter at the far end. A hooded figure wearing a khaki jacket steps into the aisle. By the build, I guess it's a man, but he doesn't remove his hood. He sits in the far corner seat, his face shadowed.

A chill runs across my skin.

He settles himself, gets out an apple, and starts working the skin with a pocket-knife. Creepy as fuck.

No way I'm falling asleep again with this dude watching me. I have to change carriages, but if I go now, he'll know I'm scared.

The train clunks into motion again. Slow pulses of its mechanical heart shake through me.

Biting my fingernails, I hide behind my book. Secretly, I watch the man's reflection in the window. He keeps working the apple. Its peel snakes down in front of him.

My head jerks back.

Fool. You're dropping off again. Go now.

Calm as I can manage, I head to the doors. The train slows, groaning.

Tucking my hair over my ear, I sneak a peek at the hooded man. Still peeling, still staring. How long does it take to peel an apple?

Is there a security camera? Surely someone's going to see this guy's got a knife. Not cool.

Lamp-posts flash by, flickering in the rain like they're spitting fire. Dizzy, I grip the yellow support rail, trying to steady myself. The train stops. Doors open and I stagger out into the downpour. Racing to the next carriage, I step back on board, hoping the man fell for my ruse. Part of me feels like a total jerk, assuming the worst of strangers, but I'm not taking any chances now.

Sinking into another seat, I re-shape the woollen python around my neck and sigh.

*

'There you are, Sleeping Beauty, you dropped this.'

Batting eyelids, I take a moment to focus. It's the woman again, holding out my book.

'Thanks,' I croak. 'I thought you got off at Porirua?'

She sits opposite me and pulls a newspaper from her yellow-leather handbag. 'I just went looking for a magazine, but this was all I found.'

I nod and slip my book into my bag. No use keeping up the reading charade now. We're the only two passengers in the carriage.

'Is it that bad?'

'Pardon?' I say.

'Your book? It seems to be putting you to sleep.'

'I've got a condition.' I give a polite smile, trying feebly to make up for my snappy tone.

'Let me guess: narcolepsy?'

I raise a brow. 'Yeah. Most people don't know what it is.'

'I'm a counsellor. I've worked a bunch of cases with sleeping disorders, they're more common than people think. Do you have cataplexy and hypnogogia, too?'

'Only when I get … stressed.'

'Do you have a support group?'

'Used to.'

'It's important. You should keep it up.'

I sigh. 'I was stable for a while. I guess I got lazy and stopped going. Haven't been this bad in years.'

'Something set you off?'

Cursing the tears that are edging from the corners of my eyes, I nod. 'My boyfriend and I...'

She twists the newspaper rolled in her hand. 'I'm sorry.'

'It's okay.' I shake my head and pull out a tissue. 'He was sleeping with someone else. Probably because I was too busy sleeping. Ironic, huh?'

'I know it's none of my business, but you can't use your condition as an excuse when things go wrong.'

I blow my nose. 'I know, but it's been a crap day. I found out this morning. It's not every day you discover the man you love is actually a cheating piece of shit.' I swallow back the salty lump in my throat.

The woman knits her fingers together over crossed knees. 'You need to take control of your life. Stop escaping your problems by going to sleep.'

I narrow my eyes. 'Excuse me? You don't even know me.'

'Are you ever truly awake?' The woman smiles with her mouth, but not her eyes. Smug. I've had therapists give me the 'wake up' speech before, but lecturing a stranger on a train? Is she for real?

'Thanks for the *advice*.' I stand and grab my bag.

'Do you think Ben cheated on you because you're always sleeping? Or because when you're awake, you're always complaining?'

Slowly, I turn back. 'I didn't say his name was Ben.'

She lifts her hands and starts clapping slowly.

Clap. Clap...

*

Snap. Snap. Snap.

The train jolts and I wake, heart racing. The hooded man sits at the far end of the carriage, flicking his pocket-knife open and closed.

I never changed cars. It was a dream.

Shit.

I shake my head to clear the drowsiness. It clouds me like fumes of liquor, tickling the thirst of a drunk. Not now.

With shaking fingers, I pinch the back of my hand – yes, I'm awake. The Provigil will take effect soon.

Yeah, you just keep telling yourself that.

Where are we?

A sweeping roar envelops the train – the muffling growl of rock. The tunnels. Paekakariki station must be next. I stare out the window. I barely recognise the bedraggled reflection, superimposed on a wash of black motion.

Should I try switching carriages again?

Go, or stay … you'll fall asleep either way.

The train brakes begin their screeching wail. Picking up my bag, I stand and move to the door. I wrap my arm around the support rail and waver with the rhythm of the clattering train. A shuffling sound startles me. I flick my head around and gasp. The hooded man moves through the carriage towards me, his face visible now. Sharp blue eyes rake down me, catching on my chest.

He might be innocent. This might simply be his stop.

It doesn't matter. Icy terror cracks through my chest and every muscle in my body commits mutiny. Cataplexy.

My knees give like someone's hit them with a hammer. My eyes roll back. I don't even feel the floor when it swoops up to clout me.

*

'Would you look at yourself? Honestly, you're pitiful.'

I'm sprawled on the train floor. Paralysed. Too weak to stand up.

Clack, clack, clack.

Dark green heels circle to stand before me. The counsellor-woman. Am I dreaming again? Seriously? Wake up!

'Oh no, you're not going to wake up.' Green heels pivot. She taps her toe like a teacher who's caught a student passing notes in class. 'You know why?'

Her yellow bag drops to the floor and she crouches. She cocks her head, bringing her face in line with mine. Auburn hair sways in time with the jolting train.

'Because you're a coward. I wish you could see what you look like right now. Slumped like a sack of recycled rags.' She feels the material of my coat and frowns. 'Is this polyester? At least no one's going to mug you for your clothes.' The woman lifts my arm, drops it to the ground. 'Always an excuse for something. I can't drive a car, I can't go swimming, I can't ride a bike, I can't, I can't, me, me, me!' She pouts. 'You know what? It's not the narcolepsy, or the cataplexy, it's you. You're bleeding useless. Lazy, selfish, and now you're delusional too. Crazy bitch. No wonder he left you.' Her eyes lather me in distaste. 'But don't worry. I'll take good care of you.'

She grabs my wrist, clutches my forefinger and looks me in the eye. 'You're mine now.'

She snaps my finger backwards. Bones crack and I cry out.

*

Gasping, I wake up on the carriage floor. Pain shoots through my arm. Sprained wrist, broken finger, I must have fallen on my arm. I roll over, cradling my injury. My breath quickens and I slide myself into the corner. Nightmare counsellor-woman's gone.

Breath heaving, I pull my scarf free and stuff it into my bag.

Scanning the rows, I can't see the hooded man, but he could be hiding.

Don't be stupid. He must've gotten off. Probably stepped right over you while you were unconscious.

The train clatters onward. We must be getting close to Waikanae. If I can just stay awake…

A vibration purrs against my leg. I fumble for my phone, swiping the lock open.

My throat is so scratchy, all I can do at first is cough. 'Mum!'

The line crackles. Mum's voice distorts. 'Dana … are … you…?'

'Mum, can you hear me? Mum?' I hug my knees. 'Mum, I'm freaking out.'

Her voice is scattered. Her tone nervous. 'Your father's … rain…'

'Mum, I can't hear you.'

'… on his … meet you … but … down…'

The train slows and shudders to a stop and I pitch forward, dropping my phone. I scramble to pick it up. Lights blink on and off in the carriage.

'Mum?' The connection's gone.

We're not at a station, did the train break down? Is something wrong with the tracks? Is that what Mum was trying to tell me?

Out the window, a river runs below. White noise dashing over black rocks. It's the Waikanae River Bridge. We're just a minute out from the platform.

I push my finger to the emergency buzzer. It crackles static.

A hand grabs the back of my neck and slams my face into the wall. The smell of iron burns in my nose.

The man spins me. Hood pushed back, his shaven head comes in close. He crushes a palm against my mouth, silencing my cries. He pins me to the wall.

I kick at his shins and he rams his knee into my thigh. Pain blooms. He flicks out the pocket-knife. Steel bites against my neck and I shiver in his grip.

He drives his fist into my gut. I buckle. Everything spins in the flickering light.

Giving up, just like that? Useless. Why not take a nap and wait for it to all be over?

Breath acidic on my face, he whispers in my ear. 'Shush, sweetheart. This'll be easier if you don't fight.' He licks my cheek and I go rigid.

That's it. Just close your eyes.

My hand slips into my pocket. I seize my phone and slam it into his head again and again. He staggers back. With a scream, I send my boot into his balls and shove him away.

Turning to the exit, I yank the emergency lever. It's stuck. The doors won't budge.

I snatch my bag and stumble through the carriage.

The man strides down the aisle after me. Jittering fluoro lights cast his shape in stop-motion.

Is there a security camera? Is anyone seeing this?

No. You're on your own.

'Leave me alone!' I shout.

I dig through my bag. My finger finds the keyring and I grip the jagged cluster. He lunges for me and I strike. Metal teeth scrape his face, snagging flesh.

He snarls, blocking my second blow. He grabs my throat, crushing my airway.

I gag, dropping the keys.

Look what you've done. You could have just let him have his way, but now he's going to kill you.

Clutching at his outstretched arm, I tear a patch off his olive jacket. Boots skid on the ground. I lose my balance. Eyelids flutter.

Pass out now and maybe you'll still have a chance. Everything will be all right. Just go to sleep.

'No!' I say, more of a cough than a word.

The man smiles, as if curious. His pale eyes glow in the strobing light.

'Excuse me?' he says. His voice is light, almost polite.

'No!' I growl, fighting to get the word out. Something inside snaps. My hands dive out. I scratch at his face. He recoils. My thumbs find his eye sockets and I dig.

Screaming, he falls back. Red lines slither down his cheeks. He stumbles backward onto the row of seats flanking the carriage.

At my feet, the tip of my scarf hangs out of the bag. I drag it out and coil it around the man's neck, pulling it tight. He thrashes. I shift behind him to avoid his swinging arms.

'What're you doing?' he gurgles.

'Surviving,' I say through clenched teeth.

Who's crazy now?

'Please—' he squeaks.

'Shut up!'

'No...'

We crash to the ground, but my lock on him is firm. I twist the cloth in my fists – constricting. We worm across the carriage floor. His arms flail. Fingers claw at the scarf. He grows weak. I keep the pressure taut. Finally, he stops. One leg spasms for a while.

Gulping air, tears stream down my face. I blink them away.

*

Hydraulics sizzle and the doors open. Lights flicker back on. My eyes fix on his outstretched foot – the velvet-green heel, skewed to one side. A puddle of auburn hair spreads across my chest. I push the body away and scramble back.

Long green jacket. My tightly-wound scarf. Pale blue eyes gaze up at me, vacant. Yellow handbag at her side, contents spewed across the floor.

Throat burning, I retch.

What've I done?

My book lies open at my feet. Pages all crumpled.

A voice-over announces, 'Waikanae Station, end of the line.'

I fly from the train, racing into the dark embrace of night. My eyes no longer fight to stay open.

The Great and True Journey

Richard Barnes

With yet more effort, Voort pulled his ice axe from the concrete-hard wall of ice. He swung it back, stretched out and slammed it into the ice a little further up, then tugged on it, making sure the head of the axe was firmly embedded.

Once sure it was secure, he paused, catching his breath. Every movement was hard work. The respirator in his mask helped him breathe in the micro-thin atmosphere, but the snow-suit was no vacuum-suit and cold was still cold.

'Steady as she goes,' said Grevill, his voice coming through Voort's ear-piece. The older man hung on to the ladder behind Voort; the ladder stretched across a twenty-metre-wide crevasse, sloping up to Voort. Its top end dug into the ice wall, but there were about three metres between the end of the ladder and the top of the crevasse. Beneath the ladder, the two opposing sides of the crevasse sank straight down to deep blue depths.

A step sideways, and within seconds this hell would be over.

Everything ached. Sleep on the ice plain above would not

be true sleep, just a period of semi-warm inactivity. The pain in his muscles, and the fiercer spike in his skull, would not abate. Altitude and thin air had been steadily swelling his brain. Death was on its way. Voort had been to war. Waking up from death and not knowing what the hell had happened was hardly new for him.

But it was only another couple of metres to the top. Then another day's trek to the foot of the crater's edge. Then up and over the crater's edge and down to the final, revelatory moment of the Great and True Journey.

'In the name of Freespace,' said Vella, behind Grevill and waiting in the fissure at the far end of the ladder, 'either jump, or climb the fuck up, so Grevill and I can keep going.' Was she reading his mind?

'You're getting there,' said Grevill, 'only another metre or so, and you're over the lip.'

'Fuck you, Vella,' said Voort.

'That's better, soldier boy,' said Vella. 'I'd worried you'd died and were just hanging there, but Grevill was too polite to chuck you out of the way.'

'Right foot then, lad,' said Grevill. 'Tenzig's up there. He'll help pull you over.'

The vertical face of the ice wall stretched above them. Tenzig, expedition leader and guru of the Great and True Journey, had climbed out of the crevasse thirty minutes earlier. The short-range transmitters that enabled Voort to speak to Vella and Grevill were blocked by the sides of the crevasse, so they'd heard nothing from Tenzig since his feet had wriggled over the top.

'Of course,' said Vella, 'a drasher might have eaten him and be waiting up there for us.'

Voort didn't have the energy to throw sarcasm back at her.

Maybe Tenzig had been taken by one of the ice serpents. But the rational part of his mind, the part that had been fighting an ever-desperate battle to keep on top, reminded Voort that this ice wall he clung to would have been shaking violently if a drasher had surged to the surface and taken Tenzig.

He took a deep breath, lifted his right foot and kicked the ice, his crampons digging into the hard surface. With his right foot secure and off the ladder, he moved his left foot up. Then his left hand with its ice axe, then the right again. Inch by inch, cold air streaming into his lungs and muscles on fire, Voort clawed his way to the top of the wall.

His left hand swung over the lip and he moved his arm around, shoving snow aside to dig the axe-head into the ice. A hand grabbed his arm and Voort scrambled up the last couple feet, half climbing, half pulled. On the flat surface of the ice plain, he slumped onto his back, gasping and looking up at Tenzig.

He couldn't see the expedition leader's face; like Voort's, it was behind a mask, and his whole body was covered by the snow-suit. But it had to be Tenzig. There was no one else but the four of them on the icy ball that was Tunga.

Tenzig dragged Voort a little further from the edge. 'Brother, if it's any comfort,' wheezed Tenzig, 'I have climbed over that crevasse forty-two times. It hasn't got easier at all. And I am so fucking glad it's the last time.'

Voort sat up. 'Oh, great Guru,' he said. 'You're not sounding very spiritual. Where's your enlightenment?'

'Over there,' said Tenzig, nodding towards the crater wall that awaited them. He slapped Voort on the shoulder. 'Come on, let's get Grevill and Vella up and over.'

They crawled to the edge of the crevasse.

'How's the head?' asked Tenzig.

'Splitting,' said Voort.

'You'll make it, okay? Only another day, brother.'

'Sure,' said Voort. 'This enlightenment had better be worth it.'

'It is, brother, it is,' said Tenzig. 'One more climb. Then comes the twin star rise, then the shuttle, then your mind-state will get copied and you can die. So stick with me.'

Voort wanted to lay down and die right there, but Tenzig kept crawling so Voort kept going, too. They reached the edge of the crevasse. Voort hoped Grevill had reached the top. He really didn't have the energy to haul the big old guy up.

An axe smacked into the ice beneath Voort's face.

Voort jerked back. It wasn't Grevill's axe, nor his hand wielding it. Tenzig had already grabbed Vella's arm and was pulling her up. Voort grabbed her other arm.

'Grevill?' said Tenzig.

'Gone,' said Vella, gasping.

'What? What do you mean?' said Voort. A moment later, Vella was sprawled next to them on the ice.

Voort rolled and looked over the lip, to the far side and the dark fissure they had climbed from. Down the sheer ice face, he saw the grooves and gouges where the ladder had dug in, and the marks of their ice axes and crampons. There was no ladder and no Grevill.

'The ladder slipped as he started climbing,' said Vella. 'He tried to climb faster, panicked, then he slipped sideways and…'

'Oh man,' said Tenzig, sitting up and looking over the crevasse and the vast plain behind them to the distant peaks of other mountains. 'He'd made it so bloody far.'

Voort felt sick. What little energy he had recuperated

evaporated. Grevill had been a giant, letting himself get older, insisting any time he was regenerated that they kept him at the same physical age as when he'd been killed. Like Voort, Grevill had come from a combat zone. Unlike Voort, Grevill had been a veteran of a dozen combat zones, but he'd done his last tour and come to Tunga for the true life, as Tenzig called it. Now he was gone. Voort's vision slipped to a dizzy white. His hands shook on the ice beneath him.

'Shaking,' said Vella.

'What?' said Voort. His mind swam back to reality. The ice was shaking.

Tenzig was on his feet first, grabbing Voort and pulling him to his feet. Vella bounced up next to them.

'Both of you, run,' said Tenzig. 'Run towards the crater. I'll break away along the side of the crevasse. I've got the gun.'

Vella grabbed Voort, who was about to topple over. 'Come on, soldier boy,' she yelled, 'you heard the guru, let's run.' She started dragging him. The ground gave a hard jolt and Voort found some energy mixed in with the fear. He looked for Tenzig. The leader was sprinting away from Voort and Vella, piecing together lengths of steel pipe as he ran.

The ice shook hard enough to throw Voort and Vella to the ground. Jets of steam shot out of a crack. The steam froze into tiny ice crystals and hung in the air for seconds. A larger chunk of ice broke from the surface, spiralling through the thin air and crashing down barely a foot from Voort.

Again, adrenaline kicked in and Voort scrambled up. He tumbled towards Vella, reaching for her, but Vella jumped up and took hold of Voort's arm instead. Her next jump carried them both a couple of metres further away.

The ice where they had been split apart and the huge,

triangular head of a drasher burst out, spraying steaming water, huge jaws open showing rows of ragged teeth. The drasher thrashed, stretching its massive, scaly body further out of the ice. Its trunk was more than a metre thick, and where it slid against the ice, the ice melted and steamed away. The beast shrieked a high-pitched screech that filled Voort's already splitting head.

Voort screamed before another chunk of ice slammed into his head and blackness took him.

*

Blue. Voort lived in a universe of deep, dark blue. Far below him, Tunga slid around the dark side of the blue gas giant, Tangaka. The icy moon with its super-dense core of iron, giving it a gravity that belied its small size, took eighty-four standard days to orbit the swirling mass of blue clouds. Half of that time was spent away from the sunlight of the twin stars, Tirana and Telyse, which Tangaka itself orbited. The distant third star, Tuul, circling the twins, but much, much further out, provided dim light for the dark half of the orbit, casting the moon's icy surface in shades of blue, grey and black.

Voort's journey, the Great and True Journey on which the six had set out, began as Tunga drifted across the terminator on Tangaka and into its dark time. From Voort's strange vantage point, high above Tunga's surface, the terminator couldn't be seen, just the great dark bulk of Tangaka, looming to Voort's left. To his right was a line of light at the edge of Tangaka.

They had started forty days earlier, aiming for the vast crater with the cleft in its eastern wall. The twin stars rose in a perfect line when seen through this cleft. This, it was said, was a vision of true, natural and profound beauty that could shatter and rebuild even the jaded, undying souls of Freespace citizens.

But to reach the star-rise and enlightenment, one had to live. Live free of the securities of Freespace, live knowing that to die on the journey would be to die as real a death as possible. To die, knowing that none of your experience on Tunga would be recalled by your regenerated self.

Voort looked at the line of light, spreading across the massive horizon of the gas giant and realised that he'd miss all that enlightenment, if he stayed in space. This wasn't death. The drasher hadn't got him. Death would mean waking up in a regeneration pod on a ship several light years away. He looked down and, despite being hundreds of kilometres up, spotted their tent, huddled close to the crater's edge.

*

He wasn't dead, just felt like he should be. The fabric of the tent hummed as the harsh surface wind pummelled it but the tent, unlike three of the original members of their group, had survived the grim trek so far, assuming that Tenzig and Vella had not been torn apart by the drasher. If Voort was still alive, surely Vella and Tenzig – both fitter and stronger than Voort – were too?

Tenzig's shot may have killed the drasher, but the gun may have just blown up. Voort wondered if Tenzig's luck had run out. What a shitty end for Tenzig's truly great Great and True Journey. Forty-two journeys of forty-two days each. Nearly ten years without dying or mind-state back-up.

The gun was not what Voort would call a gun. It was really nothing more than tubes of steel and gunpowder and explosive balls. Having done what so many young citizens of

Freespace had done, and signed up to fight in the war against the terrorists, Voort had learned a thing or two about guns. The terrorists of the various so-called insurgent worlds may have been happy fighting with mechanical projectile weapons, but the good soldiers of Freespace used energy weapons.

Yes, let Voort have a solid plasma rifle and he'd sort out a drasher. Maybe the beasts had scales that burned at over 150 degrees and jaws big enough to swallow a man whole; a few blasts of super-charged plasma bolts would still take the fucker's head off.

And while he was dreaming about the comforts of home, how about some battle armour? Temperature-controlled so there was none of this non-stop cold, and with augmented nano-motors to lend additional strength and endurance to his arms and legs.

But no, no tech or bio-enhancements of any kind were allowed on the Forty-Two Days of Enlightenment of the Great and True Journey. For one, electrical impulses attracted drashers to the surface, but more importantly, the journey was meant to be *pure*.

What a great idea, Voort had thought as their shuttle had landed on the wind-blasted plateau of ice. After six months of fighting and dying and re-starts and fighting and killing and dying all over again in the Offensive Corp, Voort needed to find something else.

'He's not going to make it,' said Vella. Voort had been aware of the rumbling of voices for a while, but they had seemed far away. Vella's voice now sounded much nearer, although it still seemed that Voort's ears were stuffed with wool.

'We are not leaving him in the ice,' said Tenzig.

'Do you want to make it to the star-rise?' said Vella. 'We

can't bloody carry him. And you're the one who's done this forty-one times. Do you really want to miss the forty-second?'

Voort thought he might as well play nearly dead for a while longer.

'I could bust his head in with my axe,' said Vella. 'At least then, he's not freezing to death.'

No immediate response from Tenzig once more. Voort couldn't be bothered to wait. He pushed himself up and opened his eyes.

'Thanks Vella,' said Voort, with a voice that sounded and tasted like cold gravel. 'If it looks like you're a bit tired, I'll happily smash your skull in too.'

'Still with us, then, brother?' said Tenzig.

Voort sat up fully, but let his head slump. His headache remained, like a spike through his skull. 'You got the drasher, then?'

Tenzig nodded. 'You should thank Vella for saving you, though. She may be keen to bludgeon you to death right now, but she scrambled both of you out of its way before I could get a shot together. She gave the bastard a race before I finally got the gun to work and blasted its brains out.'

'Letting you get eaten alive seemed a touch too far,' said Vella.

'How's the head?' asked Tenzig.

'Like my brain is about to squeeze out of my ears.'

Tenzig nodded.

'And we've got to climb even higher,' said Vella. 'He's not going to make it.'

'I'm not asking you to carry me,' said Voort.

'Hey,' said Tenzig. 'Everyone calm down. Even you, Vella.'

Voort saw Vella sit back, saw her shoulders unbunch.

'This happens, believe me,' continued Tenzig. 'This

tension. We've had a rough day. We lost Grevill, we nearly got eaten by a drasher. But we're so close to the end.'

'I can't believe Grevill's gone,' said Voort.

'The Great Journey tests us all, brother,' said Tenzig. 'We will honour Grevill, and Scoby and Sorin. We will honour those who started the Great Journey; we will find their truth.'

Vella nodded, her expression calmer now. 'Sorry, brothers,' she said. 'The others, even though they didn't get this far, I think they still found something. They'll know they set out. They say it's impossible, but I know part of their journey will be with them.'

Tenzig gave a small smile, reached out and took Vella's hand. He took Voort's hand too, then Voort and Vella joined hands to complete the circle. Tenzig and Vella closed their eyes.

Before Voort closed his eyes, he saw Vella's face fall sombre and reflective. His head pounding, he thought he saw a smirk behind the downturned mouth. He blinked. Her face was as before, sober and serious. He closed his eyes, but still saw Vella's nasty smile. Hallucinations now.

He tried to settle into the meditation. He focused on a vision of the twin stars coming up above the far crater's edge. He had no idea what it would look like; only those who made the forty-two day trek would ever know, but he pictured a deep blue expanse suddenly lightening, becoming sapphire, then sky-blue, and finally all the colours refracted through the ice.

By the time he made it to the end, Voort would probably have no idea what was reality and what was just his deluded and dying brain. Hopefully, the hallucination would be as good as the real thing.

*

'He must be cheating,' said Vella. Sarcastic Vella had soon shoved spiritual Vella aside once Tenzig was out of transmitter range. She trudged up the steep slope, about two metres ahead of Voort. Voort's eyes had been focused on the ground, just trying to keep his feet plodding on, one step at a time. He raised his head and looked up beyond the hunched form of Vella, towards the highest point on the ridge where he could just make out the dark-suited Tenzig.

Maybe Tenzig *was* cheating, somehow using stimulants or tech or bio-enhancements. Surely Vella was cheating somehow, too. Both were in far better condition than Voort. He found it hard to believe that anyone, no matter how fit and strong, could possibly make it so far and not feel like death.

'Seriously,' said Vella. 'Look at how quickly he made it up there. "I'm going to check out the route ahead," he said, and he bounded off like a Mimbinite Argut.'

'A what?' muttered Voort.

'An argut,' replied Vella. 'One of those cute furry things with the springy legs. They live on Mimbinus, a mountain world. And they bound up slopes as easily as, say, our spiritual guide, Tenzig. Taste great, too.'

'Sure,' said Voort. Arguing with Vella had been pointless nearly forty days ago when he'd had the energy for it. Now, all that mattered was placing one foot in front of the other. An argut bounced past him, paused for a moment to stick its tongue out, then bounced to the right of the ridge and straight down the sheer slope into the crater below. His hallucinations were mocking him.

He slipped, coming down on both knees. His right hand went out, finding nothing but empty air. For a moment,

Voort started to topple forward, the spiky grey rockface and white cloud swirling about twenty metres below. The view offered him a sudden moment of clarity, and he leaned back, away from the drop.

'Oh fuck, look at you,' said Vella. She was further up the ridge now.

'I'll be okay,' said Voort.

'Shall I make it easier and just kick you off the side?'

'I can kill myself all on my own if I have to,' said Voort. Vella had stopped and was staring at him. Beyond Vella, Tenzig was coming back, but was still at least a hundred metres beyond the transmitter range.

Vella glanced over her shoulder at Tenzig. 'Maybe not,' she said. 'If the guru sees me knocking you off, he'll be wary when I go for him.'

'What are you on about now?' said Voort.

'You've killed people, haven't you?' she asked. 'I mean, real people. People who actually die when they're killed.'

Voort didn't answer, partially because of the non-stop spike of pain in his skull, partially because he didn't want to dwell on his army days.

'What's it like?'

'Screw this,' said Voort under his breath.

'What's it like? Knowing that when you pulled the trigger and blew some terrorist's head off that that person would never be coming back. That everything they were was gone, all because of you.'

'It sucks,' he wheezed. 'It's shit, it's awful. Why do you think I'm here?'

'It sounds amazing,' she said.

'Then join the fucking army,' said Voort.

'Nah,' said Vella, checking over her shoulder to see how

near Tenzig was. 'I might die that way. I've never died. I'm not going to either.'

'Can we stop the philosophy and just get to the fucking end?' said Voort.

Vella shrugged, turned and started up the ridge towards Tenzig. 'Bad luck, guru. It will be nearly ten standard years of his life. And I'm taking it away.'

'Don't,' said Voort. 'Don't do it.' Vella trudged away.

'Don't fret, I'll be back for you. I'll be the only one coming back from this journey.'

Voort pushed himself to one knee and his head pain flared up again. White filled his vision for a few moments, before the world swung back into view. Vella was getting closer and closer to Tenzig.

The other leg. He had to get up to his other leg. Another surge of pain. He cried out, but made it to a standing position. Once his vision cleared, he saw Vella had reached Tenzig.

She pointed back at Voort. Tenzig took a couple of steps. Vella let him pass. She reached out, grabbed Tenzig's shoulders and tried to shove him off the ridge.

Tenzig didn't go so easily. Somehow, he regained his balance and flipped Vella. Things escalated. Vella threw a punch. Tenzig kicked back. The two traded blows, right on the precipice of the terrifying drop, buffeted by howling winds. Vella had been right: Tenzig was definitely enhanced. But so was she.

The leader caught Vella with a backhand swipe. As she toppled, Tenzig caught her right arm and delivered a hammering kick to her side. She fell back down the ridge, leaving her arm in Tenzig's hand. Sparks sputtered from her shoulder, the white goo of cybernetic fluid spurting out. Voort found he was not shocked.

Tenzig jumped after her, going into a slide which should have knocked her over the edge. Even though her arm had been torn off, Vella still moved with lightning speed. She rolled back from the edge and hit Tenzig with enough force to send him flying into space. He seemed to hang there for a moment, then time caught up and he plummeted from view.

Vella sprung to her feet and started walking back to Voort. The argut bounced back up to the ridge and gave Voort a wink. It bounced ahead of Vella and landed at Voort's feet.

'I told you, didn't I?' said Vella, very upbeat, and with her shoulder spitting blue sparks. 'He must have been enhanced.'

The argut winked at Voort and nodded towards the drop. Cute hallucination. Did arguts actually look like that?

'Don't feel so bad,' Vella said. 'I came here to kill everyone on the journey. It really is nothing personal.' She gestured to the crater. 'How good can this star-rise be? Is this really enlightenment?'

The argut chirped at Voort and then flipped over the side and away into the clouds. The pain in Voort's head cleared. He gave Vella the finger and stepped out into space.

'Bastard,' was the last transmission he heard from Vella.

*

The cloud swallowed Voort. He felt his descent slow. All was white around him and his thoughts remarkably clear. The whole experience, this plummeting to his death while his brain swelled and exploded, was actually quite calming and pleasant. If he hadn't felt so relaxed, for the first time in forty days, he'd have felt annoyed because soon he would be waking up in a regeneration pod, light years away, and with no memory of what had happened.

The gentle descent into white came to an abrupt halt as Voort slammed into something hard and cold. His right knee exploded in pain, sending shock waves through his body. The calming white became thick, suffocating clay. The hard, hard landing didn't stop him. Voort rolled over and over before he was suddenly falling again.

This time, the white scattered as he fell. Voort toppled through the air for another few metres before hitting another solid surface, banging his already mashed knee once again.

He passed out briefly, coming to while he was sliding off an icy slope and into a thick wad of snow.

Above him stood a series of huge blocks of ice, all jumbled on top of each other. The pile reached into the swirl of clouds just below the crater's ridge. Off to his right, more blocks of ice formed a colossal causeway stretching down to the black circle that spanned most of the crater's floor. Far off, the other side of the crater formed a black line against a thick ribbon of stars. His gaze settled on a V-shaped cleft in the crater wall.

The cleft where the twin stars would rise.

Not dead yet then. His head was no longer pounding, but his right leg was a white-hot rod jammed into his hip. Odd though, the pain of his shattered leg was horrendous, but it seemed like it belonged to someone else. The argut jumped down from a higher block of ice. Hallucinations were still going strong.

'Still with us, brother?' said Tenzig.

Voort wondered if the voice could be a hallucination, but the leader jumped down beside him. Without Vella's arm anymore, Voort noticed.

'How's the head?' asked Tenzig.

'Fine, actually. The best I've felt for ages. Apart from my

leg being smashed to bits.'

Tenzig nodded. 'If your head is clear, you're close to death. The swelling will have advanced to destroy the nerve endings, so you don't feel the pain anymore. Are you seeing things?'

The argut gave a wink and a nod to Voort. 'Oh yes.'

Tenzig patted Voort on the shoulder. 'Man, oh man. You haven't got long left, but I'll try to get you down to the crater floor. Maybe you'll live long enough for the shuttle to pick you up. They should be able to capture your mindstate before you finally die.'

'I thought you were gone, Tenzig.'

Tenzig looked up. 'Vella didn't wait for me to tell her that we could climb down from where you had stopped. That's why I went up the ridge, to check out the best way down.' He pointed at the massive jumble of ice blocks. 'When Tunga comes round to the light side of Tangaka, the bergs break off and fall in to the crater, so it's never the same way down into the crater twice.'

Tenzig pulled Voort up, putting an arm under Voort's arms to help him stumble along. Voort watched the argut bounce along, off their ice block and then out across the others. Tenzig, holding on to Voort, jumped the three or four metres down to the next block and then across to the next, and the next after that.

'You're enhanced,' said Voort.

'Obvious now, I suppose,' said Tenzig as he carried Voort down another series of blocks. The drop between each block was diminishing as they progressed. 'Just bio-stimulants. Nothing too powerful, but good enough to give a few boosts when I need it, recover fast and not get the altitude sickness that you're dying from.'

'Great,' said Voort. 'My guru is a liar and my co-searcher for enlightenment is a psychopath.'

'Grevill was bio-enhanced, Scoby had refitted lungs and Sorin had nano-regenerators,' said Tenzig. 'You though, you impress me. In the forty-one times I've made this trip, only three people, like you, have done this stripped back to merely human. None of them made it.'

They stumbled on, finally jumping from the last shattered remnants of the ice blocks and onto the smooth ice surface of the crater lake. Their crampons bit into the ice, making the going slow, but not slippery. Up ahead was the stubby, bare surface of a hill, poking through the ice.

'Vella's catching up,' said Tenzig. 'We'd better get to the island.' He shuffled them along faster.

Voort looked back and saw the dark shape of Vella, bounding down the tumbled causeway of ice, moving fast.

'You cheating bastard,' came a cry from Vella.

Tenzig swore and swung Voort down to the ice, then shoved him hard, sliding him away. 'Crawl as far away as you can,' said Tenzig. Voort pushed himself backwards so he could see the coming fight. He might as well enjoy himself. Vella was clearly mad, but Tenzig, oh-so-pure Tenzig, wasn't his favourite person either.

Tenzig pulled the gun parts from a side-pouch and snapped the steel tubes into place to form the long barrel. He clamped the firing mechanism to the end of the barrel and snapped open a chamber. Holding it under one arm, he found a pair of cartridges in another pouch, slammed them into the chamber, then snapped the thing closed. As he brought the barrel down and wrapped a hand around the firing mechanism, Vella landed right by him and kicked him in the guts.

The gun went flying, spiralling over and over to land a few metres from Voort. Tenzig didn't skid quite so far. He lay, rolled up in a shaking ball nearer to Vella. She stepped up, reached out with her remaining arm, grabbed Tenzig by the neck and hauled him up.

'How am I going to explain this?' she screeched, nodding to her shoulder, still sending out showers of sparks.

Voort stopped as he reached the gun. The ice was shaking.

'Don't,' moaned Tenzig, 'don't use your bio-electrics.'

Vella shook him. 'You'd like that, wouldn't you? Hardly a fair fight, though.'

The ice cracked apart.

Once again, the awesome form of a drasher burst through, accompanied by a cloud of fast freezing steam. Vella and Tenzig fell sideways. The beast swung its head round and bit into Vella.

Her legs flew off in a burst of blue sparks. The drasher shook her body around and flung it away, a plume of blood flying through the air after it.

Not all tech then, thought Voort, ever more detached from his situation.

He managed to get into a sitting position and aim the gun while the drasher dived for Tenzig.

The shot exploded out of the gun with enough recoil to knock Voort flat on the ice again. His skull cracked against the hard surface and everything went dizzy for a moment. When his head cleared and all was silent, he sat up.

To his far left, what was left of Vella lay steaming on the ice, not moving. Straight ahead, a great cloud of steam rose and fell around the drasher's body. Tenzig crawled, painfully, towards Voort. One of Tenzig's legs had been nearly torn off.

About a metre from Voort, Tenzig slumped to the ice.

Lifting a hand, he pointed over Voort's shoulder. 'Star-rise,' he gasped. His rasping breath was the only noise in Voort's ears.

Voort looked round. The stars in the cleft faded as the sky lightened from deep black to velvety indigo. The first of the twin stars broke up from the bottom of the V. A few minutes later, the second followed it.

'Is that it?' said Voort.

'Sorry,' hissed Tenzig. His body stopped shaking. The rasping breath fell silent.

The pain in Voort's leg had vanished. All sensation was fading. A movement in the sky caught his attention – a star getting brighter. Was it the shuttle?

A chirping beside him made him turn his head. The argut. Voort reached out and tickled the cute little critter behind the ears. It licked his face as the night sky faded to white.

BlindSight

AJ Ponder

ROSIE HUGS THE BOOK CLOSE, FLINCHING AS HER MOTHER rushes to her bed.

'What did you do? What did you do!?' she screams, ignoring Rosie's little brother whimpering in the corner.

Wynter, his body bloody and singed, trembles as their mother tears the pages of Rosie's book, and shreds the cover. She throws the pieces out the window. *The Tell-Tale Heart, The Raven*, the stories swirl about in the cold Wellington wind, down the cliff to the beach far below. All Rosie's books are destroyed now. All, except the pretty red and gold-edged Bible squatting in her drawer.

'But, Mother,' Rosie says. 'It was a just a book. I didn't—' The blow is inevitable, but Rosie can't stop arguing. Books are something to cherish, something to throw her life away on. They tell her things she wants to know. And things she isn't sure she should know.

'Please. The teacher says—'

'Listen to me. For God's sake, just listen. It's your sight that distracts you from the real world,' Rosie's mother screams, tears streaming down her face. 'Books are not for you. Remember your brother?'

Rosie sighs. Her mother locks the door and Wynter looks up with his face that never ages beyond a cherubic three. His right shoulder is half torn apart by Wild Things – half burnt. The monsters that attacked him had erupted into flames when she'd stabbed them with a knife.

For days, she makes believe she's a princess locked in a tower by a witch. But the game soon tires – even with her mother making appearances as the witch, muttering and sprinkling angelica around the room – and Wynter's ghost playing the role of reluctant knight. Rosie looks across to the flowery old couch where he's huddled. Once upon a time her mother would sit on it and read them stories from the Bible. Now, the couch reeks of burnt fabric, pain and bewilderment.

Rosie wonders if she'll be locked in her room forever, when two truancy officers come knocking.

'I'm sorry, Mrs Mitchell,' the lady shouts, loud enough to be heard through walls. 'It's against the law to keep a thir-teen-year-old girl at home. Either she goes to school, or we'll take this further.'

'Get out of my house,' Rosie's mother snaps, slamming the front door.

Rosie's mother turns from her door. Seconds later she is at the lock. 'You can go to school today. But be very careful, young lady. No reading. And come straight back home.'

Rosie hides her grin. 'Yes, Mother. Thank you, Mother.' She skips out of the house to the relative freedom of school, where it's lunchtime. She heads straight for the library, ignoring the other children's whispers. She thinks of them as books with pretty covers, where the insides don't reflect the outside at all.

'I heard she burnt her brother to death, and that's why she doesn't come to school.'

'I heard it was her mother.'

'Rosie's crazy. She came up to me last year and started talking to *my* mother.'

'Your *dead* mother?'

'Yeah, crazy eh?'

Rosie grimaces and walks on, ignoring the insubstantial woman trailing behind her obnoxious son. Besides, there's a book she desperately needs. Rapunzel. It might give her clues about how to free herself from her mother.

The bell rings, and the students leave. She trails after them, empty-handed. The teacher doesn't say anything as Rosie straggles in late, just points to a desk butted up against hers. And there, nestled in the muddle of papers and binders on the teacher's desk, is the book she's been looking for. On the cover, a beautiful girl looks out from a tower surrounded in gold and green ivy. Rosie has to read it, own it, possess it. Listen to the pages as they whisper words only she hears. She reaches out, and slips it into her bag. Maybe if Wynter comes out of the shadows he, too, will enjoy this story.

'Wynter, are you there?' Rosie whispers. But he's too scared to talk here in this strange place, with the teacher glaring at them, her marker pen poised in mid-air. That, or like Mother, he's still too scared of books. Which is silly. This time she will be more careful.

After school, she runs home. White-faced, her mother opens the door and shoos her inside. There's no food except a mostly-eaten packet of chippies. Rosie grabs it and retreats to her room.

Wynter is waiting for her. 'You're not going to do it, are you?'

'I'll be very, very careful.' Listening for sound on the landing, and keeping her eyes on the shadows, Rosie retrieves the forbidden text from her bag, and lets the pages fall open.

Rapunzel, Rapunzel, let down your golden hair.

The dark shadows other people call words call to her like a golden prince, enticing themselves into her head. They're more dangerous than demons, colder than the ocean roaring at the bottom of the cliff. Wynter is crying, begging her to stop. She slams the book shut, tucks it under her pillow … and fails to fall asleep.

Rosie's hands pick at the binding, while her eyes pick at the shadows lying in wait along the walls. The book's pages rant and rave; sometimes falling into silence, as if begging her to begin reading again.

Sliding the book into the moonlight, she means to have just one more peek. The shadows move, pulling danger from the stories, screaming encouragement from the darkness.

More screaming comes from the door. Rosie's mother.

Too late, Rosie shoves it back under her pillow.

Through her tears, Rosie watches the pieces fluttering like broken butterflies down to the windswept beach. One dances back into the room, the straggly hair of Rapunzel's captor on one side. On the other, is moonlit print that blazes into Rosie's brain … *until one day Rapunzel said to her, 'Frau Gothel, tell me why it is that you are more difficult to pull up than is the young prince…?'*

'Listen to me. For God's sake, just listen.' Rosie's mother's hands claw at her eyes. 'It's your sight that distracts you from the real world.'

Tearing pain overwhelms Rosie. Her eyes burst. Her world turns to shadows. Wynter stands amongst them, clearer than ever, his small body flinching. But her bed, the floral couch in the corner, and everything else is gone.

Horrified, Rosie pushes him. 'Wynter! Can't you see the shadows? Run!'

Somewhere in the distance, Mother says, 'Wynter's not here. He's not anywhere.' She grabs Rosie's hair and pulls, breath hot on Rosie's face. 'Look at me!'

'I am, I am!' Rosie screams. A lie. She can't see her mother's face, only the ink of her words, like a silver pen against the darkness.

Rosie covers her ears and eyes so tight, warm eyelid-red leaks into her brain. Even the pain of losing her sight cannot stop her wondering what will happen to the pretty girl in the tower, waiting for her prince.

An actual prince forms from the shadows. A finger to his lips, he tiptoes to where the window is banging against the wall. He reaches, arms outstretched.

Rosie calls a warning to her mother. Too late. The shadow-prince reaches out. All it takes is one little push. A scream. And it is done.

For a long time everything is still, except the ocean below and the wind rattling at her window. Rosie tries to cry, but she has no tears. So she sits and picks at the scabs forming where her eyes should be.

Police arrive, sirens first. They don't listen. They don't hear the prince calling for his princess. Will he come back and save her again?

'Are you all right?' the police demand over and over in their hard, clipped voices. 'We're calling an ambulance.'

'Can you hear the shadows?' Rosie asks. 'I think they've taken my brother. Or he's run away like I said to. He'll come back one day. Or maybe Mother will bring him back for me.'

'We'll do the best we can,' someone says from the darkness.

Mother's ghost glowers at her. Admonishing Rosie with gouts of salty tears. Her disapproval follows Rosie from foster home to foster home, but the waterworks really flow when Rosie finds a family that encourages her obsession. They're awed as Rosie's hands trace their way along the silky ink, picking out words. The more she reads, the more she realises her mother is right. Books are dangerous. Horrors lie within their pages. Their call stronger than ever. She reads under the covers, not needing light as she runs her fingers along the text. When there are no more books, Rosie runs her fingers along the walls of her room, reading the horrors there.

Rosie tries to keep the shadows at bay. She yells at them to leave her alone. Tells them she doesn't want rescuing, that she doesn't need princes or demons. She doesn't want to attract the attention of the evil characters lurking in the walls.

The other children in the foster home laugh at her when she tries to warn them of the danger.

'See!' she points at the shadows lurking in the walls all around. 'There's death everywhere. I've been thrown out of my tower. We're in the wastelands, and we have to be careful.'

She tries to shut the books. But she can't shut out the walls. She needs them to find her way in this wilderness of shadow. She needs them, or she starts to pick at her empty eye-sockets. She turns to the Bible, but the words are not the sweet stories her mother had told when she was little. The shadows laugh back as she reads the grisly tales. But she cannot leave the Bible alone. She's the only one who can break its seals and prevent the demons from tearing the world apart.

Revelations says so.

It says a lot of things. Fortunately Rosie knows cold steel is the one thing that can save her.

After the screaming is over, Rosie's mother has a whole

family of corpses to keep her company. Only it does not seem to make her happy. She sits on the ghost of her old flowery couch, cradling Wynter and scowling at the world until someone knocks on the door.

Rosie puts the catch on. 'Don't come in, it's not safe. There's still a demon here. The one with seven heads and ten horns. The feet of a bear, the mouth of a lion, and the general appearance of a leopard.' She lowers her voice. 'It's very, very dangerous.'

The knocking goes away.

The door splinters. There are so many police, they can barely move in Rosie's small room. They pick their way around. The starch in their clothes whispers secrets the owners will never hear. *I have a sore leg. I have a headache. The wind outside is too cold for me. I think I'm going to throw up.*

'…a grown man twice her size…'

'The smell.'

'…she just – tore him apart.'

'And the kids.'

Rosie shakes her head. 'No. It wasn't like that. I—'

They don't listen. Words like, *sick*, *evil*, and *psychotic*, are thrown around, punctuating the policewoman's recitation of her rights, like fists against a punching bag. She absorbs each blow. Her fingers trace across the bloody wallpaper, until her arms are yanked behind her back. Plastic bands tighten against her skin.

The word *murderer* almost bowls her over. It's new and, somehow, much heavier than the others, especially with her mother's voice, *killing is a sin*, echoing around her head.

'Listen,' Rosie says. 'The beast tore its way through. It just came.'

The silence is absolute. Not even the shadows move.

'So I stabbed it. I had to.' Rosie's voice is high, pleading against hope that they might understand. She can't see their faces. Although she suspects they're as terrified as she is of the blood. Of the bodies.

To Rosie, her foster family are more visible now than they were in life. More real. She can see the digger on the boy's jersey. The girl, lips bright with lipstick.

Rosie's mother frowns. 'You did it again,' she says. 'Weren't we enough?'

'It wasn't me!' Rosie protests, although she knows her mother will not listen. Neither will the police.

Struggling, the plastic bites at her wrists as Mother turns to Rosie's foster sister. Her gnarled finger burrows into the girl's sternum. 'Harlot, put some clothes on!'

Rosie can't protect the ghost from her mother's accusation, but the father tries. 'My daughter can wear what she likes!'

'Stop it. Stop fighting,' Rosie warns him.

'Those too tight?' A lady's voice, coming from the darkness. There's something about her. Something nice, even though the demon whispers that her shell is just as hard and blue as the other police. Maybe it's just the spirits of her two babies yet to be born, floating within the blue shell.

'The demon. It's standing right there. Can't you see the hole in the wall? Feel the indentations? I never realised demons bleed, but they do. Screaming and screaming before they go up like torches.'

'You know we're here to take you away, don't you? Somewhere you can be safe.'

The lady sounds so very sincere. And underneath it all, so very horrified.

'Wasn't I talking?' Rosie asks. 'Hardly matters. No one

ever listens to what I say.' Still, the woman did say she was taking her somewhere safe. 'Safe?' Rosie echoes, momentarily hopeful.

'Very safe,' the woman says, her words sounding like a smile.

Rosie twists her arms. 'I don't feel safe with these cuffs on. Not with the beast so close.'

The policewoman's breath changes. Quickens. She's scared. Has been the whole time. Blanketed in fear.

Rosie tries to explain. 'They come to kill. You do understand, don't you? They won't stop. Not until you're all dead.'

'Harry, this one's on something,' she yells. 'Take blood and urine samples. You ID'd the bodies yet?' The whisper of fabric tells Rosie she's wrapping her arms around herself, not as unconcerned as she's trying to sound.

'Nope. The burns are severe. One's barbequed to a char,' he replies. 'We'll be lucky if there's enough dental on it. Frankly I'm amazed the whole house didn't go up.'

'They do that. They just burn,' Rosie says. She's not really talking to them anymore. It's clear they've only ever seen one world.

The demon laughs. 'The walls for these *obscuro* are so thick nothing could ever burst through from the other side. Not much can get through their tough hides from this side either, 'cept a bullet. And me.'

'A bullet would kill you, too,' she mutters to the creature. 'It's gotta be steel, well, good silver or good steel. And not one speck of rust. Just one, and that puppy flames back to life, instead of burning to a cinder, which always has to be the plan.' She'd read that somewhere. Books were dangerous, they brought danger. And salvation. 'You know, lady,' Rosie says, desperate to scratch the scabs of her eyes, 'free my hands and I might be able to protect you. And your kids.' Rosie can see them, clear as the dead family begging her to save them.

The policewoman snaps. 'Don't be ridiculous.'

Nutto, she's thinking. *I don't have any kids.* The thought is so clear in Rosie's mind, the police officer might as well have said it.

'You're blind,' Rosie whispers. 'I see them clearly now. A boy and a girl. They're crying. Fading. If you're not careful they'll never be born.'

'Shut up.' The woman's voice is tight.

'But you have to listen. The shadow came through the walls. Through the gaps in the world,' Rosie insists. 'Nowhere is safe. Not for me. Please. Please. Let me go.'

The demon laughs. 'It's been fun playing this game with you.' And Rosie closes her eyes and prays.

'Let's get her out of here.' The policewoman prods her out of the room, down the stairs, and out of the house. 'In the car,' she says as soon as they're outside. She opens the car door and pushes Rosie's head down.

Rosie fights back, but the door closes, shoving her the rest of the way in. Almost.

Through the mesh windows, Rosie sees the woman's first child die, feline teeth wrapped around a body with chubby fists flailing. Rosie screams and pushes at the door that never quite closed, trying to stop this. The other child is torn apart as Rosie falls from the car. 'They're dead. I'm sorry, they're just gone…' Rosie cries, but there's no reply.

Footsteps rush toward her, and with sightless eyes she sees the body rise from the ground, hands pushing guts back into its abdomen. It's the policewoman. She's not only kind, but very pretty, with long dark lashes smeared black against the tears.

'You killed her!' a policeman yells.

Rosie shakes her head. But it feels like nothing more than a lie. Maybe if she hadn't allowed the family to die, if she hadn't read about the beasts in Revelations, then this woman would still be alive. But how can you hide when the only world you can see is the world of the dead?

All the other officers will die too. Rosie can't help it. Unless, and here's the thing: unless it was her that let the demons in. Unless the demons really are all her fault, because she can't leave the stories alone, she can't stop looking for answers, and she can't stop picking away at a story, even when there isn't one. Perhaps if she'd realised books were dangerous…

Funny that, even when they're wrong, mothers are always right.

The demon's lion mouth grins as it swipes the heads from the remaining blue shells, noisily sucking out the marrow as if it were ice-cream.

When it and its fellow monsters are completely finished, they look up, tongues lolling between their teeth like happy puppy dogs. They lick the spatters of blood from Rosie's face. As their rough tongues hit the empty spaces where her eyes should be, Rosie remembers her mother screaming. *'Listen to me. For God's sake, just listen. It's your sight that distracts you from the real world.'*

The monsters snarl, their teeth ripping the plastic manacles from Rosie's hands so that she's free. Free to run with monsters. Her heart soars. She realises it's what she's wanted all along.

'Wynter,' Rosie calls to her brother. 'Come with us.'

He shakes his head, reaching out his arms for their mother. 'Wynter!'

'You killed me,' Wynter says.

Rosie is overwhelmed, but can find no tears. 'No, no. That wasn't me. Come, we can be together again. Better than before.'

The police step in, more solid than ever now that they're dead. They take her back to her old house, and push her inside an iron cage dangling from her tower. If she picks at the scabs in her eyes, and listens carefully, she can see the beach far below.

Her mother's corpse, washed in salty tears, neck broken from the fall, sits very still on the old flowery couch and reads her Bible stories. The sweet ones she used to read when Rosie was a child. It makes Rosie want to scream. She prefers the Old Testament.

And so she grows her hair. Maybe one day it will be long enough for her demon prince to climb up and rescue her.

In Sacrifice We Hope

Keira McKenzie

VicParkers were mostly a stolid lot, bastions against the bandits and ferals who roamed the hinterlands between the City and the Hills, but they didn't venture into the Burswood ruins. Of course they didn't believe anything, but still, tales of Burswood had extra – disquietingly plural – dimensions, like all that rot about dimensions intersecting when the Earth tilted on its axis during The End – as if! Such talk was common in the early years, but now only lingered in areas like the Burswood Ruins. Surrounded by the toxic sludge the river had become, it was a poisonous place, dangerous and deadly.

The talk certainly didn't deter two boys who lived in VicPark, near enough to be familiar with the stories as well as the site itself. The allure of the forbidden, plus the (remote) possibility of material gain, added up to be irresistible. It called to them. The boys took their chance. It was winter, no hellish heat or chance of a storm. Perfect.

So, they told their respective parents that morning that they were joining a class for peer group study after school, and promised to be home before dark. After school, they crossed the ancient Causeway (biochar-fuelled traffic was very thin), slipped through the fences surrounding the complex, and expertly divined which solar-secure system was actually secure. Slipping through one of the many defunct others as the sounds of the village faded into the background, they soon stood on the boundary of the forbidden.

The ruin loomed against the late afternoon sky, a hulking silhouette against emptiness, luring them on with its reputation. While stripped of fixtures, fittings, furnishings and anything of value, it had never been stripped of the knowledge that it had been a great gambling den. It had in turn become the source of the most powerful of all urban legends: buried treasure. So who would be the first of this generation to find those tunnels backstage in the Dome that led directly to the upper? There, the ancient machines were still full of gold coins because no one had found them.

Yet.

The boys were off, running over the waste ground to the ruins proper, avoiding the old gambling halls' ground-level entrances. Those gaping doorways of the mostly roofless structures held populations of rumours that hunted, rustled and killed the foolhardy in various painful ways, so not even the most hardened treasure hunter went in that way. No one wanted to see the bones of the fallen. The boys skirted the restaurants where dead trees punctuated broken floors, their skeletal remains distorted into monstrous shapes by ivy fattened and weirdly verdant from tainted groundwater or the poisoned river. The ground was damp enough for toads. The boys followed barely discernible paths to where the Dome hunkered in the shadows beneath the ruins of the immense hotel.

This was the other entrance to the gambling dens (though

why they were called dens when they were on the upper floors was something no one had ever explained to the boys), a secret entrance that was known even if rarely used.

The boys clambered over lumps of masonry, shattered stairs and unrecognisable stuff subverted into ecosystems for snakes, spiders and scorpions which blocked the massive doorway. They negotiated more rubble choking one of the gaping entrances with little more than scraped knees or knocked elbows, till there they were, looking over the edge of the vast empty, echoey spaces of the auditorium.

Too easy!

The yawning roof sucked at the day, darkening and reducing it. Inside it was dry, as dry as bones, dusty and twilit. Wind thrummed around the gaping roof space in testament to bygone times of mass entertainment, when thousands of out-of-control fans crammed in for the concerts, the gigs, the bands. These boys were big on cultural history.

They descended the steps between tiers of bare benches rising tall into darkness like some ancient pyramid they'd read about in pre-history, squinting against the dust they raised, momentarily pausing at the scrabble of hurried movement whispering beneath the echoes. They sprinted the last few steps across the blank area before the stage, then leapt the side stairs leading to the stage itself. Once there, slipping a little on the dust coating the stage floor, they moved front and centre, standing in almost respectful silence, facing out over the shattered auditorium. They'd seen the pale printed screen-shots taped onto covers of rare textbooks, and for a few minutes, they jammed their air guitars better than any old-time cultural icon.

Laughing, they turned their backs on their roaring audience and walked through the dust to the rear of the stage, their performances ringing in their imaginations but fading into irrelevance as they found their way through a maze of sliding partitions to the backstage area of rooms, corridors and hopefully some interesting mementos of the complex's past life. But once in, they paused.

They hadn't reckoned on the utter darkness of the internal rooms and corridors. Then bravado set in again.

'Carter,' whispered Colin. 'It's like Carter in the pyramids.'

'Bingham,' Justin countered. 'Machu Picchu.'

They grinned at each other, and yes, if they'd been going under that pyramid of concrete benches, then they really could be Bingham or Carter avatars. Still creepy, though.

The boys walked forward into the darkness, the flashlights on their solar phones sketching the arrangement of walls and doorways.

'We gotta keep an eye on the time,' Colin said.

'We got more than two hours,' Justin, slightly older and also slightly more foolhardy, scoffed. 'Hey – we find the tunnels, we've saved ourselves time.'

That put a patina of motivation over their unease. Being the first to find the tunnels would give them kudos to last their entire lifetimes.

Mounds of dust and cobwebs glittered in patches as their lights tangled in it, shapeless things morphed out of shadows. Deeper in, detritus became scarcer; soon there was only dust, thick and sparkling every now and then in their flashlights. Walls closed around them, the ceiling pressed darkness over their heads, like an Incan or Egyptian tomb.

It was when all sense of the stage had faded that they heard noises apart from their own. They paused, playing their flashlights ahead, behind, all around. Shadows jumped and danced in the wavering light.

They couldn't identify the sound. Were they steps? Not quite. But it wasn't a slipping, sliding, or slithering sound either, which ruled out snakes or insects or rats. In unspoken agreement, the boys took a slight step backwards.

Maybe whatever it was heard them because sudden silence made the darkness a sentient thing.

What was worse? Hearing the sound, or nothing where there'd been something? Did that mean something was watching them?

They took another step back.

The silence grew more intent. They could imagine it cocking its ears, tilting its head to one side.

Colin couldn't decide whether the sound had been ahead of them or not. Justin slipped another step backwards.

'Justin,' Colin whispered and jerked his thumb to indicate ahead and behind and exaggerated a shrug. Justin edged closer to Colin, their shoulders brushing.

The sounds continued and both boys realised they were ahead – and behind!

Unthinkingly, they reached for each other. They didn't go as far as holding hands, they were too old for that, but did grab each other's nearest shoulder. Neither wanted to admit that maybe they shouldn't have come. All those stories – animals' bodies, people's bodies, people never seen again. They'd all paid their pounds of flesh which, in the boys' minds, became rotting flesh dripping from the bodies of the recently dead. Poison. That's what the teachers said. It was a place that took away pounds of your flesh.

Colin shook Justin's shoulder and indicated retracing their steps. Colin's back prickled as they turned, as though something watched them from the stage. Their lights picked up their own prints in the dust and prints of something that might've been insect, rat or snake, maybe cane toad (and large!), sometimes overlapping theirs, mostly running alongside. Whether they'd been there on the way in, Colin and Justin didn't know. They'd been looking at walls, not the floor. That they mightn't have been alone all that time was too terrible to even think.

It seemed to take too long to get out of the corridors and back to the stage. Surely it had only taken them minutes to get this far?

Both boys were almost running, breathing in old dust through open mouths, sweat trickling down their backs and ribs. The air was uncomfortably close and stale and stank, something else they hadn't noticed before.

When they burst onto the open stage, they let out a whoop of triumph, their sneaking terror dissipating into the wider open air. Somehow, with that gaping roof, it wasn't as dark, though it *was* darker. Early evening colours filled the gaping doorway, individual pieces of masonry stuck out, touched with gold. They walked to the edge of the stage and sat, legs dangling.

'I wouldn't mind coming back when we got a whole day,' Justin said.

'There's toads in there,' Colin said.

'I saw.' Justin's tone was sober. 'But you can't get poisoned by the footprints.'

Revulsion was gaining the upper hand.

Colin nodded. He sensibly turned off his flashlight to conserve the battery. Justin did the same, then switched it back on. The boys looked at each other, pale and frightened as whispers died around them. Silence returned. They got to their feet and clattered down the stage stairs, ran across the now darkened space in front of the stage and just as they began clambering up the Mayan pyramid of benches, Justin stopped. Colin, a step above him, stopped, echoes dissipating towards the stage. 'What?'

'I heard ... thought I heard—'

Colin looked along the beam of light towards the stage. 'Keep it still,' he hissed.

But Justin was too jittery and shadows shifted, slid, shivered, shouldered each other out of the way. 'I heard a name,' he whispered.

'That's just a story,' Colin hissed. 'Let's get outta here.' He turned on his own light and started up the steps, relieved as Justin's steps grated in the dust behind him, his panted breath sounding in time with his own. Colin almost ran up the last few and, reaching the top, sucking in dusty air, he turned to express triumph to Justin.

Justin wasn't there.

For a couple of seconds, Colin held his breath in horror, then just as he was about to shout, saw a wavering weak line describing Justin's path over the stage.

'Justin!' Colin's shout bounced and echoed and shivered the dust. The light continued moving towards the backstage.

'Oh – fuck!' he muttered, very low, cos if anyone heard him saying that there'd be hell to pay. He ran back down the tiers, light jerking in his hand, startled shadows leaping away or up in front causing him to stumble, slow down, and all the time Justin's light was getting farther away, then vanished into the corridors behind the stage.

Colin reached the bottom. He sped across the flat space and pelted up the stairs to the stage, backpack slamming his ribs. He stumbled over the last step, fell, knocking his solarphone from his hand. It skittered across the stage, churning dust and particles into a sparkling frenzy.

With a whispered wail, he scrambled on all fours, ignoring the sting from skinned elbows and scraped palms, almost running on feet and hands to scoop up his phone, but his backpack unbalanced him – his other hand slid out from under him and he fell forward, slamming his chin into the floor, almost biting his tongue. He picked himself up then reached for the phone and aimed it towards the backstage area, light jumping and snatching at shadows that slid around and parted to reveal a scuffed area.

Prints. Lots of them. Things like insects, and those cane toad prints.

He scrambled to his feet and moved quietly to where the dust was so disturbed. There were their own prints from before, but had they moved around so much just here? He stepped into the corridor, darkness enfolding him. 'Justin!'

His sharp whisper fell flat in the dust. Playing his light all over the walls, ceiling and floor in continuous, methodical sweeps, Colin proceeded up the corridor. At each black doorway he listened and moved on, and finally reached the spot where he and Justin had stopped. In the wavering light, the confusion of their footprints raised ridges and steep valleys in the thick grey dust, amidst the thin tracks of maybe an insect or snake. But there were too many cane toad-looking ones (and they were so big!). Beyond, shoe prints. Justin was ahead.

'Justin?' he called and his voice sprang back and bounced around him, jagged and torn. The walls were stone, not plasterboard. Was this actually one of the tunnels? The back of his neck prickled.

He heard nothing. 'Fuck you, Justin.' He tried to be angry, because he was really, really scared that maybe Justin had heard his name. But that wasn't right – it was a story, made up to keep people out. Toads didn't call anyone's name. Except – and he stopped a moment, guilt and horror enveloping him, deeper and heavier than the dark – he'd said Justin's name when they were here. He'd said it. What if something had heard them?

Swallowing down what felt like a huge lump of knowing, he followed Justin's footprints on and on, deeper and deeper into the dark. One foot slipped and he struggled to regain his balance. The light from his phone was getting weaker, but still strong enough to slip over the edge of a dark, stone step before vanishing into blackness.

Colin bent forward, shining the light down.

Justin's footprints were plain on the stairs, and handprints smeared the dust coating the walls as though he had been caught by surprise and had staggered down the steps. The smudges in the dust were big, confused, probably Justin's butt-prints.

That was almost too much. Butt-prints. He stifled laughter as he started down the steps, but his laughter faded when he saw only handprints on both walls and butt-prints on the stairs. No footprints. That meant—

A glint caught his light about two steps down. Justin's solarphone. Colin stepped down and picked it up. It was really dusty; there was even dust behind the cracked glass, as though it had been there for years. It wouldn't turn on.

Colin shone his light down the stairs. There was no laughter in him now. Justin must've slipped and kept falling. What if Justin was lying hurt at the foot of these stairs, unable to move or call out for help? Colin moved faster – still cautious, but faster, down, going down into the dark, following Justin's butt and finger prints, handprints on the walls and the steps, smeared and unclear as though he was slipping, sliding.

How would he get him up the stairs? How would he get him up all those old tiers and out past the rubble? No way could he—? Colin remembered he had more than a flashlight in his hand. He quickly pressed in his father's number, but there was no signal. Of all the times he could've used it.

He needed to see Justin before going for help. Panting with urgency and concentration, Colin continued down the stairs, concentrating because they were so rough and uneven, as though recently hacked out of bedrock. This strangeness didn't occur to him for a few minutes, and when it did, he stopped, leaning on the cold, old wall. It wasn't as if the Dome was part of the ancient world. For all their jokes about Incan and Egyptian tombs and tunnels, the Dome was – well, he wasn't sure how old it was, but his neighbour's house was older, old even before The End, they said, and its old brick stairs were still smooth. But these were … Maybe they were unfinished. Maybe they'd been going to build a tunnel under the river, before The End.

He stumbled as he reached the end of the stairs, his left foot slamming hard against the level ground. The air smelled old. Rotten. He shone the light around. On the far wall, it slid across a smooth space interrupting the rougher dark. He walked towards it, the dust in front pitted and ridged.

The rotten odour thickened around him. And was that a sound? Whispering or something? It was familiar, but he couldn't place it. He shone the light towards the smooth space and saw a handprint clear in the dust on the ground. Justin's? But there was only the one print, everything else was too mussed. He stared at it, throat tight. He wanted there to be more than that one handprint. Where was the other? That frightened him, though he wasn't sure why.

He stepped to where he could see more clearly and leapt back with a yell of shock.

It was an opening in the wall and, beyond, something like a river tumbled past the doorway: foul green and veined in red, stinking with a terrible acidic reek overlain with rotten eggs. There were things caught in the lazy current, turning slow circles before vanishing beyond the doorway.

Were they screaming? There was a sound, distant, as though it was miles away.

It couldn't be the river. Not a drop came out. Not a wavelet encroached past the threshold. But it was liquid. Those things in it.

He edged towards the stairs, keeping the light aimed at that greeny-flaring, stinking stuff, hearing those whispered sounds, though he wasn't so sure he wasn't hearing the smell, or smelling the sounds (whispers, whispers names and places secrets and promises). And heard something. A word? Was – had it been his name?

Reflected green light glanced up from his solar phone to sting his eyes.

Colin let out a yell. He was so close to that poisonous green.

He skipped, tripped, scrambled back, light dancing, catching a shape against the far wall. He shone the light on it.

A toad. Huge. Its oddly pallid skin was marred with monstrous shadows, its eyes voids of darkness.

Colin shuffled backwards. His foot hit the stairs and he spun, running up them, not knowing he was sobbing.

He and Justin were the world's best friends. Had been since – well, since the beginning of all things. Daycare, kindergarten, primary. High school next winter. Same class. They'd done everything together. They spent as much time in each other's houses, with each other's families as their own. If Justin was gone into that … that … whatever it was, then…

His sobs and panted breath sounded the same, breath coming harder because his nose was running like his tears were and he didn't care.

He reached the top of the stairs and pelted, careless of the dark, of whispers and screams, of snaking tracks or anything else, out onto the open stage beneath the gaping roof of the Dome. He walked across the stage, wiping his face with the back of his hand. Above him, sunset swirls flared across the sky.

How would he explain to his father about Justin? About that door? Was it the river he had seen? That moving green with those things turning round and over in slow-mo somersaults? Was Justin one of those things?

He had to get out. The solarphone was dying and the thought of clambering through the jumble of masonry outside in the dark, and crossing the complex to the Causeway? His breath hitched his eyes stung. He really wanted to be home and—

The hair on the back of his neck suddenly prickled. He held his breath. Something scraped behind him. Rat? There it was again. Something moving, in plops, scrapes and slithers. That wasn't a rat.

It was the toad-thing hopping up the stairs, following his tracks through the corridors. It had been following them since they came in, he was sure of it. Everyone knew they spread poison, killed anyone who touched them. A contaminant from before The End.

He turned his light off. Moving as quietly as he could, listening as hard as he could, Colin felt his way to the edge of the stage, sat so his legs dangled and inched his way on his butt towards the stairs on the other side.

He felt his way down the stairs, going as fast as he dared. He paused when he reached the bottom, but the thumping of his heart occluded all other sounds.

He moved to his right, testing the floor for obstructions before placing his feet, and kept going till he felt the wall. He inched along it, again testing the floor, conscious of that blank space to his left.

He reached the pyramid of benches and was about to start climbing when he heard something sliding slick across the space before the stage. The air belched around him, a stench as thick as the toxic river at king tide. It was something from the river, the dead poisoned river, flowing out to take him.

He sprinted up the stairs.

The sounds grew more frantic, that *something* trying to climb the stairs. Colin kept running, the tiers going on forever. He knew there were a lot of them, but shit! His chest burned, his ribs flamed with a stitch. He couldn't find enough breath.

The sounds continued to grow louder, till they filled the auditorium with whispered stinks and stinky whispers. He refused to hear his name though it was there, clicking and murmuring in the rising dust.

He was scrambling on all fours now, crying with the pain of the stitch. His backpack felt full of bricks like his big brother used for weights. He reached the top on hands and knees and, head hanging between his arms, gulped air in rasping sobs.

Finally, able to stand, he swallowed and listened hard.

Silence. He risked the light and shone it down towards the stage. The light had grown much weaker now, but it reached far enough to show nothing close behind him.

Dust hung in slowly settling clouds, sparkling and whispering. Whispering. He wasn't imagining it.

The sob that came out of him wasn't just for breathing. It was for Justin.

Colin shouldered the backpack and stepped towards the darkness waiting within the huge doorways.

Something clattered behind him.

He spun. In the auditorium, the dark had become a wall. His heart pounded in time with his whispered '*shit-shit-shit*,' a fierce whisper, as though it would protect him. Couldn't be Justin. He heard steps sliding, slipping across the stage.

His light wouldn't reach that far. Colin speed-dialled his dad but the battery was almost flat. Signal, but no power.

The footsteps were slithering down the stage stairs.

Oh whaddo I do now?

Footsteps grated across the space between the seating tiers and the stage. Colin turned and ran into the night, the fading light from his phone barely enough to get him over the tumbled wreckage. To hell with snakes and scorpions.

It couldn't be Justin. Couldn't be.

He tripped over things they'd skipped over before. He fell, got up, fell, got up, skidded – he was bruised and bloodied, confused and exhausted.

Scrapes whispered behind him.

He stopped. The Causeway was within sight, the slight glow from VicPark's security globes spilling out the sunlight they'd stored during the day. Then he heard definite footsteps and something else:

'Colin.'

Colin had never known terror before. This wasn't being frightened. Being frightened was fun, and there was nothing fun about this. All those horror stories were paper compared to the reality.

He pictured bursting in through the front door at home, his parents looking up shocked, and him all dirty and stinking, blurting out everything, and his dad calling the militia and his mum taking his backpack and saying about a doctor and him saying it was just bruises but Justin was back there and—

He felt his mother's hands, breathed in her smell, heard his father's voice, gruff and angry which he knew was fear as much as anything else and his brother coming out to see what was going on and saying they should go now and front up to the bastard who'd done this and taken Justin and his mum saying they had to call Justin's parents and what happened to Justin, dear?

That stink! Green glowed from the darkness, the dim pallid glow of another toad. He hadn't known they were white.

A figure detached from the gloom. It moved towards him. Colin tripped and fell on his butt, slamming his spine. Pain flared too bright for the dark.

Colin wanted to go to bed. His mum would treat him like a little kid. His dad would wait till he was okay to give him hell and that was okay, too.

'Colin.'

That wasn't his mum.

The figure above him bent and took his hand, pulled him to his feet. A hand slimy and cold, the same size as his, pulling him back towards the Dome, which was looming black and oddly shapeless against the sky.

A figure the size and shape of Justin.

Colin screamed. He grappled, hit, scratched at Justin, fought crazy and screaming, kicking. Justin's grip was unbreakable. He dragged him to the dark and gaping entrance.

'Justin?' Colin whispered, almost crying.

Justin's grip tightened.

He was going to take him back in, down the tiers of shattered seats, across the stage, into the corridors, down the stairs and into that green, redshot noxious torrent. And then he would come out, with a toad, and they would go up the stairs, through the corridors, across the stage, up the seating, through the tangle of rubble, back across the Causeway and into VicPark. They would part and go to their own homes and the poison would spread. Burswood poison.

Colin fought as the figure dragged him relentlessly back into the Dome. He struggled as he was pulled over lumps of concrete and twisted rusted braids of supporting steel that took great gouges out of his legs.

He didn't want to hear his mother scream. Didn't want to see his father turned to a monstrous figure with empty eyes. That's what they said people became after going to Burswood.

It was like fighting a shadow.

He fought as they went over the rubble in the doorway and Colin was abruptly surrounded by echoes of his own hoarse sobs and screams.

Suddenly furious, hating and wanting and crying for his friend, Colin swung a huge kick at him. His kick went wild. He lost his balance and fell, screaming terror and despair, clutching Justin hard, his bestest friend, all he had, as he fell screaming down the Mayan pyramid of broken tiers. An avalanche of shadows and groaning lumps of concrete followed to stone him, breaking bones and hope and finally, consciousness.

The shattered roof trembled as his screams shivered whatever mortar was left.

With a peculiar sighing sound, something shifted and the

remaining roof gave way, floated a moment in the darkening air before crashing against the concrete tiers, against the stage and empty spaces, blocking doors and shadows so only whispers flew out into the night on the rising clouds of dust.

The toad loped slowly towards the darkness of the misshapen trees that concealed the fence lining the Causeway.

Little Thunder

Jan Goldie

WHAITIRI STEPPED FROM ONE HIGH-HEELED BOOT TO the other, shaking out the pins and needles in her legs. She rolled her neck to ease the ache of driving and peeled off her gloves, slapping them across the booster's saddle. With hot palms laid bare, she reached into the cotton messenger bag for one last check, then hefted its weight over her shoulder.

'Let's do this,' she said.

The viewing platforms looked empty. She had imagined the queue snaking around the deserted railings, but nobody was keen to take in the sights at this time of year. Even now, with the sun low in the sky, the place was as oppressive as a coffin in a swamp. She didn't need to get closer to know the canyon was deep; she could smell the empty.

Turning her back, she headed out of the vehicle park, towards the bar. Squatting alone in a sea of black sand, the place looked like it had spawned fully formed from some ancient Western movie. One single-storey building with a dinky porch out front. Windows closed against the ever clogging dust, curtains drawn. Shadows crossed the slits of light, music played and laughter trickled through the cracks in the wall with sitcom regularity. On its corrugated metal roof, a neon sign broadcast a name intermittently, occasionally missing off a letter, as if it couldn't decide if it was worth it. The Edge. The Ed. The Edg.

Beyond, the dark sands stretched, a flat and lonely desert pimpled with random boulders, a haphazard acne. Did they roll there? Did they spew out of the ground?

She eased towards the building, clicked up the steps and threw a look over her shoulder. Nothing moved in the shimmer of heat and black diamonds that separated her from the gaping crevasse.

Shifting the strap of the bag so it made a diagonal stripe across her cleavage, its contents bouncing on her butt, she pulled the sleeve of her red leather jacket down over her hand and opened the door. Should have kept her gloves on.

'Welcome to The Edge Bar and Restaurant. Please place all weapons in the bin provided. Enjoy your visit.'

Whaitiri ignored the recorded invitation and stepped inside. The bar smelled strongly of onions and slow roasted beetleberries, an unusual combination. The door locked behind her with an audible clunk. Sweat itched its way down her lower back and she resisted the urge to reach back and have a good scratch. Instead, she unzipped her jacket.

'Welcome to the Crack. How can we satiate your corporeal desires this evening?'

The Multi grabbed her hand and pumped it before Whaitiri could draw away. Whaitiri stiffened, released the immediate tension in her jaw and, as casually as possible, withdrew her hand from the creature's sweaty grip. Hand sanitiser. Where did she put it?

'I'll sit at the bar,' she said.

The Multi gestured to an empty stool. Whaitiri used the short walk to scan the room. Low lights, hard to see. Two men seated at a table, one couple on a couch, a tall barkeep and the Multi. No sign of Ellingham. As soon as she pulled back the bar stool, she realised her mistake. Her back was to the room.

To compensate, she climbed up and angled her body, leather pants sticking to the hot vinyl, squelching as she wiggled into place. The Multi watched, mono-brow raised.

'First time in the Crack?'

'I thought it was called The Edge.'

'A little crevice humour,' it said.

The Multi gestured at Whaitiri's trousers. 'Rarchend leather in maroon? Interesting choice for the weather we're having.'

'It's red,' said Whaitiri, smoothing them. She tried not to stare at the Multi's six teats.

'If you say so, sweetcheeks,' it said, beckoning the barkeep over. 'You here for the party? You're early, doesn't start till later tonight.'

The question worried Whaitiri. What party?

'Actually,' she said. 'I was hoping to speak to someone before it starts.'

'What'll you have?' interrupted the barkeep.

Whaitiri craned her neck to meet his eyes. Ustartion males grew one of two ways, either up or out. This one's head skimmed the ceiling.

'I'll take a vodka lime,' she said.

She swung her bag around her body so its load rested in her lap, and suspiciously eyed the rag the Ustartian was using to 'clean' the glasses. Hopefully, the pure alcohol would sanitise the vessel.

'No ice!' she remembered at the last moment. She could do without liquid recycled through the bodies of a population of no-hopers at the edge of nowhere.

Her gaze lingered on the men at the table by the window, playing Charts. They sipped on red drinks, with long straws that stayed in their mouths as they played.

'Twenty darushas to enter the game,' said the Multi, pointing at them.

Whaitiri shook her head and turned back to the bar as the barkeep snapped down a round coaster and placed the Gimlet in the centre of it and then, with a flourish, threw in a pink straw.

'Ten darushas,' he said, picking his enormous nostril.

Whaitiri fished in her bag, surreptitiously checking the package and coming across the hand sanitiser. She tucked it down the front of her top for safekeeping and hauled out her card, swiping it across the counter. The Ustartian grunted and wandered off, examining the results of his mining.

'You can talk to me about the party,' said the Multi, hovering. It took the bar stool beside her, its generous helping of body fat hanging in rolls over the edge of the circular seat.

Whaitiri kept her face straight, slamming down doors on her prejudice. This wasn't the time to piss off a Multi, outcast or not.

'I want to make an exchange,' she said, quickly. 'For the human.'

The Multi grinned. 'What human?'

Whaitiri forced herself to take a breath.

'You know, the human you're keeping out back,' she bluffed.

The Multi arched its back.

'Oh, *that* human. Why do you want him?'

Whaitiri thought about the last time she'd seen Ellingham. His face frozen in shock as she'd hauled him in to pay for his crimes. The guilt had gradually, with ever-tightening strips of self-blame, strapped itself around her middle and now she wore it like a go-to belt. It went with everything. This time was no different. He'd bailed on her again. She was here to take in the garbage and sweep up the mess.

'I've been asked to collect him for his family,' she said.

The Multi adjusted its weight on the stool, fat dripping to the other side. Whaitiri touched a finger to the blade concealed in her sleeve.

'The human is a crucial component of our set-up here. He has … certain skills. What do you have to exchange that would make it worth my while?'

Whaitiri crossed long legs and yawned, trying to ignore the obvious danger in the creature's voice. 'I have a treasure. Something old. Something precious.'

'Something pre-occupation Earth?'

Whaitiri raised her eyebrows in a quick *yes*.

'Well, show me!' it demanded, agitation wobbling its teats and disconcertingly swelling the mound of flesh in its tight, gold g-string.

'I'll show you once I've seen that Ellingham is alive and well.'

The Multi curled a tendril of coarse hair around the third finger on its right hand, a surprisingly coquettish gesture. It gazed at the ceiling as if trying hard to decide.

'Ellingham,' it purred. 'I've heard that name somewhere before…'

'One too many buttons, "sweetcheeks".' Whaitiri lurched off the bar stool, ignoring her repulsion, to grab a handful of the Multi's meaty flesh. It slipped in her grip but she got enough to hang on to.

The men at the table by the window were startled at her sudden move, hands flying instinctively to empty weapon pouches. Out of the corner of her eye, she saw the shorter of the two leap to his feet, sucking gulps of air through the two thin slits in his cheeks, ready for a fight.

Pleebards. Dammit, easy mistake to make in a dark room, but now she thought about it, she could smell them. The slight whiff of week-old fish with a side of milk left in the sun. What were cold-dwellers doing here, when they could be enjoying the spoils of occupation on her home planet?

Infuriatingly, the Multi laughed and waved the short outlander away. 'I can handle Miss Maroon Leather.'

The creature sat down, carefully puckering his mouth over his straw. Batting purely feminine eyelashes at Whaitiri, the Multi pouted.

Whaitiri narrowed her eyes and tightened her grip, ignoring the slick flesh and hot, sweaty texture. The longing to wash her hands was a storm, crackling at the back of her mind.

'Look, I'm not here to muck around,' she hissed, pushing the Multi back against the bar.

'Ooh baby, I love me some rough foreplay.' It gave her a suggestive smile.

Whaitiri rolled her eyes.

'This is how it's going to work. I have something you'll want, something important to my people. Taonga, treasure. I'm willing to give this to you if you hand over Ellingham in one piece. Now where is he?'

The Multi moved before she could take another breath. It slithered out of her grip and made a grab for the messenger bag, missing. Whaitiri grasped a handful of hair, but fell off balance and landed in an ugly heap on the floor, carrying the Multi with her, arms flailing. The full body slam was more than she could bear. She pulled the Multi's head towards her and, using the bag strap to encircle its neck, she squeezed till the creature rolled off her to the floor. But just as she released the pressure and unwound the strap, the Multi brought its head up against Whaitiri's nose. She let out a yelp, tears streaming down her face.

'Last bloody straw!' she yelled and withdrew the heavy green weapon from her bag. Using all her strength, she slugged the Multi across the side of its head and watched it hit the floor, out cold.

'Get to your feet. Slowly.'

The gun pointed at Whaitiri's head was small and deadly. Outdated police issue Ustartian. The barkeep's huge hand almost engulfed the powerful weapon.

'Place the weapon on the floor,' he said.

Whaitiri obeyed, her eyes on the gun.

'Now, put your hands above your head and walk to the front door.'

She walked, carefully avoiding the Multi's sprawled body. On some distant level she registered the music playing, the Charts coins flipping, the occupants of the bar looking away.

'Place your hands against the door and spread your legs.' The Ustartian frisked her efficiently, sliding large hands down her arms, legs and checking under the long hair that fell down her back. Lastly, he ran a portable scanner over her entire body and started pulling off knives.

'Dammit,' she whispered.

'Okay, we're going to take a walk. Tesslah, please look after the bar,' said the Ustartian, speaking to the couple hidden in the shadows by the couch. 'Gentlemen, please accept a drink on the house for this disruption. I hope you'll stay for the party.'

The Pleebards looked pleased. The 'couple' took its place behind the bar and began mixing drinks.

The Ustartian pushed Whaitiri through the door and out into the airless evening, shoving her down the steps and propelling her forward with a hefty kick to the back.

'Hey, use your words, big boy!'

'Shut your cake hole!'

'You didn't learn that one on Ustart.'

'I had the displeasure of serving on Earth before it was … renovated.'

Whaitiri grimaced. Any reference to what happened on Earth felt personal, leaving a painful physical sensation that started at the top of her head and ended somewhere low, clenched around her perineum. Not cool. She tried to turn, but the Ustart's gun formed a cool circle on the back of her neck. She bit back her retort.

The bike sat where she'd left it. No way to make a run for it. The big guy manoeuvred her towards the Edge.

They skirted the railings and approached a gap in the tourist trappings. As they drew closer she could feel the change in atmosphere. As if this enormous canyon had its own weather system. For all she knew, it did. Older than any natural feature back home, the Edge was a void, an impenetrable fissure that stretched the length of this continent. A drop off that millions of years ago might have been covered in water but was now a sightseer's paradise. Approaching its brink, she could see why. The vista spread out in waves of earthy brown and tangerine, the sun now sinking in the sky and bathing the scene in gold. Winged reptiles circled far overhead, on an endless hunt for small prey. Sweat stung her eyes. She took it all in. The Ustartian's gun remained glued to the back of her neck, the metal warming with her body. She had to stall him.

'Where's Ellingham? Give me back my patu.'

He pushed her closer to the Edge.

'My guess is that's not your weapon. My guess is you're here out of some ridiculous sense of duty or love or family. Humans. What's the damn point anymore?'

Her toes stopped at the edge of the canyon. She refused to look down.

'Duty is for arseholes,' she replied, turning to look at him despite the gun. 'Love is for teenagers. I'm neither.'

The Ustartian brought the gun close to her temple.

'Family then.'

'I have no family.'

'Yeah, well, I may be Ustartian but I'm not stupid. Either way, you're not having him because we can get more darushas in an evening with this guy than you've seen in a lifetime, and you're getting in the way of my retirement fund. Accidents happen all the time around here and no one's got the fuel reserves to go pick up the pieces.'

'You're full of shit.'

'Really, well that's original.'

'Where's Ellingham?'

'Why do you care?'

'He's mine.'

'Does he owe you money? I've heard he owes many.' The Ustartian laughed and the sound bounced off harsh angles and hard rock. 'Debt is universal. Can't live without it, can't pay it off.'

'Well said. But I owe her nothing.'

The Ustartian whirled and she took the chance, grabbing his long cloak with two hands, dragging him to the edge and pushing him over. It seemed to take an age for the giant to fall. As if time wanted one more slow-motion scene in the movie of his life. Jowls quivered, robes billowed, his arms propelled, but in the end he slipped silently into the crack.

'No need to thank me.'

Ellingham's stubble had grey in it now. His sweep of hair receded a little further up the slope of his forehead, like a cave eroded by the sea. Whaitiri's gaze flicked to the wide nose and high cheekbones he shared with her mother and rested on the swagger in his dark, gleaming eyes.

'Fancy meeting you here, Little Thunder,' he said, grinning.

She winced at the clumsy translation. Behind her, a distant thud echoed up from the darkening canyon.

'You okay?' said Ellingham.

'Fine. You?'

She'd spiked it with sarcasm, but he answered anyway.

'Ka pai.' He winked at her, swapping the club, the smooth green mere pounamu, from hand to hand. 'I'm glad to hold this beauty again. It was a good idea to use it as bait.'

'But something tells me you're not exactly being held here against your will…'

'Against my will?' He raised a faux-shocked eyebrow. 'I'm being paid to do a job and I'm having a ball. I'm not leaving, if that's what you're asking. And you and your maroon leather will be staying here too, if you know what's good for you.'

Whaitiri reached down her top for the hand sanitiser and squirted a small, phosphorescent ball of liquid into her palm. She smoothed the cool gel across her fingers, massaging it into damp hands, all the while inching away from the edge. When she'd finished, she popped the bottle back in the messenger bag and swung the cotton hold-all to her back.

'My leathers are red.'

Ellingham laughed. The sound poured lemon juice on something raw in her gut. She took a step towards him.

Ellingham's eyes narrowed. 'What you going to do, Thunder? I'm not the weak man I was last time. A bit older and greyer maybe, but these white hairs are signs of wisdom and a fat pay packet in a few months' time.'

The auto-lights flicked on in the vehicle park, backlighting Ellingham in a dirty glow.

'Stay here with me and you'll earn riches you've never even dreamed of,' he said. 'You can't go back to Earth, and that holding pen they call Neo Terra is an insult, even for you. I bet your job pays you peanuts. If you stay, I won't report you for murder.' He pointed over the edge.

Whaitiri snorted, taking time to curl her hair behind her ears. 'That wasn't murder. That was staff management. The guy couldn't make a good vodka lime if you took him to Russia with a lime tree.'

'Your mama wouldn't have put up with that kind of bull-shit talk,' he said.

Whaitiri came at Ellingham with her head down, using her shoulder to barrel him to the ground. The club flew out of his hands and she scooped it from the sand, holding the weapon to the older man's teeth.

'Don't talk about my mother like you knew *anything* about her.' His acrid breath coloured the air around her until all she could see was red. 'Get up!'

She hauled him to standing and made him walk the few steps to the drop off. When his footsteps faltered and he glanced behind him, she stopped.

'What do you do here?!' she demanded. 'How do you earn this money?' When he didn't answer, she thwacked the weapon across his chest. Flecks of black sand stuck to his white business shirt.

'Okay, hold onto your undies. I came to facilitate a few events.'

She kept the patu pointed at his mouth. 'What sort of events?'

He shrugged and looked away. 'Entertainment.'

'What kind of entertainment?' Her voice held steel.

'Suicide parties.'

'Suicide … parties?' she repeated, unable to wrap her head around the juxtaposition.

'You know, all the rage. Black mood, goth human teens wanting to leave this life. Desperate to piss off their folks, or depressed out of their minds. Elder Pleebards and drunk Multis and outcast Ustartians and the like come to watch. Gives them a stiffy. Or whatever those bastards get. I facilitate.'

Whaitiri felt bile rise like a burning tsunami in her oesophagus. 'You mean you throw them off the edge?'

'No, idiot. It's suicide. They jump. The audience love it! No mess, you see. Straight down. No smell. It's too far. Nobody has the money or the inclination to make the trip to collect the bodies.'

The burn turned to ice and Whaitiri fought the urge to bend and put her head between her knees.

'But what if they don't die when they fall? What if they're down there, for days?'

'It's a two-k drop, sweetheart.' A smug smile pulled the corners of his mouth.

Whaitiri clocked a green-tinged moon rising behind Ellingham. The reptiles had roosted and the heat of the day was rapidly departing. She couldn't hear the tinkle of music from the bar, but out of the corner of her eye she could still see the blink of the neon sign.

The Edge.

Th Ed e.

The E g.

'Look girl, I'll be honest with you. You're literally stand-ing in the arsehole of the universe,' he said, gesturing. 'Most people come here to look at the arsehole or forget they're an arsehole. But if you join me, I'll give you a fair percentage of this game. For whānau, you know?'

Tears welled in his eyes.

Whaitiri had to give it to him, he was the best in the business. She smiled.

'So what's it going to be? Going to give an old man a break?'

Whaitiri reached out a hand. Ellingham took it. But in-stead of pulling her to him, he brought a hard knee into her midriff, winding her and folding her like an ironing board. The mere pounamu thunked into the sand. Ellingham leaned down close to her ear.

'You know what, I changed my mind. I'm mercurial like that. One minute I'm sharing, the next I'm a selfish wanker. That's the way it goes when someone you thought you knew hunts you down and puts you away.'

He thrust her to the ground, so close to the verge that her head hung over the side. He kept the mere close, malice darkening his gaze.

'You're a sick bastard who should be ashamed of himself,' she snarled.

'Why? Because I meet a need? Wasn't it your own daddy who told me to get control of my life? And guess who's pulling the strings now, Whaitiri?' He reached for the mere pounamu and jabbed it into her throat, cutting off her air.

'You always thought you were better than me, didn't you? All of you did. But now they're dead and, bitch, you're nothing. Lost in the last place anyone will think to look for you…'

Fighting for air, Whaitiri grabbed the club, her fingers slipping on its smooth surface.

Ellingham smiled, knowing she couldn't hold on.

'My daddy didn't name me Whaitiri for nothing, Uncle,' she rasped, and pushed the hidden button on the ancient weapon's side.

An ear-splitting burst of noise and electricity emitted from the mere, thundering over Ellingham in waves of pain. He staggered, propelled backwards by the force and landed on a small boulder, something in his collar bone or maybe his shoulder snapping audibly as he fell. Squealing and shaking, his ears bleeding, her uncle shuddered back onto the sand.

Whaitiri struggled to her feet, brushed the grains off her leathers and picked up the mere. She pushed the release and stopped the blaring noise before tucking it away in her bag. Then she plucked the tiny gel plugs from her ears.

'Guess I did give an old man a break,' she said.

Her uncle moaned as she clicked the auto-cuffs in place, but Whaitiri ignored him. Leaving him, she strolled to her bike, hit the comms and radioed in. 'He's ready,' she said. 'Target subdued.'

'Roger that, Thunder and Lightning. Retrieval in ten. Over.'

The Multi appeared on the bar's porch, leaning its weight against the picket fence surround. A welt the size of a small egg rose from the side of its face.

'Do you have to take him, sweetcheeks? He was the best MC we've ever had. He really knew how to get in those jumpers' heads, tell them all the crap things about the world, how bad their lives were.'

Whaitiri pulled on her gloves, threw a leg over the bike saddle and wiggled into place, kicking the stand.

'What are we supposed to do now? We've got a bus full of jumpers and a bus load of audience arriving in an hour.'

'How about telling them the world isn't so bad? How about telling them to go home and sort out their problems?'

'Are you kidding me, Maroon?'

Whaitiri grinned. 'Yeah, even I don't believe that bullshit.'

The Multi returned her smile.

'Your backup is coming to clean us out, right?'

'You've got five minutes. Want a lift?'

She revved the bike into life. The noise carried over the edge, bouncing in infinite echoes. Moonlight bickered with the parking lights for dominion over the shadows, and the neon bar sign made a half-arsed effort to join in.

The Multi got within five metres before Whaitiri threw the bike into gear and squealed off.

Screamed curses carried over the noise of her engine until the dust clouds blurred all sight of The Edge in her rear-view mirrors.

Street Furniture

Joanne Anderton

I DRAG MY DESK CHAIR TO THE KERB, AND SET IT UNDER the dingy gum tree. It's the one Dan found for me at the tip. It has rusty legs and chipped wood painted an ugly green. The goblin sitting in it the next morning is not what I expected.

'The fuck do you call this?' he says. He's wearing torn jeans and a singlet, thongs, and a cigarette droops from the corner of his mouth. His hair is a mess and his eyes are red.

I gape at him as he stands. He's taller even than Dan, and he stinks like smoke and beer. If it weren't for the pointy ears sticking out of his hair and the fact that he just feels like a goblin, I wouldn't believe it. You ever seen a goblin, then you know that feeling. Like the air's all humming around him, and he's a little transparent around the edges.

'You don't look like David Bowie,' I say, before I can stop myself.

'Fuck David Bowie.' He spits the cigarette out onto the dry grass, but even in the heat it doesn't catch alight. It just burns away, hazy and a little unreal. 'Do you actually want anything, kid? Or should I be on my way?'

'Wait!' I cry, terrified he might leave. I did what I was supposed to do – put out my furniture and caught a goblin all of my own. He can't just disappear like that. 'Yes, I do want something.' I take a deep breath to calm down, the way Mum does when Jessie's fussing. 'I want you to kill Dan.'

'Who's Dan?' he asks.

'Mum's boyfriend.'

He lifts an eyebrow, then shrugs. 'Fine,' he says. 'Your name?'

I hesitate. In the movies and the books you're not supposed to give up your name so easily.

He rolls his eyes. 'I thought we'd been through this? Want me to stay, or not? Need a name if we're going to make a deal.'

'Emma. What's yours?'

He shakes his head. 'Anything you want it to be. Your furniture, you get to decide.' Then he turns to point at the chair. 'But I need something better than this piece of shit to kill a guy.'

My heart drops. 'I don't own anything else.'

'Not my problem, kid.' He digs a pack of cigarettes out of his pocket and lights a new one with a flame that appears when he clicks his fingers. 'But I'll tell you what. How about I give you a chance to get me something decent? I'll hang around a bit. You find me a nice sofa or an armchair – oh, and a bloody lamp, thank you very much – and then I'll kill the boyfriend for you. Fair?'

Where am I going to get a sofa? 'Okay.'

'And be quick about it. Don't want to hang around this shitbox place for long.'

That night, Dan's in a foul mood because he's been out with his mates, and because my chair is gone.

Usually, Dan doesn't pay much attention to me. Only when I'm in the way, or make a mistake like this. I don't want him to notice me. Not the way he notices Jessie. Jessie's his little man. He's going to make sure Jessie grows up strong. Dan will teach him. Jessie's not even *his* kid, but Dan will teach him anyway. Like his own father did.

'How did she lose a fucking chair?' he screams at Mum, like it's her fault.

He rounds on me. 'What did you do with it, you little shit?' Reaches down to grab me.

And suddenly, he stops. He frowns, and then gasps, like he can't breathe. He bends forward, hand pressed to his side. And my goblin is there, right behind him, grinning at me as he slams a bunched fist into Dan's ribs.

Dan shuffles into the kitchen, complaining, wheezing. The goblin winks at me, then leaves the house, passing right through the closed door, back to his chair.

Mum watches me for a minute, her mouth moving like she's got something to say, but doesn't know how.

'Sorry Mum,' I whisper. I didn't mean to make Dan angry. Most of the time, he takes his angry out on her.

I don't really remember my dad, but I'm sure he never felt like this. Jessie wasn't around much before he died, so he's never known any different than Dan. Sometimes, that makes me sad. Bet it makes Mum sad, too.

'You need to be careful, Em,' Mum says, voice as soft as mine. 'You don't always know what your choices will lead to.'

I don't remember my dad all that well, but I remember life without him. The time before Dan. I remember moving from place to place with Jessie, tiny, screaming, and always sick. Mum looking so tired, Mum looking so worried. I remember being hungry.

I remember Mum crying.

Dan changed all that. Dan came with a house to live in and food to eat, and even clothes to wear when I started school.

Dan changed all that, but then Dan changed.

He's mean to her, but she won't do anything about it. He's mean to Jessie, but I don't think she sees it. I remember being hungry and cold, with nowhere to stay, and I wonder if that's why. Because Dan's horrible, and I hate him, but since she's been with him, we have a home.

'Don't worry, Mum,' I say, and take her hands. She's been biting her nails again. 'I'll look after us this time.'

She squeezes me tightly. 'But sometimes,' she whispers. 'You don't realise the cost—'

Dan interrupts, demanding a glass of water from the kitchen. She drops my hands, and is gone.

*

I press my face against the window of Vinnies. There's a sofa inside and I know, just *know*, that it's the one. It's small, and seventies-looking. Thin wooden frame and sagging cushions covered in yellow and brown fabric. I don't need to be able to smell it to know it stinks like old cigarettes and mothballs. My goblin should feel right at home.

It's also fifty bucks. Which is not very much money for a sofa, even I know that. But it's fifty bucks more than I have.

I turn from the shop with a sigh, hitch the torn strap of my heavy school bag onto my shoulder and continue home. The walk home takes me past the small, rundown houses with ramps and handrails, where the old folks and their electric wheelchairs live. There's a lady who usually sits out the front of one. Joyce. She's decent, gives me barley sugars from her purse, but she's not here today.

The usual pile of junk on the curb has grown, and I pause to stare at the goblin who lives in it. Why doesn't my goblin look like this? He's tall and handsome. Hair dyed in funky colours sticking out at cool angles. He's wearing an old leather jacket patched in just the right places, and no shirt underneath. Dark jeans torn at the knees. Tattoos down his chest and piercings in his ears. He's lounging on an old leather couch and footstool, thumbing through an even older looking book, and being just generally magic and awesome.

'You again,' a gravelly voice grunts behind me. 'Thought I told you to piss off.'

I turn so quickly I stumble under the weight of my bag. An old stooped man carrying a plastic cup of tea and a packet of biscuits scowls at me from under enormous eyebrows. He's filthy, his clothes tattered and torn, the skin of his fingers so dirty they're black. And he stinks.

'Sorry!' I squeak and try to get out of his way.

'Leave her alone,' the goblin says. His voice is deep and drawling. Something about it makes me shiver. He puts down his book and stands in one motion, so smooth he could be liquid.

'I—' I stammer. It's difficult to speak to him. The old man shuffles past me and hands the tea to his goblin. 'I did it.' And now I sound like an idiot. 'It worked.'

'Of course it did,' the old guy mutters. He puts the biscuits on a small table. This goblin also has a couch, a desk, a shelf full of books, even a collection of records and something to play them on.

'Didn't we tell you?' the goblin says. He holds out a hand to me. The old guy watches as I weave my way through the rubbish. I'm not sure why, but he's never liked me. Not when

I thought he was just a homeless bum, living in rubbish. Not that time after a bad night with Dan, and a horrible day at school, when I was bruised and hungry and really didn't want to go home. That was the first day I realised that what had always looked like a random pile of junk was actually an entire room of street furniture. That was the first time I saw a goblin.

'You see us when you need us,' the goblin says. He takes my hand and bows over it, kissing my skin. His lips are cold, like an ice cube. His hands are strong. 'Put your past on the curb, and we will sense it. Your need. Your desire.' He does not smell like cigarettes. He smells like incense. 'And we come running.' He smiles at me and I'm all shivery again.

'So piss off back to your own one,' the old man snaps. He's scowling at me so hard I can see veins across his forehead. I tug my hand out of his goblin's grip, feeling hot.

'I don't think that was necessary,' the goblin says. 'We can at least be civilised, can't we?' He peels open the packet of biscuits and bites into one, slowly. I glance over my shoulder as I hurry away. The old man coughs loudly, the noise thick and choking, his whole body shaking. The goblin just watches, and continues to eat. I wonder what the old man asked for when he called his goblin. And how can he be so dirty, when his goblin has such a wonderful room?

I find an old IKEA lamp in a bag next to the charity bins at the servo. A plastic one with a clip on one end and a long bendy neck. No idea whether it works, or if that even matters. Not like my goblin's got anywhere to plug it in. He grumbles a bit when I give it to him, about how it's a desk lamp and what the fuck is he supposed to do with a desk lamp, but takes it all the same.

After dinner, Dan's watching the footy, so I play with

Jessie in our room. Out the window I can see my goblin, the lamp attached to the back of his chair and shining a spotlight on the driveway. I wonder if he'd like a book to read?

'Time for Jessie's bath,' Mum says, softly, from the doorway. She enters and scoops him into her arms. He giggles, and she flinches at the sound.

'Mum,' I say, just as softly. 'Can we watch a video on the weekend?'

All we've got is this old video-player, doesn't even play DVDs, just worn-out tapes. There's only one I want to watch anyway.

Mum perches on the edge of my bed, Jessie balanced in her lap, and reaches back to touch the poster stuck to my wall. David Bowie glowers from the faded and folded paper, crystal ball in hand.

'There are other movies in the world, Em,' she murmurs. 'It's not healthy to be so obsessed. Believe me. I know.'

'I don't care.'

Labyrinth is my favourite. It used to be Mum's favourite too, when she was growing up. It used to hang on her wall, when she was a kid, and she passed it on to me. The video's hers too, the tape is fuzzy, and hitches, because she watched it over and over again. Just like me.

'We'll have to see what the weekend brings,' she says. 'Whether we have time.'

She means, what mood Dan is in.

I nod. 'Okay, Mum.'

With any luck I'll have found a sofa, and he'll be dead by then.

*

I wake to the noise of our bedroom door opening. Jessie's

sound asleep, I can hear his regular breathing. Mouth open, snotty nose, I can tell all that just from the sound. I'm pretty used to hearing it.

Dan sneaks in through the door and goes to Jessie's bed. I'm pretty used to hearing that, too. I squeeze my eyes shut but that makes no difference. Because it's dark. And I can hear him breathing.

Dan doesn't ever notice me. But Jessie's his little man.

'Please,' I whisper. 'Stop him.'

'Can't do it,' my goblin whispers back. His voice is close, his breath smoky against my face, like he's lying right beside me.

'But I got you the lamp.' My voice is so quiet only he can hear it. 'And you stopped Dan last time.'

'That's because it was you, Emma,' he breathes. 'Furniture's yours, so I'm here for you. Not Jessie. Not no one else.'

'But you can't.' Tears run down my face now. Dan would be so mad. 'You can't just lie here. You can't just … just…'

I can hear them breathing.

'What else will you give me then?' he asks. 'The sofa and the lamp are for Dan's life. What will you give me for your little brother?'

I don't even think. 'Anything.' I mean it, with all my heart, and I hope he can hear it in my whispered voice. 'Anything you want.'

'Now that's an interesting bargain.' His fingers are cold and slightly damp, as he traces them across my cheek, down to my throat. 'I can hardly turn that down, can I?'

The mattress shifts. I hold my breath and stare into the darkness. Dan grunts. I hear rustling, bodies moving. Then the door opens. There's a faint light in the corridor, the moon peeking through the glass panels in the front door, and my goblin is silhouetted against it. He's holding Dan, all limp, by the back of his shirt.

The next morning Dan's got this black eye and a terrible green look about him. But he's still alive. Jessie's smiling and happy to eat his breakfast. It's worth it, I know, as I watch my little brother shove toast and jam into his mouth. He's worth anything the goblin asks of me.

*

'Not just any old sofa either. Not some piece of shit like that lamp, you hear? Something nice. Something with style.'

My goblin followed me to school today. I didn't realise he could do that. Spent all day lecturing me about the kind of sofa he wants, and listing all the things wrong with the chair and the lamp I got him. He seems animated, energetic, and I wonder why. He hasn't given a shit until now.

Don't do much listening or talking at school anyway, and most people can't see him. There's this one teacher who went all white when he entered the room, but she didn't say anything. If she can see him it means either she's got her own, or she needs one. Just like I did. Makes me wonder what for.

I glance at the old bloke and his pretty goblin as we walk past on the way home. The goblin's sitting back in his chair, and the old guy … I stop, squint at them. He's stretched out across the goblin's lap, his filthy shirt and layers of jackets unbuttoned, opened. The goblin's doing something to his chest but I can't see, I don't understand.

'Just keep walking,' his goblin says, without looking up. He doesn't sound so sweet today.

'Unless you're planning to steal some of this shit for me,' my goblin says, crouched and whispering right by my ear. 'This ain't got nothing to do with us.'

'But—'

He gives me a little shove. 'Absolutely nothing.'

Then Joyce calls from her front door. 'Emma!' Her voice is warbly and thin. 'Oh, Emma. There you are.'

I turn into her driveway. My goblin sighs and rolls his eyes. 'No thank you,' he mutters. 'This you can do all on your own.' He digs cigarettes out of his pocket and vanishes as he sets one alight.

The silence is strangely deafening. Suddenly my ears feel full of cotton wool.

Joyce fusses over me. 'Put your bag down, sweetie, you'll do yourself an injury.' She's always got her handbag out the front with her, and digs around in it. She thinks *I'm* carrying too much stuff? I've never seen a bag so full of crap as hers. Lollies of so many different kinds, tissues, tissues, millions of tissues. Lipstick, hand cream, plastic bags rolled into balls and an ancient-looking purse.

She hands me a barley sugar and I'm staring at that damned bag. That ancient purse.

'You look tired, dear.' Joyce drops the lolly in my hand and folds my fingers around it. 'It's no good nowadays, all the books they make you carry and the homework. Kids your age should be running around outside.' She always worries about me, does Joyce. Once, she saw the bruises on my arm and went all quiet. Just kept giving me lollies, one after the other.

'Now then.' She pats my hand. Her skin feels like paper. She's losing her hair but combs it over like a man to try and hide it. She doesn't do her lipstick very well, and her eyes are always watery. 'Now then.' Sometimes, she gets confused. Loses track of whatever story she was telling me. Repeats herself. 'Would you like a juice?'

I never say yes to the juice. I usually just sit here and eat her lollies and pretend to listen to her stories that make no sense.

'Yes, please.' The words come out in a squeak.

'Oh!' She seems surprised. 'Well, yes then, of course.' She pushes herself out of the wicker chair with a groan. 'What kind? I've got apple, and orange, and cranberry.' She walks slowly, limping. One of her shoes is bigger than the other, and has a brace attached. 'And apple.'

'I don't mind,' I manage to say, as she shuffles past.

'Just a moment. Just a moment.'

She disappears into the house and I stare at that purse. I sit on the floor, back against the wall, draw my knees up, tuck my skirt in. Feels like the world is watching me.

I slip my hand into Joyce's handbag, and unclip her purse. The amount of money inside is a bit of a shock. Never seen so much in one place in all my life. Mum used to complain about Grandma, back when they were still talking, about carrying all her pension money around and how it was just asking for trouble.

Well, I don't want it all. More money than I've ever seen but I don't want it all.

I finger through until I find a fifty. It slips out easy, and I tuck it into my pocket. Purse is back in her bag and it looks like nothing's the matter long before Joyce returns. She walks so slowly, with her strange shoe.

She's brought me a glass of milk.

'Here you go, sweetness.' She settles back into her chair with the same groan, but smiles at me. 'Good for the bones.'

I drink as quickly as I can, and listen as she murmurs nonsense. Feeling hot the whole time. Feeling like it must be obvious what I've done.

The next day after school I head to Vinnies. They don't care how I got the fifty bucks, they just want to know how I plan to get the sofa home. I take it in pieces, the cushions in a couple of big plastic bags, the frame I half carry, half drag. Lucky the sofa is old, and cheap, and not as heavy as it looks. No one offers to help, and I wouldn't accept anyway. The street furniture is my offering, and mine alone.

My goblin says nothing as I set up the sofa under the tree, beside the chair with its clipped-on lamp.

Together, we wait for Dan to come home.

*

He insists on being close, right up against me, so our legs are touching. I'm nervous, but I try not to show it, tangling my fingers in the hem of my skirt.

'Second thoughts?' the goblin says. He's leaning back and looks calm, relaxed. Smoking slowly, drawing each breath in deep.

'No,' I say, quietly, my voice calm. After today, Mum won't be sad anymore. After today, Jessie will be safe. We'll all live in Dan's house, and we won't be hungry or cold, just he won't be there.

Dan's car rattles down the street, and I straighten. My goblin places a hand on my bare knee. 'Any preferences?' he asks.

I shake my head, and stare intently at the driveway as Dan pulls in. His old station wagon is spewing black smoke and the engine makes this squealing noise. He can't see us. Not yet. I'm not sure where the line is, between the hidden world of my goblin's room and the out there where anyone can see. Turns off the car, gets out all whistling and slightly pissed. I know Mum's at the window, watching him, sussing out his mood. She can't see us either.

I'm glad about that. My goblin will do what he needs to do but she doesn't need to see.

Dan passes by the chair and my goblin's up, moving faster than the wind, stops right in front of him and slams a hand down on Dan's shoulder.

'Excuse me,' he says, with a grin. And I realise he's got these little sharp teeth, at the back. Never noticed them before.

It's over quick.

Never seen a man die before. He flinches, shocked. Then my goblin spins him, wraps an arm around his neck, and drags him into the room. Dan kicks and he gasps and he struggles. My goblin's grip on his neck just tightens and he lifts Dan up, feet off the ground, until he stops moving.

My goblin lets him go and he falls heavy, onto the grass. I stand slowly, legs shaking, and stare at his body.

'He didn't know it was me,' I say. 'He didn't even know why.'

'That's all a second-hand IKEA lamp gets you,' my goblin says, and lights a fresh cigarette.

'Can you get rid of him?' I ask. 'I don't want Mum to find him here.'

'Not part of the bargain, kid,' he says. He starts poking Dan with his foot, shoving his body away from the furniture. 'Remember, it was a couch and a lamp to shuffle him off the coil.' He stops, and turns to me. 'And anything else I ask, for Jessie. Because I kept him safe.'

I nod, but swallow hard, suddenly unsure. 'He *is* safe now,' I say. 'Without Dan, he will be safe.' Even as I say the words I've got this terrible sinking feeling. He would have been safe anyway, once Dan was dead. It was only one more night. I promised my goblin whatever he wanted, just for one more night.

'Pity you didn't think of that at the time,' he says. And suddenly he's right up against me. His face is in shadow, the cigarette a burst of flame at the edge of his terrible, sharp-toothed smile. I know how quick he is, I know how strong he is. I just watched him kill Dan.

'What do you want then?' I ask.

'All of you.' He breathes out smoke and strokes the back of my head. His fingers feel strange, long and cold and dragging me closer, closer. 'You promised me, anything I want. And I want all of—'

He gasps, suddenly, and staggers back. The hand that held me moments ago is pressed to his side. There's blood, which seems so strange, because there was no blood when Dan died. My goblin's blood isn't even red, it's black, and it spills across his singlet and his torn jeans like a stain. He drops to his knees, stares at me, mouth open. Then he falls forward, and it happens so fast he nearly lands on me. But an icy hand grips my shoulder and pulls me out of the way.

I look up, and can't believe it. David Bowie stares at me. It can't be. But he's got the hair, and the make-up, and the jacket with all the sequins. He releases my shoulder, and glowers at me with disdain.

'There,' he says, glancing over his shoulder. 'It's done.'

I step to the side, look behind him. Mum's there. She looks pale and thin in her trackies with a stained apron over the top. Her hair's pulled roughly back so the yellowing bruise on the side of her face is visible. She doesn't usually wear it like that.

'Mum?' I whisper.

She's looking at me, but not with thanks. I got rid of Dan.

I protected Jessie. And yet…

'So, this is your daughter.' David Bowie glances between us, and smirks. 'She's hardly got your sense of flair, has she?'

Mum's got a goblin?

'Oh, Em,' Mum says. She's shaking, her hands knotted together. Her nails are bitten so far down they're bleeding. 'I didn't want to do this. Never, ever again. But you made me.'

'I—' I hold her gaze, not sure what's happening.

'I knew your mum a long time ago,' her goblin says as he crouches in front of me. 'She filled my room with beautiful furniture, even made me this jacket.' He tugs at the sequins. 'Wasn't much older than you are now, at first. But we were friends for years and years.' He laughs, and I feel like someone's dumped cold water all down my back. It's not a friendly sound. Not a nice sound at all. 'Really good friends.'

'I finally got rid of him,' Mum whispers. 'When your Dad came along. Paid off my debt, paid it well and truly. Left him to his pretty fucking furniture and got the hell away.'

'But why?' I ask. 'If you had a goblin all this time, why not ask him to get rid of Dan?'

'Why indeed?' the goblin asks, with another laugh.

'You think Dan was worth giving yourself to a goblin?' Mum shakes her head sharply, almost violently. 'Because you don't understand what you're offering. You don't know what it's like to be trapped in the room you created, with the creature you summoned, at his mercy. The world walking past you and not seeing, not knowing. You offered him everything. In the end, that's what they always want. And that's what they take. There are pains worse than bruises, Em.'

'But Jessie—?'

'I could not go back there!' she cries. 'Not for Dan, not

for me. Not even…' she lets out a little sob, chokes on her words '…not even for Jessie. Not until you put this stupid chair out on the curb. I gave my childhood to him.' She very nearly spits at her goblin. 'Could not let you do the same.'

'Enough with the hysteria,' Mum's goblin interrupts. 'You called me, I'm back. Too late for regrets now.' He picks my goblin up by the hair. 'You know the deal. I'll have a new room, thanks, for getting rid of this.' He shakes my goblin roughly, and he groans. His eyes are open and he stares at me with hunger, with anger. I take a step back, and Mum's there. She wraps arms around my shoulders and holds me tight.

'Prettier than last time,' her goblin continues. 'And bigger. And right here.' He stamps his foot. 'I want one right here.'

Mum's nodding, and crying, both at once. 'And what do you want to keep him?' she asks, little louder than a whisper. 'So he can't get to her. Even if she calls again, no matter when, he can never get her. She will be free. She has to be free of him. Forever.'

'Just like last time,' Mum's goblin says, with that same hunger, with that same smile. 'Anything I want.'

Call of the Sea

Eileen Mueller

Selina's pudgy legs race towards the slide, wind whipping her hair across her eyes. Turning, she smiles. 'Nudda wun, Mama?'

'Of course you can.' I push Aihe on the swing with my paint-smudged hands. Sea hisses on sand.

Fat fingers grasp metal rungs as Selina climbs to the top and manoeuvres her bottom onto the plastic chute. My dark skin, his light hair. Something from each of us. A gust flings sand grains across the playground. Squeezing her eyes shut against the sudden assault, Selina shoots down the slide, laughing.

Enjoying herself.

'Nudda wun?' Up she goes for another turn.

Wind moans through the tunnel on the deserted playground. The ropes on the massive climbing frame jerk. Grey waves thrash the shore, flinging spray over the naked sand. The pōhutukawa dance, the silver underskirts of their dark green leaves flashing, like shy debutantes – as if to tempt an unsuspecting fool into loving them.

My hands itch for a brush and canvas.

Breathing deeply, I shove the swing harder than I need to.

'Higher, Mum,' Aihe calls, swinging her legs for momentum. But she doesn't get far. The gale is against us.

I can't believe he did it. After all these months, I still can't believe it.

I push Aihe again.

What classic timing. Womb still raw, he'd decided to shred my heart too.

'Nudda wun?'

Nodding mechanically, I push the swing, reliving bitter accusations, angry revelations, the wind no match for my hurricane of emotions. Great clouds scud towards us, looming like the deadline on my mortgage payments.

The empty swing next to Aihe's careens into me. Selina flies down the chute and walks back for another turn. Buffeted, she falls to her knees, then crawls, mouthing, 'Nudda wun?' The wind grabs her words, tossing them against a concrete wall.

Running over, I snatch Selina up. She hides her face in my breast. Back to the swing to get Aihe, who clings to me in a crinkle of rainwear. Sand gritting my eyes, I stumble towards the car park and—

Where is Pania?

She's wandered off again. At sixteen, she thinks she's old enough to go anywhere, do anything, without asking. She wasn't like this before. Before he cheated. *Stop it! Focus. Find her.*

Out beyond the grassy verge, waves crash over the jetty. She's not there.

The car park is empty, save my old Holden. No one else is mad enough to brave this storm. Kids still clinging to me like gladwrap, I struggle along the promenade to the boatsheds, and battle my way down the stairs.

On the narrow strip of concrete walkway between boat-sheds and the floating jetty, Pania dances. Above her, gulls are tossed on the wind, their plaintive cries counterpoint to her inner rhythm. She pirouettes in her skinny jeans and sneakers and leaps through the air. Upon landing, she spins and leaps again.

The jetties, instead of bobbing on the water's surface, are submerged, roller-coastering in the wild ocean. My graceful daughter dances. Oblivious.

After the stillbirth, when Terry left and I sank into depression, Pania told me dancing had saved her. Transfixed, I stare. Sea surges over the walkway, splashing the boatsheds' brightly coloured facades. Pania dances in the receding surf. Rain, a few drops, then a splatter. Pania still dances, face upturned and arms wide, summoning heaven to earth, drinking in the rain.

I inhale the energy of the storm, the churning ocean. A moment later, black clouds are directly overhead, pelting us. Selina whimpers and Aihe's fingers dig into my palm.

'Pania!' My cry is unheeded, perhaps unheard. 'Pania, get away from the—'

Wet-haired, she springs high into the air and spins, beautiful and defiant.

A violent wave erupts from the sea, towering above Pania, still spinning in mid-air. The wave surges, opening a streaming maw. Drooling jaws snap around her. Foaming eyes mock me. Throat tight, I can hardly believe my eyes. The ocean growls. The watery monster retreats, whipping Pania out to sea.

'Pania!' The crash of the surf drowns out my cry.

Thrusting Aihe and Selina onto the bottom step, I dash

along the gangway, sliding on slick concrete. Spray splatters off my jacket. Sea drags at my boots. I scramble to the jetty, placing one foot on the surging wood. Wet to the knee, I cling to the walkway and position my next foot. The jetty heaves.

'Mama!'

Behind me, my toddler reaches for me, face contorted into a scream – barely a mermaid's whisper in *this* wind. Aihe yanks Selina's jacket, trying to hold her back. She slips, losing her grip. Selina dashes forward. To me. And the sea.

One last desperate glance seawards. Cavernous grey troughs and surging peaks. Pania's arm breaks the surface. Then she's swallowed.

'Mama!' Right behind me.

I spin, stumbling on wet planking. Selina leans over the edge, towards the jetty, arms outstretched above the roiling sea, mouth open, howling, 'Mama!'

Save Pania? Or Selina?

Chest tight and tears flowing, I grasp my baby as she falls, snatching her before the sea does. I clamber off the jetty, scraping my knuckles red, and stare out to sea.

No sign of Pania.

Aihe stumbles to me. Gasping like a landed fish, I clutch Selina, dragging Aihe back to the car. The girls tremble. My hands shake, fumbling the keys. Aihe takes them off me and clicks the beeper. *Pania. Pania.*

Drenched, Selina is screaming – no mermaid whisper now. I strap them in their seatbelts. Lock the door. And run.

Heart pounding. Across the car park. 'Pania! Pania!' Along the promenade. Sobbing, screaming, I plunge onto the gangway. One deep breath. And dive into the sea.

*

Terry's cell phone vibrates against the dining chair.

'Not in the middle of dinner!' Sue sighs, making her huge belly rise and fall like seaweed on the swell. Only four months to go, and she still looks great.

Terry shrugs. 'It's the price we pay for my on-call allowance.' A generous allowance, worth a couple of overseas holidays a year. He shovels another forkful of *risotto ai funghi* into his mouth and fishes the phone out of his pocket.

Unknown number. Not the call centre then. 'Hello.'

'Is that Mr Lenton?' a woman's gravelly voice asks. 'Mr Terry Lenton?'

Mr? Definitely not work. 'Speaking.'

'This is Inspector Turner of Wellington Central Police.'

Terry clears his throat. 'Yes?'

'Sir, we have your children in custody.'

'What? My kids!' Terry's pulse bounds, fork clanking onto his plate.

'Could you come down to the station right away, please?'

'What's happened? Where's Kendra?'

'We were hoping you could tell us.'

*

Inspector Turner's shoes snap on the grey linoleum of Central Station's corridors, a staccato rhythm almost as fast as Terry's heart. She ushers him to a small room, containing nothing but a few chairs and a table.

'My kids,' he stares around the empty room, jaw clenching. 'I want to see my kids. Where's their mother? What has she done *this time*?'

'Take a seat, Mr Lenton.' Inspector Turner takes a cautious

breath, as if he's about to bolt from the room.

Terry sits. Raises his eyebrows, breathes.

'Your children were found in a locked car at Oriental Bay an hour ago. Apparently they'd been there since the storm started around 4 o'clock this afternoon.'

'What?! That dumb—'

Inspector Turner raises her hand. 'Hear me out, please, Mr Lenton.'

Terry snaps his mouth shut and nods. Nothing to be gained by being belligerent. 'I'm sorry. Go on.'

'They'd been in the car. Both are in shock, and—'

'Both?'

'Selina and Aihe. They're pretty shaken up.'

What did she mean *both* kids? 'What about Pania?'

Inspector Turner adjusts a button on her uniform. 'Pania and your ex-wife are still missing.' A pause. 'The six-year-old keeps saying—'

'Aihe. Her name's Aihe.' What did it matter? He should keep his trap shut. Find things out faster that way.

'Yes, Aihe. Aihe says a wave swept her sister into the sea.'

'What in hell's name?' Terry leaps from his seat, smacking his palms down the table.

'Mr Lenton, please sit.'

Terry obliges. Hell, this woman is as cold as an ice bucket. Makes him wonder what else she's seen.

'It's important you don't quiz your children too much. That you don't ask questions about what happened. Listen if they talk. Comfort them. Reassure them. But please don't pass verbal judgement on anything they say. It could affect evidence if your wife—'

'Ex-wife,' Terry spits. 'Bloody ex-wife, thank heaven.'

'We need your children's evidence to be untainted, in case

your wife and daughter don't turn up.'

To hang with the evidence. 'Sure. Listen, comfort, reassure.' His mouth works on autopilot while his mind spins.

Inspector Turner stands. 'Come this way.'

Terry lurches to his feet, the risotto squirming in his stomach, and follows her down the hall to another room. A female officer is sitting on a sofa, and his kids, dressed in oversized unfamiliar clothing, are playing with a pile of toys. Despite the heater, they look cold. Selina's cheeks are pale, her blonde hair in dark damp curls against her scalp. She pushes matchbox cars along a road on a traffic mat.

Aihe leaps to her feet and rushes into his arms. 'Dad!' Her cheek is icy. Freezing hands cling to the back of his neck. She shoots a sidelong glance at Selina and whispers, 'A giant dog took Pania. Mum jumped in to save her.'

A giant dog? What sort of crap was that? Listen. Comfort. Reassure. 'It'll be all right. Mum and Pania will be home soon.'

At the sound of his voice, Selina looks up. 'Daddy. Wuff-wuff got Pani in a sea.' She pushes the car along the mat, right through three buildings. 'Brmm brmm.'

Pania – his treasure, his first baby – dragged into the sea *by a dog?* Where is she? What happened? Anxiety gnaws at Terry. There has to be some other explanation.

*

That night, Terry is on high alert. Not from being on call, but from minding his damn kids because Kendra is AWOL.

Selina refuses to sleep in the portacot, finally burrowing in between him and Sue. Not that there is any excess space with Sue's pregnant belly. Aihe has nightmares, whimpering in the room next door, until Sue moves onto the sofa and

Terry brings Aihe in with him and Selina. Not ideal, but at least he gets a few winks in between the kids snuffling and Selina flinging her arms in his face.

The next morning, Aihe has a fever and Selina is coughing. Their bed turns into a sick room, a menagerie of stuffed toys keeping the girls company. And Terry. They won't let him out of their sight.

The news is out. *Woman and Daughter Missing in Oriental Bay* splashed across social media, the front page of the *Dom-Post*, and on radio and television. A wave of calls flood in. Sue fends them off while Terry reads fairy stories to the girls, pretending everything is normal. Except it's not.

Pania is missing. His Pania, his eldest, so full of promise. Hands shaking, Terry turns a page.

At 10am his cell phone rings.

'Mr Lenton?' It's Inspector Turner. 'We may have found Kendra, but we need positive identification.'

So Kendra is dead. Has she taken her life? And Pania's too? Knowing it would hurt him, selfish cow. He shakes his head. Focuses. 'What about Pania?'

'No sign of Pania, yet, sir, but your wife is at the hospital, still alive.'

Alive? Something fierce surges in his chest. That means Pania could be, too. At last he can do something other than sit and read fairy tales.

'Daddy?' Aihe's brown eyes gaze at him. The same eyes as Kendra. 'Where are you going?' Her voice trembles.

Terry pats her glossy hair.

*

The murky water is awash with debris, stirred up by the storm. No sign of Pania. Lungs burning, I surface. Gasp.

A wave slaps my face. Salt searing my throat, I tread water, searching for a sign of her – a glimpse of flesh between the choppy peaks.

Something yanks my ankle, dragging me down. A quick gasp, then my head is sucked beneath the surface. I struggle, but the shadowy tentacled monster would rip my limbs from their sockets before it loosens its grip. The grey sea blurs, becoming darker than the day Terry left me. I'm dragged into the belly of the harbour.

Chest aching, I glimpse a fist-sized glow ahead. Anglerfish? Can't be. Wellington Harbour's too shallow. It grows into a shining orb, looming as we speed along the seabed. Indistinct figures swim inside the sphere of light.

The tentacle flings me forward. Plunging into the light, I gasp, choking on water. Throat filled with brine, I thrash.

A figure approaches, eyes as green as sea lettuce, and fishy-tailed. The merman enfolds me in his arms and kisses me. A warm current runs through me. The tightness in my chest eases, and I inhale.

Breathe? How can I, in water? Bizarre.

He smiles. 'Kendra, we've waited for you.' Beard threaded with thin kelp stands, he's wearing a necklace of living seahorses.

Inside, the globe is larger than it appears, a world unto its own, lit by a yellow glow. Around me, figures swim. Fish-tailed people – mermaids and mermen. A pod of dolphins swims by, a girl astride one, her feet against its pale underbelly. She laughs, a trail of bubbles streaming behind her as the dolphins cruise away, her dark hair swirling in the water.

Her laughter penetrates deep into my being. I *know* her.

A watery dog bounds over, a seaweed bundle in its jaws. My merman takes the parcel, extending it to me.

'Look and rejoice.' His voice, as deep and sonorous as the sea, thrills through me.

The seaweed layers peel back and dance away in the water, revealing a baby. My baby. Matiu – bigger, chubbier than when he was stillborn. Matiu beams, his eyes lighting up like candles on a birthday cake.

He's alive. Grinning, he swims off, chasing fish. My boy. My only boy, alive. My chest surges with sweetness.

The merman grins, lifting me onto his dog. Although it's made of shimmering water, its back is solid beneath me. Real. When it barks, vibrations run through its ribcage against my legs. This place is surreal.

We're off, the dog bounding through the water – merman swimming alongside – following the dolphins' wake. The dark-haired dolphin rider laughs, sending tickling fingers of recognition down my spine.

Pania?

'Yes, your daughter has chosen to live here, with her brother, with us.' The merman's voice flows through my mind like a lazy ocean current. 'You can, too.'

I turn, his gaze warming my cheeks. I tumble off the dog and fall against him, tugging his arm around my shoulders like a blanket. We drift in the current. The ripple of his laughter shimmies through me, making my toes curl in pleasure. The glow of new love flowers inside me, a rare orchid in a hot house.

'But Pania—' I turn.

He plucks a seahorse from his necklace and whispers to it. The creature unfurls, writhing through the water after the dolphins, emitting a high-pitched whinny.

Now it's my turn to laugh.

He grins, taking my hand, and I swim at his side. The

dolphin carrying Pania wheels towards the seahorse, which nickers a greeting, and leads the dolphin to its master. Nudging my companion, the dolphin bobs beside us. Pania stands up on its back, touching my shoulders.

'You won't lose me again, Mum. I'll be here.'

She pirouettes, and dives off the dolphin, into the sea. Moments later, she reappears, Matiu in tow, the dolphin circling her protectively. Placing Matiu in my arms, Pania kisses me. 'Come, join us.'

But Aihe, Selina…

The merman's eyes are grave. Stroking Matiu's cheek, then mine, he says, 'We'll love you, no matter what choice you make.'

*

Damp reddish-brown locks are splayed across the hospital bed, among the tubes and wires. At first, Terry doesn't recognise Kendra. She's dyed her luscious black hair – the one thing he'd still loved about her when he'd left. Well, that and her art, although she'd never sold many paintings. A thick tube snakes into Kendra's mouth, jamming it open, her chest rising and falling as air rasps in and out.

Her skin is the worst. Years ago he'd loved her mānuka-honeyed complexion, smooth against his hand. Now she's bloated and swollen with sea, blotchy.

He turns away, sickened.

Their separation had left him estranged from the kids. Not that he'd had much time for them before. He'd been too busy *working late* – with Sue.

And Pania? Terry shudders as he thinks of recent shark sightings off Kapiti coast.

One of the monitors starts to beep in rapid-fire. A nurse

approaches him. 'Mr Lenton, we need you to leave, so we can treat your wife.' She ushers him out.

His ex-wife, not his wife. He doesn't even have the energy to correct her.

*

Something crisp and soft touches my cheek. The brine is chased away by the tang of fresh starch. Hiss and sigh. Hiss and sigh.

Beeping. Somewhere nearby. Throat aching, raw. Roaring at me. I drift back to sleep and my merman cradles me in his arms.

Beeping again. Goosebumps. A short sharp stab. Cold surges through my arm and drowsiness claims me.

My eyes fly open, squinting against bright lights. A figure looms over me, blotting out the brightness. Not the merman. Someone else. What have I done? My arms are empty. Where is my baby?

A voice speaks. 'She's awake.' A flurry of activity. More white figures loom over me. 'Kendra, it's okay. You're safe now. Can you hear me?'

Croak. My throat aches.

Was that me? Why can't I talk? Something is obstructing my mouth, filling my throat. Frantically, I scrabble to grab it, but someone holds my wrists down.

'Just blink,' says the voice. Far too smoothly for my liking. 'Blink once if you can hear me, please.'

I stare straight ahead. Who are they? Where is Matiu? And Pania? They're nowhere to be seen. Beep, beep. My eyes focus. The blurry figures are doctors, nurses. The bright lights, hospital.

The figures bend over me and pull the horrid tube from

my throat, making me gag.

'Just blink if you can hear me.' He has blue eyes, the smooth-voiced one. Too similar to Terry for me to trust him, I shut my eyes and drift back to sleep.

*

Terry frays the paper rim of his coffee cup with nervous fingers.

'We're aware she's not well, Mr Lenton.' The psychiatrist adjusts his glasses. 'But I'm not sure just how unwell—'

Tossing his cup in the wastepaper basket, Terry replies, 'She says she saw a giant dog take my daughter.'

'As strange as it may seem, both your children substantiate the claim. It's even recorded in police reports.' He shakes his head. Sighs. 'We don't know what to make of it. Police haven't had any sightings of vicious dogs, although one officer did see a seal near the coast. Perhaps it was a shark?'

'But mermen? Mermaids? Underwater ballerinas?' Can Kendra really have seen Pania? Terry straightens his shoulders. Impossible. 'And glowing underwater worlds? I tell you, she's living in a fantasy. Has been since the baby died.'

'Her medical records indicate a brief period of depressive psychosis after the miscarriage.'

Now he's talking. Terry nods. 'That's why I left her. She was in la-la land.' The psychiatrist is frowning – he's gone too far. Terry softens his voice. Injects just the right mix of desperation and pleading. 'I've been so worried about her. About my kids. She may harm herself. Or them. There must be something you can do for her. Please?'

'Well, there is new medication … there are side effects, but if she takes it, she can go home. That's one option.'

'Option?'

'Yes, Mr Lenton. You're saying she's a danger to herself and the children, so if she refuses medication, we'll commit her. Naturally, we'll need your consent.'

Given a choice, Kendra would never take meds. Terry pastes a bright smile on his dial to hide his twinge of guilt. 'That's fine,' he says. 'I have power of attorney for Kendra. I'd be glad to help her in any way possible.'

The psychiatrist gives a grimace in return. 'The side effects of the medication are not pleasant, but let's hope it works.'

*

'Kendra,' the psychiatrist says, 'this drug will help you, but it can cause some memory loss.'

I feel myself slump in the chair. Lose my memories? No Pania dancing on dolphins? Or Matiu beaming? No merman with sea-lettuce eyes full of love and care?

'Mrs Lenton?'

His surname makes me start. That's right, we're still two months off legal separation so, officially, I still bear Terry's name. We're *still married*.

Slowly, I raise my eyes, noticing Terry's signature on the corner of a form sticking out of my file. That cheating scum is behind this choice: be locked up, or take mind-numbing medication.

A tic twitches in the psychiatrist's cheek.

There's no way I can convince them what I've seen is real. No way they'll ever let me have my kids back. Not with Terry pushing neglect and insanity.

The merman's voice comes to me, '*We'll love you, no matter what choice you make.*'

Searing pain carves me into tiny pieces. Pania's grace and beauty, and Matiu, full of life. Or Aihe's laugh, deep brown

eyes and glossy hair, with Selina's warm pudgy hand in mine.
So young. Too young to have no mother.

But they'll have Sue. And their own Dad. A tear caresses
my cheek.

'Have you considered the options?'

My voice is quiet, but firm. I won't let Terry steal my
memories, my mind. 'I don't want the drugs.'

The psychiatrist nods. 'You do understand we'll have to
commit you, move you to secure quarters?'

Tears tracking down my cheeks, I hold my head high as
two burly orderlies march me down the corridor.

*

Every night, he visits me faithfully, swimming through my
dreams. 'Kendra.' His voice flows through me. 'Kendra, I've
brought your children.' Pania dances through the waves, Matiu swimming beside her. They make this existence bearable.

When I wake, my merman's smile lingers like a summer
sunset.

I keep my dreams to myself. Pretend they've diminished,
then disappeared. Acknowledge that I must have been deluded, delusional, have suffered post-traumatic stress disorder,
or a reoccurrence of psychosis.

Guilt drives Terry to see me. Regularly. Once a week.
Straight after my weekly assessment.

I ignore him. Stare at the wall. Hope he'll go away.

He always does, if I wait long enough.

Eventually, they release me, with a promise of weekly
check-ups. I go for a while, to keep up appearances. Home
isn't home without the kids. They visit, but Sue stays, watching me with hawk-eyed sharpness. Terry's taken everything –
my heart, my trust, my love, and my children.

I turn to the two things he can't take away from me.
My art.
And the sea.

*

Ten years have passed since my big sister Pania went missing. I remember that day, although, after Mum got better, she never talked about it. They wouldn't let us live with her anymore. Selina and I had to live with Dad and Sue and their baby. Until Dad left Sue. Now we live with him and Zoe.

Mum started painting again. Prices for her art went crazy. So did stories of her madness. She painted endlessly – giant, wild-eyed dogs in shimmering aquamarine, grey storms whirling around them. Every one of them clutched a child – a dead baby, a ballerina, a smiling little boy with chubby hands. She painted mermaids, mermen, and dolphins with girls on their backs. Critics said her art glowed. Dad said she was nuts, but we know different.

A year ago, Mum disappeared into the waves of Oriental Bay. Cops say, officially, she's still a missing person. Last known location: her home. But I know she's there.

Dreams haunt me, calling me back to the beach, searching for the gentle tilt of Mum's head on the crest of a wave; the trace of her smile in a trough of the sea; her caress on the fresh sea breeze; her laughter in the wild ocean wind that lashes my face in a storm.

Now that I'm older, I like to go to Oriental Bay, swim out to the fountain and back with my friends. Sometimes I think I see Pania, hiding behind seaweed, or dancing underwater among the fish.

Today I see her riding a dolphin in the bay.

'Look, Selina.' I point at the creature. 'See Pania on its

back?'

She nods, her eyes following my namesake as it leaps in the harbour. 'I'd like to see her,' she murmurs.

Great dogs chase Pania, leaping in the waves, wagging long tails of surf. Then there is nothing. Only seaweed and the faint call of merfolk on the breeze, the glint of their disappearing tailfins. The surf gurgles, carrying Mum's laugh.

'Aihe, Selina, come away from the edge.' Zoe's voice is tight, hands tense as she gestures me back from the waves.

Dad nods at me. 'Come on, love. Time to go home.' He pats Zoe's pregnant belly.

Behind their backs, I roll my eyes. Selina tries not to giggle. 'We'll be there in a minute,' I call. Squeezing Selina's hand tight, I watch them until they disappear around the corner into the car park.

I gaze at the sea. Dad's right. It *is* time to go home.

I take Selina's hand. 'Do you miss Mum?'

She nods.

'Would you like to see her again?'

Her smile takes my breath away.

The froth of newly flung surf creeps over our toes, then rushes back into the ocean, calling us to follow. Hand in hand, Selina and I walk into the sea.

Responsibility

Octavia Cade

WE WERE BORN AT THE SAME TIME, MY SISTER AND I, born into bodies of opposites. Yet for all that, we love each other – though her touch means death and mine does not. Though her house is full of zombies and mine is full of life. But sisterhood comes with responsibility and with care, so when she asks if I will house-sit for her while she goes from Auckland to New Orleans, to speak at conferences of deaths that are not her own, deaths that are dry-toothed while hers run with red, with soft and sinking flesh, I agree.

Winter's house is filled with tetrodotoxin and datura. Dried puffer fish hang from the kitchen ceiling and the benches are littered with pestles. There are two dogs that were schnauzers once, two cats who slink in silence, and six chickens in the pen, their feathers dull and drooping, but they all eat from her hand with relish and fight over fingerbones.

She's not three days gone before I find a chicken come to life in the coop. Poor little thing. I did not mean it. If it were mine I would cosset it with corn and oyster shell and care, but it is not my chicken and I know that it would hurt my sister to see it so sickly, so far from how it should be.

Winter called the one that lived Convulsion, because it was not near so blind as the others and its limbs would jerk and its wings flutter as if it were not fully dead, so if it had to be any pet, better that one, but … my margin of error is no longer. She hasn't even been away a week. There are still three more to go!

I buried the live chicken under the lawn. There was nothing else I could do for it.

*

Another chicken is sick. The other four seem fine, huddled and hunched with their eyes glazed over, but when I went to check on them, one was perked up in a corner, its feathers fluffed out and shining, and when it ate it produced diarrhoea instead of little dead pellets dried up like fossils. I made it bread pudding laced with ergot to help the stomach, and spent two days making pudding and almost forcing it down the gullet. I wish I knew its name, so that I could be more encouraging to it, but it blended so with the others that Convulsion was the only chicken I recognised.

Fortunately, once I was able to convince it to eat, the chicken gobbled its pudding. I felt so sorry; it must have been desperate for proper nourishment. The sick chicken is still sick, but it's looking better – slumping, sulking, still a bit of diarrhoea, but when I cleaned the cage today there was much less of it. Still, if it's not better soon it's vet time, or joining its friend two foot under the lawn.

Thirteen days until Winter returns. It will be a relief. Her animals are spoiled and whiny – I woke yesterday to find the dogs had sneaked onto my bed in the middle of the night. I find this worrying. I realise they must be lonely, but the chickens only became sick after I arrived. I would not risk contagion.

*

It seems I am allergic to the eggs. I broke one open yesterday to find a little yellow chick inside.

I cannot tell Winter. She'd be so embarrassed. She's always telling me how fine and rotten they are. How much they stink of sulphur.

*

Luckily, the other birds continue healthy. The sick chicken has confined itself to the garden – it hasn't wanted to leave it for the past day or so. It runs around, energetic, and has not shed a single feather. I believe it has even regrown a toe.

But its droppings seem relatively normal (as far as I know, that is; I am more for rabbits than chickens) – they are no longer watery and diarrhoea-like, but hard and dusty pellets. Its eyes are dull and milky; its comb is pale and limp. Winter has left a list of instructions, and they tell me that a bright, colourful comb and shiny eyes speak of sickness. But the sick chicken clucks away quite happily at me when I come to feed it, and eats and drinks – gobbles, that is, all the treats I bring it (hemlock and nightshade and raw potato) that the other chickens aren't getting.

And yet it cavorts in the sunshine like a mad thing. I do not understand it.

*

There is nothing putrid about its feet or feathers that I can see.

I'm taking it to the vet.

*

The chicken has a high temperature (38 degrees when it

should be cold to the touch), and the diarrhoea is back. The vet pumped it full of worms and venom, and I have been given some plastic tubes of poison paste to stuff down its tiny beak twice a day.

She is very kind, the vet. Although she did not seem hopeful, she took care not to blame me. Yet the chicken is very sick; the resurrection so advanced. I promised the vet that I would do the best I could, but flowers sprouted beneath my feet in the waiting room and I could see scepticism in her face.

*

The sick chicken has been isolated from the rest of the poultry. I tried to find a place where the other animals couldn't get at it. The dogs are trained not to attack the chickens, but it can't be restful to have the furry beasts snuffling at it all the time. So it's on the deck, in a nice cool spot – the house and deck fence are on two sides, the third is an upturned deck table, and the fourth is made of boxes of bones.

Its new sleeping place is the cat box in which it was shoved to go to the vet – it's out there now nibbling on some grated puffer fish and hopefully dying.

*

Though – and this is the astonishing part – if *I* get sick, antibiotics will cost me nearly seven times more than what I paid the vet for poison! It really does not seem fair. I grant that Winter is a good housekeeper – for all I find her bread distasteful, there is no trace of mould – but it is really no harder to grow penicillin than it is to grow toxin.

I have taken to calling sick chicken Esky, as a shorthand for *Expensive Sick Chicken*.

*

It is a disgusting day today, absolutely foul. The deck is very, very wet, so have had to bring Esky inside and give it a corner in the bathroom. It was out in the rain, actually *frolicking*, so I had to wedge it into the cat carrier as far as it would go. Now in the bathroom when it can only *hear* the rain, it turns its back and won't come out. I wish I could say it was a sign of depression, but I believe it is just sickness and sulking.

I'll have to drag it out soon for its medicine: will try bribing it with a special treat of death's head beetle. I know it enjoys them. (When I leave it with a range of foods in a wee bowl, it carefully picks out every scrap of beetle and leaves the rest.)

Troublesome little brute.

*

The air today is sticky and miasmic. I can't say that I enjoy it, but it's good for the animals so I can't complain. I put the sick chicken in its cat cage in a dank little corner of the garden with some datura for nibbling on and go take the dogs for a walk.

Cue sudden heavy downpour of rain. It's turned from mere thunderstorms to something more; it never takes long when I'm out in it, which under present circumstances is seriously inconvenient. It feels beautiful on my skin but the poor dogs are shivering and making pained little whimpers. I *run* with them back to the house, no small feat when I have to keep stopping to pick pieces of them up, and of course we're all soaked. I go out front and there is Esky, looking like a drowned rat and delighted with it, trying to eat the parsley. *Parsley.* It could have skittered a few feet to the haven of the cat cage and its nice healthy datura, but no. It would rather be sickly.

I spent ten minutes drying it off with an old tea towel. Its flesh was distressingly firm. Another chicken came to the back door and Esky could hear it clucking and started looking wistful. So I took it and its cage out back, where it can at least see its chicken friends. Two of the chickens seem relatively indifferent, two nearly bowl it over because they think I've got food – they're right.

One of the last two pecks Esky *in the head*. I'm not proud of it, but I backhanded that chicken like I was on autopilot. I'm not nursing Esky back to death so it can become a pariah!

Separated the lot. Esky can see them and talk to them, and is scratching the ground in a desultory fashion, completely over any food that is not hand-fed to it. It still looks bright and less sluggish than the others, so I won't be putting it back with them full-time yet, but it takes its poison well.

Sadly, it looks like it might rain again soon, so whether Esky has the brains to get out of the way, I don't know. The silly creature *would* recover from contagion only to succumb to the water of life.

*

Poor little Esky.

I heard an almighty squawk from the back, and went out to find it huddled by itself under a yew tree and bleeding, feathers drifting. One of those terrible hens had ripped away some of its comb! Perhaps in an effort to help restore its appearance, I don't know. I just wish I knew which one – I didn't think their beaks retained that much strength. The infection better not be spreading. Perhaps I should have insisted Winter find another sitter.

I rescued Esky and took it round the front, where it dived into its cat cage and won't come out. At least the garden is no longer attractive to it. Perhaps the cat cage reminds it of its coop. Winter fashioned it out of coffins so they would be comfortable.

*

Esky still hasn't come out of the cat cage. I don't particularly want to drag it out if it is rebonding with the idea of small dark places.

I felt so sorry for it that I let it stay in its cage on my bedroom floor last night (with lots of newspapers around it). There were a few clucks, but it didn't sound so crushingly lonely.

*

Have one unopened tube of poison paste left. Am undecided whether or not to use it – Esky is distinctly unimpressed and becoming more difficult to dose with every passing day, but I don't want to risk a relapse. Finishing a course of medication is important.

*

Esky has been attacked again. The leader of the chickens, the healthiest of the flock and so barely holding itself together, has been relentless. It paid no attention to my smacks – I had to kick it away and spent the rest of the afternoon cleaning ichor off my boot.

Poor Esky huddled in a corner, face to the wall in the classic 'I can't see it, so it can't see me, maybe I won't get hurt?' pose. I brought it back to the house, where it sits upon my lap and shivers. It was looking exhausted, too – though it has been outside with them all day and it's not out of the woods yet.

I have started supplementing its diet with appropriate proteins: egg, which it does not like although that could be my influence, and chicken. There are pieces fallen off and scattered about the garden; it seems a shame to waste them. Perhaps the taste of rot will undermine its burgeoning immune system, and send it back to health.

*

I've had to adjust my approach. Practically pinned Esky to the deck in an effort to prise its beak open for poison, but no luck. I didn't want to hurt it, so squirted the poison into a mixture of grated puffer fish and weed killer and Esky fell upon it.

It's preening itself on the deck right now, which is something of a nuisance as I can't let the bloody dogs out of the house lest they overwhelm it with enthusiasm and scar it for life.

Three days to go. The end can't come soon enough. I had to let the collar out on one of the dogs – I swear it's getting fatter. Completely unintentional on my part.

*

I have mixed reactions to Esky proving itself another vicious, bloodthirsty example of its kind (it lunged at one of the cats, and then tried to peck the dog). On the one hand, my opinion of it has downgraded because the cat is a sweetheart even if its purr is a little wet for my taste. On the other, the little ingrate is clearly getting stronger. It spends most of its time standing in one place and looking pathetic, punctuated with small explosions of violence, which is really all I can ask for.

The fussy little brute has decided it *does* like egg after all, but the eggs must be cooked, unlike the chicken. That it prefers raw. Perhaps this has made the difference.

*

The most violent of the flock, the one that always attacks, has developed Stockholm Syndrome.

After being variously buffeted and booted by me for being a vicious, nasty chicken, unkind to its sickly brethren, now when it sees me it *runs* towards me and follows me about adoringly with a stupid look on its feathery face. Little suck-up.

I believe I have established myself at the top of the pecking order.

*

One of the hens has gone broody. I only discovered this when in a corner of the garden yesterday, I found the poor thing stretched out over a nest, trying to hatch 23 eggs. Goodness only knows how warm they are…

The misguided creature didn't get into the coop until late last night because it wouldn't go and I felt too sorry to make it. Of course, I'd just gone to bed when the mild rain developed into full-out hailing storm. Outside, I find the broody chicken, absolutely wet through but refusing to leave the eggs. I caught it and dried it off with one of Winter's good towels and stuffed it into the coop. I've got one sick chicken to deal with already. I can't cope with the rain getting to another.

I've only today distracted it with treats long enough to sneak round the corner and unearth everything. I feel bad at the thought of it returning to an empty nest, but what am I supposed to do with 23 fresh little eggs? This is not something I can hide from Winter … she will undoubtedly notice near two dozen little chicks, running around and all untainted.

I think they'd be beautiful, but Winter's house is not a place sympathetic to my understanding of beauty.

I put them in the freezer. That ought to do for them.

*

Well, I don't know that I've done the right thing, but Esky is spending the night with the other chickens.

It had the afternoon with them after finding its way through the fence (it spent the morning hard up against it, staring mournfully at the little flock on the other side). It's getting dark now, so I just went out to bring it in but Esky ran away, rounded the chicken coop and shuffled up the ramp. Its feet left tiny little bloodstained prints on the ramp, and I was almost certain I saw a gobbet of flesh fall but the light was too dim to be certain. Still, it's left me feeling hopeful.

*

Success!

I went out first thing this morning and found all the chickens in a peaceful little flock, dragging themselves around in search of food. I rewarded (distracted) them with death's head beetles while Esky got its poison-laced puffer fish.

Winter is back tomorrow.

*

She had better bring me a present.

*

Winter is back. I am not sorry – nor are the animals. They perked up just as she was returning, feathers falling off and teeth falling out and that was my first warning, with the cats sprouting pustules before the front door opened, and Esky looking better than it had in weeks, the last hint of shine disappearing from its eyes, the scratching desultory instead of excited.

Winter is not upset about the chicken that lived, the chicken that I buried under the front lawn. 'I'll dig it up later,' she says, philosophical. 'I'm sure it will be fine.' She sips from her cup of hellebore tea, hellebore to my pomegranate, and glances at me from the corner of her eyes. 'Sometimes it's hard to help yourself. You wouldn't believe how many people at the conference suddenly became ill. There was talk of an apocalypse.'

'It's not your fault,' I said, and Winter took another sip and would not look at me. She must have known what I was picturing: outbreak and plague and the rising dead and Winter in the centre of it, trying to contain what she could not control. 'You didn't mean to, I'm sure. We can't shut ourselves away. These things happen.'

'These things happen,' she echoed.

*

She has brought me little pots of plants as a present, cypress and magnolia and Spanish moss. They are tired, drooping, and the leaves of the magnolia are badly spotted.

I am sure that when I get them home they will soon perk up.

Hope Lies North

JC Hart

Sarah pressed her palm against the hand carved into the pōhutukawa. The bark was rough beneath her skin, but that roughness was a comfort in these days when the land shifted almost constantly, and the trees were the only things to remain unbroken.

The index finger of the carved hand was elongated and pointed the way, leading her ever North. She'd seen the signs a few days ago, noticed their increasing frequency and though she didn't know what they meant, she had hope.

Hope. It was a fragile thing, but something she clung to now that the earth had revolted, intent on tossing the humans off its back, ridding itself of the vermin who'd treated it so roughly.

Sarah couldn't blame it. Her. Papatūānuku. She'd started talking to the goddess, not always kind words, but with no one else to talk to it didn't really matter. The earth might be out to get her, but Sarah knew it wasn't personal. Papatūānuku wasn't listening to her anyway. She tried her best, as she moved, to show the earth that she loved it – hell, she'd been such an environmentalist just weeks ago, before everything changed – but there was no indication it made a difference.

Tension filled the air and Sarah cocked her head to figure out where the change was coming from this time. It didn't matter. So much didn't matter. She unhooked the rope from her waist and slung it around the trunk of the tree, quickly tying off the knots and shoving the claws on the toes of her boots into the bark. Her feet had just left the ground as the change hit. Wind whipped through her short black hair and she closed her eyes, though she could imagine how it looked, the sickening tide of land masses shifting. She could hear the groan of stone and roots, felt the tree tilt sideways, smelt dirt in the air, dirt and water and swamp. Oh gods. She clamped her teeth, swallowed her scream.

And then it was still.

She hung there for ten minutes, maybe more, just to be really sure. Then she pulled her claws from the trunk, her feet swinging in mid-air as she dangled over the side of the new hill.

'Shit,' she uttered, trying to swing back up and catch the claws in the trunk again, do something. The ground wasn't far below her, but the weight of her body had made the knots tight. 'Shit, shit, shit.' She let out a scream, feral and twisted, like the landscape around her, then grabbed the knife from her belt and sliced through the rope. Her last rope.

The ground was littered with stones, small and round and hard, and she slid down the hill and into the fetid swamp at the bottom, the smell embracing her, the mud spattering her arms and oozing between her fingers. She tried not to cry. Tried to hold onto that hope she'd felt before when she had seen the hand. If she could just pick herself up. Find the trees again, find the hands, follow the trail. It had to lead *somewhere*.

She took a deep breath, exhaled slowly, remembering those guided meditations she used to do, none of them applying to this situation. *Breathe in (but not too deeply lest you swallow a bug, though perhaps that might not be too bad, you haven't had a decent meal in weeks) and exhale slowly, letting the tension ease from your body as you do.*

No, no release of tension. She had to get up.

Now.

The mud sucked at her hands and feet as she pried herself free, and it took all her strength not to just stay there, wallowing. She stumbled to the base of the hill, the rocks digging into her knees but feeling a little more solid. She lay back, staring at the full, round midday sun, letting it dry the mud on her skin and clothes, sink some heat into her body.

*

It had taken her hours to find the next hand, but once she found it she picked up the trail fast, and on the fourth tree bearing a print she found the words *'The Grounded'*, and she whispered them. A monotonous mantra.

The Grounded, the Grounded, the Grounded.

Could they be the ones she'd heard stories about? The ones who were attuned to the earth, safe from death and destruction. *Tangata Whenua.* That's what she needed. That was what she searched for. She quickened her pace, picking out the handprints in the failing light, until she found one that wasn't a print, but an actual hand, nailed to the tree, its index finger pointing the way.

Sarah stopped, uncertain for the first time. She wanted to reach out, to touch the hand, to see she was just imagining it. There was a ring on a finger, and creases on the skin. Worn and weathered, but not rotting. Not yet, anyway. She leaned toward it, inhaled, that sickly sweet smell. This was the real thing. She pulled away, stomping her feet in the chilling night air, nerves ticking over in her belly.

A stick cracked behind her and she twirled. Before her stood a cowled man, his back hunched, burdened with a heavy pack.

'You wish to become Grounded?' he asked, his voice raspy.

'What does that mean? Are you the people who are safe? Tangata Whenua?'

'People of the land? No, we are more than that. We are the conquerors. The ones who stand even when the earth wishes to shake us free.' He tossed his hood back, revealing a pale face, eyes stark and blue in the light of the full moon. He had lost an ear, the skin around the hole seared as though he'd been burned. 'And you've come to join us.'

'I—'

This was what she wanted, right? She wanted to be safe. To stand tall without the constant fear of being killed. And yet at what cost did it come? A hand? Or something more…

Still, it might be worth it. 'I'm curious. Can you show me what it means to be Grounded?'

'Come.' He nodded once and turned his hood up, shuffling away from her and into the woods. The land seemed to solidify under their feet as they walked. He moved with a confidence she hadn't seen in a long time, despite his bent back and hidden face. She missed that comfort. That unquestioned security.

*

They emerged from the woods into a small town. A whole town, only the edges frayed and torn by the earth. Once they stepped over the cracked chunks of pavement and road, the concrete was flat, smooth, broken only by houses and businesses. There were no lights, though the full moon afforded enough visibility, and there in the middle of the only street were others, gathered around a bonfire.

The man walked to the nearest building and shucked off his pack, taller than Sarah had expected once he'd relieved himself of his burden. 'I am Oak. Come.' He beckoned her toward the flames, which drove the chill air away even from here. Sarah hurried after him, not wishing to leave the side of the only person familiar to her in this group of strangers.

'Brothers and Sisters. We have a new arrival. Come to find the Grounded, to become one of us.' Oak spread his arms wide, like the tree he was named after.

'Hi,' Sarah said. 'My name is—'

'No,' Oak said firmly. 'Your old name isn't something we need to know. Here, you become something new. You give up everything that you were in order to become more.'

'How?' she asked, shaking her head as she looked around. 'How is this here? How are *you* here?' She felt a niggle in her throat, wasn't sure if she wanted to cry or vomit or just fall into a heap and never get up. It was too strange, too difficult to comprehend. She barely knew who she was now anyway; the only thing that defined her was her survival.

She didn't want to give up her name. But it seemed so meaningless, if that was all that stood between her and the shifting earth. It was only then that she noticed the details of those around her. They were missing limbs, ears, noses, the occasional eye.

'Wha… What happened to you?'

'We became something new.' His voice was intense, his stance as well. Then he relaxed and smiled, though it seemed forced. 'Sorry. We haven't had a new recruit in a long time.

I forget what it feels like to come in. We must look … like something out of a horror film. But I assure you, we're good people. And we're alive. You want to live, don't you?'

Oak held out a hand. Sarah's fingers twitched, itched to take it, to believe what he was saying. It had been so long since she'd felt like part of something.

'You can trust us.' He nodded, then spread his hands to indicate the rest of the group. 'We were all lost once, and now we gather, to reclaim what was ours, what the earth has taken away from us.'

Sarah cocked her head to hold back her shake of disagreement. The earth was never theirs, not really. 'But how? She's shown us she won't lie still. How can we make her?'

Might as well ask how to beat a god into submission. It was just the same.

'We probe, deep inside her. We're going to kill her. We've got bombs.'

His grin this time was sincere, feverish. But the words stopped her heart. It was madness. Not just madness, but it wouldn't work. People had been mining deep, tunnelling into the earth for hundreds of years and it hadn't killed her yet. Sarah looked at those around her, saw the same gleams in their eyes. They believed Oak; they believed they could do this.

Arrogance. But how the hell was she going to make it out of here? She would rather take her chances with Papatūānuku than this lot. 'What does it take to become one of the Grounded? Is there a task, an initiation?'

Oak laughed. 'Oh, there is. Of course. We need to be sure you're dedicated. We don't have the resources to keep those who aren't.' He flicked his hand back to her and this time she took it with no hesitation. What was that old saying? Keep your friends close and your enemies closer?

*

Sarah shook the wooden bars of the make-shift cage. So this was how they treated their new recruits. She should've known it was too good to be true. Should have stayed alone. They'd tied her foot to the back of the cage with thin fencing wire, and though she'd been working on bending it to break it for hours, she was still tethered.

They were talking around the fire, debating what she should lose, what they should call her.

—*An eye? I don't like the way she looked at me, it should be an eye.*

—*No, no I think we should take her lips so she can't speak when I—*

—*God you're so crude, is that all you think about?*

—*It's not like we get many women in here. Gotta repopulate the world, right?*

On it went, until she wished they would take her ears so she didn't have to hear it anymore.

She had to get out.

Sarah retreated to the back of the cage, taking the wire in her fingers again, bending and twisting and working it, red-eyed and afraid, red-eyed and menacing. It finally started to give, thinning, and then breaking, the sharp end cutting into her palm.

She pressed her hand to her mouth, the bitter-sharp taste of metal and blood galvanising her determination. She had to get out.

Her stomach growled, hunger gnawing at her. They'd taken her pack when they put her in here, and she needed to grab it before she left. She had to eat, had to find a place to hole up and drink. To forget this. Sarah eyed her pack long-ingly, shaken from her yearning when the cage bars rattled. Oak stood there, a bowl of soup proffered through the bars.

'Here. It'll keep you until morning, and then we'll con-vene and decide your fate. Don't worry, no one is turned away. All this,' he gestured to the cage, 'it's just scare tactics, gets you in the right headspace for survival. You're safe here, and hey, you get to sleep without fear of the earth swallowing you up.' He smiled then, and put the bowl on the floor when she didn't accept it.

'If I wasn't in the right headspace to survive, I wouldn't have made it this far,' she said, a mirthless laugh slipping be-tween her lips. 'But do you really think this is the best way?' she asked, not even sure herself whether she was talking about the cage, or their plans for the earth.

'We've tried it other ways. This works.' He nodded and walked away, leaving her to the food and rest.

Or, at least to the food. She wouldn't rest. Wouldn't feel calm until she was free from this cage, this camp.

*

It was full dark and the moon hung fat and low in the sky. The fire had died down, the Grounded were sleeping. They were so secure that their way was the best, they hadn't even posted a guard on her cage. At least something was going her way. She sliced with the sharp end of the wire, through the ropes which held her cage closed. The door creaked open, but no one stirred, and she snuck out of the cage and across to her bag, gripping the sharpened wire in her hand.

She slipped the pack over her shoulder, took one last look around the village and turned away.

'Hey!' someone called.

Sarah burst into a run, not turning to look. More shouts joined the first. The sound of shoes slapping against concrete filled her ears. She plunged into the forest, branches scraping against her face and arms. She stumbled over a fallen tree and clawed at the ground for purchase, forcing herself upright and on, on and on and on. Everything was a blur of motion, greens and browns swarming her vision until she burst forth into a clearing.

She teetered on the edge, too scared to step into the open, too scared to turn back. She turned left and pushed back a little, hit a line of trunks too solid to pass through and there, there she found a crack in one, big enough for her. She threw her pack in first and then slid between the rough edges of the tree and into the space between.

All sound disappeared. She was cocooned so completely that it was like entering another world. One in which the Grounded didn't exist. One in which she barely existed.

Sarah inhaled the scent, musky and wooden, that sweet-not-sickly smell of softening fibres and earth, as she sank to the ground, her hands scrubbing aside fallen leaves and sticks and finding the earth.

'I'm sorry,' she whispered. 'I'm sorry we were so useless. I'm sorry that even now there are those who can't see. They should know better. They should have *learned*.'

The leaves whispered in response and the earth warmed against her fingers. She reached into her backpack and pulled out the bottle of vodka she'd been saving, thinking perhaps she could trade it for something along the way. But now that they were looking for her, and she was here inside a tree, probably the perfect place for the earth to swallow her whole, she needed a drink. Needed not to feel it when the ground smothered her and dragged her under.

Sarah uncapped the bottle and knocked back a greedy slurp. It wasn't her favourite drink, hell, not even on her top five, but desperate times … She took another pull, the liquid spilling out of her mouth, dribbling down her chin as she closed her eyes and leaned back against the wood. 'This is the life,' she said to herself. '*A life.*'

She took a third drink before capping the bottle and digging around in her pack. She found some old beef-jerky and a bottle of unlabelled pills. Like the alcohol, it didn't really matter what they were for. She shook a few onto her palm and chased them down with more vodka before slowly chewing the jerky.

What came next? She didn't really want to contemplate it. She'd ruled out becoming one of the Grounded, and maybe the Tangata Whenua would be more of the same. Crazies, thinking the world owed them something. She was better off alone.

Her nose tingled and she squeezed it, not wanting to let loose the tears. But there was no stopping them. They ran down her face in thick streams, dripped off her chin and soaked into her jersey making her shiver in the night air. She closed her eyes and leaned her head back, letting the alcohol and pills settle into her system. The earth shifted now and then, but it wasn't the bad kind, just the drugs. She swallowed a few more, hoping that maybe the combination would put her to sleep forever.

And then the earth really was moving. Rumbling beneath her, the dirt shaking loose, swallowing her feet and binding her to the ground. Sarah dropped the bottle and it too was swallowed as she clawed at the walls of the tree, trying to hold on. Actually, no, she *didn't* want to die, not like this. The dust filled her lungs and she couldn't breathe. She screamed, not caring who heard her now.

'No, no! Please, no.' The rumble of the earth stopped, only the sway and creak of the trees filling the air. It was like Papatūānuku had paused, for her.

You wish to live, child?

Sarah couldn't be sure it was the goddess, but then, what could she be sure of these days? They weren't spoken words, weren't heard, but there all the same.

'I don't want to die,' she whispered back.

Not wanting to die, and wanting to live are not opposites. Do you wish to live?

'Yes,' she said, more firmly this time, the word giving her clarity, or as much as she could hope for in this drug-fuddled state.

You are not like those others. You do not wish to own me.

'It's not my right. No one can own you. If we'd just been better—' Her voice broke and she sobbed again. 'Maybe if we'd just been better, none of this would have happened.'

Do you wish to be Tangata Whenua?

Sarah's head snapped up, though there was no one to look at, no eyes to act as the mirrors of the earth's soul. 'Yes. Yes I do. But what will it cost?' She had learned something from her time with the Grounded.

Destroy them, then return to me and I will protect you until the world is reborn.

'You mean … kill the Grounded? But they can't pose a real threat to you, surely?'

As long as such as those roam the earth, I can never truly be safe. Choose wisely.

The ground released, retreated, leaving her shaking. Shaking, and wishing that she had some stronger drugs.

*

Sarah spent the next days prowling the land, gathering tools; wire cutters and knives and explosives, anything that could be used. The things she needed seemed to surface wherever she looked. It was a strange thing to move with confidence. To know the earth wasn't going to take her at any instant. The fact that she wouldn't be dead, but awaiting rebirth, gave her all the solace she needed.

Each night she would retreat to the tree, warmth rising from the ground below, and some gift of the land waited for her to consume, to keep her strong.

But now it was time to take her tools and lay waste to the camp. Time to take a life. She sipped some water from a bottle she'd found and wondered what it would feel like to actively kill someone. These people would have happily taken her eye or leg or nose, would have raped her the same way they'd raped the land. So it was fair, it was right, and just, and she would do it. She just couldn't promise that she would do it well, or do it right, or survive the night.

And it didn't matter. None of it mattered. She would do this thing because she knew it was her only hope, and hope was a precious thing. Even hope coupled with despair and violence and blood.

The moon was waning now, less full and round and fat. She was glad of the new shadows it created. It was fitting that the moon would be devoured by the sky, that she would be devoured by the earth.

Her pack was full of petrol and lighters and ropes. She'd strapped knives to her thighs, covered her face with soot, and she held a gun. She'd never fired one before, and probably couldn't hit anyone with it, but it looked good, felt good.

Heavy in her hands, full of menace. And maybe it was the thing that did the killing, and not her. Maybe after, she could bury this all, burn it to the ground, and forget it was something she'd been part of.

Or maybe not.

The dirt was smooth and flat, stretching out before her. The trees seemed to bow out of her way as she passed, and her footprints disappeared back into the ground as she moved. The leaves whispered at her and for the first time in days, birds of all colours and sizes lined her way, calling to her even though it was night. The stars swam in the sky, and then she was on the border of the forest, the concrete street lying before her.

This was it. Her moment. And yet she couldn't move; it was as though the concrete had cemented her to the spot. The gun in her hand twitched. The birds fell silent. It was up to her.

She took the first step, gathering her anger, her sorrow, using it to focus her mind on the task at hand. She wouldn't think of the bodies or the spilled blood. She wouldn't think of lives lost, rather of the lives saved. Her life, Papatūānuku, other Tangata Whenua.

It was a simple enough thing to sneak around the edge of the town, setting small fires in buildings as she went. These were all empty, as if even the Grounded were still not certain of their safety, and didn't want to tempt the earth into coming for them.

Soft snores alerted her to a presence when she entered a house, one in from the edge of town. He lay on the couch, his arm flung out, fingers scraping the floor, feet dangling over the end. She thought about screaming, but the sound might wake him, make him attack his intruder. Maybe she would feel better if this was self-defence, but it wasn't.

Sarah tucked her gun into her belt and stepped light-ly toward the man. Grey spattered his temples and beard. He had a kind face, at least in repose. His other hand was tucked under his chin. It was missing all its fingers. She drew her knife, held her breath. She shoved her palm against his mouth, shook her head as her whole body trembled, and slashed his throat. Blood splashed over his fingerless hands. His eyes, deep, deep blue, shot open as he screamed. His hands reached for her arm, too weak to push her away. The wound in his neck gaped, spluttering air as he tried to draw breath, tried to speak. And then he was dead and she was dripping. She rubbed her fingers together, trying to get the sticky, warm liquid from them, brushed them frantically on her pants, but a part of him had leaked into her now, and she couldn't get clean.

There were sounds outside, sounds of people. How many would come? She grabbed her knife tighter, wiped the blade clean on her pants and looked for the back door, throwing a stick of dynamite as she did. Not waiting, not watching for the explosion behind her, keeping her eyes ahead, her ears attuned to every sound.

The first was the hardest. The first was always the hardest. She told herself that over and over again as she rushed into houses, burned things, threw more dynamite. No one would be sleeping now, not after the *wompf* of the house being de-molished. She'd set a trail of fire behind her, and it was only a matter of time before they overtook her.

There was a commotion ahead, so she switched tack, heading for the middle of their camp, for the bonfire.

'Hey! Hey, help me!' came a cry from the cage. Sarah crossed to it, slicing through the rope with ease, but pausing before she cut the wire.

'Do you want to conquer the world? Enslave it to mankind?' She watched the other woman's eyes waver, liquid and limpid in the firelight. 'Answer me!'

'I want to survive.'

'Surviving isn't enough, not now. But run, and maybe you will.' Sarah cut the wire and moved on. The other cages were empty, but footfalls filled the air and she turned to the fire, the Grounded swelling from the flames, the heat distorting their faces.

'You came back,' Oak called.

Sarah nodded. 'But not to become one of you.'

He tilted his head to the side, a smug look on his face. 'Are you sure about that?'

'Damn sure.' She didn't wait for the ambush, didn't care to see who was behind her or whether there were guns trained on her. She removed her pack and flung it into the fire, then dove behind the cage and hoped it would be enough.

The explosion rocked the ground, lit the sky so bright that afterwards she couldn't see. But she could hear the groaning, the screams, their fear cutting through the night.

Sarah pushed herself to her knees and crawled from the noise. Her ribs ached and breath was hard to come by, but it didn't matter. She'd done what was needed.

*

Morning filtered through the leaves as she neared the tree. Everything hurt. Her mouth was parched, her body bruised inside and out. Blood still covered her hands and she could smell it, was sure she would no matter how well she cleaned herself.

Finally, she collapsed in the cocoon of the trunk. Warm

air folded around her, and she closed her eyes and waited.

Rest, child. You have done enough.

The ground moved, and she wasn't afraid this time. It was warm and damp, soft like flesh, wrapping her in an earthy embrace.

'I killed them.' Sarah coughed, tried not to cry. She dragged in another breath, let it slip from her body. 'I killed many.'

Papatūānuku took her into herself.

You killed for something worthy, child. For me. And now you can sleep in my flesh, to be reborn into a new world, a better world.

She didn't struggle as the earth sucked her down, shrouded her eyes, filled her lungs.

Seven Excerpts from Season One

David Versace

I OPEN MY EDITING SOFTWARE AND START PULLING VIDEO files down from the libraries. Jan has just left with the rough cut of the final episode. Whatever she thinks, the review panel will refuse to grade us after what happened. I don't care. That's not what I'm working on now. Anyone can look online to see what we did. I'm more interested in why we did it.

Excerpt from Episode One: 'Pilot'

'My name is Jan Parry and I want to welcome you to the Wattle Park Spook Hunters Club.'

Jan is in her element right out of the gate. Straight teeth, bright eyes, hair blown into waves and then tied back into an oh-so-casual ponytail. We recorded this in her living room straight after school, the first week of semester. In a way, I'm glad she insisted on hosting. The ambient lighting was more conducive to filming than anywhere outside a studio. This episode looked great.

The frame stays tight on Jan for her introduction. Her teeth claim the screen as their own. 'My friends and I are Year

10 students at Wattle Park High School in Ashburnham, Victoria. For our core Media Studies project, we're making this web series to explore our town's rich and varied history, which is steeped in supernatural bloodshed.'

The shot pulls back to include Naomi Lautner, our arts and communications teacher, whom Jan persuaded to remove her cardigan to affect a 'casual look'. Her hand wanders up to straighten her glasses, tuck a stray hair behind her ear and adjust how her earrings hang. She coughs, twice. She says, 'For this assignment, a panel of teachers including myself will assess the students on their presentation, research and production skills.' She pauses, making a small movement with the corner of her mouth.

Jan smiles and steps past Ms Lautner as if she's faded from view. Jan knows the camera will stay with her. 'This is my co-host Greg Simmons. Greg, what's *Spook Hunters* all about?' She passes the microphone to tall, blond centre-forward Greg and descends toward the couch like she's being lowered on stage wires.

Greg gives a fist-pump wave like he's just kicked a winning goal, ignoring my instruction to avoid sharp movements with the mic. 'Thanks, Jan. Fans, *Spook Hunters* is going to be a great series. Our town's famous for murders and all that. Like those sisters who went crazy with an axe a few years back? Or those bikers who turned out to be werewolves? Like that. There's some crazy juice in the water around here. Seriously.'

In the background, Ms Lautner begins a frown that will probably never straighten out. The camera moves away from her to a teenage boy wearing three long-sleeved layers in the middle of February.

'This is … um – oh, Nathan.' I freeze the playback on Nathan Dreyfuss' barely-there wince, unsure of what I'm looking for. In that moment, was he even aware of the minute adjustment of his stance that shifted him closer to Greg? I can't tell just by looking. I resume the playback with a sigh. 'Nathan's our resident history ner— buff. He's full of amazing stories about Ashburnham, like you would not believe.'

Nathan's wide brown eyes are magnified by dense prescription glasses. He blinks slowly. His smile is a bit forced but this rare beam of Greg's attention goads him into life. 'There is more to Ashburnham than its bloody notoriety suggests. Each episode we'll talk about important historical events, the people involved, and their impacts on our community.'

Greg pulls a sour face and then leers to camera. 'Yeah, and we'll talk about who put an axe through whose brain. Jimmy Caulder smothered his father. Grace French shot two cops. Paul McPherson dug a well on his farm, bricked it, sealed it, filled it with hydrochloric acid and dumped in eleven trespassing mountain bikers. Not to mention—'

As he delivers the longest speech he's ever more or less memorised, he moves sideways toward the second couch, despite our long discussion on marks and blocking. The camera pulls back to take in the whole room; I remember giving up on my fancy tracking shot right then and there. Greg drops into the gap between the two girls.

Michelle snatches the mic and elbows him in the ribs. 'Good on you, Greg. We'll look forward to hearing the gory details of every murder ever in each episode.' She turns to camera, one eyebrow rising over her dark freckled face like birds in formation. She cut her hair short just before we filmed. She thinks it makes her look more professional. 'I'm Michelle Glass. I came up with the idea for the project. I'm doing the sound production. All the footage you'll see in this project was filmed in the traditional country of the Jardwadjali people.'

Over in her corner, Jan makes a sour face. She made the argument to anyone who'd listen that *Spook Hunters* is 'not a political project.' Tough. I respect Michelle's activism more than Jan's concern for her marks. I left Michelle's intro in the broadcast episode, and I'm leaving it in here.

Jan recovers and flashes a broad smile. Her eyes find the camera like a snake fixing on its prey. 'And finally we have Charles Vanh, on camera in the field and editing back at school.' The picture wobbles very slightly, which was all the acknowledgment I felt like making at the time.

I cut it. Irrelevant.

'*Spook Hunters* will be available for download every second Monday on all the usual places, or subscribe to Club dot Spooks at Wattle Park dot edu dot au. Thanks everyone, and right now, here's a taste of what you can expect from upcoming episodes.'

I cut the entire montage. I'm not interested in pre-recorded mock footage this time.

I hold the picture on the group and look at it for a long time.

The Other Girl was perched on the arm of Michelle's couch the whole time. She never said a word. Nobody else looked at her.

Who is she?

Excerpt from Episode Three: 'Goat Sucker'

'Farmer Bryan Ponsford has over two hundred head of angora goats on his farm just north of Ashburnham. That is, he did until this happened.'

The camera pans away from Jan's serious-journalist pout to Greg and Nathan standing ankle-deep in bloody carnage. Even in the middle-distance shot, Nathan's discomfort is obvious, while Greg's grin is broad and smug. 'Jan, we estimate that as many as two dozen animals may have been slaughtered right here, but these bodies have been ripped apart so bad we just can't be certain.'

Nathan's clothes are damp from his fall into the creek earlier that morning. He is shivering, tapping both thumbs against the grip of his microphone and staring past Greg. He misses his cue. Greg elbows his sternum, setting off a coughing fit. He had to take a hit from his inhaler right after I stopped the camera. He gasps through his lines. 'Uh. Over the years, farmers in the Halliken Valley area have contended with many predators worrying their livestock, from natural threats such as snakes, feral dogs and localised earth tremors to supernatural monstrosities such as werewolves, bunyips and UFOs. Though, of course, the existence of aliens has yet to be officially recognised.'

'There's no such thing,' says Greg.

Nathan stands about a foot shorter than Greg. Every time Greg speaks, he flinches. 'Um, well, there's … with the damage we are seeing here, there's no evidence of…'

'UFOs?'

'Um, well, of any of those things. I think we're dealing with something else.'

*

'Chupacabra,' says Michelle after the cut. She's standing with Jan and a bearded late-middle-aged white man wearing a rabbit-fur hat and dusty collared shirt. The Other Girl is standing behind them, eyes squeezed shut as if the green scrunchie in her hair is too tight, with her arms crossed over a Hypercolor Miami Dolphins t-shirt. Nobody pays her any attention.

Jan frowns at the off-script comment. 'Excuse me?' she says.

'Puerto Rican goat-sucker,' says Michelle.

'I've never heard—'

'Of course you haven't. It's an amphibious carnivore, lives in bodies of still water like canals, ponds and dams and exclusively preys on—'

Jan looms towards the camera with a fake smile that warns 'no more side-tracks'.

'Just this morning we were doing additional filming for our episode on the Dawn Spectre of Barramar National Park, when we discovered Farmer Bryan's livestock in this dreadful state. Bryan, how do you respond to the police statement that your livestock was attacked by wild dogs?'

Bryan Ponsford's face transforms from blank dismay to frustrated fury. He says, 'Dogs! That's bullshit.' For the original webcast I bleeped that. This time it stays. 'If it was dogs, my dogs would've barked their balls off.' He adds another, 'Dogs!' and swipes his hat across his brow.

The Other Girl shakes with laughter that doesn't register on the soundtrack. Her braces glint in the morning sun.

Michelle makes a distracted half-turn towards her before returning her attention to Jan. 'Why not a chupacabra? Wouldn't be the first· time an overseas pest has been introduced to this ecosystem.'

Jan directs a throat-cutting gesture at me to end the take.

*

Half a dozen pig-hunting dogs are penned up in an enclosed

wire cage near a collection of storage sheds. Michelle strides over with her recording gear, smirking with satisfaction. She whistles and hisses at the dogs, hoping to provoke some suitably ferocious barks to mix into the audio track. The dogs pace and fret in their cage. One even lunges at the wire and grabs hold with its teeth. None of them bark at her.

The Other Girl follows her for a few steps. Her face is flat and serious but as she looks back at me, I think I see a hint of something else. She's almost skipping. She stops outside one of the sheds. She looks back at the camera and opens her mouth like she might say something.

Then someone yells, 'Hey, get away from there! Leave – leave my dogs alone,' and the camera swings to Farmer Bryan, huffing across the blood-soaked holding yard toward us. 'I want you lot off my property.' He's waving his arms so hard, he almost rolls his ankle on a decapitated goat head.

That was the episode where *Spook Hunters* took off online.

EXCERPT FROM EPISODE FOUR: 'THE DAUGHERTY THEATRE'

'The Daugherty Theatre staged its first play in October 1902, a production of Boothby Chambers' notoriously unlucky and subsequently banned play, *The Light across the Billabong*.'

Nathan's glasses reflect like full moons rising over his lips. I borrowed a night vision attachment to compensate for the abandoned theatre's poor lighting, but it was difficult to get the correct settings. I abandoned it after filming this background segment.

'The opening night was a fiasco. The leading lady broke her leg and six patrons contracted cholera from drinking spoiled champagne. The theatre's owner, John Abercroft Daugherty, was undeterred by the setback. Over the next eleven years, he produced some of Australia's greatest theatrical works, making Ashburnham a prime location on Victoria's cultural map. Daugherty was the rock-star producer of his day.'

Jan takes up the narrative. 'That ended when John Daugherty and his brother George volunteered for the First Australian Imperial Force in November 1914. John was killed at Fromelles. George returned after the Great War and took over the theatre.'

Greg is standing so close to Jan that the weird illumination makes it look like two heads sharing one body. He takes a sneaky glance over her shoulder at her cleavage.

'Nobody knows how or when George Daugherty got his secret taste for human blood, but we do know he was a full-on cannibal by the time he got home. Local historians reckon his interwar body count was eighteen, most of them day labourers.'

Michelle adds, 'Only three murders were proven at his 1938 trial, which was enough to send George to the gallows. The Daugherty Theatre was declared hazardous by the town's authorities and closed the same day England declared war on Germany.'

Jan says, 'For a building that's been condemned for over seventy years, the Daugherty Theatre is in good shape. That's because the Ashburnham Historical Society raises funds to restore it every ten or fifteen years. Public-spirited carpentry is not without its risks. Nathan's dad hurt himself falling from that catwalk back in 2007, right Nate?'

Nathan's father spent nine months in traction and walks with a cane to this day. His injury forced him into early retirement. He is a kind man, but he tires easily.

Nathan does not reply. The Other Girl puts her hand on

his shoulder.

Even though it's a rare example of them all working as a team, I would cut this scene as irrelevant if not for where they are standing, in the side aisle of the partially restored auditorium. The Other Girl is in her usual position, unnoticed at the rear, shrouded by the hanging shreds of a long-ruined velvet curtain.

Nathan confusedly wanders back a couple of steps, giving voice to a small croak, until he bumps into the wall. Not noticing the Other Girl, I thought nothing of it at the time and paused the recording.

*

'Come on, what do you say we give this a run? George is probably still here.' Greg produces a plywood sheet painted with letters and numbers. He never holds it still long enough for it to be recognisable as a Ouija board. In the original episode, I inserted a still-frame image for the audience's benefit but that doesn't matter now.

With the introduction done, Michelle's interest in cooperating evaporates. 'Okay, two things about that. One, why would anyone want to talk to the spirit of a guy who murdered people and ate them? And two, what the hell is wrong with you?' Greg's look of surprise is understandable. They used to get on much better.

Nathan is pushing the curtain around and knocking on the wall through gaps torn in the fabric. He ignores the others. The Other Girl shows a glimpse of amusement at Michelle's speech, but is more interested in Nathan's investigation.

Jan scowls and pushes close to Michelle's face. 'What makes you think we're not going to try to contact the dead? That's what *Spook Hunters* is all about.'

'As if you have any idea what this is all about, you pushy little show-off. You just read your palm cards and show some pasty white skin and try not to get any of your drool on him.' Now it's Jan's turn to look shocked. I doubt anyone has ever stared her down like that before.

Greg steps between them before Jan thinks of a way to escalate. 'Hey now, ladies,' he says, and his grin suggests he might believe they are fighting over him.

'…distasteful.'

'What?' Michelle turns around to the Other Girl with a frown like someone snuck up from behind and pinched her. The sound on the original recording was terrible. Michelle and I spent half a day trying to clean it up for the webcast. Nathan's voice had some weird echo artefacts we just couldn't isolate. In the end, we got him to record a voice-over.

'What did you say?'

Nathan coughs. 'I said, ghosts. They don't like being summoned. They think it's impolite and distasteful. Anyway, I found something.'

He's standing in a doorway that wasn't there before. 'I think this is George Daugherty's kill room. What say we give our viewers a first look inside?'

I slow the playback again. As he holds the door open for us all to clamber forward, it's easy to miss the slight bulge of something long and flat stuffed into his shirt.

Excerpt from Episode Five: 'The Ghost of Clarice'

'Jan, some of the feedback from our regular viewers has been a bit critical.'

'How so, Greg?'

They are flushed and keep exchanging furtive smiles they must imagine are invisible to the camera.

We waited for them for an hour, making uncomfortable small talk with the old woman whose lounge room we had invaded. Jan assured us she had called ahead to make arrangements. It transpired that she left a message on an answering machine that has not been checked since 1996.

'A few commenters have complained that the *Spook Hunters* project is a failure.'

'A failure?'

'Right. Because so far'—she glares what must be intended as daggers penetrating through the camera to its operator—'we haven't captured a single spectre, cryptid or otherworldly horror live on film.'

Little do they know.

'Well then, tonight they're in for a treat.' Jan steps back with a ringmaster's expansive wave.

The old woman, Mrs Gretel Stone, tries to rise too quickly from her armchair. Nathan and Michelle take an arm each to prevent her toppling. I hold the shot on her countenance of confused gratitude. She really had no idea why we were there, but she didn't complain. Manners are paramount and at least we were interesting company.

'Vanh! Camera!' For the webcast, I cut Greg's deep-throated stage whisper out. I feel no obligation to make him look good this time.

The picture veers to Jan by an old-fashioned fireplace, where fading photographs in tarnished silver frames sit atop a faintly scorched mantle. 'This,' she announces, gesturing with both hands at the stuffed and mounted remains of a tortoiseshell cat, 'is Clarice.'

'And this,' she says, reaching out to steer the camera

towards a window, as if nobody else has read her very detailed running sheet, 'is also Clarice.'

A cat – the same cat, though warmed through with a translucent amber glow – is sitting on the window sill. It considers the camera with thoughtful disdain for a moment. Then it raises its head to accept a stroke from Jan's hand, which passes straight through to stop with a gentle slap on the windowsill. The cat's ears flick. It rises, arches its back, and slips out the closed window, disturbing neither dusty glass nor lacy curtains.

Jan swears loud enough for our inadvertent host to hear. As she begins to react, Greg asks, 'How did Clarice die, Grandmother Stone?'

Our host's baffled cordiality freezes on her face. 'I won't talk about that while she's here.'

We all turn to look at Jan, even Greg. 'Not her. Her!' The old woman is pointing into her own little galley kitchen. The camera pans slowly. I didn't want a wobbling shot.

Nathan is carefully pouring the contents of a steaming kettle into a porcelain tea service, while the Other Girl watches, drumming her hands on the table. Startled, he spills hot tea on his fingers as he looks up. Her mouth drops open and she flaps her hand like a bird taking flight.

'Who?' says Greg. 'I don't—'

'Mum? What's going on? What are they doing here?'

I happened to be by the front door at the time so I didn't need to move. Mrs Lautner walked straight into the shot. The camera is so close up on her ear that you can see it turn red. She says, 'Jan, why are you all in my mother's house?'

Count one, two and there is Jan, in the shot with Mrs Lautner. Whatever else you can say about Jan Parry, she has fine spatial awareness. 'Fans, you remember Naomi Lautner, don't you? She's the clubs coordinator at Wattle Park High and she was just indispensable in helping us set up the Spook Hunters Club in the first place. Mrs Lautner – well, no it's out of school hours so I guess we should call you Naomi, right? So, Naomi, what can you tell us about your mother's spectral pet?'

'Jan Parry, I told you about Clarice in confidence.' Mrs Lautner turns to look to the camera. Her disappointment still feels worse than a punch to the stomach. 'This is an invasion of my family's privacy, not to mention a breach of trust. I would like you all to leave immediately. I will discuss this with you after school on Monday.'

Jan persists, putting a hand on Mrs Lautner's shoulder to angle her slightly towards the camera. 'Do you think it's possible your mother poisoned her own cat in order to—'

There's no more footage. That's when I stopped filming.

EXCERPT FROM EPISODE SIX: 'WISDOM STREET'

'This green marker shows where Robert O'Reilly fell after he was stabbed twice in the neck, and the orange one is where Mrs Katherine Morris bled out after Constable Ernhardt emptied his pistol into her chest.' Nathan is speaking very quickly and will not hold still while he speaks to camera.

He was still upset after the meeting with all our parents. His father asked him to stop making the documentaries. Nathan argued with his father, which I don't think he had ever done before.

Despite his nerves, he completes his recounting of the details of each murder without pause. The camera follows him on a wayward route down the street, checking in on a series of numbered plastic markers. Each is a memorial to an unlucky bystander picked off in Lidija Hummel's branch of the 1893 rampage.

Michelle falls in step alongside him. Her glance to camera, no more than a blink, is heavy with emotion. The rebuke that followed Jan's stunt was still fresh in our minds, as was the implied threat that our grade would be withheld. Michelle does not care to hide her anger.

*

Nathan arrives at a patch of dappled shade beneath a stand of thin white gum trees. In two upturned palms, he raises a flat, curved blade covered in wriggling marks like the scribbled bark patterns behind him.

The Other Girl stands beside him, her tied-back hair and oversized shirt unaffected by a light breeze that ruffles Nathan and Michelle. She frowns and often glances away to one side as though she is waiting for a late bus.

'What sparked the Wisdom Street massacre, we don't know for sure,' Michelle says. 'When Lidija Hummel hanged herself from the branches just above us, she took the answers with her. None of the other participants in the bloody all-in brawl outlived her by more than an hour.'

'Eyewitness accounts agree that a strangely shaped blade changed possession several times among the Wisdom Street killers. Some historians hold that an argument broke out over its ownership. The suggestion remains unconfirmed and no such weapon was ever found. Until now.' Nathan holds a knife, which I believed until that moment to be a replica.

As Michelle takes over to recount the bizarre circumstances that drew seven previously unconnected townsfolk into unexplained mutual butchery, a man in a grey suit with an emerald-green tie joins them in the shot.

He listens to their presentation with an expectant look. He does not appear perturbed that neither has acknowledged him.

The Other Girl's pinched face registers hostility. She pulls at her hair with some ferocity, retwisting her scrunchie like a sailor securing loose ropes in a storm. The man in the grey suit ignores her.

As the historical presentation ends, the man in the grey suit leans towards Nathan and whispers something in his ear.

Nathan looks at the knife and runs his finger along the edge, where a dark red smear appears. The man in the grey suit smiles like an encouraging teacher.

Nathan raises his eyes and looks into Michelle's as if he sees her for the first time. Michelle is looking at the knife and at the blood dripping from Nathan's fingers.

The Other Girl touches the man in the grey suit on the shoulder. He reacts, shaking his head at her without turning, a disdainful dismissal.

The Other Girl squeezes, the coil of bangles on her wrist shivering against one another. Smoke or perhaps steam curls from the collar and cuffs of the grey suit.

Michelle swears and snatches the audio bud from her ear. She slaps a hand against the side of her head, grinding her palm against her ear.

The man in the grey suit disappears. The Other Girl falls to her knees and coughs. Michelle's equipment does not pick up the sound of her coughing.

Nathan puts the knife down. He looks at his hand and squeals in pain. 'Oh hell. I need stitches.'

Jan and Greg never showed up for the recording. When they recorded their introductions at school the next week, Greg told Michelle that they had been grounded by their parents. Jan told me that they lost the address details.

I don't know why they bothered lying to us.

Excerpt from Episode Eight: 'The Farm' (episode not broadcast)

I have tried every trick I know to clean up the footage from the hay shed. I have run a stabilisation filter. I have cut the worst bits. I even tried centring each image frame by hand. It's no good. I couldn't stop my hands from shaking when we recorded.

The cut on Greg's forehead is deep but the flow has stopped. Except for the bite on his shoulder, his clothes are more torn up than his skin. He is sitting on the hay-strewn floor of the shed, legs folded, holding his foot with both hands. He stares at everything with a bewildered fury held in check by shock. He says nothing. He does not understand what has happened.

Jan is so pale her eyelids and lips are almost blue. 'Charles?' she says, to camera of course. 'Charles?' She still wears her head microphone, carefully raising and lowering the pickup arm every time she speaks. 'Charles, where is he?'

Michelle grabs Jan's bare arm and squeezes until a halo of red skin surrounds her hand. 'He went to get help,' she says, flat and merciless. 'He went because you told him to. You selfish—'

Jan slaps her hand away. 'Me? We wouldn't be here if not for your stupid club. Think about that.'

Michelle drops to her knees and starts unscrewing the boom stand into its component metal rods. 'Sounds like your problem to me. I don't remember inviting you.'

She shakes her head. Her hair has grown out since the

first episode. I didn't remember that at the time, but now the contrast is striking. Her flat curls have stretched and dangle, reaching for her shoulders. Her skin is too dark to show signs of shock. But then, she shows no other signs of shock either. She looks to the camera. 'We can't broadcast this footage, you know. It'd mess up the court case.'

'What court case?' says Jan. 'He's going to kill us. He'll kill us and he'll get away with it because he always has.'

'Speak for yourself,' says Michelle. She hands one of the dense metal tubes toward the camera; my hand extends forward to claim it. 'This is just to keep the dogs off, okay?'

We can hear the baying in the distance, getting closer. I think Greg might have managed to kill one of the dogs, or at least hurt it badly. There are at least six others, not to mention Ponsford himself.

The camera pans around the interior of the feed shed. Hay bales are stacked ceiling-high against the corrugated aluminium interior walls.

The Other Girl is not with us, which must mean she's outside with Nathan. I think that's where she's been for a long time.

'Why did we come back here?' I reframe on Greg, who has raised his hand to ask the question. I freeze the frame to get a better look at what I saw a second later. The floor's discolouration is obscured by leg movements and patterns of dirt and hay. Did I really see it on my own or did I have help? I still can't tell.

'Get up. Get him up.' My own voice sounds tinny and hollow. Michelle half lifts, half drags Greg out of the way. I set the camera at floor level. My feet appear, kicking a clearing in the straw, stomping to sound out which parts are concrete and which parts are a grey vinyl sheet camouflaging an iron manhole cover.

The Other Girl brought us here. Nathan claimed it was all his own idea. Maybe he was just trying to protect her.

'Help me with this.' Michelle takes one side of the metal ring handle and together we lift the manhole cover. The lid flops open with a crash and the two of us look inside.

I drop to my knees and vomit on the straw. Michelle's legs buckle a little but she keeps her feet. Jan can't resist. She comes over to look. Her cry is cut off with a thick sound as Michelle's hand claps over her mouth.

There is a crash at the shed door. 'Let me in,' calls Nathan. More shakes. The footage of Michelle reaching out to lift away her improvised door bar is unwatchable as I unsteadily retrieve the camera.

Nathan falls through the door, holding Greg's mobile telephone. The Other Girl steps through behind him, looking like she is queued up for a Duran Duran concert.

'Did you—?' Jan's voice is guarded to the point of despair. She lost hope quicker than you would expect.

Nathan nods, catching his breath. He is not a good runner. Another reason Greg would have been preferable. 'I got a signal near the ridge. I called the police. Greg's father, too.' He bites his bottom lip and shrugs when Greg does not respond.

Michelle gets it first. 'Where's the goat farmer?'

'He's busy with his dogs. But he's nearly done.' The dogs' barks have reached a primal ferocity. Their chorus is getting closer, but contains fewer voices.

Jan starts turning to each of us. 'He's coming. He's coming. Why did we come back here?'

The Other Girl kneels by the open manhole, looking down with an apologetic expression. I didn't take the shot until much later, but it's no mystery what held her gaze. One of the ruined gelatinous faces staring back from empty sockets wore braces over shrunken gums and a green scrunchie in its matted thicket of hair.

Greg's mouth moves but his expression does not change. 'You killed his goats. That's why he's angry at us. You killed his goats.'

Nathan shrugs. He did and didn't. He wasn't in the driver's seat then, any more than he was when he threw himself into a creek to wash the blood and gore away.

I'm the first to notice what he's missing. 'Where's the knife?'

'I gave it to him,' Nathan replies.

'You what?'

'I had to, otherwise he wouldn't have murdered his dogs.'

There's a final helpless yelp from somewhere nearby and then the noise steadies into a ceaseless monotone mutter of swearing and violent threats. The sound comes closer. The shed door thumps once, shaking the whole structure.

Michelle takes up a spot beside the door. She has a short metal pole in each hand. She gives the Other Girl a hard look and I think it's the first time she's ever seen her. 'You got us into this, chicky-babe. You got what you wanted, now you do right by us, hey?'

Nathan and the Other Girl reach out together for the door handle and pull it open.

The goat farmer is there, eyes wide and mouth dripping red, holding Nathan's knife like a short sword. In person Bryan Ponsford was just in his blood-soaked working clothes. On film, he's wearing a grey suit with an emerald tie.

He sees the Other Girl and he takes a half-step back. Michelle slams his wrist with her improvised club, hard enough to break skin and bone. She put her weight into it.

The knife drops in front of Nathan and the Other Girl. They kick it across the floor into the manhole.

Ponsford howls unintelligibly and grabs at Nathan. The Other Girl grabs his arm and stops it from reaching Nathan's throat.

Michelle hits him again, this time on the back of his head. Ponsford's hat spins off into the straw. Ponsford takes one more step and collapses forward. His face bounces off the rim of the manhole. He stops moving, his face hanging into the hole like he's vomiting into a toilet.

Michelle says, 'Let's go now.'

For some reason Jan picked that moment to start screaming so I stopped recording then.

Excerpt from Episode Nine: 'Final Report' (episode not broadcast)

When we filmed the final episode two nights ago, Jan wanted everyone to sit in the same places. She gave up when Greg pointedly refused to give up his crutches and sit down.

Her webcast-host face is gone, replaced by serious-student face. It is no less insincere. In comparison to the footage I was looking at a minute ago, her transformation is unsettling.

'We've had an amazing semester,' she says. The frame tightens on her face; I wanted to get through this in one take and I didn't want anyone else's expression to distract attention from her. 'The Wattle Creek Spook Hunters have looked Ashburnham's darkness right in the eye and brought it into the light. We're so proud that you've been able to join us on this journey. Your emails of support and encouragement have kept us going in the past few weeks. I wish I could thank every one of you in person.

'This series started as an extracurricular project for credit towards our final Year 10 certificate. But it's become more than that. And I'm not just saying that because Ms Lautner abandoned her teaching responsibilities and convinced the principal to cancel our bonus marks. That doesn't matter anymore because the great news is that our last episode had over seventy-five thousand downloads. You banded together to create a real community. You've all rallied behind us and I know that this is just the start of something big and important. I just know that when the legal injunctions on our latest episode come down and you finally get to see it, you're going to lose it. You guys can't get enough of *Spook Hunters* and I love you for that.'

The camera pulls back as she speaks. Nobody is looking at anybody. Nobody says anything with their eyes. When Jan finishes, she leads an infectious round of applause that nobody catches.

Greg nods once and settles his crutches into place. He turns his back on Jan and makes a painstaking, lumbering circuit towards the front door.

'Where are you going?' Jan seems too surprised to be angry.

'Coach says I have to keep up physical therapy if I want to start training.' With a little shuffling manoeuvre to get the crutches out of the way, he opens the door.

Jan tries to save the moment. 'Don't you want to tell the viewers about what's coming up in Season Two?'

'I can get graduation credit from footy. Can't get anything I want here.' Greg closes the door behind him and for once Jan's media presence doesn't rush to fill the vacuum.

'I'm gone too,' says Michelle, picking up her bag.

That snaps Jan out of it. 'Fine, you bugger off on walk-about or whatever. We can do this without you.'

Michelle stands, breathing quietly and holding herself very still, for a long time. She says, 'I'll see most of you at school on Monday. Good night.'

I pause the shot just as the camera pans past Jan's face. Her flaring nostrils look out of place at the centre of a cracked mask of bland good cheer.

I admit it. I enjoyed the moment. Maybe I'm not as good a person as I tell myself.

I restart the footage.

The pan resumes to the floor, where Nathan sits cross-legged. To his left, the Other Girl wears a sweet smile and, for the first time in our acquaintance, she has changed out of her old clothes into stonewash jeans and a Spin Doctors t-shirt.

Nathan puts an arm around the Other Girl and says, 'This is Sally. Well, that's what we're calling her right now and I'm sure she'd let us know if she minded. I don't know if you see Sally. Not everybody does. But she's been with us for a while and she's planning to stick around from now on, helping us to help other people.'

Jan looks at Nathan like he's on fire and ignoring it. 'Who are you talking—?'

Nathan goes on. 'We have a debt to repay to Sally. The first thing we're going to do is find out her real name. Who she was.'

Nathan looks to camera. His replacement glasses are so fine they almost vanish from his face. 'We're going to make another change next season. Together. All right? Together or not at all.'

The picture wobbles just a little bit. I don't intend to fix it.

I walk around and take my place next to Nathan and Sally. See you next season.

The Island at the End
of the World

Paul Mannering

In the evening, the village gathers on the beach at sun-fall to watch the sky burn. Mother brings lumps of coconut meal and rice to eat. It's padded together to make the sticky balls that leave grain-crumbs like tiny maggots on my fingers.

Sarny toasts fish on the embers of the fire while we sit with our backs to the glow, so as not to miss anything on the horizon. We eat, drink kava, and talk until the sun vanishes into the abyss and the sky lights up in rippling curtains of bright green, purple, and red. Amongst the shimmering waves of fire are streaks of white light. Mother says the streamers are the souls of the dead, passing through the veil and going to the beyond. I wonder if it hurts to burn like that once you are dead. Most nights you can see as if the sun was still shining and in the flickering fire of the dark sky everyone's skin glows with the colours of a polished pāua shell.

I sit next to my friend Gilly and Mother approves. She talks about how Gilly and I will marry when we are old enough. I asked her once what marriage meant and she said it is having one special friend. I guess that means Gilly and I are married now, cos we've always been friends.

After a time, the sky-fire fades and Sarny scoops white sand onto the dying embers and snuffs them out. We go home, under the smear of the moon. Sarny says that the moon used to be like a coconut; round, white, and full of milk. Now it's spread across the dark like a bird splat on a rock.

Our village is small, like the world, which is big, but not as big as it was. Sarny says you can go to the horizon, but then you will die because there is nothing beyond that. I didn't understand what he meant, so I asked Mother. She said no one knows where the world went, but that the ocean around us is all there is.

They say my father went to the horizon. He paddled his canoe out through the lagoon and raised the sail and waved to the people watching on the beach. He took coconuts for food and drink. He took fishing hooks and lines. He took hope, and he took Mother's heart. He never came back and now Mother is like copra, the dried coconut. Sarny doesn't mind. He loves her even though she can't love him back.

In the morning the sun comes back. Sometimes it rises up behind the village, other times it comes up in front. Some days are over quickly, others drag on forever. The sun doesn't care. It doesn't have anything important to do. It just wanders around.

The pigs wake me with their grunting. I give them leftover fish and coconut-rice balls. They squeal and push to get the best bits, though I try and share them out.

Bara, the sow, wriggles to get up from her litter. They are pumping her pig-udders for milk and she is hungry. I feed her a special mix of banana, coconut chunks and fish-meat, then I scratch her ears and she grunts and sniffs me for more food.

We are going to eat the piglets, but first they have to grow up enough. Sarny says we have to feed the pigs like we have to plant the fields. All these things keep us in food, for one day the sky might burn the sea and all the fish will die.

He says that happened before, when the moon died and the world was lost. The people of the village picked up so much fish they couldn't eat it all. Lots of it went on to the fields and made the taro, the coconuts, and the bananas grow. Everything grows good in our fields because Sarny made people feed the ground with all the extra fish.

The canoes go out each morning to set nets and drag the fish from the water beyond the reef at the end of the lagoon. Sometimes they find things that aren't fish. Sometimes the things that aren't fish drag a fisherman out of his canoe and I guess he becomes a streak of light in the fire-sky at night.

When the pigs are fed, I walk down to the beach, past the coconut palms and the other huts. Gilly comes out of his hut and we burst into a race. He's taller than me, even though we're the same age, both born under the same fire-sky.

Gilly's father got swallowed by a whale. He was in his canoe, going fishing, when a big wave came. He paddled through it and then the whale in the wave opened its mouth and the canoe went inside like it was a cave in a cliff at high tide. Swallowed him and his canoe whole. Whales scare me with their tentacles and the stink of their breath when they blow. I wonder if a whale ate Father, or if he really sailed off the end of the world.

I reach the water's edge, the border between worlds, half a step behind Gilly. I push him in. By the time he's come up, I'm swimming across the lagoon. There are little fish in the water, turtles sometimes, too. Looking down, we see crabs, snails, sponges, and things that should not be.

On the other side of the lagoon is the reef. Inside the reef, there is the village, the lagoon, the fields, the streams, and waterfalls. Inland, past the fields, there are the jungle trees and the high mountain where the carved stones move in their slow dance.

Rolling onto my back, I look towards shore and the mist shrouded mountain top. Raising my head higher, I see Gilly as he dives for something on the bottom of the lagoon.

I float, my head sinking back, feeling the cool water stroke my skin. The nudge of waves tells me that Gilly is coming closer. I try not to grin or squirm. Instead, I wait until I am sure he is close and then I flip over and splash him. Except it's not Gilly coming up from underneath, it's something with a pale face and dead eyes.

Its lips peel back and bubbles rise out of its mouth as long arms reach for me. I scream into the water and thrash, getting my arms and legs in order to swim. The easiest thing to do is dive down, past the thing coming up at me with bared teeth and slack grey skin.

I twist aside, feeling the graze of its clawed hands as I plunge. The surface water is warm but a body-length down, the cold grips like dread.

I'm fast in water, born in the shallows of the lagoon under the burning night sky while Mother wailed and the women sang waiata to call me forth from her body. Swimming hard, I pretend I'm a fish, faster than a whale, faster than a spear, faster than a wraith, zipping through the burning sky. No fish can catch me. Not even a dead one with white lips and teeth of polished grey stone.

I can't see Gilly. I hope the white-faced thing didn't get him. Grabbing a coral ledge, I pull myself under it, hiding like an eel. The seeweed swirls, dark fronds of brown and green reaching out to taste my skin, the pods along the stalks opening and the eyes inside turning to look at me.

The white-faced thing floats down, its head turning this way and that, while I lie still under the cover of the weeds, so scared I forget to breathe. The seeweed eye-pods look at the intruder, ever watchful, but unable to do anything.

After a bit, the strange fish swims towards the beach. It looks rotten, with ragged strips of grey skin waving in the current. I hope one of the older boys hunting along the shoreline sees it and stabs it with his fishing spear. When the coast is clear, I slip out from under the ledge and slowly rise to the surface.

Gilly yells and waves. He is standing on the reef, a big pāua in each hand. Good meat lies in their flat shells. I swim quickly and climb out onto the rocks, the spray of the big-sea waves splashing over us. Gilly hands me one of the shellfish and scoops the meat out of the other shell.

'Didya see it?' I ask.

The pāua shrieks in wordless terror until Gilly bites its brain off at the stem and spits it into the lagoon.

'See what?' he asks.

I strip the second pāua out of its protective shell and bite the brain off. At home, Mother fries the brains in coconut oil and sprinkles them with flakes of dried chili. Out here, we just spit them out.

'Strange fish,' I explain and bite into the firm meat of the pāua. It grips the rocks like a limpet, so they're all muscle.

'You're a strange fish,' Gilly replies.

'Nah, there was a fish, with a weird head and it looked like it was dead, but still swimming.'

Gilly looks out into the lagoon. The water is emerald

green and still in the sunlight. 'Dead fish?' he echoes.

'Yeah. It looked half rotted, but still swimming.'

The sea, always such a safe place and a part of everything I know, now feels filled with unknown dangers. Gilly shivers as if he feels it too.

'Maybe it washed over the reef in the high tide?' Gilly says. We both look out past the breakers and the swell. The deep water is shades darker and the fishing canoes are laying their nets.

'We should tell Sarny,' I say. We should tell Sarny. He says he's the smartest person in the village, so he must be.

'Did it try and eat you?' Gilly asks around a mouthful of pāua meat.

'Maybe.' It had teeth. Things with teeth always want to eat you. I tear a chunk off my own pāua and chew it.

'Wanna work on the boat?' Gilly asks, his pāua chomped down already.

'Sure.' The boat is our project. A canoe of our own, one we can take past the breakers on the reef and maybe, one day, sail to another island. Sarny says there are other islands, so there must be.

We stand together on the wave bashed coral, neither of us ready to dive into the lagoon and swim for the beach.

Gilly laughs, 'You scared?'

'Nah.' I try to laugh too, but my throat has closed up.

'We gonna stand here till high tide?'

I manage a loose smile. 'You can wait till the canoes come in, ask them to rescue you.'

'Or when they come by, you tell them you forgot how to swim,' Gilly suggests.

'Last one back has to sled the pig mud to the far field!' I spring off the rock and into the lagoon. I dive deep and swim hard. Arms and legs curling and dragging me through the water. Faster than a spear. Faster than a striking fish. Faster than—

Gilly swims up beside me, his eyes slitted against the water. We race, both of us reaching out and pulling hard. The sand turns white under us and we run out of the water and on to the beach, laughing at our fear.

'Beat you,' Gilly says, his chest heaving with the exertion of the swim.

'Only cos I let you win,' I reply. Gilly just shakes his head.

Little Oolee comes running down the beach. She's half our age and I remember when she was new. Wrinkled, dark, and fresh as a warm egg.

'Hey! C'mere!' Oolee yells, waving her arms. We walk towards her, old enough not to run just because a little girl demands it.

'What?' Gilly says as the three of us come together on the sand.

'Booa killed a fish. It come up outta the water. Was on the beach and walking to the village.'

Yesterday, we would have laughed. Told Oolee that Booa was full of it. Not today though. Not after what I'd seen. 'Was it dead and rotten looking?' I ask and Oolee's eyes go wide.

'Yeah…' she breathes. 'Wait, how'd you know that?' She scowls at me, hands settling on her hips in imitation of Mother.

'Cos we're older,' I reply. 'Where's this funny fish?'

Oolee turns on her heel and skips down the beach. We follow and take the path back through the trees and to the village.

Everyone not out fishing has gathered round Booa and

his catch. He's standing there, shaking his fishing spear and looking like he killed a whale on his own.

I ignore Booa and stare at the carcass. The fish is long and draped in loose skin. I crouch and look at it in detail. The head is on an angle, but it has a neck, like some of the things that swim but don't make good eating.

'You seen anything like that?' Booa asks, expecting us to be impressed by his trophy.

'Yeah,' I reply. Looking up, I stare at Booa, answering his challenge with one of my own.

Taking a deep breath, I straighten up. 'I saw it. Came up on me in the lagoon.'

'Nah,' Booa waves my words away as if they were flies.

'Yeah it did,' Gilly comes to my defence. He's good like that. If he told Booa the sand was green, I'd agree with him, too.

An elder shuffles forward and pokes the corpse with her stick. 'Is gotta bad smell to it,' she warns.

'It was dead before Booa speared it,' Gilly says.

'Nah!' Booa snaps.

'Where'd it come from?' Oolee asks.

'Deep sea,' I reply. 'Out by the horizon. Same place all things come from.'

'And to which all things return.' Sarny has come from somewhere, and will tell us what he knows.

'What is it, Sarny?' I ask.

'It's a dead soul, returned to the sea. Didn't burn up in the sky-fire, so got washed up here.'

A murmuring goes through the villagers. We all step back, even Booa looks less pleased with his catch.

Sarny stares at the thing's sagging skin. 'Burn it. Burn it to dirt and take what remains out past the fishing grounds and let the sea take it.'

We stack wood, coconut husks, and branches to make a fire. Sarny brings hot coals from a cooking fire. No one volunteers to bring the dead fish to the pyre.

'Booa killed it,' Gilly says. 'He should drag it over.'

'You scared?' Booa asks him. He knows what to say to make Gilly do something stupid.

Gilly walks over to the dead fish and grabs it by its twin tails. Walking backwards, he drags it through the sand to the fire. 'Give us a hand,' he says to me. I look at the thing's head. Remembering those teeth and the way it came at me.

'You take the tails, I'll get the head,' Gilly drops the thing with a splat and walks past me. I don't say anything, feeling stupid for being afraid. I grab the tails; they feel soft and slimy under my hands. Gilly's trying to get a grip on the head. The soft body sags in the middle. He sets it down and gets a handful of the loose grey skin. Together, we lift the body.

'Gah!' Gilly lets out a yell and the fish hits the sand.

'Too slimy for you?' I tease him. Gilly is staring at his hand and I see blood dripping.

'You okay?' my arms are getting tired, so I drop the tails and give the dead thing a wide berth on my way to check on Gilly.

'Yeah, there's spines in it. Under the skin, they slid out and got me.'

'Well, be careful.' I examine his hand. There's a line of four punctures running from the heel up to the base of his webbed fingers. Blood oozes out as he pushes at the flesh.

'You'll live I reckon.'

'Let's burn this thing and work on the canoe.' Gilly shakes the last of the pain out of his hand and takes a more careful grip on the fish.

We watch it burn, black smoke twisting in the air and giving off a choking stink.

'Smells like Booa,' I say, and Gilly grins.

We leave the fire to do its work. We can come back later and scrape up the dirt and then one of the fishermen can take it way out and dump it.

Our canoe lies in the trees at the far end of the lagoon. We have spent months charring and chipping the heart out of a fallen tree. It is good to work and see the log become more boat-shaped, it keeps us going knowing we are making something that will always be.

When we arrive at the canoe, it is infested with crabs. They hiss at us so Gilly uses his axe and scrapes the smaller ones off the log. The crabs have long arms with pincer-claws that can snip off a finger. The bigger ones rise up on their legs, standing as high as my waist and they charge at us. Their claws sing and crash. We smash them with our axes and drive them back.

At night, the crabs come out of the rocks and shallow water of the lagoon and gather up the charcoal scraps left from our work hollowing out the canoe. They use the charred black chunks to mark symbols on the round stones under the trees. Even Sarny doesn't know what the crabs' writing means. Once the crabs are swept aside, we get to work. Yesterday, we burned more of the tree, and now we chip the charred heart-wood out of it. Each cut releases a scent like burning blood and we settle into a rhythm of chopping.

By the time the sun is high overhead, my arms are aching from the work and I straighten, stretching my back and squinting in the bright daylight. Gilly is still chopping, each blow like the thudding pulse of a heart. The beat falters and a moment later, Gilly crumples. I drop my axe. 'Gilly?'

I rush to his side and crouch down. My friend's face is grey and his eyes are clouded. 'Gilly?' No response. I shake him, feeling the slick coolness of his skin under my touch. The crabs have gathered again, they clack their claws in a drumming rhythm that sounds like a burial chant.

I yell for help until everyone comes to lift Gilly and carry him home. I spend the rest of the day sitting with Mother and Oolee outside the hut where he lies. As the sun descends and the sky burns, Gilly dies.

No one drinks kava or watches the streaming lights in the curtains of green fire that night. I hear the songs of grief and sorrow, the waiata that mark the passing of one of our own. In my pain, I cannot tell if it is the women of the village singing, or if the keening wail comes from my own throat.

In the morning, Gilly's skin is slack and pale, like the strange fish that poisoned him. Sarny gathers wood and rebuilds the pyre. I stand watching, my eyes streaming from the acrid smoke as Gilly burns to black dirt on the white sand.

'We must take the remains out towards the horizon,' Sarny says to the gathered village. 'We will be rid of the curse when the last of the ashes are lost in the sea far from here.'

I take a gourd and scoop up Gilly's ashes and the white sand. When I am done, only the swirls in the beach remain for the tide to devour.

Our canoe smells of burnt blood. The crabs have written all over the wood in rows of charcoal symbols. I take a paddle from one of the beached fishing boats and put the ash gourd into the canoe. It is too heavy for me to slide down the beach, but I cannot ask for help. Sarny, Mother, and the elders will tell me to stay in the village until my grief washes away on the tide.

Sitting in the canoe that Gilly and I will never finish, I cry. I see his face when I close my eyes and I hear his laugh in every brush of the waves on the sand.

The canoe rocks from side to side and I grab the edges in panic. The prow of the narrow boat rises and then I feel it move. The sand around the boat is thick with crabs. They move in silence, burrowing under the boat, rocking the canoe as they lift the dugout with me in it. Passing from pincer to claw, I am carried on a rippling tide of red shells to the water. The canoe floats. I take up the paddle and push out through the low breakers of the lagoon.

I follow the path of the fishing canoes through the narrow gap in the reef where the ocean surges. I paddle hard, alternating between sides and watching for the moment when I will be caught by the outward flow of the sea. If I do this right, the water will carry me beyond the reef's coral teeth. Time it wrong and the coral will eat my canoe and me, too.

I should be afraid; paddling out of the lagoon is dangerous and only experienced fishermen do it. The boys learning to set nets and handle boats on the open water always crouch in the prow and try not to scream when they go out.

Spray erupts in a howling geyser as waves explode against the coral jaw of the reef. My paddle strikes air as the sea drops away. I almost fall on my face. Kneeling in the bottom of the canoe, I watch the sea and brace for the crash. The water hits the bottom of the canoe like it were a flat stone. The slap of it jars my bones.

I paddle hard as my canoe climbs the slope of the next oncoming wave. The carved tip of the boat rises almost vertical and I have to stop paddling and grab the urn of Gilly's ashes to save them from falling into the storm of white foam.

Then the water calms and the canoe bobs in the swirling current until I take up the paddle again. Rhythmic strokes push the canoe through the water. I tell myself it is like swimming, I am faster than a fish, faster than a spear…

Away from the boiling sea, howling in the throat of the reef, I push on, turning and heading parallel to the island that has been my entire world. Driving the canoe forward, when I look up again, the land is gone and the sun is moving low across the sky. I must let the burning orb travel without me; to follow it would be to go in a circle or go blind. Sarny has many theories about what the sun will do to those who try to make sense of its wanderings.

I paddle until my body aches and the skin on my palms has swollen into bubbles from the friction of the oars. The searing day has dried the skin of my arms and back into rough scales.

The sea is endless. The horizon is a lie. Have I gone far enough to die without returning to the shore as a rotting fish? If I scatter the sand and ashes of Gilly here, will it be far enough away to keep my village safe?

I keep paddling: the horizon is where I must go. Far enough to have no doubt and no grief. During one breath, the sun is a tumbling red circle of spinning fire, the next it has plunged into the sea and I am sure I hear the hiss of its quenching. The sky burns in a searing curtain of green and purple light. The smear of the moon twists like an eel and the streaks of light, the souls of the dead being cleansed or punished, fall through the veil.

The bottomless water around me, so dark in the light of the sun, now shines with the reflected aura of the burning sky. Things rise, and bring their own luminescence with them. Worms as long as the reef twist and turn as they rise to the surface. Their bodies glow with a bright blue light. Clouds of fish, each one a disc no larger than my hand, move as a single body. A side expands, becoming a point and then, like stretched seeweed, what remained below springs to catch up. Where the cloud flowed a moment before, a dark mouth snaps shut and my blood runs cold.

Feeding whales.

Each behemoth could easily inhale my tiny canoe and devour me without chewing. A ring of tentacles surrounds each gaping maw. Those mouths, as wide and dark as the pit, reach out and snatch fish from the swarm of fleeing creatures.

Terror paralyses me, and I can do nothing except await the fate rising from below. A mountain of black flesh breaks the water and I choke on the stink of its exhalation. Salt water and mucus rain down from the whale's blow. The creature is an island in the night, cloaked in strange weeds and writhing polyps that seem to speak in a myriad of voices. Do they sing and cry under the water? Or is it only when the whale breaks the surface that they are given voice?

I dare not listen, the voices are too close to my own and I am afraid of what they will tell me. I lift my paddle and cut the water, again and again, pushing the canoe away from the mass of black flesh that is larger than the sun.

In my wake, the whale finishes its cycle of rise, exhale and plunge again. The waves of its passing make a new current and the canoe zips through the shimmering water so fast my eyes water from the wind. I paddle on. There is nothing else to do. I wonder about diving over the side and swimming down until I can no longer see or feel. What is down there in the endless darkness of the deepest ocean? Are there other worlds? Does the water have a different surface, with canoes like mine skimming across it under the same staggering sun?

The unmeasurable cadence of the sky, the solid certainty of the water and the land have not always been. Sarny tells me this and I believe him. There is change and the forms of our world are fluid. We come from the sea and to the sea we will return.

The current of the whale's wake has faded, though my speed has increased. A new force is drawing me forward and when I look up, the sky is closer. Rows of rippling green light wave overhead and dip to touch the sea. Lightning arcs between sky and water in blinding forks of dark-light. The other worlds are not beneath my canoe, hidden beneath an abyss of ocean; they are above me. I am at the bottom of the sea, looking up through the unfathomable depths and wondering at the surface world.

I stand up, my paddle extended for balance as I reach towards the sky. The vault of the heavens twists, spiralling into a sinkhole, a swirling darkness that sucks all water and all life into the black centre. I drop my paddle and snatch up the gourd of Gilly's ashes.

'Let us go on together,' I say, and the canoe tilts into the sky.

There is no falling or rising for me, instead the sky and the ocean moves around the fixed point of a single star, blazing in the void. Then everything flies apart. Air becomes water, water becomes fire, and fire becomes earth. I am lying on a beach of black sand. I crawl away from the foam-lipped edge of the sea, which hisses and reaches for me. There are squat trees here that lean in close to each other, and carry the whispers of the waves to unseen ears.

I find Gilly's urn in the sand, the clay seal still unbroken. My grief drowns the instant of hope that perhaps here, he would be again.

This is far enough, the sky is dark at last. Populated by a scattering of tiny shards that glitter with a cold disdain.

The black sands will take Gilly's dark ashes and make them their own. I claw at the seal. It refuses to tear and there are no rocks to smash the gourd.

Standing, I carry the vessel inland, passing the silent sentinels of the trees. I do not speak to them and I do not listen to what they may say.

Beyond the trees, I find the stones. They are carved in familiar shapes, faces and silhouettes of Sarny, Mother, Oolee, and the rest of the village. Sinking to my knees at the rounded feet of Gilly's stone likeness, I dig with my hands into the soft earth. Then I lift the gourd and break its neck on the base of the statue. Pouring Gilly's ashes into the dark hole fills it and the surface becomes the same as the black sand.

Now he is part of this land and too far from home to come back or to burn in the streamers of white flame. Here, Gilly will become part of the dark island and in time, he will return to the sea. I hope his soul will join the endless points of glittering light that look down on me as I return to the water and crouch, washing my hands in the white-foamed surf.

I slide forward into the first row of waves and the sea strokes me as it always has. I take comfort in the water's embrace and swim through the darkness as I have swum through the lagoon since first night. The ocean flows through me and my gills open, drawing air from the water and turning it to fire in my blood. Where my skin has blistered and cracked from long exposure to the sun, the ocean sloughs it away. I shed strips of dead scale and flex my arms, feeling the stroke of the water against the webbing that runs from my arms to my body.

The moult is a great easing for my itching dry skin. My new adult form is stronger, more suited to the long swim through the horizon and into the distant ocean where the whales watch for the unwary. I can make it home now, back to the island where Sarny and Mother wait. Where we will drink kava, eat fish, and watch the sky burn while the crabs write the history of the world in the fluid script of charcoal on stone.

Back When the River had No Name

Summer Wigmore

REY HAD BEEN YOUNG WHEN THE WORLD ENDED, AND he didn't remember much of the before times. He thought he remembered sleeping next to his mother, the shape of her beside him, but it wasn't a comfortable memory. He didn't like to think about things like that. Everything was beautiful and the world was good, but only if you tried hard enough.

He cycled up the hill, standing on his pedals to push. His mountain bike wasn't as good as a motopaika for power, but it didn't need gas and it was better than a car for swerving around the cracks and potholes. Once he was at the top of the hill, he rested with one foot on the ground. The road ahead was cracked too, but there were no real big holes, and no traps. He kicked off and swept down it, like he was flying with the wind in his face. He stood on his pedals and whooped. The framework of his bike juddered with each hole, but held.

He got to the bottom of the hill too quickly, but at least there was another one to climb. He pushed up this one too, legs burning, his pack heavier on his back. When he was nearly at the top, he had a bad feeling, so he got off and walked quietly.

He was glad he had. From the top of this one, he could see a camp of travellers, probably here, like he was, to cross the bridge and bargain with the Baron. They were a few hundred metres from the base of the Baron's bridge, and had a fire. Rey went back and hid. He could be quiet when he needed, and the chipped plastic beads and things on his bike were easy to hide with the blanket from his bag, so if they had heard him they might not see him even if they came to look. He hunkered beside the bike and waited.

This was the only bridge across the River he knew of. Over the River there would be ruined houses and old supermarkets to raid. All the food was long gone, but there would be some bright plastics to scavenge, for his bike and hair and clothes, and maybe there would be proper dye that was better than the bleaches he used sometimes. They were bad for him, but it was good to know *why* his hair was falling out, and he liked it being colourful. It helped him keep happy and it was important to be happy. But the Baron was said to ask a high tax to cross their bridge, and Rey didn't have much to give. Maybe the travellers would?

He waited until the sun vanished and the long thick cloud that was always in the sky went dark purples and blacks like a bruise instead of grey and grainy like dust. Once it was truly dark he left his bike and, keeping low to the ground, sneaked to where the travellers were.

They didn't have scouts. It was a big party, two motopaika and a quad. No cars. Cars were good for carrying big loads, but you needed more people than this to get them through tight spots and out of muck. This was more people than he'd seen in a while but still not all that many, less than ten. More than five. He counted until he remembered the number, proudly: eight.

He scanned their resources. Big tins of gas for the bikes, blankets and knives, but no guns. One person had a knife lashed at the end of a stick, like a spear, and a few had jackets, but every single person had their own plate. The smell of food was good, even if the River stink ruined it. Rey crouched and watched, eyes gleaming. Food would be good, supplies. He could ask, maybe, or steal. Or kill them. But he hated doing that, even when it was people who weren't people any more, like ghosties, and these were all still people, though some had wounds with that shiny look that meant they weren't healing. He scratched at the scabs on his own leg, which bled a bit, so that was fine. One of the people didn't have any legs, but that might have been from before the world ended. He sat near some of the others, playing cards. One was a child. Rey hadn't seen a child in ages.

They looked cosy, like a family gathered around a TV, and it made something in his chest feel painful like it had got caught there, like a big splinter or bit of metal that needed to be pulled out. They looked nice, a big mix of people, the guy with no legs and a thin white girl and others. Maybe he could just go up and ask.

The scrape of forks on plates got quieter, and Rey sat straighter, like that was a signal, like something was going to happen. The oldest man there placed his cards down and cleared his throat. After he cleared it he had to cough, again and again, but at last he talked, and his words rumbled, strong despite the cough.

'In the old days before the cloud came and the lifeless things,' the old man said, 'my people still lived near Oldland. Their waka was Tainui. My dad always had enough food and beer. He could invite friends to watch the game.'

'*To watch the game*,' the others murmured. It felt warm and close and reminded Rey of something. He ran.

He brushed through the rough grasses, but there wasn't any shouting from behind him. He found his bike, pulled the blanket off it and laid it on the ground to sleep on later, underneath a bush so he would have shelter from the rains. He couldn't make a fire this close to the travellers.

The story had been in English, which was good because Rey only knew a few words of the old tongue. They said in the old days people could speak it for a whole conversation. Sometimes they said there were people who still spoke it, them by the lakes that had sunk when steam came up from the earth: people who still spoke it, and spoke nothing else.

To Rey it was like the world that had been lost. It wasn't a language he could use even if he remembered it, because the world it described was no longer there. He still reached for it sometimes without knowing why, the pieces sunken, too, beneath his memory.

'My mountain is…' Rey said aloud, but if he'd ever had one he couldn't think of it. He paced, then tried again. 'My mother's name is…'

He huffed out a breath and crouched, giving up. He'd passed a deary a few weeks back, with some food inside. He had no meat left, but he still had a stick of candy. He chewed it slowly, hunkered over the emptiness in his belly, and afterward tied the wrapper around one spoke. Then he lay down and slept.

The bridge was grey and old-looking, big and broken and pitted like a tooth. Once there had been arcs of stone along each side like the back of a beast through the water, maybe for rituals. Now the pillars that had supported them were mostly broken off. It was the only way to cross the River unless you had a good boat, and no one had a boat; the only bridge still standing, though it was snapped in two pieces, one veering out over the other.

There, the body of the bridge and its grey arcs angled down. The travellers made their way slowly across, and Rey followed them. He had left his bike behind, but he could go get it later. Bikes made noise, and Rey could be quiet. None of them saw him, not the people who were crossing the bridge, not the man with no legs either, left with a spear and the supplies at the bridge's base. He hid behind pillars and inched down one of the thick ribbons of stone. The party reached the break-off of the bridge and stopped to talk to the Baron, and Rey crouched behind a pillar, and listened.

'We need to cross, Baron Taniwha,' one of the women called. Her mouth was twisted like she tasted something sour, like some of the meat Rey had taken from the deary, which had twisted his stomach for days and made him sick up and see things. Maybe it was the smell.

The Baron stood on her higher piece of bridge. Rey tilted his head to look at her better. She was like a ghostie, with her skin so pale and blue. A long gun hung from her hand in a casual way. She wore a tattered suit. 'I control this crossing,' she said. Her voice was flat, and grated like glass. She gestured with her long gun. 'What do you have to trade? What do you have to give me?' She looked to where they had left their stores. 'Food?'

The woman who had spoken first stepped in front of the kid who was there. The old man cleared his throat, coughing, and said, 'We need all the food we have.'

The Baron straightened and pointed the tip of her gun at them. 'Get out,' she said, the way you'd speak to roaches or rats, all disgust.

A man in a jacket pulled a small gun out from under it and pointed it at her. The air was silent and thick as stew.

'I can pick you all out from here,' the Baron said. Rey thought her back looked less straight than it had.

The man with the gun said, 'Not before I hit you. Wing you at least.'

That was when Rey hopped down behind the travellers. 'But you're cornered!' he said.

The kid and its guardian whirled. So did some of the others. The man with the gun and the other women didn't move their eyes from the Baron. She had flinched her long gun a little in his direction when he came out, but now it pointed back at the group.

'That's right,' she said, and gestured with the tip of it. She looked confident again now. 'Get out, I said. Don't come back without a toll if you know what's good for you.'

Rey stepped to the side to let them pass, beaming at them. None of them smiled back. Like they didn't know how important it was, being happy.

When they'd passed, he tilted his head to look up at the Baron on her ledge. 'Is that worth the crossing?'

She didn't say anything. She stepped back. After a second, the rope ladder dropped across the gap, only big enough for one person at a time. He climbed up.

There was a pile of stuff on the other side, more guns and vests and blankets, food.

'Baron Taniwha?' Rey said. She didn't nod, just looked at him unmoving, the gun ready in her hand. She wouldn't have let him across if she thought he was a threat, but no one survived long unless they acted like everything was. 'You shouldn't have a name like that.'

The Baron smiled without anything in it that a smile should have. Her lip cracked and a dribble of blue dripped down it. 'Cry me a River.'

He looked back at the drop half a step behind him and the water beneath that. 'There was a saying once, about this River,' he said and frowned. 'I don't know what it was though.'

'A lot of things have been forgotten,' the Baron said. She didn't sound upset by it. She raised her gun a little and gestured with it, between him and the bank. 'Get going and keep going. I'll welcome you back across if you pay the price. But friend, touch my storehouse and you'll regret it. Or won't.'

Rey stayed where he was. He felt rooted with wonder. 'Friend?' he said. 'We're friends?'

She stared at him. Her eyes were blue too, or grey, like dead fish. There were blue veins beneath her skin. Rey beamed at her.

The Baron's eyes flicked to the water sludging below, then up.

'Will you help me with something?' she said, slowly.

'Of course!'

You couldn't trust anyone out here, not these days, not ever. But this was different. They were friends.

'Then yes.' She lowered her gun, and jerked her head for him to follow. 'Come eat … friend.'

If he thought her pile of gear by the bridge was riches, then the stuff in her base underground was more than riches, was treasure. Rey wandered around, looking at the piled cans, the shelves of wood for burning, the food wrapped in plastic, crackers, biscuits, most of it still good. He bent to look at a stack of big squashy bags, touching the shiny plastic.

'There's nothing you can eat there,' the Baron said. Rey

snatched his hand back. He knew that smell.

He sat cross-legged across from the Baron and nodded in thanks when the Baron passed him a can of beans and a fork – a real fork, so he didn't need to use his hands! He did anyway, scooping up the cold beans and eating them quickly.

'Been a while since your last meal?' the Baron said in her dry creaking voice. Rey set his emptied can back down, ashamed. He wiped his mouth.

'My mum always fed me good when she was around,' he said, because he didn't want anyone thinking badly of his family. The Baron nodded without saying anything. She didn't eat, just watched as Rey did, watched him like she hated him, but she couldn't, because they were friends. 'It hasn't been that long,' Rey said. 'I'm sixteen.'

'All right,' the Baron said.

Looking for something to say, Rey smiled wide, wide enough that his mouth hurt, and waved the bean can. 'You're very generous.'

'Ha,' the Baron intoned. 'Ha.' She stood up and went somewhere. Rey rolled his can on the ground, batting it between his hands, until he got bored and just sat.

He gave a start when the Baron came back. She moved more smoothly, but her skin was paler and peeling, blue underneath.

'You addicted to it?' he whispered. 'Pickle-juice?' It was good for the people who needed to fight off illness and keep living, could clean your wounds out, and it preserved the dead, but if you took it all the time … he'd never even heard of that. 'You mustn't even feel alive anymore.'

'What's so great about living?' the Baron said. 'This is better.' She kicked at Rey's ribs to get him to move. 'Sleep,' she said. 'There's work for you tomorrow.'

Rey curled up on the cold concrete and did. He slept much easier that night. There was no chance of the rain getting him down here, and the rain sometimes bit like fire or insects, and made skin go red and blistery and fall off.

He woke up and didn't know if Baron Taniwha had slept or eaten. She was still wearing the same clothes. She led him out, and stopped to show him another wonder: a whole stack of clothes, new and used and in all sizes, none with bad holes or stains. He felt them with his hands and whistled. 'You could give clothes to everyone in the Islands.'

'Give?' the Baron echoed. There seemed to be a lot of words she didn't know.

There were some trees growing near the Baron's storehouse, and the hidden entrance they left it by. She took him out to the edge of her side of the bridge and pointed. 'There. Do you see?'

He nodded. The River bent past the bridge, and in the crook of it the water seemed deeper, pooled, a patch of stillness. They went back.

Nearer the River the grasses grew smaller and brown. Several metres before the water's edge they stopped and there was just mud. Looking up and down the bank Rey could see where the old town had gone into the water.

'I need supplies,' the Baron said. She levelled her long gun at Rey, who blinked at it. 'Get down there and find what you can. Bring it back up. If you try to hoard it and run, I'll shoot you.' Rey nodded. The Baron looked at him, pale-eyed. 'Do you know what a gun is?'

'Sure,' Rey said. He pointed.

'Have you seen one used?'

He shook his head.

The Baron pressed her cracked dead lips together. 'What

about this?' she said, pulling a flare from her pocket, and Rey flinched. Those could hurt if they were let off too close to you, burn your skin worse than rain. 'There,' the Baron said, and pointed it at his face. 'Do it or I'll shoot you.'

Rey shook his head and laughed, turning his back on her and picking across the mud towards the water. His friend, the Baron, sure was a joker.

'Food is good,' she called after him. 'Jewellery to trade. If there's any bottled water that isn't tainted, bring that back first.'

'Okay,' he said, focused on the River water. It was brown and thick, and didn't move how water should. After the mud bank it dropped off steeply, so he didn't wade in, just curved his arms above his head and dived into the water.

It swallowed him with barely a splash. Rey kicked his way down, then opened his eyes wide against the strain of the water. All his body stung, but his eyes were the worst. It was worth it though, because he could make out shapes further in, where the water was deeper.

He swam with all his body then, kicking like mad and making scoops of his hands to pull through the water, which was thick, making it hard to get through but easier to go against the current. He kicked his way down, eyes straining. Murk and darkness. There was a shadow, maybe a drowned building, maybe a rock. He closed his eyes and opened them again, and swore when that hurt.

Air bubbled thickly from his mouth, and he closed it quick, shuddering and going still. It felt like probing fingers had pooled into his mouth, not water at all. He wanted to spit it out, but he didn't want to open his mouth again.

His lungs pressed hard against his chest. He should've taken more clothes off before he dived, but the problem was probably his lowermost vest, and he hated taking that off, except sometimes on girl days, and he hadn't had a girl day all week. Besides, he didn't trust this water.

He couldn't just hover here, losing his bearings. The Baron, his friend, was relying on him. He ignored the taste and kept on choppily swimming.

The deeper water was kept still and silent by the buildings buried in the muck, rearing up sudden when he approached them. A chunk of city drowned in shadows. Rey hung in the water in front of it, staring around. Did Welltown look like this, under the sea?

He touched a wall and kicked forward, using it to guide him. He came to a door and smiled at how it was sideways, rearing at an angle from the River mud. Rey kicked closer.

Something lunged at him, slimy and scaled, and he reared back at the touch of it and screamed. All the air left his lungs in big thick bubbles, and he clawed up after it as though he could get it back. He looked from his vanishing air to the doorway, and wanted to scream again in frustration. It wasn't a dead body or ghostie or monster, just a big fish, a koi. It dipped its fat head out around the edge of the door, regarding him, then with a swish of its tail was out of its hiding place and away, sending great puffs of mud when it touched its legs to the riverbed.

Rey's lungs burned worse than the rest of him now, and the edges of the River were thickening at the edges of his eyes like swarming black dots. He had to get treasures. He kicked forward again, shoving through the door, but it was dark as dark inside. He groped around, and touched something sliming and dead, useless. Reaching out, he couldn't feel or see anything else. He had failed, and it felt like exhaustion, like the last of him giving up.

No. He had to be happy, all the time. He had to, or they'd catch up.

Desperately Rey towed himself through the water, using his arms because his legs felt weak and exhausted. His lungs more than hurt now. There were bands squeezing at him, wracking his lungs so his body shook, wanting him to breathe in. He shut his eyes and opened them. There was a dead body watching him from one side of the door, long hair drifting limp in the water.

Rey pulled himself past, through a swirl of hair, and out, struggling, his limbs hard to move. His chest squeezed, and without meaning to, he glugged in a breath that was water. The taste of it was foul as a memory. Rey spun, desperately moving, then stopped. He hung in the water.

She stared at him. *Who are you?* she seemed to say. He felt the words like a crushing inwards of his ears. *Where do you come from?*

I don't know, he whispered, *I don't know. I don't remember anything. I don't remember my mother.*

The pressure pushed against his ears, hungry like anger, and he knew it was a lie. Rey did remember. He tried not to, but he did. He remembered his mother lying beside him, protecting him, and he knew what was wrong with the memory. She was cold.

There was more that was wrong. There was all that was wrong.

To eat your ancestors is the worst desecration, the dead woman said, and Rey cringed.

I had to, Rey whispered. His mind was fuzzing now and shutting down. *I was so hungry. There was nothing else to eat…*

In front of him something flashed and trailed away.

He wanted to move, to get out, but the water felt solid

around him, like it was holding him there. Like it knew his guilt. He closed his eyes.

Something rushed up beneath him, pushing him up, up, something cold and rough under his dim fingers.

Rey woke on the riverbank, and stared up with eyes that burned. The sky's red grey was the best thing he'd seen.

He turned over and was sick. He remembered what he had been trying not to remember and vomited again, his whole body shaking with it, bringing up nothing more than acid and a taste of mud. Rey wanted to roll away from the sick, but he could barely move. He flopped back in the mud.

He was able to raise his head, just. In the water something moved, fast and sharp. The creature's back pushed up massive through the water, with great cracks in its skin where pale flesh showed through and pale fish gripped and fed. There had been taniwha in this River once, he remembered. That was what the saying was.

This thing was huge, bigger than a log, bigger than three logs together. The fin on its back, cutting through the water, was a shape he remembered from stories.

Squelching footsteps and toneless cursing came from somewhere near him, and he craned his head. The Baron walked past, dragging one of the squashy plastic bags behind her, slippery through the muck. She stopped by the riverbank, then pulled, heaved, and with one great effort tossed it out into the water. She slipped on the mud, but got up again. The shark slid at it, barely two metres from the bank, its great mouth lunging up and tugging the bag soundlessly beneath. There was tearing and thrashing, flailing. Shreds of plastic floated up, and bits of the body.

The Baron did the same with the other bag, then walked back and sat, fell, on the ground near Rey. He blinked at her. Her suit was a mess. 'Whenever I call him I have to feed him, and there isn't anything else,' she said. She looked more human like this, all covered in mud so he couldn't see the blue stuff in her blood. 'One of these days I'll be eaten instead of being helped.' She shrugged, as though to say it was what it was.

Rey struggled into sitting up. The shark fed, then nosed at the bits of bag in case anything was left. Tears pushed up behind Rey's eyes, and then he was crying, sobbing, his lungs feeling like they were being squeezed again and pushing the tears out, water coming from his eyes and nose, shoulders shaking. The Baron sat stiffly beside him.

'I hate this world,' Rey whispered, 'I hate it, I hate it.' It was true, mostly.

After, he felt better. He wiped his face with his sleeve. The water was smooth now.

'You made me use my flare,' the Baron said.

Rey ducked his head. And he hadn't even found anything. 'Sorry.'

She said, 'No.' He glanced at her in surprise.

She frowned a little. 'I was using you, of course,' the Baron said tonelessly. 'It's dangerous to swim in that.' She brushed some mud off one sleeve, and she wiped her hand on the ground, but the ground was just as dirty. 'I still don't care, not like I should. In the old world I would've been a monster. I'm actually suited better to this one.'

Rey didn't know what to say. 'I like you,' he said.

'You're insane,' the Baron said. Rey bobbed his head. That was probably true.

Using his fingers, he combed the worst of the mud out of his hair. He'd need to put more dyes in it. When he couldn't find proper dyes, he would crush flowers and rub them in, and those had all washed off now.

His hair was thick and knotted, and he didn't remember it growing this long. He doubted, now, that he was sixteen or anything close to it.

Rey glanced at the Baron and dug at the mud with one hand. 'Those travellers,' he said, and she turned her head slowly to stare at him. 'They probably have more flares.'

The Baron sat with her arms laid over her knees.

Rey scratched his nose. 'They won't be far. And there's plenty of them,' he said, not quite meeting her eyes. He looked over her shoulder instead, at the bridge, upriver, then focused somewhere around her chin. 'They could use the shelter, and the food in an emergency, and we can all fight together when ghosties come. All together. *Whānau.* I know *that* word.' And if families didn't exist the same way anymore, well, they could just try to make new ones.

The Baron turned to look at the water. Had he failed? She said, 'Ugh,' not a throat-sound, actually saying it. Then she said, 'If we must.'

Rey smiled, not broad enough to hurt. They should go back, but he didn't feel like moving yet, and the Baron just sat there. She was quite slow moving, with her addiction. She'd still come after him.

Rey lay flat on his back, arms beneath his head, and looked, rusty, into the future, which he had not thought of in a long time. They could all work together. He could hunt, and ride, and scout. He would get the Baron off pickle-juice and everything would be fine. Or it wouldn't be fine. But his mother would be … proud.

'My mother's name was Maia,' Rey whispered to the sky like a prized secret, like getting rid of something heavy. He closed his eyes. 'And this river, this used to be the Waikato.'

The Architect

Phillip Mann

PART 2

LET IT BE SAID, THERE WAS NO LOVE LOST BETWEEN THE Architect and the administrators who managed the mining operation on Meredith. While the Architect had built his city, he had watched the crews come and go. To the enlisted men, Meredith-duty was synonymous with banishment. It was five years of thumb-twiddling; five years away from family and friends; five years of synthetic air and hydroponics food. For the most part, the commanders of the Meredith torus were professional officers coming to the end of their careers. Some just wanted a quiet life and time to build up their pensions. Others took pride in what, to the Architect's way of thinking, was mindless efficiency. Such a one was Commander Aaron Shelley.

From the moment of Commander Shelley's arrival several months earlier, there had been friction between him and the Architect. Their two styles of thinking rubbed against one another. This instinctive antipathy had reached its climax in a fierce row during which the Architect, never a politic man in his negotiations, had told Commander Shelley that he would have been better employed managing the garbage chute of a prison moon! To which Commander Shelley, an Australian by birth and no stranger to verbal debate, responded with remarkable restraint by telling the Architect that he and his city were 'a quaint and costly hobby'.

That did it. That one word: 'quaint'. No single word could have taunted him worse, not even 'hobby'. The Architect had made a rude noise in reply and switched off the communicator. He had not switched it on since, and hence had missed the occasions when Commander Shelley had tried to make amends. Instead, the Architect had worked. Worked harder than ever before, and in that time he had completed his city. Quaint indeed! He would show them.

The result of his anger was that the completion of the city had come upon him almost unexpectedly. Intellectually, he had always known just where he was in the overall plan, but emotionally he was not ready. He had not faced the question of what he might do *after* the city was made. Now the reality was upon him. In a few hours the last piece, the final small chamber with its flashing light, would be finished and sliding down the delivery chute, thence to be guided to its final resting place by one of the construction monitors.

Before opening contact with the world above, the Architect gave himself a shot of his *Aqua Mirabilis*. He knew that he would have to contact Commander Aaron Shelley soon of course and tell him the news. But not just yet, eh? Time for a bit of a party first. Very private. Exclusive. 'Here's to me. Here's to the City. Here's to all who will live here.' He awarded himself an extra dose of *Aqua Mirabilis*. In the olden days, the Architect was in the habit of drinking when he needed to. His favourite tipple had been whisky.

Once, he had managed to stay drunk for several days. That was when the inspiration deserted him. Sometimes he didn't know whether he was drunk or sober. That was when the inspiration was on him. But now, the *Aqua* was all he ever craved.

The warm flush made him shiver, but not with cold. The *Aqua* mellowed him. Perhaps he had been a bit hasty in his dealings with Aaron Shelley. The man did have a certain crass sense of humour. In any case, the Architect needed to tell someone that the work was done … and then of course he would have to contact those who had commissioned the City in the first place. They would need to come to see it. And … and … The Architect felt a deep and sudden sadness well up inside him. 'And then? What will I do then?' Unbidden, verses he had known when he was a student came to him.

Fear no more the heat o' the sun,
Nor the furious winter's rages
Thou thy worldly task hast done,
Home art done, and ta'en thy wages:
Golden lads and girls all must,
As chimney-sweepers, come to dust.

He sighed, blew his nose and approached the communication console again.

Much to his surprise, the machine chattered the moment he switched it on. A long paper message snaked from the printer. This was unusual. Most exchanges were verbal. Paper messages were more formal. The Architect guessed that the present message had been stored in the memory for some time. He ripped off the paper flimsy and read.

CCSED-RR-3/l 1717-a
Attn. Cdr Shelley.

By order of the Central Council for Space Exploration and Development, all activities connected with the colonisation of Planet Meredith are terminated as from receipt-date of this order. Construction of surface habitat to cease immediately. Standard closedown and evacuation procedures apply. All CCSED personnel will be reassigned upon return to HQ.

Closedown time-frame to follow. Confirm.

An indecipherable signature was appended.

The Architect read the message twice and it still did not make sense. What did 'Construction of surface habitat to cease immediately' mean? Did that mean *his* City? And what was this about the colonisation being terminated? None of it made sense.

He looked at the date and saw that the communication had been dispatched some six standard days earlier. That meant...

The Architect did not bother to complete his thought. He slammed home the relays he had removed to stop the machine plaguing him and pressed his automatic call sign. Within seconds the call was answered by a young man in a smart uniform, whom he did not recognise.

'Where's Aaron Shelley?' asked the Architect without preamble.

'And who are you?' asked the young man, staring at him with cold eyes. He then glanced to one side and checked the origin of the call. 'Ah. The Architect. The one who won't answer calls. Well, I hope you got the message. I hope you've nearly completed your clear-out. You should only bring absolute essentials. Too costly to bring out the big gear.'

'There isn't going to be a clear-out,' said the Architect, mustering his anger but feeling himself strangely unimpressive before the young man with the cold eyes.

'Wanna bet?'

'Who are you?' asked the Architect.

'Lieutenant Samuelson. Security and Intelligence. I'm here to see the Meredith enterprise closed down smoothly.'

'Where's Commander Shelley?'

The young man took a few moments before answering. 'Well now, I thought he was with you. He's on his way down to see you with the decommissioning crew at this very moment. When you didn't reply, we had no option but to take action on your behalf. Anyway, his team should be with you shortly. You'll be off planet in two days. Only bring essentials.'

He reached forward to break the communication.

'But…' The Architect looked at the young man as though he were speaking a foreign language. 'But what does it mean?' he asked finally.

'Mean? What do you mean, "What does it mean?" Can't you read? You're being closed down, old man. The whole operation. I'm surprised that you seem surprised. It's been on the agenda for years. They've found a better planet. Better climate. Just as rich. Less overheads. Meredith will be mothballed. It's a good and sound decision.'

'But they can't just…'

'Wanna bet?'

'What about the people?'

'What people?'

'The ones who are going to live in my city?'

Samuelson looked at him, and shook his head. 'You don't get it, do you? The project's over. There won't be any people coming to see it. Finished or not.'

'But—'

'Tell Commander Shelley to contact me as soon as he is

ready to close the main generators down. Okay?'

The young man reached forward again, and this time he did break communication. The screen died.

*

The Architect staggered back until he was sitting on his bed. None of it made sense. He felt a sharp pain in his heart and he beat his chest with his fist – pain killing pain. 'But they can't do this,' was all he could say.

The communication machine chimed again, and the Architect opened contact cautiously.

Was it all a joke or a misunderstanding or…

In front of him appeared the face of Commander Shelley. 'So, there you are. Good to see you're still alive. Just to let you know, there's been a slight delay. We'll be with you in about twenty minutes. We're just clearing the elevator now. Have all your personal effects ready. Okay?' The Architect did not reply. 'I have an electronics expert with me and she'll be closing the machines down, so please have the manuals all ready.' Still the Architect did not reply. There was a pause. 'I guess you're pretty upset, eh? But I did send you warning as soon as I knew.' Still no response. The Architect just stared. 'Okay. Well anyway … And I have a photographer with me who wants to take pictures for an article he's writing. So … okay. See you soon, I guess.'

And there the communication ended. Twenty minutes! After forty years! Twenty minutes! Well, he would make it as hard as he could for them.

He hurried from his room, past the design consul where lights were blinking, calling for attention, and into the corridor which led to the wide doors of the supply elevator. The elevator was up aloft somewhere, in use no doubt, and the access doors were closed.

Attached to the wall beside the elevator was a cabinet containing a first aid kit, a fire extinguisher and an axe. The Architect picked up the axe and used it to destroy the electronic door controls. Now they would have to smash their way into his quarters. He jammed the blade of the axe under the door and kicked it into place. Then he retreated into his control room and locked the door behind him. For good measure, he opened the main control cabinet and snipped some of the wires which controlled other doors.

All the activity had tired him and he stumbled back up the stairs to his bedroom. Almost by reflex, he reached up and found the catheter and connected it to the valve in his neck. The rush of the medicine into his veins made him gasp, but it eased something too. All shall be well. But his mind was now fuzzy. There was something … something he needed to do before … before what? He gave himself an extra shot and noticed that the reservoir was empty.

The Architect turned and slowly made his way down the stairs and into the control room. Everything seemed normal. Peaceful. He crossed to one of the walls and dragged back a heavy curtain. Revealed was a window. It was located high on one side of the vast dome and gave him an eagle's eye view of the entire city. The slim, beautifully shaped tower standing at its centre was almost complete: all that was needed was the final block. Every available construction monitor was in attendance, clustered round the base of the tower. They were like guests at a garden party or mourners at a funeral – he could not decide which. They were still now, their big mechanical mitts resting on the ground, their work almost done. But one was waiting, its rubber claws open. Very soon the tower would receive its final … What? Crown…?

Block…? And it would contain a light which could be seen from any part of the city. A symbol of some sort … of triumph perhaps.

Behind him, the Architect heard a shuffling sound.

He turned in surprise. At his design desk a progress report was unfolding from the printer. It had been doing this for some time and the folded pages had spilled out onto the floor. The report gave a detailed mathematical description of every aspect of the tower's construction. The fact that the report was printing now signified that the ultimate stress values of the whole building had been finally calculated and verified. The printer would chatter one last time when the final piece of the construction was in place and its light switched on.

The Architect gathered up the pages carefully, placed them in a binder and carried them to his records room where he slid the binder into place beside the thousands of other files which documented the building of the city. The room was almost full. He was aware how suddenly everything seemed ceremonial. Every action was significant … like eating the last breakfast at dawn before…

Interrupting such thoughts, a bell began to ring cheerfully in the design room. It was informing him that the cistern in which the final block would be frozen was now full and awaiting his attention. The small vanes, each no bigger than a fish scale, would already be gathering and locking into place, forming a perfect cube. Ha! Amazing. It was all coming together. The Architect rubbed his hands, suddenly boisterous, as though he had awoken from a bad dream to find the sun shining.

He crossed to the window again. This time he was amazed to see there were lights on in his city. That stopped him in his tracks. There were people too, and a fairground with music and dancing. He could hear singing. Only the tower was not lit and that was his job. That was something important he still had to do. He was glad to be reminded.

At that moment, he heard a noise from beyond his doors – the scream of metal on metal. Aaron Shelley and his evacuation team had finally arrived at the disabled elevator.

That noise. It set his teeth on edge. He could not think clearly. Who were they? Why were they here at this important moment? Did they want to destroy his city or claim it as their own? That must not happen. Hands over his ears, he hurried to the design desk and checked the Construction Programme was still active. It was. Everything was ready to go.

*

Inside the elevator, Commander Shelley smiled. 'Well you've got to give the old bastard credit. He's stuffed up the door. I thought he wouldn't go without a fight. Okay. Block your ears, everyone, and look away. There's gonna be a lot of sparks.' He hoisted the cutter and attacked the door lock of the elevator. He cut round it, through the door guides, and when he stopped the door sagged and fell outwards.

Moments later, Shelley and his team arrived at the inner door. Locked, of course. They discussed briefly whether it could be booby-trapped. But to settle matters, Shelley gave it one booted kick and it flew off its hinges. They surged into the control room. The Architect was nowhere to be seen.

*

No sooner had the shrieking of the saw stopped, than the Architect heard their voices at his door. He ran to the narrow, twisted passage floored with raffia which led to the freezing pits. As he ran, he sometimes bumped into the rugged stone wall, but he did not tumble.

He came to the red door. It was standing open. Now that was strange. How had that happened? Then he remembered … Yes, he'd cut some wires. Perhaps he'd cut the wrong ones and … Well, it didn't matter now.

He entered the space between the red and blue doors, but found that he couldn't shut the door. The green button which activated the hydraulic arm was dull and lifeless. He heaved and tugged but the hydraulic arm was stiff. Then he kicked it and finally he stepped onto the hydraulic arm and jumped up and down. The arm came away from the wall. Over forty years of alternating hot and cold, hot and cold had weakened the connection. The arm now dangled, loose. He pushed and the door closed.

Immediately the second door opened smoothly and silently and he entered the Freezing Chamber. Behind him he heard another sound; it was the smashing of the door into his room. Then he heard voices calling … calling him by name.

Quickly, the Architect closed the switch which would activate the freezing. It would happen now in five minutes.

Inside the Freezing Chamber, the Architect stepped away from the door, intending to hurry over to the small pit where the final block would be waiting, its vanes all locked and the surplus water drained away. From where he was he could see the still surface and the reflection of the roof lights.

In his haste, The Architect neglected to step into the magnetic overshoes. Inevitably, as soon as he tried to hurry, he slipped on the thick oily jelly which coated all the metal structures. He fell and went slithering and sprawling across the floor. His head hit one of the uprights for the safety fence, and for a moment he passed out. But his body skidded on and only stopped when it was at the very lip of the cistern.

He began to struggle to his feet. He was aware of a trickle of blood.

Behind him, in the wall of the cavern, the blue door opened slowly and Commander Aaron Shelley stepped through, accompanied by one of his team, a man who had visited the vast cavern years earlier as part of an honour guard.

The Architect was now struggling to stand. He was holding the safety rail and staggering like a drunk.

Commander Shelley was about to set out towards him when he was stopped by his companion. 'Wear these, sir,' he said, pointing at the magnetic clogs. 'Or you'll slip like he did. That jelly stuff is lethal, and it burns.'

Other members of Shelley's team arrived at the door, ogling in amazement. But one of them, an electronics specialist, touched Shelley on the arm. 'I think we only have a few minutes before this place blows,' she said. 'He's tampered with the electrics and the safety override may have collapsed. Just to let you know.' Aaron Shelley nodded. Then he set out, clunking awkwardly towards where the Architect had now sunk to his knees beside the shimmering pool.

Arriving at the safety rail, Shelley reached down and seized the Architect by the hand. 'Come on, old man. I'll pull you back.'

But the Architect shook his head and Shelley could see he was crying. 'No,' he said, his voice breaking. 'For pity's sake. Let me be. This is where I belong.'

For a moment Commander Shelley hesitated. Then he released the Architect's hand and gave him a gentle push.

The Architect fell back, almost in slow motion, his arms spreading wide as he fell into the water which billowed round him. The Architect gave Shelley a crooked, child-like smile before he sank.

*

'Sir. Sir. Hurry. She's about to blow.'

Commander Shelley turned and clunked his way back to the door. He kicked off the clogs, entered the small chamber and closed the blue door. The team hurried out of the temperature lock, and pushed the red door until it closed. The electric bolts slammed home.

Seeing Commander Shelley's surprise, the electronics specialist shrugged. 'I repaired the connection,' she said. 'Or we'd all be dead by now.'

Any further explanation was cut short by an explosion and a massive shock-wave which blasted the blue door off its hinges and shook the red door to its very foundations. The last block was on its way.

*

Some time later Commander Shelley held a meeting in what had once been the Architect's design room. His team were quiet and thoughtful, gathered in a circle. He regarded them, uncertain how to begin. 'I tried to save him,' he said. 'But…'

'You did everything you could, sir.'

'We all saw that, sir.'

'You have no reason to feel reproach, with all due respect sir.'

'It was what he wanted, sir. It was why he was there.'

'Okay,' said Commander Shelley. 'If we are all agreed.'

'We are, sir.'

'Well, I guess we'd better start clearing this place up.'

And this they did, gathering the notes and sketches and

the vast pages of data documenting every building in the city. One member of the team stood at the window marvelling at the complexity of the city below him, and he noticed something moving.

'Commander. I think there's something you ought to see here.'

Shelley, who had just finished speaking to Samuelson, explaining what had happened and why they were delayed, crossed to the window.

'There. Do you see, sir? The rail path down the main street leading to the tower. There's a block being moved along. A cube. If you look closely you can see something of interest. Use my binoculars.'

Shelley focused on the block which was almost perfectly translucent. At its centre he could see the sprawled figure of a man, spread-eagled as though caught at a moment of falling. A red stain, like frozen silk, surrounded his head.

'Good God. It's him.'

The others came to join, and one by one they shared the binoculars and expressed their astonishment. They watched as the block was manoeuvred inside the tower and then hoisted up. They could follow its passage through the clear ice walls. At the top, they saw the sparkle of lasers as the block was annealed into its place and deep frozen again. It filled the top of the tower perfectly, completing the structure.

There was a moment of stillness and then a light at the apex flashed on and began a steady blinking – on off, on off.

On off, on off…

Splintr

AJ Fitzwater

One Body.

IT'S THE LAST SUNSET ON EARTH. AGAIN.

Yes. I chose to stay and look death dead in the eye. I prepared for a swift end. What I didn't know, when I stumbled home dirty and bloody from the Hagley Park evac zone that yesterday of six months ago, is that I would die over and over. Six months of facing the shell, the convex nothing, that swallows me every night from the South Pole around.

My deaths are nothing so soothing as sleep. They slip the knife of stars in under my defences, readying to flick away another piece of me in the morning. Everything stops: the baleful red eye peeking between the eyelids of the shell; the stars; the tracery of my thoughts; my heart.

And in that last knowing wink from the universe, as the Earth is cut off from the rest of it, there is hope. Hope that the last sliver of silver light gives out for good, that the Collective's ships are beyond reckoning. Hope that tomorrow I'll wake up dead and this will *all stop ending*.

Stop. Stop these new memories. Of a world I didn't know,

didn't ask for. Stop reliving. Stop dying on these southern cliffs.

That, or at least put the puzzle pieces of myself that break off every morning back together. To make some sense of why it keeps ending.

Aeron, m'girl, people would say, *making sense has never been your strongest quality.*

Well now, there's sense in giving death its due.

Now they don't say anything. Now they don't even people. What did the Collective promise those eight billion to save their souls? Everything. And nothing. A future, but not one here. All because these greatest minds in the universe, who we didn't even know existed until a few short weeks ago, couldn't quite say what the future looked like inside the planet-eater, though they'd been saving civilisations from it for millennia. There's no adequate name for it, in their languages or ours. The Dark suffices, along with the promise of letting humans become more than human.

Promise, or threat?

I might not be the brightest biscuit in the tin, but I know liars when I see them. None of the Collective could truly show us their faces. They couldn't survive in our atmosphere outside special suits, so they said. Yeah, some of us cried wolf. The Collective were perfectly, infuriatingly, reasonable to that. Those who didn't want to Ascend were given the choice of asteroid ships that housed other Questioner factions.

So, gods don't all think alike.

So, how do I die today?

Picking a spot takes careful consideration. It's the only thing I have any control over on this day on rewind. Waking at 8am in my old cold Christchurch flat, filling the banged-up station wagon at the Mobil where the pie warmer is always turned on and full. I resist, but this all happens as it should.

No need to shower. Who's gonna smell my stink? Theoretically, I had a shower late last night to remove the triumphant emptiness smeared on my hands and face. Shower today, and pieces of me may be sent out to sea too early. Lost count of how many pieces of me have broken off. Takes only a few moments for another piece of myself to flake away each morning, like shaking off the hangover from a bad dream. This shed reptile skin acts as if I'm not even there, fragile derma that could crumble to dust in the merest breath. It goes wherever it pleases on walkabout to the edges of the South Island. Just hope they don't fall off.

I'd like to say the pain is bearable. If pain is all I can offer, then let's do pain the best way possible. Raw skin. Screaming nerves. Absorbing every last moment and micro-meteorite puncture wound. Still, not sure what is more painful: the roaming pieces of my skin, or the growing blankness when I reach out for old memories. Everything else from that first last day onwards is intact. And on that new day when they crack open the shell in a thousand, a million, a million million years, they can excavate the archaeology of my dust and discover what truly went on here.

Continuity. Yes. Be careful of distractions, losing track of time.

I always point south from Christchurch. Want to be as close as possible to the border between flesh and blood when the Dark comes. It's the best I can do in what little time is left. Sometimes I go as far south as State Highway One will take me, right to the dead end of Bluff. Sometimes I sit out on the Fortrose Cliffs or near the Waipapa Point lighthouse, kicking my feet over the edge, not wanting to go before I have to.

Right now? That border is the cliffs just beyond the Curio Bay campground. Tattered awnings and rusting Zephyrs hunker at the arse end of anywhere. Antarctic fury has pushed trees into arthritic angles, and carnivorous summers hide cicadas ready to scream seventeen years of sexual frustration.

Now the cicadas hold their bows and the wind holds its breath. The smashing grey water has stilled, listening for the onrushing tide of star-crossed nothing.

The deathly cold puckers the edges of my raw wounds. I pull the sunset around me like a blanket, but it doesn't suffice for the lost layers of armour. Would be nice if my skin could come back and tell me what death does to their pieces, what they think of our choice which wasn't a choice at all. Would those skins fit any better after their sixteen hours of freedom, with their divots and hastily sewn rents?

I'm being punished for wanting to leave the road marker of my DNA here. I'm the spanner in the works, the bacteria in the petri-dish, the cat perhaps, or perhaps not, in the box. The Collective wouldn't risk turning back for one mere speck. They've gathered the motes in the corners of their eyes, done their good deed.

Look, there it goes. Losing the fight above the horizon of the upper shell. The silver star, shrinking so quickly over the course of the day, quicker than should be possible. It'll be back to thumbnail size come tomorrow morning, if I'm unlucky. Do they look behind while I look ahead?

Only the molten red eye watches now. Pushing down. Waiting for the crust to splinter off. A singular thought bouncing off the inside of the empty skull. I don't do thoughts well. I lift, I hold, I tear.

How will death feel tonight? Short and sharp, a snapping of teeth? A slow peeling back of the layers; flesh, then nerves and arteries, bone, organs, ash? I can never quite disappear. We always return to stardust.

Goodnight. Die well. I'll see you in the morning.

*

Two Minds.

Fascinating. The last sunset on Earth is happening. Again.

You've been searching for the perfect equation to explain this phenomenon that has you stuck in the same day over and over, but not even science fiction has the answer. Maybe there isn't one, even the Collective expected that. Entropy happens, as simple and complex as it wants to be.

Aeron, people would say, *you think too much.*

Now no one is here to add their collective brainpower to the equation. They have bigger problems to attend to, like getting the hell out of the Solar System in time. And Ascending.

Sure, the Collective made promises to the human mind: faster, better, more. But there's nothing like good old fashioned on-the-ground observation. Go West Coast, for the best worst sunsets around.

Gather data. Analyse in that superb organic computer. Archive neatly for retrieval. *They* EQUALS human or post-human AND/OR Collective AND/OR species unquantified AND/OR all. Death EQUALS the dark shell devouring all PLUS x. x EQUALS unquantifiable. x does not have a soul/spirit OR anything useful beyond the barrier of heat death.

IF only you could put your body back together like a puzzle, make everything function at full capacity. Those pieces of you that slough off every morning must have collected some good chunks of raw data by now. They're everywhere, never in the same place as you, searching for their own truth, oblivious to any other of your selves.

You hope they find what you're looking for. You would like to make a useful observation one of these days other than the shell looking like a closing eyelid.

Choosing the right spot to die takes calculation, good timing, and the precise angle of the bars of sunset through that eyelid with its star-less greed.

Luckily, no South Island coastal edge is more than eight or nine hours drive from Christchurch, giving you plenty of time to walk out further. Marfells Beach, Punakaiki, Bruce Bay. Even the sandflies know what's up and hang in sad little clouds of welcome. It's not cockroaches that survive the end of the world, it's the blood suckers. They've tasted everything. It's in their DNA now.

Farewell Spit is always a nice choice, though it doesn't give the perfect angle. It's the golden sand, the hesitant blue of the water as it reluctantly leeches away to grey, to the liquid obsidian knife edge cutting the world open along its ley lines.

Yes, you know you're holding on to humanity with too firm a grip. There's nothing left to do. The choice was taken away from you. You wanted to go. The Collective in their strange suits said, 'Go, collect what is important to you. We have time. We'll wait.'

They lied.

It's a mistake you don't intend to make again.

If there are places devoid of data, it's the evac zones. The centre of everything until they were violently, silently not. You watch yourself run back to your seventh-floor apartment on Victoria Street to fill hard drives, flash sticks, e-readers with science texts. Had the Collective uploaded the world's entire digital store of knowledge to their great library ships? There had been so little time, mere weeks, and humans had to compete for space with thousands of other Ascended species. How useful would all that information be, once they'd gone post?

You ran back to the park, not that far away. And you shouted *wait, wait*, but that final evac pod had gone without you. Within moments Christchurch was all quiet. Not even the sagging oaks and willows, hugging their branches about themselves along the Avon, murmured farewell.

You stood for hours staring at the shrinking silver hole in the sky. There was no use screaming *come back*. Screaming is so pointless.

The silver star got small impossibly quick, as if they knew what they had done.

Oh yes, you firmly believe this is an experiment. The Collective's arrival was too damn convenient. No time, just go. No use sullying the monster with romance. This world-eater was bigger, hungrier, more random than them. *Here is the way home*, they said, pointing away from one darkness into another. At least, there were stars in their direction. A faction of the Collective could not abide unpredictability; you agree on the specious concepts of luck and coincidence. Everything is quantifiable, even if the answer isn't immediately obvious.

The Dark must really annoy them, then.

And now … the silver finally winks out. You know the damage their backwash does as it swarms over the planet, over you. It takes energy to retreat from death that fast. The Collective hadn't been entirely forthcoming about many things. But there was no looking a gift escape in the eye. Maybe that backwash is what triggered these months of

Sundays. Maybe that's what they intended.

Data, dammit. Too many variables, too many holes. Solve for x.

Here's a variable: are there more like you, left to collect data? Not the pieces of you, but others wandering other countries, watching parts of themselves fall off. It seems likely, but only you and yours are what remain on the South Island of New Zealand. There are no ways to contact the rest of the world, they made damn sure of that. They vacuumed the vacuum. No satellites, no stations, no junk. The night is the clearest you've ever seen. Convenient.

The great eye is getting real tired now. The southerly has shuddered to a halt, and the sand rubs listless at your feet. These are just emotions, clouding observational facts. Turn your back on the east. You don't desire to mourn yet another sunrise, but desire has nothing to do with it.

Watch out. Here it comes.

It's the same as always.

A last tui tolls a death knell from the sweet-salt-smelling bush, but is cut short.

Good night. Die well. You'll see everything in the morning anyway.

*

Three Lands.

Aeron is watching the last sunset bury itself into the Earth. Again.

There is no choice about looking death dead in the eye. It is what it is.

Aeron m'boy, people would say, *you hate that phrase. You're always the master of your destiny.*

Now they don't say anything. They chose to abandon this land for new ones carved out of asteroids by the Collective, persisting with the new plate tectonics of this universe.

Picking a spot to die every day takes careful consideration, good map reading, and careful driving. He doesn't want to die before he has to, before he's saluted every last rock that he can. No GPS now all the satellites are gone. Riding the backbone of Te Waipounamu gives the best view: Mount Cook, Arthur's Pass, Cardrona. Everywhere below and beyond is crimson-flecked white wave tops, the grinding rock tide of the Kaikouras and the Southern Alps. Throwing pebbles from that high up won't start an avalanche.

Today, regrets fall one by one into the valleys below the Island Saddle.

But he shouldn't be able to see all the way down like this. He can't quite shake the feeling he's standing on someone's shoulders, watching the walls from all angles as they crumble.

It must be those pieces of him that chip off like shale beneath a chisel every morning. These rolling stones must be a side effect of what's happening to the planet in its death throes. An attempt at species repopulation in spite of the harsh climes. Too late, too soon.

He can't hold the land together with just his hands and willpower. It would take an intervention of god-like proportions to stop the Earth being encased by the Dark. And the gods that did a drive-by were out of time and ideas.

Just when humans had crawled out from under the delusion that they were special to the universe, they get a mere few weeks, a whisper, a glance, of undivided attention from the parental unit. Then they're thrown to the dogs of vastness again.

The gods looked away.

This, whatever this becomes, would require new gods. Or none at all. Hands were just as good at shaping clay.

Had enough about Earth geography been uplifted to the Collective's great data storage ships? Many didn't think information about a soon-to-be-dead planet would be relevant. Humans had barely scratched the surface. The Collective were experts by millennia of default.

If they ever wanted a *hope* of putting the puzzle pieces of Earth back together, they were going to need atlases and textbooks. So that had been his task in those weeks locked away in his tidy 4-bed 2-bath in flat-land suburbia. Sorting and choosing relevance. The weeks of civility and resignation gave no sense of urgency. Why riot and loot, hurt and maim, when you can't take it with you, when borders were moot?

By the time he decided he was prepared, the last shuttle was clawing a hole in the sky, the evac zone in Hagley Park scorched and empty. He'd stood there for the longest time, shaking a fistful of flash drives, shouting *wait, you forgot these…*

Maps. Desire lines. The best and quickest routes. Linkages. Drawing a line from there to here. These are what he's good at. And by god, if that's all he's got left, he'll etch them on his skin with needle and blood if he has to. What else is going to survive the forever night as the shell closes its eye on the world? Paper will burn. A signal will degrade the further it travels. There'll only be his skin left, those pieces of him stretched across the continental plates, stitching the Earth together until someone comes to scrape the palimpsest clean and start anew. He is cartographer, witness, bacteria, thief.

He examines his hands, the ones that can't pull up the anchor of Maui to let the waka float away into the milky stars. There must be something in this DNA, the random collection of wrinkles and calluses, lifelines and scars that have moored him so securely to this land. Maybe just the right amount of nothing, maybe just the right amount of skin. There's certainly plenty of him to go around, if the dust on the floor every morning is anything to go by.

And now: the sunset, with its encore of darkness. It gets cold very quickly this far up once the shroud smothers his face. There is no worry of freezing to death. Every last moment counts, etched into his flesh by near-invisible dust particles attracted early to the inside of the shell. At that speed, the dust looks like anti-meteorites, stars pummelling at the nearby heaven in a futile gesture to embrace their siblings.

He blinks, and for just a moment the three islands have joined hands. He's so large, he could step from one mountain top to another, across the Cook Strait and keep on going, striding over the Pacific to batter his fists against the walls of other continents. And then he is small again, with a perfect view down to the west. If he can see to the coast on a night like this, death is worth it.

He imagines approaching the planet like one would a map, two dimensions curved by the hands of gods upon and over. Is this how the Collective saw him, clinging to the top of the bottom of the world?

He thinks of all the names for this place – the ones before, the ones now – and tries to imagine what those names would become after.

What names did the Collective have for their places, solid and in-between, before they too were eaten by the Dark? He knuckles his eyes. The skin stretches aching across his bones, washed clean. There is no use for a name when there is nothing to attach it to. 'You Are Here'.

The atmosphere shudders as the silent lullaby sweeps it clean. The Earth is tired. Soon it will be too hard to breathe.

He counts every vertebra of the alps, the peninsulas dipping their dragon heads into the sea. He is the master of their destiny, at the end of it. He etches their names into his skin with his teeth and fingernails, a gift to his descendants.

The great red eye looks away.

Good night. Die well. Please don't be there in the morning.

*

Many.

Here we are. The last sunset on Earth.

Time to pull the sky from the sky.

We drift down the gravel road towards the Curio Bay camp in ones and twos, Aeron pretending to be oblivious of the other Aerons. We are full of sunsets and skies, rocks and bones, carbon and oxygen and nitrogen. We have left our stardust on everything.

The salt-rusted caravans hunch, prepared for the bitter southerly; it's the bitter end they're getting instead. Trees stretch their branches, ready for a farewell embrace.

We stare over the Southern Ocean, the cliffs falling at our feet. Eyes strain, waiting for that first glimpse of onrushing death. The sky, its copper tang sweet on our tongue, weeps blood.

The great eyelid droops. It winks. And winks again. The silver hole diminishes, but is not gone. It is a needle. We, the thread.

This is not how this day of days goes.

A light brush on the shoulder, like a hand resting there, soothing. Some of us stand close. Others still dot the far edges of our vision, imprinting those last images and impressions. Everything matters, and nothing.

The inside of our elbow itches still, like all the raw places on our skin before. Eczema. Pieces of us still wanting to flake off, go wherever they please. Road markers. Souvenirs. Reminders. Maps. Memento mori.

To what purpose?

This.

We beckon each other closer. Tell us what we know, Aeron. What have we seen out along the barricades? We are all coming back, to clothe Aeron against the endless night. Skin upon relentless skin, our armour. We shall come together and apart, a step forward, a step back, hesitating on the lintel of death. We shall spread our knowledge along the ground and out across the convex shell that is about to become our universe.

The Collective left us here. We are humanity in one name only. No. We *are* the Collective; we joined their ranks in that last moment when we made that choice, when they chose to leave us behind, when they left us here by accident. We are their eyes, their ears, their dozens of other senses, some of which we are yet to discover.

We shall become. We are here to witness, if only for ourself. And one is enough.

We are their experiment. They are ours. A closed system. One day they will crack open this shell and feed upon what has gestated inside, gorge themselves with millennia of good nights. And we will nourish them with what has been writ on our skin, what we imbibed of this infinite, this few dozen, this one sunset.

We won't be able to give of what we know of death, because of death we have not received.

The wings of the shell are almost together, the tendrils along the edges reaching out to interlace like hungry, searching fingers. Only patches of the space beyond remain. Only moments until death.

The familiar lethargy does not push us towards the gentle drift of sleep. We huddle closer, so many of us that our edges overlap, blurring, and we cannot tell where we begin and end.

So it shall be.

We hold our breath.

Once the lungs start burning, we let it back out again.

Nothing.

The edges of the shell meet.

We arch the neck back. The sky is complete, a rare treat.

Complete, except for the new stars.

These stars are not the purple-blue diamond scatter of the Milky Way. They are much closer, pinholes to another reality, etched on the inside of the shell. They are not constellations we recognise, but, given enough time, we hope to. Some of the stars are so close we comprehend their yellowness, their blueness, their inward gasp of black on black. The largest, the brightest, the closest, is a perfect silver.

For the first time in the many deaths we've set ourself to observe, we look behind.

They wait patiently for our instruction: What do we do in death?

Do as you always do. Run. Hide. Observe. Wonder.

Or do nothing, if it so pleases.

But beyond us, more are coming. They are us, but not us; us from above and below, beyond and before. They're a new puzzle piece, a new iteration, a re-evolution to add. Their edges shimmer ice-blue, dust-grey, oily green and purple, liquid silver in the remaining Cimmerian light.

Their curiosity has killed them. They have come back.

One Life, No Respawns

Tom Dullemond

THE OLD JACK LAUGHED DRYLY WHEN HE SAW THE MOTTO behind me. The sharp sound of it, his little coughs of appreciative mirth, bounced around my small office.

'Man, I used to hear about you guys all the time.'

I didn't need to turn in my chair to look at the wall, but I did, despite the pain, just to set him at ease. I didn't *really* look at it though.

'They made, like, five VR shooters about you guys. That's how they trained you, too, right? Virtual shooters? No respawns.' He laughed like no one had ever made that joke before. 'You're almost like … a mascot for the recruitment agency. Company must've paid a fortune for the rights to use that. And you!' He laughed again.

I turned back to him and crinkled as much of my face as I could in a smile.

'Hah, yeah. Good times, my friend, good times.' The plastic of my cheeks felt tight, but I don't think the jack noticed. I tapped my false nose conspiratorially. 'Still got my one life.'

But not my one job. I forced myself to keep the edge of

frustration out of my voice. As if my screw-up was this jack's fault.

You're right, I'd said to my boss, parroting his lecture. *I don't think I'm a good fit for this organisation anymore. Vets can be pretty touchy and what I did to that guy … yeah some people can take it, but I should have known better, of course, I understand. Yeah, he's in a frakkin' psych ward now, I heard. So there's that.*

I didn't say any of that out loud. The state cut my pension again and I really couldn't afford to lose another job, this job of 'giving other vets jobs'. I was scraping the bottom of the office work barrel, and now I'd scraped so far I'd fallen through the bottom and what was there, in the beyond, beyond the barrel? I guess I'd find out.

'So how long have you been working here?' asked the jack.

'It's my last day, actually.'

'Oh?' The little vowel hung in the air and instead of answering it, I pushed the sheaf of e-forms and a stylus across the desk, a quiet reminder to the jack of why he was here. 'There's a placement on offer with a private security company. They have a pretty good psych on staff locally, and a couple of Earth-based professionals available over priority solar network links.'

Something shifted in the jack's eyes and I could sense that I was skating close to whatever his private hell was. Back in the corps, we were all pretty hands-on, maybe the last hands-on soldiers in the system, and I couldn't really imagine what might break a jack. None of the ports in his neck looked damaged, but their kind of free-running through hostile computer networks came with its own horrors.

'Yeah, I get a lot of chatter in here,' he said, touching his face. His eyes were suddenly wide. There was a tremor in his voice. 'Lot of flashbacks, you know? You mesh pretty tightly with the tech.'

'No to the links, then.' I smiled, more broadly this time. 'That's why they employ a local.' I struggled to think of a real world analogue for a winky-face. That's what that sentence needed. A stupid smiling winky-face stuck right on the end of it. *I'm on your side, buddy. I'm no different to you, man, we've been through the same things. Wink.*

But of course, we hadn't. Him with his booth and wires and shooting his consciousness out across the networks and through and around high tech ICE; me holding Anka's brains inside her head as though it was just a bleeding flesh wound I could staunch with pressure, Kolain's tired shake of the head as she pushed me aside and put a bullet in the rest of Anka.

One life, no respawns. Both an invective spat into the eye of our enemy-of-the-day, and a promise to the last of the hit-dirt-and-pray soldiers.

Our roles reversed then. The jack must have seen my own face shift, a difficult thing considering how inflexible most of it was. He wasn't trained to deal with vets like I was, so he just ran his stupid mouth.

'Probably saw some crazy stuff in your time,' he said. 'I did some work with the corps once, 2057 clearing out tour.' He laughed, and I thought, *No surely that's too much of a coincidence,* and then he said, 'New Sydney, it was, or what was left of it,' and, of course, that opened the gates.

'Hah, yeah, I remember that.'

I tapped at a screen to flick through stats. Everything had seemed clear, plenty of power left in the units. My team was picking through the New Sydney rubble still, so it was unexpected when Kolain called us back via the emergency channel.

Most of the ruins had simply sagged over the decades, hunched their shoulders and settled into the dust and debris, over forgotten, desiccated civilians. Hidden in the dust lay countless fragments of depleted uranium ammunition, pushing the Geiger counter readout in my helmet to almost 1,000 times normal background radiation levels.

I snapped my hand sharply across the sensors in my chest and my mechanised units stopped picking through the rubble and stood to attention. On my heads-up display, I saw the icons of Anka's team first freeze, then head inwards from our perimeter, back towards Kolain's safe point. In rapid succession, Moria, Jacques and Gert-Jan's teams followed suit. There were only nine dots left in Gert-Jan's squad, which made me wonder what resistance he'd encountered.

I hesitated to follow the order. My units had uncovered a piano – a dry, cracked thing that would've been stuck under the rubble for a decade – and underneath it a skeletal mummy in the shreds of a military uniform.

Kolain's glyph in my visor flashed red. A brief message blinked beneath it.

HTFU

One of the politer ways Kolain used to hurry me up.

I directed one of the scout units to document the find and waved for the others to follow me back to the safe point. It was autonomous enough that it would come back when it was done, but worst case one of the jacks at HQ would find it during a map scan and guide it back manually, assuming no enemy e-war algorithms found it first.

Gert-Jan's units started disappearing off my visor. *Aw man*. They blinked out, one at a time. I couldn't hear anything over the crunch of my own feet in the dirt and the padding of my squad. I sent a scout and three infantry units across the rubble in the direction of Gert-Jan's position, but I cautioned them. Something had ambushed him, there was no other way he could've lost three, now four, units that quickly.

Everything was so quiet. The sound of steps in dirt, the occasional whir of the fans in my helmet kicking up. Somewhere out there was mute warfare. Gert-Jan's units were gone and it was just the glyph of him now, moving across the HUD map projected into my eye. Then, that too vanished; all silent. One life. I couldn't abide that silence.

I blinked very slowly. The jack looked back, mouth slightly open, gaze flicking around my face.

After another moment, he took my stylus and filled in his application e-forms for the security job. 'Not too often you get to reuse your skills in a civilian company,' he said, breaking the silence. 'So many things I picked up out there, even just on the networks. If I tried that stuff now I'd go straight to jail.' He paused. 'What did *you* leave behind, out there?' He asked it so casually, initialling *here* and dating *there*.

'I just love that idea, man,' he added, even though I had clearly ignored his question. 'Just … being able to use your skills to the limit again, but back here in the real world.' He paused apologetically. 'This job seems cool, though.' He finished signing. 'Job hunting skills are really networking skills, they say.' He tapped his forehead, tapped all the tech hidden inside that skull somewhere. 'I can do networking.' His smile cracked a little.

I thanked him and stayed seated as he left. I wasn't ready yet for the metal pain of standing up and seeing him out, the spear in my spine with each step. *Always be as efficient as you can*, Kolain had said. *No point charging through jungled streets when all the automated defences run full-spectrum cameras and can tell a loitering baboon from a macaque at three hundred metres.*

'No frakkin' respawns,' Anka yelled in response, laughing manically. Her grandfather used to call her 'Yolo' and cackle like it was some secret generational joke. I looked it up once; it was just some stupid acronym.

Jacques helped me with the Chlorin e6 eyedrops and because we were on such a time constraint, I was still blinking into my night vision when Kolain took the team further towards the compound. Our remote jacks disabled the nearest security cameras and our mechanised units swarmed across the streets, firing precision bullets and shaped EMP bursts at enemy placements. I flicked on the camo suit and moved in, perfectly visible to the rest of the team, but with the heat profile of a bunch of confused cats. We only had to fool artificial vision, after all.

When the weapons fire started I didn't even realise I was hit; I was behind Anka, and she was silhouetted by sudden whitesmoke deployment, frozen for the briefest instant before the hard *pak* that knocked her helmeted head sideways, and then me running towards her crumpling shape, oblivious to the gaping tear in my thigh and the wetness blooming there, and the gas canisters raining down around us, and each breath burning a gash deep in my chest, stripping me raw, skin and bone and heart.

I tried to calm the ache in my lungs, pulled some reports and glanced at my watch. I waited for the ex-jack's footsteps to fade. It was almost time to go home.

You know it's pointless, Kolain's tired voice, and then the muted *crack* that finished Anka.

You know it's pointless, my own inner voice anticipating

the exit interview feedback.

customer satisfaction is low and you need to do something with that face prosthetic is a problem but can't you get a surgeon just to clear it up so we can't see this working out for everyone because these vets are sensitive and with your attitude is a problem and we really don't think

Decent hit rate today for placements. End of business day imminent. Pain levels nominal, which was nice because the doctor kept telling me I'd eventually become resistant to some of the stronger pain relief, the kind that got me to sleep through a solid night.

The lights dimmed on cue and I struggled to my feet, leaning heavily on the desk. I caught a glimpse of the wall behind me: Anka, Gert-Jan, me. A goofy group high-five on a battlefield I recognised but couldn't remember. I wouldn't miss it.

One life, no respawns, the motto said beneath it.

It was supposed to be a curse to the enemy and a promise to the troops, not a corporate slogan. Not some shiny promise to burned-out high-tech soldiers, scrabbling to make sense of the normal world, whatever the hell that meant.

I sucked an anticipatory breath against the pain and lurched towards the door, where Kolain and I regrouped, spinning in the centre of our units. Four-legged hound artillery cleared out the horizon beyond our line of sight, while several scouts wheeled out to telemeter the targets and locations to our visors. We fired single smart shots whenever the reticules on our helmet displays agreed with the tiny virtual intelligences in our guns, taking out barely visible enemy units before their scrambled visual systems could lock.

A single contrail cut across the clear sky and then a silver confetti bloom burst above us. Kolain swore. 'That's it, jacks are out. EMP flak killed the whole damn network.'

The units dropped back to local and autonomous modes, which suited me fine. I called back the infantry units, sent them left to flank an embedded cluster of targets, while I searched for cover in the smoke. I didn't have a visual on Kolain, but her green blip in my visor reassured me.

I spotted a tunnel opening to my right, hurried in while I shot commands to the artillery to lay a wall between me and the infantry. Stung by splinters of stone, I reached safety and tumbled into the elevator, leaned heavily against the wall to catch my breath.

Before my units had cleared the field, Kolain's green blip flickered, and I lost sight of her on the visor. I rapped at the helmet, the ancient ritual that miraculously realigned sensitive electronics. Gone.

With my fingers still pressed to my temple, I pushed myself off the wall. When the elevator doors slid open, I stepped onto the sidewalk, tapped my wrist to summon an autocab, and tried to ignore a faulty streetlight sizzling in the rain. My own visual systems were almost entirely electronic and something in the frequency frizzed my left eye. Half my body was constantly on high alert, burning through my mental reserves, while the other half always felt like it ran a few milliseconds behind the rest of me, like watching your own hand through a digital camera lens. I closed my prosthetic hand ... and my prosthetic hand closed. My brain had never let me obscure that lie.

I checked the time, which was an excellent mission-critical obsession to have, and moments later the autocab pulled up. I clamped down on the urge to crouch for cover, to tap instructions and push units to the front and back to escort us home, send scouts around to divert traffic, artillery to lay down an exclusion zone. The autocab waited in the silence, mute to my frantic strategising.

I took a careful breath. I leaned down painfully to climb in and shuffle onto the seat. 'My place,' I muttered, and the cab accelerated and drifted into the light traffic.

No respawns was a lie. *One life* was a lie. I died out there and respawned back here, in this haphazard fan-made level.

I glanced out the tinted windows, watched dimly lit buildings float past. I confirmed my team had me properly escorted, scouts running ahead, tracking enemy targets and sending back analytics in tiny encrypted bursts. 'Yolo!' Anka yelled hard in my earpiece, crackling through the static in my head. I twitched the softer corner of my mouth in a thin smile.

That's when the explosions started behind me in the office building. I counted the sharp sounds of them, the little destructive coughs.

AND STILL THE FORESTS GROW though we are Gone

AC BUCHANAN

THE HERO MUST ALWAYS FIND HIS WAY THROUGH THE enchanted forest. You can take the pick of the dangers that may lurk there: dragons or cannibalistic witches, nixies luring you to the river, or the forest itself, slithering into traps that bind you to your fate. The prize is usually a woman, of little interest to you, but you may still find wealth or a crown upon your head. There are many possibilities. This is your forest, after all.

*

Overhead you hear through your dreams the drone of engines, the Hercules filled with the last of the refugees – stubborn, to have left it this late – leaving the South Island. The North is already gone and the forest is closing in. You don't know how long you'll have left.

*

For the first time in years, you're sharing the house with someone. Not just with someone, but with strangers, three of them, who've taken the spare bedroom, library, and office for their sleeping quarters, who cook in your kitchen and sit at the dining table playing cards in the evenings. You've let your house become a hub because it has a rainwater supply, a generator, and a septic tank, because you can't really live alone and because Glenn built this house himself for you both and you can't bear to leave it.

You've learned, by now, to recognise these strangers' footsteps on the hardwood floors, and that was Lauren who just walked past; hers are heavy, determined. She's usually first in the shower – not that it matters, it's always cold.

It's dark outside. You switch on your torch and pull on an old, but good-quality, pair of jeans and button up a shirt. The others will get breakfast in their dressing gowns, but you're liable to be considered a doddery old man if you do, and if they doubt your capacity you may end up evacuated without your consent.

There's still bread left from the last food drop, so you can make a good breakfast with eggs and toast and canned beans. It's not all bad. But as the light grows you can see kelp shoots pushing up through the grass, some no more than fifteen, twenty metres away. You'll go and burn them off, of course, but they'll come back. You're not stupid enough to think you can win this war. There's no breadcrumb trail out of this one.

'Smells good.' Wiremu Meihana squeezes past you to grab a plate. He's a big lad – rugby player, you assume, when there were still enough people around to make more than one team. Bright too, a scientist. He worked on the kelp farms, in research and development. Perhaps that's why he stays. Guilt. Or perhaps he believes he knows enough to solve this problem.

You don't tell him that you're just as guilty.

After a while, Lauren eats too, her hair smelling of floral

shampoo she must have hoarded somewhere. You don't care for yourself; you barely have any hair left, but it worries you. Selfishness, secrets, have the power to undo you all.

'Nari up yet?' Lauren asks. Wiremu shrugs. 'We were going to go wring the necks of the chickens that have stopped laying.' There's a hint of pleasure in her voice. Nothing like making a guy raised in the city squirm.

'Well, before that,' you say, 'let's go burn back some of that kelp.'

Lauren rolls her eyes. '*Already*? We did that yesterday.'

'In case you hadn't noticed,' Wiremu says, 'that shit grows pretty fast.'

She slides into her walking boots and laces them tight and the three of you walk out into the dawn. There's a hint of frost on the ground and it's just cold enough to see your breath as you walk. Another party, parents and two teenagers, signal to you in greeting. If you look carefully, others are doing pretty much the same thing, walking the perimeter with blow torches, small fire extinguishers at the ready. Hoping to keep this last piece of land, hoping that by some miracle the kelp forests can be beaten back and the land can be saved.

But the cities are in ruins and your time is short. Even over the past few weeks you've found yourself increasingly short of breath. You'll be seventy next year and have resolved to die here, but that time may come sooner than you'd hoped.

For now, you keep up with the others and hide any signs of exertion. Around you, against the horizon, the kelp forests are closing in, fifteen metres high and more. Brown slippery leaves towering against the sky, beckoning towards you in the gentle wind, filling the air with the salty, metallic scent of iodine.

You're not sure why this rugged section of Southland has

been saved. Perhaps your efforts have helped, burning back each new shoot, but there were more than a million people in Auckland, with the Defence Force and aid from Australia behind them, and yet the city was still overrun by the seaweed. It pushed through cracks in the concrete, entangling itself around traffic lights and trees and then into the buildings, shattering glass as it grew through apartments and offices.

'Maybe even the JAFAs were glad to see the back of it,' Lauren had said, once. You laugh at anything you can these days.

While the chickens are meeting their fate outside, you go round and collect the sheets from the beds. It's been a while since they were washed and you think keeping up with chores like this is important for all your wellbeing. You pause when you get to the library, where you'd sat and read when Glenn was alive. It still has its rimu shelves – he made them himself – and many of the books, but it's Nari's bedroom now. So much of the past has been sucked away. You tell yourself that at least he didn't have to witness this happening to the land he loved but, selfishly, you really need him here right now.

*

Your mother told you tales of the Black Forest, of the darkness beneath its evergreen canopy, of the ruined castles and the creatures which lurked within its depths. Of cottages that could transform to a palace, or the scene of your grisly death. Of dwarves and werewolves and virtuous peasant girls with selfish sisters.

But that was hundreds of miles away, and the forests you grew up in were those of broken stone, bombed out shells of buildings, the debris of destruction and slow reconstruction.

You were born as the Battle of Berlin drew to a close, shielded from the worst of the aftermath by a mother who fed you first, as mothers often do, and yet there was a slow trauma reverberating in you all your life. You were told your father died before you were born; perhaps it was true, and either way it was likely for the best.

You were following a boy when you came to New Zealand, of course you were, but you were also looking for a place where the dust had settled and the air was still.

*

Sometimes you try to think back to the days before. It's a guilty process with one question at the heart: *what could we have done differently?* But it would have been hard, even for those who ran the kelp farms, to predict how this would unfold, let alone for you, a retired small-town accountant.

In those years the inevitable end was taking the form of rising temperatures and rising sea levels. A trajectory the world has not unshackled itself from, you remind yourself, though of course these islands have more immediate concerns. But then you thought salvation was an option, and kelp was just one potential saviour amongst many.

You still got newspapers delivered, right up until the printers stopped and the family who owned the nearest dairy left the country. You liked the texture of them, spreading them out across the table in the morning. In those pages you saw the first pictures of the farms, and though you had limited interest at that stage, you had to admit they were spectacular and, more than that, they were tangible, evidence that something was finally being done.

On television there were adverts, competing power companies desperate to prove their concern for the environment. In the evenings, over an imported beer, you saw the film recorded by underwater cameras navigating a path between the towering stalks and then the image softly fading into that of a child switching on the light and grinning at the new future open to them. This new biofuel, the voiceover said, had limited CO_2 emissions and would not take up valuable land or fresh water. All Natural, All Safe, All Ours.

And then Glenn's cancer came back. The future seemed not just irrelevant, but a brutal, mocking presence. What happened next, you caught up on only after he was gone.

There were five large developments off the coast of New Zealand, along with other research centres, and it's generally agreed the problems started in the largest, east of the Coromandel peninsula. Was there a defined point in time when it began? Perhaps not, because if the seaweed was growing faster than expected, or pushing the boundaries of the designated area, no one was too worried.

Over the course of a year or so, it came closer to land, close enough that they closed the beaches for swimming in case people became entangled in it, dragged down beneath the waves. The area became jokingly referred to as Sargasso, and while there were calls for government intervention, and the energy companies lost some of their environmentally friendly credentials, it took a while before people were truly concerned.

The generally accepted theory is that a genetic modification experiment, designed to increase the hardiness of the kelp and expand the range of conditions in which it could grow, had been more successful than intended. Before long, it was poking above the surface, and then higher, as if the sea were populated by bushes and then trees, growing closer to the land until you could walk amongst it at low tide. A marvel of nature, they called it, beckoning tourists to these shores.

But warning signs grew and the excitement deteriorated. People started to talk about management, and then about herbicides. Shipping lanes were disrupted and the fishing industry was all but destroyed in some regions. The kelp continued unabated, spreading around the country's coastlines, growing higher, closing in.

*

Lauren and Wiremu take the quad bike out to the supplies drop. There are fewer people there each time they go. They say the RAAF offered to take them out on that very flight, and that they won't be able to keep bringing in supplies indefinitely.

Wiremu seems disconcerted by this prospect, but Lauren isn't worried. 'I told them the chicken we had yesterday was pretty good, and that we have leftovers. And there's a good vegetable garden going by the marae,' she adds. 'There are maybe thirty people living up there now, heaps of kids running round. I asked someone there, she said if we help them out we can take some food. It's community, eh, helping each other. That's a good thing.'

You want to have faith in community, but the parcels, whether you need them or not, are more tangible. Sausages, cheese. Large sacks of rice. Panadol and antiseptic cream. You eat the rest of the chicken for lunch and Nari makes a casserole for dinner. You hang around as she cooks, half-heartedly cleaning up then trying to work out how to use the satellite phone. You wouldn't touch it in front of Wiremu; show a moment's hesitation and he'd snatch it off you, but here you have the time you need to work it out.

'How are your daughters?' you ask after some silence.

'Very good.' She drains the cans of beans into the sink. 'Sophia is starting her Master's degree. Moving to California. And Melanie – she says nothing but I think there might be an announcement soon. Very hopeful.'

'A baby?'

'A marriage. Then babies. She's old fashioned.'

You're tempted to ask the obvious question: *Why don't you leave, Nari, be with your daughters?* Wiremu has his guilt, and Lauren has barely been as far as Wellington, can't conceive of another land. There are some for whom this whenua, this land, cannot be separated from themselves, or who believe they are duty bound to stand guard over it, and others whose nerves are so shredded by fear they simply cannot leave. For you, it's stubbornness, an acknowledgement that your days are already numbered, and that you've little appetite for starting again and no ties anywhere else. The Berlin of your childhood is unrecognisable; the few visits you made to your mother revealed a different city, and she is long gone. Your only known relation is a much younger sister who you barely know.

But though you're curious about Nari's motivations, you hate being asked the question yourself, and so you refrain from inflicting it on her. You're immigrants both, and despite all your combined decades on these islands, you're used to thinking of yourself as transitory, rootless. And yet you're holding firm here, when so many have gone.

And for the moment your lives are good enough. You eat decently, sleep well. That won't last forever, but it lasts for now.

*

You don't miss the cities, exactly, but there was a comfort in knowing they were there, anchoring you to the rest of the world. Now they're crumbling buildings and shattered glass, fallen into a forest of kelp. They say that up north you can catch glimpses of the Sky Tower among the leathery strands of seaweed, grown and woven together, but that's all.

Auckland fell first, then Wellington, the harbours turning to forest, the shoots growing inland, breaking up Wellington's reclaimed shore and then up the hills faster than they could be beaten back. You mentally check off cities: Christchurch, Tauranga, Dunedin. Hamilton was the last major centre to fall, but the kelp came up the river ahead of its progress across the land, and they evacuated, jets taking off in quick succession to Sydney, then returning for a new load of refugees. Soon after, the seaweed broke through the runway, cracking the tarmac.

And then the entire North Island was forest. You understand, from the patchy satellite internet, that they can land teams for research, but certainly no one can live there. Let's face it, they're not hoping to reclaim the land, just trying to prevent the same fate befalling another nation.

Now the South has gone the same way, all except a patch of land maybe ten, fifteen kilometres square, around the edges of which the growth of the kelp has slowed, but does not stop. A patch of land you have called home for half a century.

*

You haven't used a gun since your Wehrdienst, a young man amongst other young men, amongst forests – forests of trees, yes, but also of tents and barracks, of uniforms. Forests of repetition which is what forests are at their essence; repetition you can become lost among. Your mother cried when you left, as if you were really going to war, as if you could not possibly be back in six months. In a way, she was almost right; by the time you returned to Berlin you'd already begun planning your passage to New Zealand.

But today you have a gun in your hand once again and Lauren is leading, gently schooling you. You tell yourself it's to hunt wild pigs and kill the cows humanely when their milk runs dry. You tell yourself that, but the supply drops are stopping in two weeks, and what you produce here can't sustain everyone forever.

Wiremu is uncomfortable around guns and not afraid to show it, but Nari seems excited by this sudden power that has been placed in her hands, whooping each time she hits the makeshift targets that Lauren and Wiremu rigged up.

Your shoulder hurts from the recoil more than you thought it would, and after a while you take a walk, while the sound of gunfire penetrates the air behind you. Your body finds new ways to ache, new ways to fail you, and though you are nominally healthy for your years, it feels like everything is pointing in one inevitable direction.

But there's a cold, clear, Southland sun above you and a pasta bake waiting to be put in the oven. You're alive for now.

*

The last flight out takes 29 passengers. Amongst them are the Lemalu family (and you're relieved because that boy of theirs is barely two years old), Jana Reid, Sione and Jenifer Robertson, Crystal Makea and her girls, and elderly Mrs Morgan. You remember being a small child, and your mother carrying you outside to watch the planes make their descent into Templehof, remember being young enough to have faith in uniforms and in flying machines. The population of New Zealand now numbers a couple of hundred, and the outside world will not be helping you any longer.

When you return home from the drop, your backpacks full of supplies, Wiremu has his laptop out, the table covered with paper. He's in his element, calculating your resources, projecting needs and worst-case scenarios, what you might trade. Lauren and Nari survey the house for vulnerabilities, places where mice might get in and eat the rice and the flour you have stored. There are guns in every room now.

Lauren guards the house while the rest of you walk the couple of miles to the community meeting. The meeting's in a school next to the marae, long deserted by children. Their artwork still covers the walls. Most made it out alive, you tell yourself. Most are safely in Australia or further afield; most, but not all. For some, the kelp will have weakened the foundations of their houses until one night the whole structure collapsed, the roof crashing in on them, crushing them to death as they slept perfectly forever, parents running through the forest in despair, in search of help that never came.

Some will have been lost forever in the forest. They'll have wandered out while playing, or perhaps they woke one morning and found the kelp growing around their house and ran in the dark looking for their parents until the dark closed in. Perhaps they sat leaning against a damp trunk and cried, or perhaps they tried eating the seaweed but found it salty, and there was no water to be found.

They say that if you go into the forest you can hear them, laughing and gurgling, as if swimming under water.

Time for you to break from this line of thought. Tragedies

happen, children die; it's just the way of the world. You can only focus on what you have: three people who were not long ago strangers, determined to cling to this rocky patch of land. No, more than that: in this hall you have two hundred and eleven people – you know this once the record-sheets go round on worn clipboards with biros attached to them by string – who refuse to leave.

After the karakia, Lorena Sánchez is the first to speak. She says she wants to thank – and here her voice quivers a little – all those who have helped them, taken care of their children. She appreciates their concern about her husband's illness but, she says, she's left one country behind and found a refuge here, and she cannot bear to leave another. The crowd applauds her, with genuine support but perhaps unease at her decision.

This fate is not so terrible, says Bethika Auld, a woman of forty or so who has emerged as a community leader in the past few months. Many catastrophes have threatened all your lives, over and over again. Is the land being reclaimed by nature so terrible in that context? *Perhaps we've found the community we never had, and now we know that each one of us can do what we once thought impossible, we can build a new community here.*

Jim Henderson pins a map to the wall behind him, a number of concentric though irregular shapes which show the progression of the kelp. You're trapped from all directions. He tries to stay optimistic, though, pointing out areas where the lines are close together, an indication that their efforts are having an effect.

In your mind, the close lines on the maps indicate a steep slope. It feels as if you could fall forever.

*

You're woken by noises downstairs. You pull on your dressing gown, grab the crowbar from beside the bed – the gun doesn't even occur to you – and go to investigate. There's someone in the kitchen, rummaging through the cupboards by torchlight. You're thinking what to do: whether to confront him, or to get Wiremu for backup, when he hears you, leaps forward, pins you to the ground with his hands around your neck. The torch falls to the floor and smashes.

You're struggling against him in the dark, the blood pressure building in your head, your thoughts blurring, when there's a light and for a split second you see Kieran Auld's face before his hands loosen and he falls onto you. Later you'll realise that the warmth you feel is his blood, pulsing onto you then spreading out over the vinyl floor.

When you pull yourself free you see Lauren, her hand grasped around a kitchen knife. The colour has drained from her already pale skin. Her hands are trembling and her face is sinking in on itself. You recognise not just shock but horror. Wiremu takes her to the bedroom, feeds her sickly, barely-dissolved Raro to get her blood-sugar up and tells her to try and sleep.

You and Nari wrap the body in a sheet and take it outside. While you soak your clothes with bleach – they're too precious to get rid of – you try and work out how to tell his family.

'I don't understand it,' you tell Nari, your fingers aching and raw, a small penance. 'The Aulds are so well prepared, and everyone likes Bethika. Couldn't she just have asked?'

Nari has the mop in her hands, ready for a third attempt at the floor.

'People don't always act in rational ways. It happens more the closer the forest comes. There are strange things out there, people not what they seem.'

You look up.

'Do you really believe that?'

'Of course not. But I think you do. You might be right, I might be. No one to decide for sure.'

In the morning, Lauren is gone. You don't see her again.

The words hang in the air, but no one says them: *If anyone could survive this, it would have been her.*

*

As the weeks turn into months, you look back on the early days with envy, as if they were filled with feasts and laughter. You're rationing yourselves now, and the food is bland, the only seasoning salt and the Italian parsley which is thriving as every other plant wilts. The hunger persists even when you eat.

Wiremu, especially, is noticeably thinner, lethargic. He pushes on with the heavy work, but without the protein he needs to sustain his muscles. You have little flesh to lose. There are eggs one day in five, at best. It'll be time to kill the last of the chickens before too long.

Another ring is drawn on the map, and then another. But you don't need those to see that the kelp is coming closer, and you're not comfortable at the meetings anymore anyway. People might say that Lauren had no choice, that he shouldn't have been stealing, but in her absence they blame you just the same. Bethika sits silently at the back now, and no longer addresses the group.

So today Nari guards the house and Wiremu goes alone. You walk out early in the morning to burn back some of the kelp shoots, which are appearing with increased frequency. You burn and burn though your arms ache and you feel uncomfortably warm from the proximity, watching the singed stalks die, taking some comfort from this minor victory despite knowing they'll be back tomorrow. You burn and burn, zigzagging back and forth between them. You reach the edge of the forest.

Even the smaller of the kelp plants – trees, you increasingly call them – are taller than you. You stand between two of them, staring into the darkness. Something is enticing you, calling you. It's the soft voice of a lost child, the cackle of an old woman, the scream of a wounded animal, the authoritative command of a guide who'll take you somewhere from where you'll never return…

You wonder, briefly, if these kelp trees soaked with the stench of fish are Tāne's descendants, or if this is an overgrowth of the sea, of Tangaroa's domain. You wonder, not for the first time, why it seems filled with stories you brought with you from another place and another time, if they've finally taken root, an infestation of sorts. You wonder if it's all your fault.

But such thoughts are their own kind of arrogance. As if you could control this land and this sea and this sky which, as you take cautious steps into the forest, becomes dappled and patchy, barely finding its way through the leaves.

A few more steps and you'll be unable to see back to the open land. Those few steps are itching at you, an urge longing to be fulfilled. But you hear Nari calling your name, she calls and you turn and walk back into the light. You blink as your eyes adjust. You're not going that way. Not today.

*

That evening Nari and Wiremu start yelling at each other. It's a stupid argument, about water conservation and frequency of household cleaning, but at this point it seems anything has the power to tip people into tension and tears. You've never heard Wiremu yell before; he's always had the presence to make himself heard without needing volume. You try to block it out, grab a book from the shelves and mumble lines of poetry you half-know by heart in the hope the rhythm will comfort you.

You're interrupted by shouts outside and the sound of a quad bike. Wiremu's needed. He's not a doctor, has nothing but a first aid course behind him, but people think his Master's in biology counts for something.

You and Wiremu grab the bike and follow. The sun is beginning to set; it sets earlier these days, falling behind the kelp which now stretches six metres high or more, enough to keep this increasingly small patch of land edged by shadow.

On the way, Jim shouts to you over the noise of your bikes. 'Accident at the Sánchez's. Their littlest is really sick.'

When you get there, you realise he hasn't told you half of it. You see bodies outlined under sheets; Lorena and David Sánchez and their two sons. Their youngest, Ellie, all of three years old, alive but barely, surrounded by a crowd.

Carbon monoxide poisoning from a barbeque in the front room where they slept, someone tells you later. No one says that Lorena and David would never have made a mistake like that, or that if they'd asked for help then they'd have probably have managed to get an evacuation team in, because what's the point?

If Ellie survives, they will tell her that her family went into the forest.

*

You go into the forest. You must always go into the forest. The kelp above you cuts out the sun and you walk by torchlight.

You feel, as you take steps too light for your heavy boots, that there is a piece of the story missing; that you should be dropping breadcrumbs or marking each fifth trunk with a knife or trailing a length of string behind you. But such things are for people who expect to find their way out.

More life has survived than you expected. *Damn possums*, you think. *How typical that they would outlast us.* They seem to be laughing at you from high above.

You keep walking. You turn off your torch to see how the darkness feels, and it seems less claustrophobic than the light. Now you could be anywhere; out on the plains, atop a mountain, standing on the deck of the ship that brought you here all those decades ago.

There are no stars. The air is too still. You switch the torch back on.

You are somewhere that is neither land nor sea, and years of stories lap at invisible shores.

You hear wolves howling in the distance. You hear the voices of children. You hear the axe of a woodcutter: chop, chop, chop on the slippery trunks.

Many have brought stories with them. It can't just be yours that have slipped out.

Chop, chop, chop.

In the distance there's a voice. It's not a peasant child, and it's not a witch. It's calling your name.

Closer, and you recognise Wiremu's voice, bellowing into the seaweed.

'Mike, please come back. They've found a herbicide that

targets the kelp. They're testing it up North and then they'll deploy it here. We're saved.'

You stay quiet, and still. You try not to breathe, hope he won't find you.

You know that he will have brought some breadcrumbs, or a ball of string, or marked every fifth trunk with a knife.

About the Editors

With five pointy Sir Julius Vogel Awards on her bookshelf, and an Australian Shadows trophy in shared custody with co-editor Dan Rabarts, **Lee Murray**'s most recent work is the military monster thriller *Into the Mist* (Cohesion Press).

The author of several novels, shorts stories and novellas, Lee is proud to be the editor of five fine anthologies of speculative fiction. Her work-in-progress is a middle grade adventure, *Dawn of the Zombie Apocalypse*. Find her online at leemurray.info.

Dan Rabarts is a multi-award-winning short fiction author and editor, podcast narrator, and sailor of sailing things. He was the recipient of New Zealand's Sir Julius Vogel Award for Best New Talent in 2014, and the co-editor of *Baby Teeth: Bite-sized Tales of Terror*, with Lee Murray, which won the SJV for Best Collected Work and the Australian Shadows Award for Best Edited Work that same year. Dan and Lee continue to collaborate on projects, including a crime-horror novel set in a dystopic near-future Auckland. His SFFH short stories have appeared in venues such as *Beneath Ceaseless*

Skies, *Andromeda Spaceways Inflight Magazine*, and *Aurealis*, on the Hugo award-winning podcast *StarShipSofa* and others, and in the anthologies *Regeneration*, *In Sunshine Bright and Darkness Deep*, and *The Mammoth Book of Dieselpunk*, to name a few. He is one head of the writing band Cerberus, which includes fellow kiwi author Grant Stone and a certain hairy mango, Matthew Sanborn Smith. Find out more at dan.rabarts.com.

CONTRIBUTORS

Joanne Anderton is an award-winning author of speculative fiction stories for adults, young adults, and anyone who likes their worlds a little different. She sprinkles a pinch of science fiction to spice up her fantasy, and thinks horror adds flavour to just about everything. Her science fiction/fantasy novels have been published by Angry Robot Books and Fablecroft Publishing. Her short story collection, *The Bone Chime Song and Other Stories*, was published by Fablecroft Publishing. It won the Aurealis Award for best collection, and the Australian Shadows Award for best collected work. You can find her online at joanneanderton.com.

Richard Barnes lives, works and occasionally writes in the coolest little capital in the world: Wellington, New Zealand. His short stories have been published in *A Foreign Country* and *Tales from the Bell Club* amongst others.

For a fresh take on Royal Weddings, with added monsters, sword fights and car chases, check out *The Royal Wedding from Hell* e-novella at smashwords.com.

And why not check out his reviews of the 11th Doctor's

era on reviewthewho.wordpress.com. And one of these days, seriously, Richard WILL write a whole novel. And he blogs at richardbarneswriter.blogspot.co.nz.

Carlington Black lives in an apartment on the Wellington foreshore with his cat Poe, and his late parent's hound, Jimmy.

AC Buchanan lives just north of Wellington. They're the author of *Liquid City* and *Bree's Dinosaur* and their short fiction has most recently been published in the *Accessing the Future* anthology from FutureFire.net and the Crossed Genres Publications anthology *Fierce Family*. Because there's no such thing as too many projects, they also co-chair LexiCon 2017: The 38th New Zealand National Science Fiction and Fantasy Convention and edit the recently launched speculative fiction magazine *Capricious*. You can find them on twitter at @andicbuchanan or at acbuchanan.org.

Octavia Cade has had stories published in *Strange Horizons*, *Apex Magazine* and *The Dark*, amongst other places. Her short fiction has been BSFA- and Sir Julius Vogel-shortlisted. She'd previously sworn never to do a zombie story in her life, but a month pet-sitting for her sister destroyed that notion when she found herself a) burying a dead chicken under the front lawn, and b) skittering back out to that lawn in a thunderstorm at midnight, to roll a heavy planter on top of the grave just in case. (She'd been watching a horror film and is entirely too suggestible).

Shell Child is a writer and a sound designer for films and VR games. Some films she's worked on include Steven Spielberg's *Tintin* and Neil Blomkamp's *Elysium*.

Shell lives in Wellington where she's working on her latest writing project, a young adult sci-fi novel series. Shell's had a few short stories published in New Zealand speculative fiction anthologies. Storytelling is her passion. She believes the world is what you make it, and so spends most of her time creating worlds. The rest of her time is consumed by movies, wine and cheese. Check out her blog at shellchild. me.

Debbie Cowens is a writer and teacher, living on the Kapiti Coast with her husband and son. She has contributed to a number of anthologies, including the award-winning *Baby Teeth: Bite-sized Tales of Terror*, for which her short story 'Caterpillars' won the AHWA Best Short Story Shadow Award in 2014. She co-authored *Mansfield with Monsters*, and her first novel *Murder & Matchmaking* was published by Paper Road Press in 2015.

Jodi Cleghorn (@jodicleghorn) is an author, editor, small press owner and occasional poet with a penchant for the dark vein of humanity. Her stories have been published locally and abroad, including the Aurealis-shortlisted *Elyora/River of Bones* and the flash collection *No Need to Reply*.

Tom Dullemond stumbled out of university with a double degree in Medieval/Renaissance studies and Software Engineering. One of these degrees got him a job and he has been writing and working in IT ever since. Tom writes primarily short fiction across all genres, including literary fiction and the occasional poem. He co-authored *The Machine Who Was Also a Boy*, the first in a series of philosophical fantasy adventures for middle-grade students, and has short fiction published in a handful of anthologies and magazines including *Suspended in Dusk*, *Danse Macabre* and *Betwixt Magazine*. He is the co-creator of Literarium, an online writing management portal.

AJ Fitzwater is a meat-suit-wearing dragon who lives between the cracks of Christchurch, New Zealand. A graduate of Clarion 2014, they were awarded the Sir Julius Vogel Award 2015 for Best New Talent. Their work has appeared in such venues of repute as *Beneath Ceaseless Skies*, *Andromeda Spaceways Inflight Magazine*, *Crossed Genres Magazine*, Lethe Press' *Heiresses of Russ 2014*, Twelfth Planet Press' *Letters to Tiptree*, Random Static's *Regeneration: New Zealand Speculative Fiction 2* and many others. Their ideal dinner party guests would include James Tiptree Jr, Joanna Russ, Anne McCaffrey, and Freddie Mercury.

Jan Goldie writes books and short stories. Her latest creation is a children's fantasy adventure about a boy called Brave and a girl named True. The book features a magical world, strange creatures and months of travel without a bath. Jan loves coffee, champagne and raspberries, so she wouldn't last long on that journey. You can find out more about Jan and *Brave's Journey* by visiting her website at jangoldie.com.

JC Hart is a mother and writer who resides in Taranaki, cushioned between the mountain and the sea. She is the author of several works of both long and short fiction, including several short stories in award-winning anthologies, of which one, 'The Dead Way', was a finalist for the Australian Shadow Awards 2014. Alongside her writing, JC is also a freelance editor, and the co-chair of LexiCon 2017: The 38th

NZ National Science Fiction and Fantasy Convention.

Perth-based writer **Martin Livings** has had over 80 short stories published in a variety of magazines and anthologies. His first novel, *Carnies*, first published by Hachette Livre in 2006, was nominated for both the Aurealis and Ditmar awards, and has since been republished by Cohesion Press. Find him online at martinlivings.com.

Phillip Mann was born in Yorkshire. After working in Drama in the USA, he and his wife moved to New Zealand in 1970 where, apart from working in the theatre, he founded the first New Zealand Drama Studies Department at Victoria University.

He began writing Science Fiction while working at the New China News Agency in Beijing. To date he has published 10 science fiction novels (all with Victor Gollancz) and his most recent work, *The Disestablishment of Paradise*, was a finalist for the Arthur C Clarke Award in London in 2014. This year, he was made an Honorary Literary Fellow by the New Zealand Society of Authors.

Further information on his writing can be found on his web page at phillipmann.co.nz.

Paul Mannering is an award-winning writer living in Wellington, New Zealand with his wife and two cats. His writing crosses the range of speculative fiction genres from horror, to sci-fi and philosophical comedy. Paul is the author of the Tankbread series; *Apocalypse Recon: Outbreak*, published by Permuted Press; and the first two volumes of the Drakeforth Trilogy, with Paper Road Press. He holds a long-standing grudge against asparagus and believes that we should all make an effort to be courteous to cheese. He appears on Twitter as @paul_mannering.

Keira McKenzie resides in the desert lands far to the west across the Tasman ditch. In the city by the sea, she spends her time torn between drawing/painting and writing. She has sold illustrations, artwork, short stories and essays. She doesn't know which comes first: the painting or the words. She has a PhD somehow, despite the cat, the would-be triffids of the courtyard, and the (mostly) invisible dragons of kitchen gardens and rain drops.

Shortlisted in the Sir Julius Vogel Awards, **Eileen Mueller** has won SpecFicNZ's Going Global and NZSA's NorthWrite Collaboration awards. Co-editor of *The Best of Twisty Christmas Tales*, an anthology including stories by Joy Cowley and David Hill, Eileen was also sub-editor of *Lost in the Museum*, the 2015 Sir Julius Vogel Best Collected Work. A New Zealander of the Year Local Hero, publicist, and marketing consultant, in 2014 & 2015 she managed Wellington's Storylines children's literary festival. In her spare time, Eileen sings in a barbershop chorus, runs community planting projects and juggles children – usually without dropping them!

Since 2011, Perth short story writer and PhD candidate at UWA **Anthony Panegyres** has had numerous stories published in anthologies and also Australia's premier literary journals (*Meanjin* and twice in *Overland*). He has also been an Aurealis Award Finalist for Best Fantasy Short Story (republished in *The Best Australian Fantasy & Horror*, 2011). His most recent stories have been published in the anthologies

The Best Australian Stories 2014 (edited by Amanda Lohrey) and *Bloodlines* (edited by Amanda Pillar).

AJ Ponder has a head full of monsters, and recklessly spills them out onto the written page. Beware dragons, dreadbeasts, taniwha, and small children – all are equally as dangerous, and all are capable of treading on your heart, or tearing it, still beating, from your chest.

Specialising in dark fantasy and horror, **Angela Slatter** has won a World Fantasy Award, five Aurealis Awards, and a British Fantasy Award. She is the author of, among other things, six story collections (including *Sourdough and Other Stories* and *The Bitterwood Bible and Other Recountings*), has a PhD, and was an inaugural Queensland Writers Fellow. Jo Fletcher Books will publish her debut novel, *Vigil*, in 2016, with its sequels, *Corpselight* and *Restoration*, coming in 2017 and 2018 respectively.

Her website is located at angelaslatter.com and she can be found on Twitter @AngelaSlatter.

David Stevens lives in Sydney, Australia, with his wife and children. He has worked in criminal law for 25 years, including a year spent in The Hague recently, working with an international tribunal. His fiction has appeared in *Crossed Genres, Aurealis, Three-Lobed Burning Eye, Pseudopod, Cafe Irreal*, the anthology *Love Hurts*, and elsewhere. He blogs irregularly at davidstevens.info.

David Versace lives with his family in Canberra. He occupies his time between meetings of the Canberra Speculative Fiction Guild with minor acts of public service. His work appears in the CSFG anthology *Next* and in the forthcoming *The Lane of Unusual Traders* from Tiny Owl Workshop. Find him online at davidversace.com or on Twitter @_Lexifab.

Emma Weakley is a freelance illustrator and sometimes writer currently living on the Kapiti Coast. Her first book, *Jack and the Beanstalk,* was published in 2010. She has won the Sir Julius Vogel award in 2008 and 2014 for best professional artwork. Emma uses a mixture of traditional drawing and digital painting.

Summer Wigmore has written many books and published one, so far: *The Wind City*, published by Steam Press. This is their first foray into sending out short stories, and shows the excellent rewards of foraying. Lately, Summer has also taken up a bewildering variety of crafts, from candle-making to drying their own ingredients for tea. A living experiment in gentle pretension.

EG Wilson cut her authorial teeth writing *Sherlock* fanfiction at uni when she should really have been studying. She fell into writing science fiction after being inspired by *Star Wars* and That Whedon Show That Was Cancelled After One Season, and has since won NaNoWriMo four years in a row. She lives in South Canterbury, New Zealand; she loves mountains, hates broad beans, and never wears matching socks.